Naughty Nuptials
oh yum!

Beth Kery
Kit Tunstall
Desiree Holt
Alice Gaines
Zannie Adams
Taige Crenshaw
Michele Bardsley

ELLORA'S CAVE
ROMANTICA PUBLISHING

What the critics are saying...

ॐ

ONCE UPON A WEDDING

5 Lips "All I can say is WOW! When I got near the end of the story, any feelings I had at the beginning were no longer in existence. I was very pleasantly surprised to say the least. *Once Upon a Wedding* is the first book I've read by *Desiree Holt*, but it certainly will not be the last! Bravo *Ms. Holt*! Bravo!" ~ *Two Lips Reviews*

BRIDE PORTAL

5/5 Rating "Michele Bardsley always gives us fascinating tales of different types and this one is no different. She shows us that good-looking men, even if they are from another planet, can love heavy women too. Makes us heavy women love and fanaticize about having a good-looking long thin man on our arm even if we don't already have one, a good-looking one that is. As always Michele does it again and gives us a steamy, sizzling, fun story to read. Just make sure to have a fan with you to help cool you off it is a hot one." ~ *Night Owl Romance Reviews*

WRONG GROOM

3.5 Stars "*Wrong Groom* will appeal to all women who are not a size 6. [...] The chemistry is instantaneous and never leaves the reader in doubt that these two characters are meant to be together. The realistic obstacles both must overcome draw the reader into the middle of the story, relating to them as if they are friends. *Wrong Groom* is a wonderful way to while away an hour or so. Kit Tunstall is an author I intend to watch." ~ *Sensual EcataRomance Reviews*

CLAIMING KATE

4 Hearts "The plot is well developed and the characters are realistic. I'm sure that you will be pleased when you see who decides to be responsible for *Claiming Kate!*" ~ *The Romance Studio*

SEDUCING A GOD

"This *Naughty Nuptials* series is one of the best series that Ellora's Cave has done to date. I love the storyline that Ms. Taige has crafted. You have a woman that wants a man, but she doesn't think he sees her, and takes matters into her own hands to make him see her. I know that most of us women can relate to that. I loved the way this author wrote this fun plot, making Markus a god of Matrimony, yummy! This author has wet my taste buds and I look forward to reading her next book." ~ *Paranormal Romance Reviews*

WEDDING NIGHT SURPRISE

4 Hearts "The reader will be drawn to these enchanting and memorable characters that stay in your thoughts long after the last word has been read. [...] The sexual chemistry, love and trust between the hero and heroine, is an engaging factor that drives the story forward to the erotically intense wedding night present. Each sex scenes between the hero and heroine are smoking hot and very frequent, but the author doesn't fail to showcase the sex as a means of emotional intimacy that is breath-taking. The wedding night between Steve, Cass and Rafe is a tempting delight, with passion, sensitivity and a touch of humor that will dazzle the reader." ~ *The Romance Studio*

GROOM'S GIFT

4 1/2 Hearts "This is a marvelously exciting, edgy tale about one night—the gift of Libby to John for his wedding gift from his friends, Malcolm and Ced. It has a surprising, though somewhat predictable, ending which is totally worth your time. I recommend it to all who might be interested in frank, bordering on bondage, sensual activity!" ~ *The Romance Studio*

An Ellora's Cave Romantica Publication

www.ellorascave.com

Naughty Nuptials

ISBN 9781419959295

Edited by Helen Woodall, Sue-Ellen Gower, Shannon Combs, Jaynie Ritchie, and Ann Leveille.
Cover art by Syneca.

This book printed in the U.S.A. by Jasmine-Jade Enterprises, LLC.

Trade paperback Publication June 2009

NAUGHTY NUPTIALS

ഇ

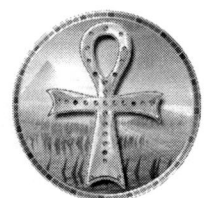

ONCE UPON A WEDDING

Desiree Holt

෬

Dedication

❧

This one is for my husband David, my prince, my hero,
the man who made all my fantasies come true and still
does

Trademarks Acknowledgement

❧

The author acknowledges the trademarked status and trademark owners of the following wordmarks mentioned in this work of fiction:

Ducati: Ducati Motor Holding, S.p.A.

Volvo: Volvo Personvagnar AB Corporation

Chapter One

&

"Well, Rainie, you've done it this time."

Rainie McIntyre sat on the beach where she'd been for the last two hours, arms resting on her bent knees and talking to herself and getting no answers. Was there another woman on the planet four weeks away from her wedding who was out looking for a man to fuck her for the weekend?

And Stuart. Was that shock or disgust in her fiancé's eyes when she told him what she needed — one weekend of wild sex before they settled down.

"Everyone's sown their wild oats but me," she told him. "I love you, Stuart, but I've got to get this out of my system."

She didn't want to lie to him. That lie would always be between them. And because he loved her he'd let her go. She wondered where he was right now. What he was thinking.

The sun dipping down toward the waters of the Gulf of Mexico cast everything in shades of rose and gold. Way out against the horizon a cabin cruiser chugged through the water. The late afternoon stragglers were gathering their belongings and the outdoor bar of the hotel was preparing for the next onslaught. Music began to fill the air through the outdoor speakers.

"You look like you're in very serious thought."

The deep voice startled her out of her reverie. She looked up...and up...and up. When she reached the top her jaw dropped.

"What—"

"What's a nice guy like me doing in a place like this?" He gave her a lopsided grin. "Trying to find some answers. And you?"

Rainie just stared, speechless.

The man was a one-eighty from the starched and pressed men she was used to, including her fiancé. He was at least six-foot-four, with a thick, tawny mane of sunstreaked hair framing a tanned face full of planes and angles. His casually unbuttoned shirt revealed a broad expanse of chest with a soft mat of darker hair. Amber eyes flecked with gold looked down at her from under thick lashes. Long, tanned, muscular legs stretched out from well-worn denim cutoffs and ended at feet shoved into disreputable deck shoes. Behind the zipper of his cutoffs a well-defined bulge made her mouth water. A lion! That's all she could think of. A lion had come to life in human form.

Rainie couldn't stop staring.

"I should introduce myself. I'm Joe."

"But—"

"It's not so hard." He grinned, showing even white teeth. "Just say 'hi, Joe'."

She swallowed. This was absurd. "Hi. Joe."

"See how easy that was?" He hunkered down next to her. The wind had tossed her dark curls every which way and Joe reached out a finger and very gently brushed some loose strands away from her cheek. "You look like a damsel in distress. Think I'd make a good white knight?"

"Y-Yes. You would." God, that smile. She felt her bones melt.

"As my first official duty, can I interest you in a drink?" He gestured toward the outdoor bar, already filling up with the cocktail-hour crowd.

She shook her head. "I'm not in the mood for people right now."

"No problem. I'll bring the drinks over here."

Rainie started to protest. "I don't think—"

"Good. Don't think. Go with the flow." He winked at her. "You never know what might turn up."

Boy, that's the understatement of the year.

He was back in minutes carrying two disposable glasses. He handed one to her.

She raised an eyebrow. "Piña colada?"

"Something told me that's your drink. Am I right?"

"Yes, you are."

He sat down on the sand beside her. "So how about telling me your name, now that I told you mine."

"Um, Rainie. My name's Rainie."

"Rainie." He rolled it around on his tongue. "Nice name." He let his eyes roam over her from head to toe. "It suits you."

"Thank you." She sipped at her drink. "Most people call me Loraine, but that has such an uptight sound, don't you think?"

"I think a name is what you make of it. You shouldn't let it define you."

She'd never looked at it that way. She'd always hated her name and waged an unsuccessful war to get her family to call her Rainie. Not even Stuart, her erstwhile fiancé, called her Rainie.

"Thank you for the drink," she said after a while, remembering her manners.

"My pleasure. So here comes the pickup line of all time. What's a beautiful gal like you doing sitting so sadly on a beach by herself?"

"It's complicated." She sipped more of the drink.

He was only inches away from her and she could feel his powerful sexuality rolling off him in waves. He wasn't even touching her and her nipples tightened and moisture dampened her panties. Her hands itched to yank down his zipper and caress what was sure to be a magnificent cock. If she closed her eyes she could imagine it in her mouth, stretching it to the limit, or sliding into her greedy pussy.

He took a swallow of his drink, tilting his head back and Rainie stared at the muscles flexing in his throat. "I've learned most things are really simple if you break them down to their basic form. Why don't you try it?"

She sighed. "I'm getting married." He stiffened slightly and she caught the tension. "You, too?"

He shrugged. "Maybe. I don't know."

"So why are *you* out here, then?"

He gave her a lopsided smile. "Working some things out. Anyway, a wedding's usually cause for celebration, not unhappiness. What's the problem? Bridegroom a disaster?"

"No." She hadn't meant to shout and lowered her voice. "He's a great guy. Better than I deserve."

"Can't be too great if you're out here by yourself."

"No, you're wrong. He's wonderful."

He shrugged. "Okay. If it's not the groom, what else? Don't want to be married at all?"

"Yes, I want to be married." She plucked at the skirt of her sundress.

"Then what's the deal?"

Rainie let out a huge sigh. "This is going to sound so very, very stupid."

Joe laughed. "You'd have to go some to beat all the stupid things I've heard. Come on, out with it."

"Okay. Here goes. Everything in my life is so…so…normal. There. I've said it."

Joe turned his head to look at her. "And you think normal is bad? There are people who would kill for normal."

14

"See? I told you it was stupid." She sipped at her drink again.

"Let me get this straight. You're out here on the beach because getting married is too normal."

She let a handful of sand trickle through her fingers. "I'm twenty-eight years old. I've always followed all the rules. The wildest thing I've ever done is get drunk the night I graduated high school and get a speeding ticket."

Joe raised his eyebrows. "Wow. Pretty wild all right."

She sifted more sand. "See? That's what I mean."

"So you want to spice up your life? What about your fiancé? Isn't he spicy?"

"He's wonderful. Everything a woman could ask for."

"Except in bed, right?" There was an edge of bitterness to his voice.

"That's not it," she said carefully. "He's just...conventional."

He turned his amber eyes on her. "Conventional."

Rainie threw up her hands. "What can I say? I should have my head examined. He's such a good catch women are lining up to take my place."

"Then what?"

She took a big swallow of her drink. "Here's the thing. In four weeks he and I are going to stand up in front of four hundred people and become man and wife. Everyone will be smiling, including both sets of parents. We'll go on a conventional honeymoon, come home, buy a conventional house and have two point five conventional children. And live happily ever after."

He shook his head. "Doesn't sound too happy to me. I'd say you're probably shortchanging the guy if that's how you look at it."

She sighed again. "Stuart is wonderful and he'll be a wonderful husband. It's just... I have fantasies like almost every other woman. I just wanted one wild weekend so I could have a chance to live them."

"Oh? And what kind of fantasies do you have?"

She couldn't look at him while she spoke. "I want to find a sexy man, have wild, uninhibited sex, do all the things I've never done and get it out of my system."

"So you can go back and pretend to Stuart everything's all right."

"I won't have to pretend. It will be." She could hear how desperate she sounded.

"What if you fall in love with this man, whoever he is?"

Rainie shook her head. "That won't happen. I love Stuart."

"Sure about that?"

"Yes. I'm positive. If only he were, I don't know, more adventurous. Less—"

"Conventional." Joe grinned. "Maybe he thinks that's what you want." He drew his knees up and leaned his arms on them. "So, just for informational purposes, what kind of sex are you looking for? Bondage? Toys? Spankings?"

Rainie felt herself redden and kept her eyes averted. "Um, yes. All of that. Don't you have fantasies, too?" *I am so not having this conversation.*

"Yeah. But the woman I want doesn't give me signals that she's into that stuff."

"So you're looking for someone, too?"

He didn't answer for a long moment. "Maybe I'm just hoping the right person will come along and I can stop looking."

"Oh." She thought for a moment. "And one other thing. I want to ride a motorcycle."

"Yeah? Why?"

"Another stupid answer. Because I drive a Volvo and I'm tired of safe and sensible. Just once I want to ride with the wind." She felt herself blushing.

Joe raised an eyebrow. "Stuart doesn't like motorcycles?"

She shrugged. "I don't know. We've never discussed it."

"Sounds like you should have a talk with Stuart." They were silent for a long moment. Joe picked up one of her hands and played with the fingers. "So Rainie-who-wants-to-be-wild. Do you think I'd do?"

She frowned. "Do?"

"You know. For the weekend fling. I'm healthy, momentarily unattached and I can promise you the sex will be better than you can imagine."

Her heart was beating in a stuttering rhythm. A flutter deep in her womb began to increase in tempo.

While she chewed on her lip, Joe made the decision for her. He swallowed the last of his drink, rose with lithe jungle grace and held out his hand to her. "Come on. I promise you an adventure you won't forget."

Rainie looked up at him. A wildness glittered in his lion's eyes, a hint of something feral and untamed beneath all those tanned muscles and that amazing grin. Anticipation rolled over her.

"All right." She stood up, hitched the thin strap of her flat purse over her shoulder and gave him her hand.

He tossed their drink cups in a trash barrel and led her toward the street.

"Where are we going?"

"I rented a house down the beach for the weekend. How does that sound?"

She paused. "I don't have any clothes except what I've got on. And my car's in the garage here."

The amber eyes darkened to a deep gold. "If things work out you won't need any clothes. And your car's safe at the hotel. Anyway, I've got the transportation covered."

They stopped at the curb where a gleaming silver Ducati motorcycle rested on its kickstand.

Rainie's mouth flopped open. "Is this yours?"

"Sure is." He winked at her and handed her a helmet. "Here. You'll need this. Don't want to splatter your brains before we get to that wild sex."

Suddenly Rainie threw back her head and laughed. What the hell. This was what she wanted, wasn't it? "Okay, Joe. Crank 'er up."

She hopped onto the motorcycle behind him, wrapped her arms around his hard, muscular body, her hands clasped against sun-warmed male skin and inhaled. A cologne so light its fragrance was almost elusive mingled with the scent of the sun, the Gulf waters, the lingering coconut aroma of the piña coladas and the male essence that was uniquely Joe. She had to squash in irresistible urge to pull up his shirt and lick his skin to see if he tasted as good as he smelled.

They roared down the street with wheeling seagulls squawking overhead and the rushing slipstream of the wind sweeping away the last vestiges of restraint.

* * * * *

The house was a two-story weathered barnwood and glass creation, at the end of a cul-de-sac. Beyond it Rainie could see the beach and the Gulf. She figured he'd paid through the nose for the location.

Joe pulled a remote from his pocket and opened the garage door, smoothly gliding the Ducati inside. He parked the bike, put the helmets on a shelf and led her up three steps into the house.

"Oh my god." She didn't know what else to say.

The house was beyond dazzling with an entire wall of glass facing the water, Saltillo tile floors and comfortable furniture in white wood and denim. A fireplace swept the length of one wall and an entertainment center took up the opposite one. Sliding doors opened onto an elevated porch that ran the entire length of the house.

Joe grinned at the look on her face. "Pretty snazzy, huh?"

"It must have cost the earth to rent. Even for a weekend."

He was standing right next to her and his hands cupped her face. "I thought maybe I'd get lucky and I wanted to impress my date." Then his mouth descended on hers.

The kiss was seductive rather than demanding. He nibbled at her lower lip, grazing it with his teeth and then brushing his lips against it. His tongue traced the seam of her lips, tasting her. When he'd tasted every inch of the surface of her bottom lip he moved to the upper one.

Rainie opened her mouth on a sigh and Joe's tongue swept inside. It felt like a feather in her mouth, lightly touching every inch of her inner flesh. When he ran the tip of it across the length of her own tongue, she met him in a graceful duet.

She had no idea how long they stood there in the most erotic kiss she'd ever had. Her breasts were pushed against his naked chest and even through the thin material of her dress she could feel the light scrape of the crisp chest hair. She swayed slightly, moving her breasts against him, her nipples burning for his touch, straining on tiptoe to press her pelvis against the tempting erection. His tongue moved in and out, a signal of what his body would soon do to her. Heat fired her blood and the drumbeat inside her grew harder.

"Your mouth tastes like rare wine, Rainie." He whispered his words into her open lips. "I'll bet your cunt tastes even better."

Moisture flooded her panties at his words. She swallowed her hesitation and asked, "Are you going to find out?"

"Oh yes. You bet your sweet ass I am. In more ways than you can count." He stepped back from her. His hand came up and traced the outline of her jaw, the shell of her ear, the slender column of her neck. "The minute I saw you sitting on that beach I wanted to rip your clothes off and fuck you senseless."

Her mouth formed a small O.

Joe swept her up in his arms. "Shall we get started?"

She was glad he was holding her because her legs were suddenly weak.

The master bedroom was upstairs at the front of the house, with a window wall similar to the living room. A huge bed dominated the room and beside it on the nightstand was a bottle of wine and two glasses. Soft music flowed from the entertainment center and candles were placed around the room.

Set for seduction.

Joe moved around lighting the candles and then picked up the wine bottle. "Drink? It's chardonnay."

Her favorite. Her head was buzzing from the one drink she'd already had on an empty stomach but she needed something for her sudden attack of nerves. "Sure. Wine would be great."

They carried their drinks out to the balcony. Rainie looked across the beach to the endless waters of the Gulf. "This is…exquisite."

He put his mouth close to her ear. "I'm going to fuck you out here, Rainie. With people walking on the beach below us. I'm going to fuck you so hard you'll scream, only you won't be able to because people will hear you if you do."

Rainie shivered at the thought. At his words. This was what she wanted. And more.

Joe took her glass from her hand. "Take off your clothes."

Her eyes widened. "Right here?"

"Right here. I want to see that body naked in the breeze."

"B-But the people..."

"If they see you they'll envy me my good luck. Come on, Rainie. The dress."

Rainie reached down to grab the hem of her skirt and pulled the dress over her head, tossing it onto a chair.

"Bra and panties, too," he commanded.

With hands that trembled slightly, she unclasped her bra, let it fall and shimmied out of her panties.

Joe stared at her for a long time.

"Is something wrong?" she asked at last. His lion's gaze was predatory.

"No." His voice was husky. "There's not a thing wrong. Not one single thing."

He set his wineglass down, lifted her in his arms again and carried her inside to the bed. Snapping on the bedside lamp, he used his hands to spread her knees wide, exposing her entire pussy to him. He stared, his eyes feasting on her as if he'd just discovered buried treasure.

"You have the prettiest cunt in the world, Rainie." He reached out a finger and traced the length of her slit. Up and down. A whisper of a touch.

Rainie shivered.

With gentle fingers he opened her labia wide, looking all the way into her vagina. "In fact, it's so pretty I don't want anything to hide it from me."

"W-What do you mean?"

"You'll see. Stay here just like this. Don't move. I'll be right back." He leaned down and placed a soft kiss right on her mound. "You have only one thing to remember. I will never do anything to hurt you."

She lay there a trembling mass, listening to the sounds of him in the bathroom. When he returned he carried two thick towels, a china bowl filled with water, a can of shaving gel and a razor. Adjusting Rainie so her hips were right at the edge of the bed, he bent her knees and planted her feet on the coverlet. He placed one towel underneath her, the other beside her and the bowl on the nightstand. Then he pulled over an ottoman and sat down.

"I'm going to shave your pussy, Rainie. Take off every bit of hair so I can see it completely naked. That okay with you?"

"Yes." Her heartbeat kicked up a notch and a tiny thrill ran through her. She often trimmed her pubic hair at home to keep it neat but she'd never been shaved completely. The thought of Joe doing it was intensely arousing.

"Okay. I want you to spread your legs as wide as you can and use your hands to keep them that way. Can you do that for me?"

She blushed but nodded.

"Good." With a light touch he moistened the entire area of her sex and then covered it with the gel, talking to her in a low voice while he worked. "I love these soft little curls, you know, but I want to see your naked pussy more. If you lie perfectly still while I do this I might have a treat for you when I'm finished. I can hardly wait to see this pink flesh darken and your cream run out of you."

Rainie knew she was getting wet just from listening to him and she had to force herself to lie still.

He moved a fingertip over her clit, a feathery caress that made her shiver. "Do you like that?"

"Yes." She bit her lip. "It feels good."

"I'm going to make that pussy feel a whole lot better." He slid one finger inside. "I'm going to feel every inch of it with my fingers and my tongue. And when I've eaten it until I've swallowed every bit of your juices and finger-fucked you until I can feel every tiny muscle inside clench and spasm, I'm going to put my cock in there and fuck you until you scream the house down." His eyes held hers. "That sound good, Rainie?"

"Yes. Oh yes." Her words came out on a whisper of breath. Her pulse was beating so fast she was sure he could hear it and she tried to clench around his finger.

He laughed and withdrew it, applying more gel. "I'm distracting myself."

Rainie's breathing hitched and she concentrated every effort on holding her thighs wide apart and not letting her hands slip. "H-Have you done this before?"

He looked up at her. "Not when it mattered. This matters. Okay, now the inside of the lips." He tugged on her skin, pulling the labia to the side. "Such pretty lips. It's a shame to keep them hidden."

The razor glided down one side of her cunt, then the other, in slow, sure strokes. She wondered if the pulse in her vagina was visible and if Joe knew how turned on she was getting.

As if she'd spoken aloud, he lifted his head and grinned. "I know this is making you hot. That's the idea. The hotter the better." He gave her his sexy wink.

When he had shaved her cunt to his satisfaction, he braced one arm against the backs of her thighs and rocked her back on her shoulders. "I'm going to shave around your asshole, too, Rainie. All that light little fuzz. I'm going to fuck that ass this weekend and I don't want anything there except that dark rosy skin."

When he spread the gel around her anus, one fingertip probed lightly at the opening and she almost lost it. Being fucked in the ass had always been one of her darkest fantasies. She'd been sure Stuart would think she was crazy if she brought it up. Or else run in the opposite direction.

"All done." Joe put the razor aside, wiped the area with a warm cloth and dried it with a towel. Then he slipped one lean finger into her cunt and his mouth turned up in a smile. "You're sopping wet, Rainie. I can't wait to slide my cock in there. But first that treat I promised you."

He rose and picked up the bowl and razor. Rainie heard him moving around, then he came back and sat down again. She'd relaxed her legs but he bent them and opened her wide again.

"I knew you'd look delicious with all that hair gone." He released her legs. "Okay, darlin'. Turn over and get on your hands and knees."

Rainie blinked. "What?"

Joe sighed. "I hope you won't be asking questions all weekend. Such a waste of time." He turned her over and arranged her the way he wanted her. Placing pillows under her head, he pulled her arms behind her.

When she felt something wrapping around her wrists, Rainie gasped. "What are you doing?"

"There you go with the questions again. These are special soft handcuffs. I want your hands behind your back." When her hands were securely fastened, he leaned over her and placed a folded silk scarf over her eyes. "This weekend, Rainie, you're going to learn to develop your sense of feel. When you can't see everything is more intense. And I want it to be intense for you."

Rainie swallowed hard. Her ass was up in the air, her cunt wide open and she was quite literally helpless. Well, this was what she wanted, right? She just didn't think they'd jump right into it.

"When I bought my...supplies for this weekend, I saw this tiny little vibrator that's supposed to work really well. Let's see if they're right."

Rainie felt something cool touch the lips of her pussy followed by a humming sound. Joe was running the little toy all around the edge of her cunt, in a trailing lazy circle. She felt herself gush again and tried to close her legs.

"Uh-uh, darlin'. I said don't move. You need to pay attention."

She jolted as an unexpected slap landed on her ass. "Hey!"

Joe placed an open-mouthed kiss on one of her ass cheeks. "Gotta let you know who's boss here." He spanked her again. "Tell me you don't like it and I'll stop." Another slap.

Heat streaked from her ass right to the center of her pussy and she felt the sensation of need building in her. Joe was right. The spankings brought her to the edge of pleasure-pain and increased her arousal.

"Okay, then. Ride with me, darlin'."

Rainie lost track of how long she lay there in that position. Joe alternated the spankings with the buzzing torment of the vibrator. When he touched her clit with it she thought she'd fly off the bed, especially when he held it there, his hand pressing down on her spine to keep her immobilized.

"God, Rainie." His breathing was slightly unsteady. "Your cunt is turning such a beautiful dark red and you're so wet it's dripping out of you. I could do this for hours and hours."

"Oh, please don't. Please let me come."

She hadn't realized she'd said the words aloud until Joe said, "In a minute, darlin'. I want to play just a little more."

Play? He was driving her insane.

Suddenly the buzzing increased, the vibrator pressed harder on her clit and Joe slid two lean fingers into her hot sheath. "Okay, Rainie. Let it come, darlin'. Feel that vibrator and my fingers fucking you and let it happen."

His words tipped her over the edge. She felt her pussy convulse around his fingers and she tried to move herself on them. Joe laughed softly and slid a third finger inside, fucking her with his hand while the vibrator drove her on and on. She shook and arched and rode his fingers until at last the spasms died away and she lay panting on the bed.

Joe rotated his fingers inside her as he drew them out, pulling one last aftershock from her. He leaned down and kissed her cheek. "Your pussy is like a soft flower, Rainie. I could leave my hand in there all night."

He removed the blindfold and untied her hands. When she rolled over she realized he was naked. Her eyes dropped at once to his magnificent erection jutting from the nest of dark golden curls.

Joe grinned and gave her that sexy wink. "See what you do to me? Come on. Time for a shower."

The shower took up an entire end of the enormous bathroom. When Joe turned it on water pulsed from every direction. The minute they stepped into the enclosure Rainer felt water everywhere, the spray as soft as a fine mist. Joe held a bar of soap under her nose. "Lavender. To relax you."

Then he pulled her close and kissed her.

Chapter Two

℘

The kiss was seductive. That was the only word for it. Joe teased at her lips, sucked them, licked them, tasted the inside of each lip. When his tongue slipped inside she tasted wine and Joe and the combination was so heady it made her head spin. He ran his hands up and down her spine, caressed the swell of her ass, moved his fingertips over her shoulders and collarbone.

Needing to touch him, she lifted her hands up between them and tangled them in the mat of hair on his chest. Her fingertips dusted across his nipples.

Joe's fingers circled her wrists and moved her hands away from his body. "This is for you, Rainie. Let me pleasure *you*."

Lathering his hands, Joe began to bathe her, stroking her body, soaping every inch of her—feet, ankles, calves, thighs—massaging them until she was nearly boneless. He paid meticulous attention to her breasts, cupping them in his palms and running his thumbs over the nipples. Then he knelt on the shower floor in front of her and pushed on her legs. "Open wide for me, Rainie. I want to wash every inch of that little cunt."

When his fingers slipped into her, slick with soap, her body came to life again. He explored every inch of her labia, the opening to her vaginal sheath, the sheath itself, the crease at the juncture of her thighs. At the touch of his fingers on her clit she started to tremble.

"I can't wait to take that little clit in my mouth, Rainie." His voice was like hot syrup. "I want to do wicked things to it." He stood up and turned her around. "Place your hands against the wall and lean forward."

As soon as she did he lifted the long fall of her hair and kissed the nape of her neck, swirling his tongue over her shower-soaked skin. Then his hands made long sweeps along the length of her back and down her legs, caressing each inch of skin as if it was precious cloth. He was as thorough with her back as he'd been with her front, kneading her muscles as he rubbed the lather into them.

When she felt him separate the cheeks of her ass and rim the tight pucker of her anus with a soapy finger she instinctively clenched. He began working one finger into that small opening. When she started to clench he put his lips close to her ear. "Relax, Rainie. Let it happen. When I fuck you in the ass I don't want hurt you. Come on. Let me in."

She closed her eyes and with an effort of will forced her muscles to go slack. As his finger moved in inch by inch a dark thrill ran through her. She had no idea how long they stood there, Joe moving his finger in and out of her ass in a slow, hypnotic rhythm. Finally he slid it out.

"Stay right where you are," he ordered in a low voice.

In a moment he was spreading her ass cheeks again. She felt something cool squeezed against the opening, then Joe was spreading it inside her, rubbing it into the walls of her dark tunnel. "Take a deep breath, sugar."

She drew in as much air as she could and while she was slowly letting it out she felt him pushing something solid into her ass.

"What…?"

"This is a butt plug, Rainie. It'll help loosen those tight tissues so you'll be ready for my cock when I fuck you here. You can take it, sugar. Come on."

With his other hand he reached around and found her clit. His fingers rubbed it and tugged at it until Rainie forgot anything but the swirling sensations. And then the plug was all the way in and that dark curl of lust grabbed her again.

He turned her around and leaned her against the wall. "Okay, Rainie?"

"Yes." Her breathing was unsteady. "Fine."

"Good. Let's get the rest of the soap out of you." He took the handheld showerhead, sat down between her legs and reached for her clit. Peeling back the protective little hood, he turned on the showerhead and directed its spray directly on the exposed nub.

The tiny needles of the shower spray made her clit throb and her vaginal walls quiver. At first the sensation was so intense Rainie tried to pull back from it.

Joe wouldn't let her do it. He crooned soft words to her, sexy words, as he worked the showerhead, stimulating her clit, coaxing her response. "Play with your nipples, Rainie. Take them in your fingers. You have such gorgeous nipples. They were made to be sucked and teased. Come on, darlin'. Pinch them for me."

Automatically Rainie raised her hands and squeezed her nipples between the thumb and forefinger of each hand. As soon as she did streaks of lightning shot to her hungry clit. Tiny spasms rippled through every inch of her body and she moaned with her need.

"Hot, Rainie. You are so hot." Joe slid open the shower door, reached out to the counter and in seconds was rolling a condom onto his cock. He lifted Rainie and slowly slid her down onto his throbbing erection. With her legs wrapped around him he took in a shuddering breath. "Jesus. Rub your clit, darlin', because I'm gonna come faster than I wanted to."

Rainie was already so stimulated she barely touched herself before she felt the ripples gathering in her body. Pulling on her clit, she rode Joe's magnificent cock as he stroked into her. In what seemed like seconds his orgasm came crashing down on him and Rainie was right behind him. With only the shower wall for support they shook as release flooded them both, the fine shower mist spraying on their heated skin.

Finally Joe reached up and turned off the shower, carried her out of it and dried them both off. The soft music was still playing in the bedroom and the candles had filled the room with the scent of lavender. Seduction of the senses, Rainie thought to herself. Well, it was working.

Joe refilled their wineglasses. "You have a very sensitive body, Rainie. It's like playing with an incredible toy. I'm curious. How come you've never done these things with your fiancé?"

Rainie closed her eyes. "Stuart sees me in a certain light. I've always been afraid if I told him some of the things I want to do he'd look at me as if I was some kind of sex addict. We're both very…conventional people."

"Maybe you sell him short." His eyes studied her intently. "Maybe underneath it all he wants the same things you do. I'd see this as a way to enhance our love, a way for me to worship you even more. It wouldn't be a turnoff. Just the opposite, as a matter-of-fact."

"You don't think I'm perverted or something?"

Joe took her wineglass and put it with his on the nightstand. "You're a beautiful, responsive woman. A man would have to be out of his mind not to want to do all these things with you. I think you're selling both of you short. In any event, this is your fantasy and I'm honored to be a part of it."

Rainie wet her lips. "Thank you."

He opened the drawer of the nightstand and took out a small satin pouch. "Pinch your nipples again for me, darlin'. I want to see you plump them up."

Curious, Rainie's hands moved up to grasp her nipples and squeeze them. She felt them harden at once.

"Do you play with yourself at home, Rainie? Make yourself feel good?"

She felt a blush creep over her and looked away from him. "Yes. Sometimes."

"Darlin', it's nothing to be ashamed of. It's great to make yourself feel good. In a little while you're going to show me how you do it. But first, I have some jewelry for you."

She frowned. "Earrings?"

He grinned. "Not quite." He took one of her nipples from her, tugged on it and then inserted it in the small clamp at the top of the jewelry and began to tighten. "Nipple rings. Your nipples were made for them."

"W-Will they hurt?"

Joe shook his head. "Only enough to give you pleasure." He watched her face as he turned the tiny screw. When she bit her lip he stopped. In a minute he had the other one fastened in place. He touched the tip of each nipple with his finger, smiling when she jumped. "Just right. Those nipples will be so sensitive you'll come just from my sucking them."

What shocked Rainie was the streak of heat that shot straight to her womb. She moved restlessly on the bed.

Joe knelt beside her, feathering kisses across her face, paying careful attention to her eyelids, her cheeks, her jawline, her neck. As his fingers traced the shell of her ear, he placed a light kiss where her neck met her shoulder, then bit it gently, and her body shook.

"So sensitive," he repeated. "Such soft skin. You taste like peaches and cream. I can't wait to get my tongue inside that sweet cunt of yours. God, Rainie, you're every man's wet dream." His voice was a low rumble in her ear. "So when you masturbate at home, does it feel good? Do you like it?"

"Yes." She could hardly get the word out.

"Do you know watching a woman pleasure herself is a huge turn-on for a man?"

He was running his hand over her body and she was having trouble breathing. She was very conscious of the butt plug and the feeling it gave her. "No. I didn't know that."

"I'll bet Stuart would like to watch. What do you think?"

"I-I never asked."

"Well, I'd sure like to watch. I can't wait to see you finger yourself and make yourself come for me." He turned away from her and opened the drawer again. This time he took out a vibrator much larger than the one he'd used before. Then he sat down cross-legged on the bed at her feet. "Bend your knees up, sugar, and let me see you finger yourself. Just like you do at home. God, I know this is your fantasy but watching a very sexy woman like you play with herself is one of my fantasies."

Her eyebrows shot up to her hairline. "Really?"

"Uh-huh. Without a doubt."

"And you think I'm sexy?"

Heat glimmered in those amber eyes and her lion leaned forward to touch her cunt. "Rainie, you are the sexiest woman I've ever known. There are so many things I want to do that luscious body of yours that just thinking of them gets me hard." He placed a row of tender kisses on the inside of each of her thighs, then sat back. "Do it, Rainie. Now."

Rainie closed her eyes, letting the soft notes of the jazz music wash over her and inhaling the soothing scent of the lavender candles. She could feel the throbbing of her nipples under the pressure of the rings and the fullness of her ass with the butt plug inside her. Suddenly she wanted to perform for this man, this lion who made her hotter than she'd ever been. Whatever he asked she wanted to do. Any lingering shyness she might have had evaporated.

Her hands moved slowly over her stomach and down toward her very naked cunt. She took her time, visualizing his eyes on her as he watched the progress of her movement. When she pulled her outer lips apart and began rubbing the tips of her fingers against the exposed inner flesh she heard the hiss of his indrawn breath. A wailing saxophone floating through the air lifted her from the bed into a cocoon of sensuality.

When she did this at home she often needed to moisten her fingers until she reached a certain peak. Not tonight. She was already gushing, the copious fluid a testament to her high state of arousal. The orgasm in the shower had barely taken the edge off her excitement. In fact, if anything it had stimulated her even more.

Lost in the rhythm of her strokes she jumped when she felt Joe's hands rest on her knees and his thumbs begin massaging the insides of her kneecaps. The slow circular motions sent electricity streaking straight down her thighs to her clit. More liquid gushed onto her fingers as she rubbed them over the opening of her vagina.

"I can't take my eyes off you." His voice was thick with desire. "Watching you stroke that beautiful pussy, open yourself up for me to see...it's like a gift, Rainie. A rare gift."

She could hardly find words to speak. "I'm...glad you like it."

"Touch your clit again," he urged. "Let me see you pull on it and rub the tip. Yes, that's it. God, you're glistening, you're so wet."

Lost in the rising tide of emotion and the wail of the saxophone, Rainie almost missed the faint buzz until she felt something touch her labia and tiny vibrations jolt through her. She tried to look but Joe used one hand to press her back against the pillows.

"Just a little something to help you along. Don't move your hands. Keep stroking yourself, no matter what I do."

She felt the head of the vibrator against her opening, pausing there for a moment, then beginning to move up and down her outer pussy lips, a slow caressing motion that brought every nerve screaming to life. This one drove her higher than the little one he'd used earlier. The more it circled her cunt, the faster she stroked her clit and her hips began a thrusting movement. Eagerly she slid two fingers into her vagina and she had just begun to set her rhythm when Joe removed her hand.

"Your clit, darlin'. Just concentrate on your clit."

She did as he told her and in seconds she felt the buzzing vibrator slide into her vaginal sheath. When it was fully seated Joe turned the speed to high and the vibrations rocketed through her body. With only a thin wall of tissue for separation the butt plug picked up the sensations and began vibrating, too. Her whole body began to shake. The nipples pinched in the clips throbbed with a red-hot heat. Her ass and her pussy could hardly keep up with the stimulating assault and her orgasm began to rise through her body.

"Faster, Rainie," Joe urged. "Rub yourself faster."

She picked up the tempo of her hand, eyes closed, one of Joe's thumbs still drawing circles at her knee. Up and up she went, more and more and as the saxophone crested on a wailing high note, her climax broke over her with the force of an earthquake. Spasms ripped through her, shaking her so hard she thought her bones would break. Her cunt clenched and convulsed around the vibrator and fluid ran from her down into the cleft of her ass.

Joe fucked her with the dildo, encouraging her with soft words and gentle touches, but not letting her come down until he was sure the last aftershock was gone.

When he withdrew the vibrator Rainie collapsed on the pillows, gasping for breath. Her body was covered with a fine sheen of perspiration and her heart threatened to beat itself out of her chest. She lay like a doll with all its stuffing gone.

"One more thing, darlin'."

One more thing? I can't take one more thing.

She jerked when she felt his fingers on her painfully swollen clit. When something pinched it lightly she moaned.

"Just a little clamp like the ones on your nipples. Keeps that sweet little clit in a high state of arousal."

Like she needed any more!

Joe moved up on the bed beside her and wrapped his arms around her, one hand holding a breast, his lips trailing kisses along her cheek and neck. He held her cradled against his strong, muscular body, one leg thrown over both of hers, his fully aroused cock pressing into the cleft of her buttocks. The saxophone was now a trumpet and its low moaning sound spread through them.

Joe's warm breath whispered across her temple. "You know the hardest thing about fucking you, Rainie?"

Rainie forced her eyes open, a tiny knot of apprehension tightening in her stomach. "What? Did I do something wrong?"

He brushed her hair back from her cheek and tucked it behind her ear. "If I fuck you with my cock, I can't watch that unbelievably exquisite cunt when you come. So you see I'm depriving myself of one pleasure while taking another."

"Oh." A feeling of warmth stole through her. No one had ever said anything like that to her before. She could get used to this. Too bad it only had a shelf life of one weekend.

"Take a little nap, Rainie. You'll need it."

"I'll try." She was sure she'd never fall asleep with her nipples and her clit being tormented as they were but exhaustion overtook her body. She snuggled against him and in seconds was asleep.

* * * * *

Joe watched the rise and fall of her breasts as Rainie breathed in and out in a quiet sleep. God, she was exquisite. Her thick hair, a deep almost midnight black, danced from her head in a waterfall of curls. Behind the sooty lashes emerald green eyes flared with fire. She was tiny, barely above five feet but a handful in all the right places. He ran his hand over the curve of her ass, admiring its fullness and texture, his cock pulsing as thought of how it would feel in that hot, dark tunnel. Her breasts made his own fantasies run riot. The nipple clips swelled them to a luscious shade of deep red. He could easily sink his teeth into them.

Careful not to wake her he stroked lightly over her stomach, teasing at the indentation of her navel, then whispering his fingertips over the naked cunt he'd loved shaving. God, that had been a turn-on. He'd had to clamp down on his control just to keep his hands from shaking.

When he started out on Friday on his own adventure he wasn't sure just what would happen, but things were turning out far better than he hoped. Rainie was so responsive, every inch of her a treasure to explore. And that cunt! He could spend a lifetime doing all the things to it that cropped up in his mind. Before this weekend was over he planned to show her that fantasy could become reality with the right person.

He had no idea what would happen after Sunday. She seemed to see her life as very rigidly defined, living up to other people's expectations of her. Maybe he could help her get past that and reach for what she really wanted.

If he could do the reaching with her.

Pulling her closer, he tucked her head under his chin and closed his amber eyes. Well, he was a part of her fantasy and he'd do everything in his power to make it an extraordinary one.

Chapter Three

∞

"How would you like a little sustenance?"

Rainie woke to find Joe standing beside the bed holding a tray laden with crackers and cheese and another bottle of wine which he set on the table.

He was still gloriously naked, the tanned and fit body all rippling muscles and sinew, his enormous erection jutting proudly. His tawny hair was disheveled in a way that gave him a wild look and his amber eyes were filled with desire.

It was all she could do to keep from licking her lips. She stretched like a cat and yawned. "I'd love it. I seem to keep expending a lot of energy." A small grin played at the corners of her mouth.

"And we've hardly started." He smiled back. "I thought we'd go out on the balcony, but there's something I need to do first."

Rainie raised an eyebrow. "What's that?"

"You'll see. Turn over and get up on your knees."

"What?" Her eyes widened.

Joe began stroking her back. "Relax, darlin'." One warm hand was caressing the tops of her thighs where they met her buttocks. "I'm going to make you feel good, Rainie. I promised that, too."

"Mmm."

He leaned down and brushed a kiss across the top of her spine, a gesture so tender she melted. "I'm going to switch this plug out for a larger one so we can keep preparing you for when I slide my cock into your ass. Okay?"

She took a deep breath and let it out. "Okay." She pulled herself up to her hands and knees as he asked and felt him slowly remove the plug from her asshole. She felt strangely empty with it gone and wondered if she could get him to spank her again. Without warning she felt a stinging slap on her ass and something dark turned over in her mind. Her entire sex was suffused with heat and she was sure liquid was seeping from her again.

"Like that spanking, don't you, darlin'?" Joe's voice was like a heated caress. "I wish you could see how pink and rosy it makes your ass."

The next slap fell and then another. And another. Rainie tried to anticipate them, but Joe wouldn't set a rhythm. Each contact of his palm with her flesh aroused her more until she was pushing back at him, silently begging for more. She felt his palm pressing down on the small of her back and the next slap landed squarely on her cunt. She thought she would come right at that moment.

Then, without warning the slaps stopped. Her ass and her cunt were on fire yet she wanted more. Harder.

God, what am I turning into?

Joe placed a light kiss right on her anus and sensation jolted her.

"Don't want to spoil you with too much of this, darlin'."

He spread more soothing gel over the tight little rosette, stroking it inside her with two fingers. When he pressed the next plug inside her she was so stimulated by the spankings she almost climaxed on the spot.

Joe reached between her legs and plunged two fingers into her cunt. "Wet. I knew it. God, sex with you is like a dream come true."

"Do-Do you keep a supply of those plugs around?"

"Nope. Bought them in case I met a woman today with a fantasy."

"Oh." A strange feeling twisted through her, one she had trouble defining.

"Now come on. Let's go outside."

"Okay. I need to find something to put on." She swung her legs off the bed, feeling slightly off-kilter with the plug inside her.

"No clothes today, darlin'. See?" He gestured at himself. "None for me either."

But when she walked out onto the balcony she instantly drew back. "There are people down there, Joe."

"It's dark. They can't see us. Besides, isn't it a turn-on to know you're up here exposed for all the world to see yet their eyes can't find you?" He lifted her hand to his lips and ran the tip of his tongue over her knuckles. "Is that unconventional enough for you?"

She laughed, still somewhat self-conscious. "I guess it is."

"Come sit on my lap." Joe patted his knees. "I can feed you like slaves used to do to their queens."

Rainie gingerly lowered herself to Joe's thighs, the butt plug pressing into her and her ass still sore from the spankings. His large, erect cock nestled against her ass. He arranged her legs so they were spread wide, exposing her cunt to the night air.

He handed her a glass of wine and clinked his own glass against it. "To fantasies."

"To fantasies." She let the chilled liquid slide down her throat, hoping it would ease her a little. Her breath hitched when she felt Joe's fingers open her folds and the night air flow into her opening. He stroked around the edges of her vagina and tugged at her labia. She knew moisture was seeping from her again.

"Try this cheese. I just discovered it and I'm hooked."

He handed her a wedge of something soft that almost melted on her tongue the minute she put it in her mouth. "Mmm. Good." All of her senses had become sharper.

"So were you always...what's that word...oh, yeah, conventional?"

"Um, yes, conventional." His voice was low at her ear, his warm breath fanning across her skin like an angel's kiss. His fingers were still busy at her cunt and she tried desperately to pull her thoughts together. How could he expect her to carry on a conversation when he was doing such wonderfully wicked things to her?

"Too bad. Everyone should have a walk on the wild side in their life. So. What about a piece of fruit?" He lifted an orange wedge from the tray but instead of handing it to her he placed it against her clit and squeezed. It pressed on the little clamp Joe had placed there and cold juice trickled inside her pussy lips. She jumped but his arm around her waist held her fast.

"I can't make that pussy taste any sweeter," he chuckled, "but I can change the flavor." He bit the side of her neck as he pushed the orange wedge up inside her.

The coil of lust inside her began to tighten. A tiny whimper escaped her lips.

"Like that?" he whispered. "Maybe we'll try different flavors, mix them up."

Rainie could feel every inch of Joe against her and his warm breath on her neck. She let her head fall back on his shoulder thinking to herself. *This must be what it's like to have a totally free relationship with someone. Let yourself go. Explore your sexuality without fear of censure.*

They sat there on the balcony, the world marching along the beach beneath them, a soft night breeze blowing over them. All the while he fed her cheese and wine Joe squeezed one of every fruit on the tray over her clit, pressing the tiny clamp into her, then sliding it into her pussy. Whenever the juice dripped onto his hand he rubbed it lazily into her cunt, stroking until she thought she would faint from the sensations rolling over her.

At last he lifted her from his lap. "Stand up, Rainie."

Turning her around, he leaned her backward and placed her hands on the balcony railing. He hitched forward and lifted her legs so they hung over the arms of the chair and plundered her with his mouth. That was the only word for it. His tongue reached far inside her vagina, licking up every remnant of the fruit he'd placed in there, while his fingers pressed against the clamp on her clit. And all the while the butt plug pressed into her, stimulating nerves she didn't even know she had.

Rainie had no idea how long it went on. Joe would lap at her, nibble her, graze her labia with his teeth and stab his stiffened tongue inside her. Then he'd withdraw, his thumbs making those insidious circles on the inside of her thighs.

"Don't take your hands off the rail, Rainie," he kept telling her. "Hold tightly."

She gripped the ironwork with desperation. Snippets of conversation from the people below them drifted up. They could have been standing in the next room for all she cared. Her entire being was centered on her pussy and the man tantalizing it. Despite the cool breeze blowing over them sweat broke out on her skin. Her breathing quickened and every muscle in her body strained for fulfillment.

Finally Joe raised his head, his lips shiny with her moisture. His voice wasn't quite steady when he spoke. "Do you want to come, Rainie?"

"Yes. Oh yes please."

"All right, sugar."

She heard the tearing of foil and the snapping of latex as he sheathed himself. Then he rose and in one swift movement impaled her on his cock. With the butt plug filling her asshole, Rainie was even more conscious of the enormous cock as it plunged into her. She felt stretched almost beyond endurance, yet at the same time she craved more.

She opened her mouth as Joe began to stroke in and out, but he captured her lips with his. She tasted herself on him as his tongue plunged inside and mimicked the action of his cock inside her pussy. He gripped her hips tightly and began to move in a slow and steady rhythm. The muscles in her cunt clenched around him, milking him, trying to force a climax, but he held her to a maddeningly slow pace.

"Please," she begged again, uncaring that people below could hear or see her. "Please fuck me harder."

"You got it, darlin'." He increased his movement, harder and faster, watching her face, timing himself with her. When he felt every muscle in her body clench and her pussy grip him so tightly he thought she'd strangle his cock, he gave one last hard thrust and hurtled them both over the edge. They came together, shivering and shuddering, each feeling the other's spasms and convulsions.

Joe fused his mouth to Rainie's, swallowing her screams. At last, when she was sure she'd never be able to draw breath again, Joe moved back and dropped into the chair, pulling Rainie with him so she straddled him, his cock still held tightly inside her cunt.

She leaned forward and touched her forehead to his, wrapping her arms around his neck. The scent of sex was a heavy cloud around them and tiny aftershocks still rocketed through both of their bodies.

Joe pulled her more tightly against him. "If I die tomorrow I'll die a happy man."

"Same goes. Except for the man part, you know." She giggled and as she did her cunt vibrated against his cock.

"God, Rainie," he groaned. "Have a heart."

"You mean you're done for the night?" She gave him an impish grin.

"Done for the night? Not on your life, sugar. Come take another shower with me and I'll show you who's done for the night."

Rainie was beginning to think she'd never be able to shower again without having sex. They stood under the fine mist from the rain showerhead, her body so sensitized that every touch of Joe's fingers sparked an electric response. He ran his hands over her breasts, teasing the engorged nipples and her body came to life again. She wanted his cock inside her again, wanted him to ride her until exhaustion claimed them both and then ride her some more.

When he slid his soapy fingers inside her cunt she pushed hard on them and begged him for more. "Please," she whispered. "Please, please, please."

He laughed, a low rumbling sound. "I wonder if all those very proper conventional people know what a sexual animal Rainie McIntyre is."

"I'll tell them all if you'll just keep doing what you're doing."

"You like that, do you? Well, let's see if I can make you like it a whole lot."

In what seemed like seconds they were out of the shower, barely dry and back on the bed. The room was heavy now with the scent of lavender, the music had changed to a mellow jazz piano and Joe's fingers inside her were making the nerves in her pussy dance.

Very carefully he removed the clamps from her nipples and her clit. At once pain shot through her as blood rushed to the tormented areas, but it was a pain that brought lightning jolts of pleasure with it.

Joe took both of her wrists in one hand and held them above her head, stretching her out so her breasts were taut and upraised. His mouth covered a nipple still raw from the clamp and sucked it into his warm wet heat, his tongue swirling around it. When he bit down on it with the faintest of bites

Rainie arched off the bed, thrusting her pelvis harder against his fingers. She knew her cunt had to be gushing and tiny tremors were racing through her body.

In and out his lean fingers moved, his thumb rubbing her sensitive, swollen clit, his mouth continuing to worship her breasts. Rainie had been sure another climax was beyond her reach tonight but soon it began to gather low in her belly, radiating through the walls of her vagina and up through her body.

"More," she cried. "Don't stop. Oh please, don't stop."

And then it was there, her juices flooding his hand, her pussy grasping at his fingers like a wet vise, her entire body quivering and convulsing. His fingers never left her until the last tiny spasm had faded and she was gasping to draw a full breath.

"My turn," he said, releasing her hands and reaching for another condom.

This time she was sure it would be an impossibility, but as soon as Joe slid into her she was shocked to feel her body begin to respond. He moved his cock in long, lazy strokes, his amber eyes now a hot gold burning into hers, his lion's mane framing his face.

"Put your legs around me and hook your ankles," he commanded in a voice taut with tension.

Rainie complied, lifting herself more tightly against him and drawing him in deeper.

"Tell me what you want, Rainie. Tell me what you want me to do." Sweat covered his face and his muscles corded as he reached for control.

She knew what he wanted to hear. "Fuck me, Joe. Fuck me hard."

His control snapped and he drove into her with such force it rocked her back on the bed. The friction of his cock in her sheath against the plug in her ass took her up the spiral again and once more the pressure built. The soft notes of the jazz piano were a counterpoint to the slide of skin against naked skin, Joe's harsh cries and Rainie's whimpering ones. When their climax came it hit them together, so strong Rainie lost all sense of presence and self. She convulsed around him as he shuddered and shook.

At last he collapsed on top of her, his heart beating so hard she felt it clear through her body. His mouth at her ear kept repeating, "Rainie, Rainie, Rainie." She ran her fingers through the tawny silk of his hair and across his sweat-slicked shoulders, dragging air into her lungs.

She had no idea how long they lay there, wrapped in each other's arms, before he moved.

"I know I'm too heavy for you. I'm sorry."

"No. It's fine," she protested. "Really."

He rolled to the side, bringing her with him. "You may kill me yet, Rain of Fire." He stroked her arm. "That's the only appropriate name for you."

She had no response to that so she snuggled closer, not wanting to break the contact between them.

"I think we need some sleep, but first I'm going to remove the plug." He kissed her cheek. "We'll let that delectable little ass rest until tomorrow."

He got up and took the plug into the bathroom, extinguished all the candles and turned off the stereo. They fell asleep to the sound of the gulls and ospreys and the crashing of the Gulf waves on the beach.

Chapter Four

∞

Rainie insisted on cooking their breakfast—fluffy omelets, toast and coffee. She blushed when she arranged orange slices on the plate, remembering the night before.

Joe lifted her hand, kissed the palm and winked at her. "Orange will have a whole new meaning for me from now on."

They spent the day on the balcony sunning themselves. Joe lavished attention on her, oiling her skin so she wouldn't burn, massaging her body to relieve the soreness from the previous day's activity. When he spread the cool gel on her anus and slicked it inside with two fingers her pussy began to clench and juice dripped onto her thighs. As he slid the third plug into her she realized how eagerly she was anticipating having his cock in there. This was something she'd only read about, tried to imagine. Soon she'd have the real thing and with a man like Joe who would treat her with tenderness and respect.

In the early afternoon, as the beach below them began to fill with sunbathers, Joe went into the bedroom and came back with a long silver object in his hand.

"Another vibrator?"

"I think you'll like this, Rainie. A lot." He leaned over her and urged her legs apart, separating the folds of her cunt and sliding the object inside. Then he lay back down on the chair next to her, leaving her to wonder what it was all about.

She didn't have long to wait. Just as she was drifting off in a light sleep the silver object began to vibrate, sending shards of heat through her pussy and her groin.

"Oh my god!" Her eyes popped open. "That feels..." Her voice trailed off.

"Good ? Stimulating?" She could hear the grin in his voice. "Exciting?"

"Yes. All of that." She started to squirm on the sun mat. As soon as she moved, it stopped. "No. Oh Joe. Don't stop."

"This is to be savored in small doses, sugar. Besides, for what I have in mind later, I need you to be right on the edge, not sated and relaxed."

"Later?" She glanced over at him. "What do you mean?"

He winked at her. "You'll see."

They lay there sunning and dozing and every time Rainie would feel herself about to drop off, the vibrations would start. After a while sleep eluded her altogether and she lay in a constant state of expectation, trying to anticipate when the silver dildo would come to life again.

Eventually, to escape the danger of too much sun, they moved back into the bedroom. Joe removed the little silver vibrator and began to kiss his way down Rainie's body but she stopped him.

"I want to do something for you."

"Darlin', you're already doing more for me than you know." He bent to his task again but Rainie rolled away from him and got up on her knees.

"No. I get to choose this time and I choose for you to lie still." A sly grin turned up the corners of her mouth. "If you can."

She pressed her mouth to his neck and licked at it with the tip of her tongue, then began trailing kisses down his chest and through the mat of golden lion hair. As she came to each nipple she nipped it lightly as he'd done with hers. She was rewarded with a sharp intake of breath. Her lips traveled every inch of his flat abdomen, paused at his belly button to lick and kiss and moved down to the thatch of dark hair at the root of his magnificent cock.

When she took it in her hand it felt warm to her palm, heat radiating through the cool skin. Thick veins throbbed on the side. The broad head was smooth and the purple skin had darkened. Now a tiny bit of fluid escaped from the slit. Rainie swiped her tongue over it, feeling Joe jerk in her hand. When she dipped the tip of her tongue in the slit his hand came down to tangle in her hair and grip her head with a fierce hold.

Rainie slid a smile at him as she slipped her other hand down to his heavy sac, cupping it and tickling it lightly with her fingertips. Without warning she covered his cock with her mouth and took him into her throat, still teasing his balls.

Joe's hand tightened even more. "Jesus, Rainie. You're killing me here."

She lifted her head. "Just relax and let me do my work. I told you it's my turn." She took her time with him, sliding her moist lips up and down his shaft, teasing his balls, swirling her tongue around the head of his cock until his body was so rigid she thought his body would snap. Only then did she begin to suck him in earnest, pumping with her hand in concert with her mouth.

She let his hands on her head guide her, showing her the pace he liked and the way she should hold her mouth. His taste intoxicated her, the salty velvet skin on the hard core of steel mingled with his natural musk. His hard muscles flexed as his climax began to build. He pressed harder on her head and she increased her tempo.

His shout was the only warning she had and then the first splash of hot cum hit the back of her throat. Her hand kept working him as he emptied himself into her, the thick liquid sliding down her throat as she swallowed every bit of it. She didn't lift her head until the last spasm had left his cock and he fell back on the pillows with a groan.

Rainie lay down next to him, cuddling close, his arm pulling her next to his body.

"You are a treasure, Rainie McIntyre," he told her when he could speak. "An absolute treasure. I'd like to wrap you up and keep you tucked away from the rest of the world."

"Mmm. That sounds nice."

"But," he sat up, bringing her with him, "we have things to do and the night's just beginning."

She cocked her head. "What kind of things?"

"That's part of my surprise. Turn over. I want to take that plug out for a while."

Again she felt bereft at the emptiness it left behind and her body began anticipating his thick cock sliding in there.

"Okay. Quick shower and then a little ride before dinner."

"Ride? What kind of ride?"

His eyes sparkled with mischief. "You'll see."

He had her put on her dress and sandals but leave off her underwear. She wondered what he had in mind and hoped he'd tell her soon. The vibrator had left her with a slickness no shower could wash away and her pussy ached for something to fill it.

He took two steaks out of the fridge and set them in a marinade. "They'll be ready when we get back."

"Back from where?"

"A little ride to see the beach at night. Come on." He led her into the garage where he handed her the motorcycle helmet again. "Buckle up."

When the bike was ready she went to climb up behind him as she'd done the night before but he shook his head.

"Not this time. Up here." He slid back on the seat to make room for her.

Rainie straddled it as best she could but when she went to settle herself he stilled her with his hands. She heard the slide of the zipper on his jeans and felt him flip up her skirt. He lifted her with his big hands and when he settled her back down his cock slid into her cunt until the tip of it touched her womb.

"I knew you'd be nice and wet after that little silver bullet did its trick and I was right."

"Joe!" she squealed. "You don't mean we're going to ride like this."

Joe chuckled. "Didn't you say you wanted a wild, unconventional weekend? Well, darlin', they don't get much more unconventional than this." He lifted her hair and kissed the nape of her neck, then bit the side of it. "Better hang on."

He settled her hands and feet, tucked the hem of her skirt in firmly on either side of her thighs, raised the garage door with the remote and they roared out into the night.

Rainie was glad the helmet had a visor that concealed most of her face because she was sure everyone was looking at them as they raced down one street and then another. Whenever they stopped for a light, Joe cradled her with his body, protecting her. He also managed with his movement to push his balls against her bare ass under the dress and rub the tip of his cock on that special sensitive spot inside her cunt.

Saturday night in a beach town is a busy time and this one was no exception. The sidewalks were crowded with people, parking slots were full, kids on bicycles raced in between traffic often creating havoc. Up one street and down another they went, streetlights and store lights a rainbow blur. The saltwater breeze blew against their skin but Rainie thought she'd needed a freezer to cool off her overheated body.

With every bump and jolt Joe's cock stroked into her. The front of the motorcycle seat pressed against her clit, the vibrations nearly driving her crazy. Her nipples were so hard she was sure they'd poke through the flimsy material of her dress and her pussy began to clench around his thick hardness.

When she began to feel the orgasm building, she panicked. "Joe?" she screamed.

"Right with you, darlin'. Hang on."

They veered off onto a side street Joe followed it to a deserted building that faced the beach. Pulling around to the side he cut off the motor and hit the kickstand. With hands not quite steady he took off their helmets and gripped Rainie by the waist.

"It's my dance, Rainie." His voice was a hoarse whisper. "I'll lead."

Holding her tightly, pressing her forward so her clit rubbed against the front of the seat, he thrust his hips back and forth with quick hard strokes.

"Grab your clit," he ordered. "Rake your fingernail over it."

She could hardly get her breath but she fumbled under her skirt, found the throbbing nub and dragged her nail over the surface. Just like that she came, with Joe pulsing inside her. Finally, spent, she collapsed back against him, her heart skittering wildly. Then something occurred to her and she sat up.

"Joe! God, Joe, we didn't—"

"Got you covered, darlin'." He lifted her up, slid out of her and stripped the condom off his cock. From a pocket he dragged out a handkerchief and wrapped the condom in it for later disposal. "A Boy Scout's always prepared."

He turned her halfway on the seat and kissed her, his tongue stroking inside her mouth, his lips caressing hers, one large hand cupping a breast. Their tongues twisted around each other, giving and taking. When they ran out of breath he lifted his head.

"I think the ride back will be a little less exciting." He kissed her cheek, zipped up his jeans and settled her back in front of him.

Rainie could hardly say a word. They snapped on their helmets and Joe kicked the Ducati to life.

* * * * *

They'd polished off the steaks, a salad and baked potatoes like two starving people. Rainie insisted on clearing the table and putting the dishes in the dishwasher since Joe had cooked. Now they sat across from each other drinking the last of the wine, eyes smoldering with the knowledge of what was coming next.

"I think—" Joe started. Stopped. Cleared his throat. "I think we should go upstairs."

"Yes. We should."

They climbed the stairs, arms around each other's waists. All through the meal the anticipation had been building in both of them. The motorcycle ride, rather than depleting them, had only built the excitement.

In the bedroom Joe flipped on the stereo again and carefully lit the fresh candles he'd set out. Honeysuckle flowed into the room. He lifted Rainie in his arms and carried her to the bed, stripping off her dress. His gaze raked her from head to toe, admiring every curve and slope. His amber eyes darkened to deep gold as desire mingled with many other emotions.

They both knew tonight was it. Tomorrow the fantasy would be over. But tonight Joe would give her something no other man ever had, take her in a way she'd longed to be taken and bring her a pleasure greater than she'd ever known.

Rainie was so moved by what she saw in his eyes and on his face she wanted to cry. Her lion was looking at her in a way no one ever had, with desire and adoration. She wished for a miracle to make time stop and tomorrow never come.

Joe reached into the drawer of the nightstand and pulled out the wrist restraints.

Rainie wet her lips as she imagined what was to come.

He bent down and kissed her, tasting the inside of her mouth, then fastened the cuffs around her wrists, first slipping the connecting chain around one of the slats in the headboard. Next he pulled out the silk scarf and blindfolded her.

She heard the sound of him shucking his cutoffs and then he was beside her, his naked body pressed against hers, his hands exploring her.

She felt his fingertips brush over every inch of her as if he were memorizing the surface of her skin. Soft butterfly kisses beat their wings on her eyelids, her cheeks, her ears, her neck. He stroked her shoulders and her arms, kissed each finger with precise care. When he began a sensuous journey at the pulse beating madly in the hollow of her throat, Rainie could only lie there, afraid to disturb the moment by so much as a movement or a word.

He spent a long time on her breasts, teasing and tormenting them until the still-sensitive nipples were dark red with desire. She felt his teeth nibbling at the hard points, his tongue tracing patterns over the slope and swell. His hands held them as if they were precious jewels, cupping and kneading and stroking them.

He'd been right. She could almost come just from this. But she didn't want to. She wanted what she knew he would do any moment.

Her ribs received the same infinite care as he drew lines with the tip of his tongue then lapped at the skin. His fingers traced a line from the valley between her breasts down to her navel where he swirled the tip of his tongue in a lazy pattern. As his tongue moved over her his hands massaged her breasts, pulling and tugging on the nipples until Rainie thought they would burst from being so hard and sensitive.

She felt him slide down her body until his head was between her thighs and his mouth pressed open kisses on her mons, the crease at the top of her thighs, the inside of her thighs. When his hands urged her thighs open she was so ready for him to plunge inside her cunt but he was intent on teasing.

"Please," she begged.

He gave a low, throaty laugh. "Don't rush me, darlin'. We've got all night. By the time I take that sweet ass of yours you'll be so hot you'll be ready to explode."

He was right about being hot. The slight roughness of his tongue as it teased at the edges of her vaginal opening sent little quakes rippling through her body. She wanted him to plunge his entire tongue inside her, to lap at her juices, to scrape the inner walls with the tip but he only kept up the maddening, tantalizing strokes. Her skin felt stretched beyond its limits and heated as if she'd stood too close to a fire.

His mouth traveled a path from ankle to thigh with a shower of kisses while his clever fingers drew sensuous circles on her knees and her calves. He traced the crease of her thigh with his tongue, his breath soft on her overheated skin.

Rainie closed her eyes and tried to will herself to relax but every nerve was firing. When she felt him roll away from her she wanted to cry out at the sudden sense of loss. Then he was back, pulling her legs apart and a faint hum signaled what was coming. The anticipation of it caused little tremors in the walls of her pussy.

He played the vibrator over every inch of her cunt as he'd done before, the outer lips, the mons, the inner flesh and the entrance of her sheath. When he moved it to the ultrasensitive skin between her cunt and her anus every nerve in her body fired and heat streaked through her vagina. And when he held it there while his mouth took possession of her clit she bucked against him so hard he had to use an arm to hold her in place.

"Please, Joe." Her voice was ragged. "Do something."

His own voice was strained. "I'm doing something, darlin'. And enjoying the hell out of it."

His hand moved away and she struggled to pull herself together. Then she felt it again, this time against her anus, rimming the opening and electricity sizzled through her. She felt her vaginal muscles spasming on air, desperate to be eased. And he stopped again.

After a while she lost count of how many times he did it. Pressing her vaginal entrance, pressing her anus, teasing the skin between, sucking her clit. He took her up the spiral and down again until she would have done anything to feel his cock inside her.

Without warning he flipped her over, the movement tightening the strap that bound her wrists to the bed. "On your knees, Rainie." His voice was low and urgent. "Come on, darlin'."

The minute she was in that position, she felt the sting of his hand on her again. She wiggled her ass, craving the feel of the slap. This time he alternated the spankings from her ass to her cunt, each one heating her more, driving her desire, until she shook with need. When he stopped and began to apply the gel to her anus, she was so ready for him she bit her lip to keep from begging.

The butt plugs had loosened the muscles or the intrusion would have been painful. As it was, the minute his fingers plunged inside her she felt her pussy gush and her nipples burn. Now. Was he going to do it now? Oh please now. Instead she felt him insert the vibrator and turn it on, sending sent shock waves through her tight asshole. He reached beneath her and began to stroke her clit.

She was beyond the point of begging and pleading. Her body wanted him and it wanted him now.

"Oh please," she sobbed. "Please do it."

He removed the vibrator and ran his fingers over her cunt. "Dripping, Rainie. You are so hot."

"Oh god, Joe." She begged as hard as she could. "Please."

"Please what?"

"Please fuck me in the ass." She almost screamed it she was so desperate.

"All right, darlin'. Here I come."

She felt the head of his cock press at her highly sensitized anus and slip beyond the tight ring of muscles. Rocking slowly he moved into her an inch at a time, all the while crooning to her, telling her what he saw and what he was doing to her. She caught the rhythm and began to move with him. As he filled her the forbidden lust inside her began to shake her with dark need.

Then he was all the way in and she'd never felt so filled in her life. Her utter helplessness only increased the heat sizzling through her.

Joe began to move his hips in earnest, fucking her ass as if his life depended on it, his hands holding tight to her hips, pressing her to him. The orgasm began low in her belly and spread throughout her body, an uncontrollable heat that shut down her mind and made her focus only on one thing. That elusive peak looming before her. One more thrust, two more, she heard Joe shout and he took her over the edge with him.

She came screaming his name, her body convulsing and clenching, juices spilling from her cunt, his hips pushing back against him to lock him inside her. She had never felt such lust or such magic in her life. All she wanted was to freeze this moment in time and never let it stop.

Joe leaned over her to release the hand restraints and yank off the blindfold. When he pulled out of her she wanted to weep. *Come back! Don't stop!* But he was there beside her, rolling her against him, his heartbeat thudding against her almost louder than hers. He kissed her neck, her shoulders, her arm and his hand sought her breast to hold in his palm.

After a long while he got up and she heard him in the bathroom. When he came back he held a washcloth and cleaned her with infinite tenderness before getting back into bed and pulling the covers over them both.

She wanted to say something but she was beyond speech. And what was there to say?

"Go to sleep, Rainie." He spooned her against him and exhaustion claimed her.

Chapter Five

ɚ

Rainie stood in the vestry of the church, her arm linked through her father's, white silk wedding gown swirling around her, veil delicately draped over her face. In a moment they'd start down the aisle.

"Don't settle, Rainie," Joe had told her. "Marry the man of your dreams."

And today she was going to.

Two moments in life were burned into her brain. The last night at the beach house was one. Coming home to her condo was the other. Exhausted mentally and physically she'd headed for the kitchen to see if there was still some wine left in the fridge when a deep voice stopped her.

"You must have hit the beach traffic."

She almost dropped the glass in her hand. Leaning back on her couch was her fiancé, Stuart Joseph Hoffman. Stuart. Joe. He was still wearing the cutoffs and open shirt.

"I drove around a little." She really needed that wine.

He stood up and came to her, resting his hands on her shoulders, amber eyes probing hers. "One question. What kind of relationship do we have that you couldn't tell me the truth? About yourself. About what you wanted. About what I wanted."

"Stuart..."

"Joe. From now on I want you to call me Joe."

"Everything about us was always so..."

"Normal? Conventional?" His mouth turned up in a wry grin.

"Yes." She gave a little laugh.

"Rainie—and that's who you'll be to me from now on—I wanted to be what you wanted. Your father, your family, all of you..." He spread out his hands, palms upward. "I'm a corporate attorney in your father's firm. I saw what I saw and made myself part of it. For Chrissake, I love you. If it meant changing myself to have you, I was willing to do it. I just wanted you any way I could get you."

"I thought you were just like all the other lawyers in the firm. And you seemed so..." She searched for a word.

"Conventional? God, I think I'll hate that word from now on."

"Me too." She swallowed some wine and held up the bottle to him.

He shook his head. "I made myself be what I thought you wanted. Because I love you so much. I didn't want to scare you away with the real me."

"And the motorcycle?"

"That's mine." He grinned. "My secret passion, next to you."

She leaned against the counter and looked up at him. "What made you come to the beach?"

"I couldn't stand the thought of you with another man doing what I wanted to do with you. To you. I hoped when I showed up you'd go along with the charade so we could find out what we really had between us."

She burst out laughing. "I nearly died of shock when I saw you. And I took a big chance showing you that side of myself."

"Me too," he said softly and bent down to kiss her. Where his other kisses had been scorching or devouring or even tender, this one was filled with so much emotion it brought tears to her eyes. When he lifted his head he smiled at her. "I changed our honeymoon plans."

Rainie lifted her eyebrows. "You did?"

"Uh-huh. A cruise was just too conventional. I rented a house on the beach for two weeks and we're not telling anyone where it is."

Rainie looked at him shyly. "Does it come with all the things the last one did?"

Dark heat flared in his eyes. "And more." He sighed. "Rainie, from now on we're gong to be completely open and honest with each other. About everything. I think we made a really good start this weekend, don't you?"

"Very good." She leaned into him, relishing the heat of his body.

He set her wineglass aside and lifted her in his arms. "I think we need to go to bed now, don't you?"

"Mm-hmm." Then she leered at him. "But not to sleep, right?"

He threw back his head and laughed. "Not for a very long time." He reached down and lifted a gym bag from the floor. "I still have some new toys we haven't used."

And now in just minutes they'd be joined as man and wife. As she proceeded down the aisle her eyes caught his and her heart turned over. Her lion was waiting for her, ready to make all her fantasies come true forever.

BRIDE PORTAL
Michele Bardsley

εꝺ

Trademarks Acknowledgement

഼

The author acknowledges the trademarked status and trademark owners of the following wordmarks mentioned in this work of fiction:

ABBA: Polar Music International

Godiva Chocolates: Godiva Brands, Inc.

Hummer: General Motors Corporation

Jell-O: Kraft Foods Holdings, Inc.

Chapter One

ﻼ

Mary Jeanne Wolmack stared at her apartment door and wept.

These were not tears of sweet longing, harbored hope, or romantic sorrow.

Her weeping was ugly, messy and loud. Sobs of complete, utter despair racked her body until she shuddered violently, feeling like Jell-O in an earthquake.

A door opened down the hallway. "Shaddap, will ya? Jeopardy's on and I can't hear a damned thing!"

"S-s-sorry, Mr. W-W-Wiesman." Mary wiped her runny nose on the torn, muddied sleeve of her new black blazer.

The door slammed shut again.

Mary sucked in breaths, but couldn't stop blubbering. She tried to be brave. Really, she did. When she got laid off this morning, she packed up her desk, smiling until her lips ached. As she exited the cubicle she'd worked in for the last two years, she ignored the whispers, mean-spirited chuckles and dirty looks. She'd left the telemarketing firm with shoulders squared and head held high.

She didn't break down once she reached her car, either. She put her box of personal items in the trunk, slipped into the driver's seat, and put on *Abba's Greatest Hits*. Belting out the second chorus of "Waterloo", she stopped at Main and 3rd Street, waiting for the light to turn green.

A scruffy young man opened her door, pointed a gun in her face, and demanded that she get out of the car. She grabbed her purse and vacated it immediately.

She walked five blocks to the police station, waited two hours to make a report, and slogged the three-mile walk home. She attempted several times to hail a cab, but as her friend and fellow tortured dieter often commiserated, "No cabbie stops for fat chicks."

The rain started after she walked the first mile home. The mud was courtesy of a Hummer that had veered too close to the curb and spun through a large puddle—which soaked her entire self. The ripped clothing was from ramming into a chain-link fence. She'd dodged two teenage boys on bicycles who both thought playing "sidewalk chicken" with a wet, angry, thin-challenged woman was funny.

Finally, Mary had trudged inside her building, up two flights of stairs, and now stood forlornly in the hallway because…*sniffle*…because…*sniffle*…becaaaaauuuse…

Her goddamned key had broken in the lock.

She wailed anew.

"Mary?"

Her open-mouthed sob turned into a horrified squeak. Oh, God. Not him. Not now. The Great and Gorgeous Matthew Adams, the demigod of lust who'd moved across the hall two weeks ago, had arrived to witness her fall from grace—admittedly, a short trip. He was really tall, at least six and half feet, and really, really buff—he reminded her of The Rock in *The Scorpion King*. He wore his black hair shoulder-length and loose. It was sexy as hell, but not exactly businesslike—unless he was a gigolo.

"Are you all right?" he asked.

"Yes, thank you. You can…uh, go." *Shoo, demigod. Go on, shoo.*

"I cannot leave you in distress."

He had such an odd, formal way of speaking. She couldn't place his accent—almost French, almost Scottish. They'd never conversed for long. He gave her such complete attention, his stare almost unblinking, that his manner both thrilled her and freaked her out.

"Please go away," she said. "I'm...I'm...thinking."

"This is how hu — er, women engage in cogitation?"

Startled by his geek-speak, she laughed. She turned and looked at him. Her face felt swollen, her eyes ached, and her body felt beaten and bruised. "What are you, a lawyer?"

"No."

"Scientist?"

"No."

"Professor?"

"No, Mary. I will tell you who I am at another time." Distress filled his gray-green eyes. "You are unwell?"

"A bad day," she admitted. "The worst day of my life, and honey, that's saying something." She clutched her purse, waved good-bye, and squelched past tall-and-yummy. She felt a light touch on her elbow. She looked at him over her shoulder. "Yes?"

"You are unable to get into your living quarters?"

"Key broke in the lock."

"I offer my abode to you. You will rest there and I will fix the door for you." He grimaced. "This lord of the land does not respond quickly to such problems."

"Lord of the land?" She grinned. The guy had a sense of humor, which was another point in his favor. Not that he needed points because she'd take him as is, right now. He, on the other hand, was a nice guy who probably had a tall, skinny blonde girlfriend who was a model or flight attendant or barista. "Yeah, the landlord is a jerk. No offense, Matthew, but I just want to get inside, take a long, hot bath, and drink a gallon of white zin."

"Please, Mary." To her utter shock, he dropped to his knees and took her dirty, scraped hand into his warm grasp. "Allow me this kindness. I have wanted to spend time with you and have been unable to gain your attention long enough to ask." He stared at her, yearning in his gaze. "Is it too much too hope that you might find me worthy?"

Mary hit the wall of her own restraint and sanity. She had no job, no car, and no way to get into her apartment. Now, the most handsome man she'd ever met was on his knees in front of her begging to know if he was worthy of her.

She giggled. The giggles turned into guffaws. The desperate hilarity was the last straw for her abused psyche and tired body. The whole world grayed as she pitched forward...right into the arms of Matthew Adams.

* * * * *

When she awoke, Mary found herself naked, in a warm bath filled with pink bubbles. Lit candles rimmed the large tub. The mild scent of vanilla entwined with the spice of sandalwood. Sitting up, she looked at the small table within arm's reach of the tub. On it sat two fizzing glasses of champagne and—dear God—a twenty-piece box of Godiva's G Collection.

"Am I dead?" she whispered.

"No," said Matt as he hurried into the bathroom. "I'm sorry! I called in an order to Zio's. You—you mentioned you liked Italian food."

He looked so anxious. Why? Because he wanted to please her? Whoa. His gaze ensnared hers. "I washed you thoroughly and cleaned your clothing. I've been watching you, Mary. You wouldn't have drowned."

She smiled and nodded. Then, as calmly as she could, she asked, "What the fuck is going on?"

He looked nonplussed. "I conveyed all there is to know. Would you like me to repeat it?"

"No," she said. Her heart thudded. Freaking Matthew was seducing her. Oh, baby! "I got the gist. I fainted, you caught me. Now I'm in a hot tub surrounded by candles and chocolates and champagne." She looked him over. He wore nothing except a thin gold chain around his neck. The chain attached to a gorgeous blue stone, which hovered right below his collarbone. It wasn't like any gem she'd ever seen. But jewelry was not the issue right now.

"Why are you naked?" she asked in a strangled voice.

"I would hope to please my lady by joining you."

"I knew it. I'm dead."

"Mary, you are not in Illania."

"Ill-whataya?"

"Heaven." He waved impatiently. "It is of no matter. Great Geru! I grow weary of these Earth mating rituals."

She blinked at him. "Mating rituals?"

He swallowed heavily then dropped to his knees again. His big, tanned hands grasped the edge of the tub and his eyes searched hers. "This is not my way. If we were on my planet, I would steal you away and I would kill anyone who tried to keep me from claiming you. You are my *harataya*."

"Oh. Well that explains everything, doesn't it?" Beautiful, muscled...and oh mama, what a package...but totally, completely crazy. She patted his hands and smiled brightly. "Would you get my clothes, please? I need to go home."

His roar of frustration seemed to shake the walls. He surged to his feet, plucked Mary from the tub as if she weighed no more than a feather, and slung her over his massive shoulder. Water sloshed, putting out the candles. Pink bubbles flew everywhere.

In five strides he was in the bedroom. He dumped her— naked, wet and shocked—onto the bed. "You are mine, Mary Jeanne Wolmack. I have traveled all the way from Kratania to claim you. I care not for what the Oracle says about wooing an Earth woman. I have tried the simpering ways of Earth males and they do not work. You have ignored me for two weeks."

Mary gaped at him. He stood next to the bed, hands on hips, a magnificent barbarian warrior assessing his stolen bride. "I...uh...what?"

"You are so beautiful," he said, his gaze roving her shivering form. "I have dreamed often of touching you, of taking you. I am tired of pleasuring myself and wasting my seed!"

Panic burbled through her, but she had to admit to some serious thrillage, too. Insane or not, this hunk wanted her. "You may have noticed I'm not exactly...well, thin." Gak. Why had she felt it necessary to point that out to him? The man had eyes.

"Thank Geru! You are well-built, my *harataya*. You are very luscious." Lust darkened his gaze. "When we return to Kratania, you will make me the envy of my brothers." He leaned over the bed, once again looking anxious. "Do you refuse me?"

"Oh, honey." She rose up on her elbows. God, he was nuts. And it would be really, really wrong to take advantage of his mental state in order to have her way with his muscled bod. *Look at that cock. It's so huge.* Lust heated her belly...liquefied and flowed to her pussy. Damn, she wanted his cock inside her. Plunging. And plunging...oh merciful heavens!

"If you could prove you were an alien, I'd let you ravish me."

"That is all you require?" His brows rose in surprise.

"Sure. And those chocolates. You can't buy a girl the G Collection and not let her have it."

His lips tugged into a half-smile. "The chocolates please you? At least the Oracle was right in that regard. So, if I prove that I am from Kratania and give you the sweets, you will allow me the honor of *ghrata*?"

"What is *ghrata*?"

He frowned, as if trying to figure out how to explain the term. "Making love."

"Yep." It was a safe response because poor, sweet, deluded Matt was one taco short of a combo platter. There was no way in...uh, Illania he would really ravish her. "I would *ghrata* the night away with you, babe."

"Then it is a bargain." He crawled onto the bed and knelt between her legs. "Let me taste you, Mary. I have longed to be near you, to touch you. Enjoying you this way will not affect *ghrata* or our bargain."

Mary's heartbeat kicked into overdrive. He really wanted to go down there and...and taste her? None of her boyfriends, what few there had been, had ever offered to give her pleasure. Her sexual experiences had always been disappointing. She stared at Matt, unable to respond. The knot in her throat was so tight she could barely breathe. He looked at her, waiting patiently. Finally, she managed a weak nod.

Mary trembled as Matt's long fingers slid up her too-jiggly thighs. He treated her skin as though it was rare silk. He smiled at her, his gaze alight with lust. With his forefingers, he parted her vulva, looking at her pussy as though he were examining the dessert bar at a buffet. His breath quickened.

Matt wasn't lying to her.

He was turned on...because of her.

Leaning forward, he kissed the top of her pubic bone. Then his tongue slid across her clitoris. Pleasure erupted, sudden and intense. She held on to the covers and shuddered. Exhaling raggedly, she tried to relax and allow herself the bliss he offered.

Matt pressed his tongue into her wet flesh, licking her inner pussy lips, teasing her entrance. Then he kissed her clitoris, flicking the swollen nub.

She nearly launched off the covers.

His tongue delved between the moist folds, lapping up the beads of her desire, always returning to tease her clitoris before flitting away like a fickle butterfly.

Parting her labia, he blew hot air across her sensitized flesh then paused as the effects rippled from her cunt to the low, heavy swirl in her belly.

He waited. Seconds ticked by and she gulped in air, her body whimpering for relief. But no, Matt left her quivering and panting and wanting.

Showing no mercy, he plunged his tongue into her pussy, fucking the engorged flesh. Mary's need pulsed hot and strong. She felt wild and raw, her fingers twisting deeper into the covers. Sweat beaded her throat and trickled between her breasts.

Once again, he stopped his sensual torture, but only for a second. His mouth settled onto her clit. She felt two of his thick fingers slide into her pussy. Curling under her entrance, he pushed up and back and then he sucked hard on her clit.

Stars exploded behind her eyes. Her hips left the bed as the orgasm seized her. Pleasure undulated over and over until it was reduced to trembles and tingles.

He sipped on her juices and soothed her swollen cunt. Then he rose to his knees, wiped his chin, and grinned.

Mary didn't care if the man was from Mars or from an asylum. She was so going to do him.

But Matt removed his hot self from the bed. She had yet to regain her breath, so she watched his buttocks flex and his muscles ripple as he took a ring from his nightstand and pointed to his left.

To Mary's amazement, a swirl of green light appeared. It grew larger and larger until it was as tall and wide as Matt. The light now looked like rippling liquid—a pond turned on its side. Matt reached toward the bed and offered his hand.

"Come with me," he demanded.

"No thanks." Her heart thudded. Was that, seriously, a portal to another world?

"We made a bargain." His eyes glittered dangerously. "Is your word worth nothing?"

"I didn't pack for a guilt trip," she muttered as she scooted off the bed. She ignored his proffered hand as she rolled to her feet. Mary walked to the green mirror and peered at it. "What are you? Some kind of magician?"

"No," said Matt. "I am Crown Prince of Kratania."

"You're what?"

She felt his big hand splay on her back then he pushed her into—no, through—the crazy green glass.

Mary landed on something big and muscled and swearing. When she managed to lift her head, which ached fiercely thank you very much, she was faced with a man looking both amused and pissed off. Yikes. She struggled to a sitting position.

"It is my lucky day," he murmured. "You have very nice breasts." To her shock, he cupped her double-Ds and thumbed her nipples.

"Who the hell are you?" she blurted.

"Vrek. And you are?"

"Insane."

The man on whom she landed gladly allowed her to remain astride his supine form. He was so glad, she noticed, that his cock hardened. The only thing keeping her vagina from touching it was the towel wrapped around his waist.

She heard a thud behind her then a string of nonsensical curses.

"That's my woman!" roared Matt. He scooped her off Vrek, holding her against his chest protectively, and glared down at the grinning fool.

"Who is to say that Insane is yours? She landed on me."

"Only because you are in my bedroom." Matt frowned. "Why are you here?"

"Your bathtub is bigger than mine and it has a waterfall."

As the men continued their argument, Mary looked around in wonder. Holy shit. Matt was an alien. This was a different world. He had proven his claims…and so, unless she chickened out, she was going to make love to him. Hooray!

"How many times must I tell you to stay out of my room?" groused Matt. "Build a waterfall in your own bathroom and leave mine alone."

At that moment, one of the massive double doors at the end of the huge room opened and two very voluptuous, very tall women entered. Both only wore seductive smiles. They sauntered toward Vrek, looking curiously at Mary and Matt.

"Is everyone here naked?" she asked crossly.

"I am not," said Vrek. He pointed at the tent in his towel and smiled broadly.

Oh, lord. She pressed her hot face into Matt's massive shoulder. Then she inhaled a breath and ventured another look. Nope. Nothing had changed.

"Leave," boomed Matt to the women. "Go to Vrek's room, if you feel the need for sport."

"We would be honored to serve you, Crown Prince Tek," said the blonde, who looked at least ten years older than the brunette. She laced her fingers through the young woman's hand and drew her forward. "Alana joined the harem today. Is it not your pleasure to welcome her?"

Mary felt a strange emotion weave through her. It took her a second to recognize the jealousy. Were those two blind? Could they not see Matt held her in his arms? So what if she'd only known him two weeks and he'd only seduced her five minutes ago? Glaring at the blonde, she wrapped her arms around her man and snuggled. The tart's eyes went molten with rage. Mary barely resisted the urge to yell *nyah, nyah!*

"Vrek," said Matt...er, Tek in a weary voice. "Did I not tell you to stop adding to the harem?"

"We have only a hundred girls," said Vrek. "And they must service all seven of us brothers. Well, six. Mek prefers men. But he has his own harem." He said this last sentence accusingly as if his sexual pick of one hundred beautiful women was a terrible burden.

Vrek looked at Mary, his expression aggrieved. "Tek keeps marrying them off."

"They deserve lives of their own," said Tek in a voice that suggested he had given the same explanation many times. "It is wrong to keep them in servitude."

"Not all of us wish to leave such service," said the blonde. "Alana is my sister. She, too, wishes to please the Crown Prince."

"Vrek, escort Rona to your room and do as you wish," said Tek. "Alana, stay here."

Grumbling good-naturedly, Vrek jumped to his feet and tugged Rona out of the room. She laughed merrily, but the sounds rang false. It was obvious to Mary that Rona wanted to stay.

"I must release you for a moment," he murmured. "I retrieved your chocolates."

He put her on her feet and guided her to the freakishly gigantic bed. As soon as she sat down, he grabbed the box from a nearby table and placed it on her lap.

"Thanks," she said. Her gaze skittered toward Alana. As curvy and tall as she was, she still only appeared to be sixteen or seventeen. "You're not gonna do anything I might have to castrate you for, are you?"

Tek blinked down at her. "Castrate?"

"If you try anything with that girl, I will cut off your balls."

He laughed heartily. "No, my beautiful Mary. This I promise you." He strode across the massive room and opened the tall, carved door on the left. He entered it briefly and when he returned, he wore a copper robe. He held two others—one that was gold silk, and the other white cotton. He laid the gold robe next to Mary, so she stood and put it on.

Tek gestured Alana forward. As the girl walked to her sovereign, she ducked her head. Her whole body trembled.

"What do you wish of me?" she asked. Apparently all her sensual bravado had gone out the door with sister. "I am versed in massage, in oral pleasure, in—"

"No," said Tek gently as he put the robe over her head. "Alana, why did you join the harem?"

"My family is too poor to pay my dowry," she admitted as she finished putting on the garment. "My fiancé would have me without it, but Father has too much pride. They think I am visiting cousins. I lied to them so they would never know my shame." Tears slid down her cheeks. "Rona told me that if I stay in the harem, I might earn enough coins to wed. She says the all the princes are very generous."

"Rona does not send any money to your family?"

Alana shook her head.

Tek glanced at Mary, grimacing. "It is customary for adult children to send a portion of their earnings to their parents. It is a gesture of love and of thanks. We call it matra-patra, which means 'mother-father honor'."

Mary seriously doubted ol' Rona had any love in her heart, much less gratitude, for anyone other than herself. "C'mere, Alana," she said. "Have a chocolate."

The girl looked at Tek, who nodded his permission, and she walked to the bed and sat. Mary opened the box, took off the paper insert, and offered the girl her pick. She plucked one out and popped the whole thing into her mouth. Her eyes widened as she chewed it. After she swallowed, she exclaimed, "It is wonderful!"

"You've never had chocolate?" asked Mary.

"We do not have cacao beans on Kratania," said Tek, chuckling. "And we really have no equivalent to your truffles."

"That's...that's...horrifying!" Mary couldn't live on a planet without chocolate. Not that she was exactly considering doing so.

Tek strode to a massive dresser against the far wall. He opened a drawer and plucked a bag from inside it. Then he returned and handed the bag to Alana. She took it, opened the drawstring, and gasped. Carefully, the girl removed a blood-red stone.

"This will buy your dowry," said Tek. "And the rest should cover what Rona owes your family. Tell your father that Crown Prince Tek honors his service to his country. And promise to never lie to your mate or to your father again."

"Yes, Prince Tek," said Alana, her face bright with hope. "Thank you, milord and m'lady."

Mary smiled and once again offered the box. "Go on, take another one."

Delighted, Alana took another chocolate. Then she rose from the bed. Tek guided her to the door. "Go see my steward. Ask him to arrange transportation to your home."

Alana nodded, hesitated, and then planted a kiss on Tek's cheek. She hurried out the door.

Tek returned to the bed and smiled at Mary. "It was kind of you to share your chocolates."

"That was nothing compared to what you did for her." Mary was still wrapping her brain around the idea that her would-be lover was a crown prince. She boxed up the chocolates and returned them to the side table.

Tek sat next to her and grasped her hands. "I have kept my side of the bargain."

"It's kinda hard to believe...you're not from Earth. And this place is real. And...and you really want me."

"Yes," he murmured, "I want you very much."

Oh, what the hell. Mary fell back onto the bed and undid the sash to her luxurious robe. It fell open, allowing Tek a full view of her nudity. "All right, baby. Let's *ghrata.*"

Chapter Two

ဆ

Mary waited for Tek to make his moves. Though his gaze feasted on her naked body, he didn't touch her. Instead, he sighed deeply and turned away.

Rejection cooled her lust instantly. Was she really such a fool? She had believed him. Tears pricked her eyes, but she blinked them away.

"I knew this was too good to be true," she said. Anger surged and boiled. "You are a shithead!" She leapt from the bed and tugged the robe closed. "Take me home, Matt or Tek or whatever your name is."

"Mary, please calm yourself."

"No!" She wanted to gouge out his eyes the way he had gouged out her heart. She had believed all this nonsense about making love and mating and...and...argh! He didn't really want her. She was fat and plain and pitiful. She sure as hell wasn't beautiful like Rona and Alana. What an idiot she was to believe even for a second that a gorgeous, kind-hearted man wanted her!

She stomped toward the double doors with every intention of leaving the bedroom and wandering the halls until someone opened a portal to her apartment. Before her hand touched the oversized gold handle, Tek scooped her up.

Mary bopped him on the jaw. The blow didn't faze him at all. He merely grinned at her. "You have such fire," he murmured. "I cannot wait for our *ghrata*."

"You'll have to wait until hell freezes over."

"Do not be angry with me," said Tek. "Beautiful Mary, I have not been honest with you. You do not understand our customs or traditions. I cannot take the next steps until you know — and accept — the truth."

He took her back to the bed and sat down, but he did not release her. Her ire had been doused by his sincerity, so she stared at him and waited for the information bombs to drop.

"When a crown prince turns thirty, he must wed. No king has ever chosen his own bride. We must go before the Oracle and ask her to choose for us."

"That sounds terrible. Like slavery or something."

"No," said Tek. "The Oracle is very wise. All matches between kings and their queens have borne love as well as heirs. It is said that as long as the kings follow the Oracle's advice, Kratania will remain a loving, peaceful planet. For a thousand years, it has been so."

"You mean...the Oracle sent you to me?"

"Yes. You will be my queen." He took her hands in his and kissed her fingertips. "The *ghrata* is more than making love. It is a ritual that binds us together, heart and soul, body and mind. Once it is performed, we will be together for always. We will rule Kratania as one."

"And if I don't agree to marry you?"

"My crown passes to my brother Sek and I must seek the robes of a monk."

Holy crap. Mary thought it would be a real shame for Tek to never again use his sexual talents. "What about my life on Earth?"

"If you marry me, you cannot go back." He looked uncertain. "Will you miss it so much?"

Mary wanted to laugh, but tears fell instead. She had acquaintances, not friends. She was the only child of parents who had passed on a decade ago and she had no other family. As of today, she had no job, no car, and no way into her apartment.

If she thought too long about her crappy days and her lonely nights, she would have to admit she'd lived an inferior life. She had never believed herself worthy of reaching for something better. And yet, something better had fallen into her lap. Or rather, she had fallen into his arms.

"I accept," she said. "If you want me, Tek. You got me."

* * * * *

"Good child-bearing hips," said the wizened old lady. She looked older than time with her gray hair, rheumy eyes, and stooped form. She wore royal blue robes and leaned on a polished staff. A blue stone gleamed from its circular top.

"Can we move on with this inspection?" Mary asked impatiently. Naked and cold, she shivered as she stood in the small chamber.

As the Oracle made her fourth circuit around Mary, she patted her ass. "Got some meat on your bones, don't you?" She cackled as she peered up at Mary. "You will give our crown prince something to hold onto when he's plowing you."

Mary stared at her, unable to believe those words had just crossed such grandmotherly lips.

The Oracle struck her staff onto the marble floor and the sound echoed throughout the circular room. "Are you worthy of our Crown Prince?" she intoned.

Mary opened her mouth, but no words came out. The woman leaned forward and whispered, "The answer is yes."

Swallowing the knot in her throat, Mary managed to squeak out, "Yes."

"Good."

Blue light issued from the staff's unusual stone and encircled Mary. She felt heated tingles zip through her body. Then an intense circle of heat fused to her skin just below her collarbone. After the light and sensations dissipated, she felt utterly at peace. She suddenly knew that she was exactly where she belonged.

"The Stone of Kratania has confirmed my vision," said the Oracle. "It has gifted you as well." She pointed at Mary's chest.

Mary lifted her fingers. Just below her collarbone, she felt the hard round edge of a jewel. "What is it?"

With a twirl of her fingers, the Oracle produced a small mirror. Mary took it and lowered until she saw the beautiful blue stone. It was lodged into her skin, but it didn't hurt or feel out of place. She touched it, wondering how the hell it had fused to her skin. "Will it stay there forever?"

"Yes." The Oracle nodded. "The Prince was given his the night he submitted to my choice for his queen."

Tek's necklace! He had probably connected the gold chain to his stone to prevent questions from Earth people. The illusion had been a good one—she hadn't noticed the gem was attached to him.

And now, she had one too.

"Come with me." The Oracle gestured at Mary to follow her. They left the little room and entered a cozy living space. In the hearth burned a lovely fire and the floor was littered with huge, fluffy pillows. On a tray positioned before the fireplace sat a tea service and tiny sandwiches.

"Here is your robe."

Mary put on the gold robe that had been taken from her when she entered the Oracle's quarters. The woman squatted onto a pillow positioned on one side of the tray. Mary took the other pillow and looked at the goodies. Her stomach growled. She hadn't had a thing to eat since lunch…which seemed like a year ago.

"Go on, my princess," said the Oracle. "Eat."

Mary didn't have to be told twice. She grabbed a couple of sandwiches and bit into the first one. It was creamy and tasted like peppered cucumber. The second one was sweet and crunchy.

"Is that all there is to this business?" Mary plucked another sandwich from the tray. "You give me permanent jewelry, pronounce me Queen, and we're done?"

"No," said the Oracle, chuckling. "Tomorrow, Prince Tek will present you to the Court and announce you as his harataya. As is our custom, any female can challenge your claim to the throne."

Mary nearly choked. "You mean I have to fight other women?"

"In my life as an Oracle, a hundred and three years now, no female has ever challenged my pick for queen. It is a mere formality."

Feeling slightly better about the situation, Mary tried a tiny square cake. It tasted like a sugared pear. Not bad. Of course, a drizzle of chocolate would certainly improve it. "What's happens after that?"

"You perform the marriage rites."

"Dare I ask what they involve?"

The Oracle chose a bright orange teacake and popped it into her mouth. After she chewed the treat, she looked at Mary. "You and Tek will bond before the King, Queen and the Royal Court. After you are pledged to each other, you must retire to Tek's chamber and perform your first sexual act as a married couple before the Guild."

"What?"

"You'll have an audience the first time you fuck the prince," the Oracle said coarsely. "The Guild is made up of five powerful psychics. They will confirm your first sexual act as a married couple and make sure that his seed has been planted in you."

"What?"

"Tek's cock must not penetrate your vagina until the night of your marriage. He's primed to get the Queen pregnant from day one and only heirs produced within the marriage are legitimate." The old woman peered at her. "It is your duty to provide your husband with plenty of sons."

"Is that all?" A note of sarcasm crept into the question.

The Oracle nodded. "Don't worry, you'll do fine."

No, I will not do fine. Mary was in trouble. As much as she wanted Tek, all these expectations were scary. She wasn't from this world, but she was going to rule it? And she was going have an alien's baby before she even had a chance to adjust to being the alien's wife. The delicious food soured in her stomach. She pressed a hand against her roiling tummy.

"I've never been wrong about a queen." The Oracle poured a cup of tea and handed it to Mary. "You are strong in mind, spirit and heart. You are the perfect match for our prince."

"Yeah," said Mary, clenching the teacup. "Perfect."

* * * * *

When she returned to Tek's rooms, Mary had her speech prepared. *I'm sorry, Tek,* she would say mournfully, *but I can't do this. It's too complicated. I haven't thought about children or marriage. You're hot — I mean you're really hot — but I can't be your queen.*

The problem wasn't the speech — it was her reluctance to give it. What kind of idiot would give up Tek so she could go home to an empty life? So what if she had to do a little song and dance to marry the guy?

Still, fear chilled her.

What was the right decision?

"Tek?" she called as she wandered around the cavernous room. She heard the splash of water so she followed the sounds to an opened door just a few feet away from the bed. She peeked inside. "Hello?"

"Mary," said Tek. "I'm in here."

82

Vrek hadn't been kidding. Designed to look like a lush, tropical jungle, the bathroom was huge. The waterfall gurgled from the wall, which looked liked chunky purple rocks. It splashed into a large circular body of water—she assumed it was supposed to be the bathtub. Flowers in wild shades dotted the large, leafy plants filling nearly every nook and cranny.

Tek was on the opposite side of the tub sitting in a chair. He wore the copper robe. His legs were stretched out and crossed at the ankles.

"How went your interview with the Oracle?" His gaze fell to her neck and he grinned, obviously relieved to see the jewel.

"She says she's never been wrong about a queen and that I'm definitely your girl," she said. "And she told me we can't *ghrata* yet."

"We can do other things," he assured her.

His promise created sparks of lust and longing, but she held off her libidinous thoughts.

"Tek, what if we..." she trailed off, licking her lips. Nerves plucked at her tummy. "We could go back to Earth and live there without all these insane rules and responsibilities. You wouldn't be a monk."

"I wouldn't be a king either," he said, frowning. "I was born and bred to rule. Though it has always been my fate, I have never wanted to be anything else. I will be a good king. And a good king does not abandon his people."

"You mean duty before love?"

"No," he said softly. "Duty because of love."

Mary felt ashamed of her selfish desires. Here was man with the heart of lion and the body of a demigod. He wouldn't abandon her or ask her to do more than she was capable. And Mary was capable of being his queen. The Oracle thought so, Tek thought so, and the damned Stone of Kratania thought so. This was the kind of second chance every woman dreamed of...did she really want to throw it away? So what if it was rough going now and then? Anything worth having was worth fighting for.

"I will stay," she said. "And be your queen."

He smiled broadly. "You will be a great queen, my beautiful Mary. I am proud that you are mine."

She blushed. She had never been so complimented before and she seriously liked it. Looking at him, she pulled off her robe and sauntered toward him. "Now, about those options…"

"Your needs will be met," he promised. Instead of getting up from the chair, he clapped his hands.

Mary stared at him. What the hell did he expect her to do now?

To her surprise, two men sauntered from another corner of the bathroom. They were tall, lean but muscled, and well hung. She knew this because like all the crazy folks on this planet, they were naked. Their skin was tinted aqua and their large eyes were black.

"These are water nymphs," said Tek. "Their semen is only fertile one month out of the year when it is time for their species to procreate. Right now, they cannot impregnate you. For them, giving pleasure is receiving pleasure. They feel what you feel and so, they try very hard to make you happy."

Mary stared at the gorgeous men then at her fiancé. "And you brought them here because…"

"I want to watch them give you pleasure. They can control the water in wonderful ways."

"I thought you didn't have slaves."

"They are neither slaves nor part of any harem. They volunteered."

Mary wasn't convinced. "I'm supposed to marry you. Having sex with other men seems adulterous."

"If your husband-to-be consents to such an arrangement and it will bring him great joy to see you well-fucked, where is the issue?"

Tek had a point. Unbelievable. This morning, she had no dating prospects on the horizon. Now she was engaged to a future king who wanted her to enjoy the sexual talents of water nymphs. Where was the issue?

"Oh, all right…if it means that much to you."

His lips tugged into a grin. "Hmm. Yes, I see how hard it is for you to sacrifice on my behalf." He pointed to the tub. "Get in there, woman."

"Yes, my liege." She rolled her eyes then took the corner steps into the warm, swirling water.

The nymphs joined her. Anticipation spiked her groin as they surrounded her. They didn't touch her, but they were awfully damned close. Their proximity made gooseflesh rise. Her doubts were not assuaged. Was she really going to give in to this crazy proposition?

"They communicate telepathically," said Tek. "They rarely speak aloud. Remember, their satisfaction increases as yours does. Just let yourself be pleasured, Mary."

"Okay." She tried to relax, but man, she felt nervous. The nymphs' gazes were otherworldly and now that she was closer to them, she could see the scaly texture of their skin.

The one behind her grasped her shoulders and drew her backward while the one in front took her legs and lifted them. As she floated on her back, the water took on a strange liquidity, feeling almost solid. The nymphs let her go, but she remained buoyant. Slowly, her body rose until her front was exposed to the humid air of the bathroom jungle. Her backside was cuddled by the water. She felt very safe and inch by inch, she relaxed.

The nymph standing between her spread legs gestured at the water. On either side of her chest, a curl of water rose. Each curl surrounded her breasts. It felt like tiny, heated fingers massaged her skin. As the water cupped and kneaded her breasts, her excitement built.

Two thin tendrils emitted from the larger ones and encircled her nipples. They pulled tighter and tighter until the exquisite pain stole her breath.

The nymphs moved to either side of her. They touched her, their hands amazingly soft as they stroked her skin. They trailed webbed fingers over her ribs and stomach, thighs and calves.

Every so often the water nooses squeezed her aching peaks. The burst of pleasure-pain coupled with the gentle touches of the nymphs' skilled hands was so arousing, she found herself panting and squirming.

"Give her more," demanded Tek. "But do not make her come."

Mary groaned at Tek's command. An orgasm would be really nice, but her body was starved for erotic stimulation. She wanted more. And she knew Tek would see to her pleasure through any means.

What a guy.

The nymphs continued their unhurried exploration of her body, building pyres of lust. Feeling dazed, she watched a swirl of water rise between her legs. The liquid vortex flowed into her pussy. She sucked in a breath. It felt good. Beyond good. Its vibrations and heat made her quiver inside and out.

One nymph leaned over and flicked his tongue, which was long, thin and lizard-like, across her clitoris.

Oh God.

Euphoria snaked through her. She bent her legs and lifted her hips to more fully take the vortex thrusts. Her hands clenched as the flickering tongue and plunging water dildo brought her closer and closer to the peak.

Before she could tilt over the edge, the nymph stopped licking her and the liquid cock melted back into the water.

"Damn it!" she cried. Her body hummed and quaked. "Tek!"

"Yes, my love?" He took off the robe. His magnificent body gleamed in the low lights. She wanted to lick him, especially that yummy, hard cock. Obviously he had enjoyed how the nymphs had revved her engines.

Tek jumped into the water and waded to them. "Your skin is flushed," he murmured, cupping one breast and squeezing. The water tendrils tugged one of her distended nipples. She moaned.

"Prepare her," he said to the nymphs.

She felt a swirling finger of water poke at her anus.

"Hey!" she protested.

Tek lifted her to her feet and embraced her. His hands slid down to her buttocks. Parting them allowed the water finger to deepen its anal exploration. It widened her pucker and increased to the size of two thick fingers.

Tek kissed her.

Her whole world became that luscious kiss. His tongue dipped into her mouth and danced with hers. He took her hostage with his lips, with his lust. And all the while, the nymphs stroked her back, her ass, her thighs.

Mary was awash in pure erotic elation.

The water plunging into her asshole curved into a vortex that entered her pussy. The double penetration tore a groan from her. Tek refused to free her mouth. His hands tightened on her ass and his kiss became even more desperate, even more ravenous.

She wanted relief from the sensual torment but Tek and the nymphs kept stoking the carnal fires. The flames burned away all her doubts, all her worries. She submerged herself in the moment and enjoyed being sexually worshiped by three men.

Mary was only vaguely surprised when the water parted. A huge air bubble formed around the four of them as they sank to the bottom. Her water dildos disappeared, leaving her weak-kneed and delirious with need. God! Would somebody fuck her already?

The water formed a cushion above the concrete floor. One nymph lay down on the "cushion". Tek helped her kneel over the blue, primed cock. Her entire body trembled as she slid onto the glorious dick. Bracing her hands near the nymph's shoulders, she lifted her ass.

She knew exactly what Tek wanted to do. She was too far gone to quit now, but she'd never had anal sex. Then again, she'd never fucked three men at once, either.

"My cock emits a viscous fluid that it is much like your store-bought lubricants," said Tek.

"That's fascinating," she said. "Now shut up and fuck me."

He chuckled as he fit his cock snugly against her anus. "Push back," he said hoarsely, "as I push in."

She did as he said. Her ass burned as he worked his cock deeper and deeper inside. His huge penis was well lubed, which made the going a little easier. The sensations that radiated from her ass and pussy tormented her deliciously. Her body demanded satisfaction, relief, a mind-blowing orgasm.

She wanted to be fucked. Now!

When Tek was fully seated, she couldn't believe how stuffed she felt. No, what she couldn't believe was that she liked the double penetration. And when both men started moving...God, oh God, oh God!

The second nymph knelt in front her. He pushed his stiff cock into her mouth and gently fucked her lips as her ass and pussy took the thrusts of the other cocks.

"More," demanded Tek.

The water nooses on her nipples squeezed harder and harder. Another swirl of water dipped into the air bubble and wormed across her pussy. The liquid tendril cuffed her clitoris and began sucking on the swollen nub.

Euphoria sparked and built higher and higher. Each double thrust sent her spiraling closer. She groaned around the cock impaling her mouth. Getting three-way fucked felt better than...better than...chocolate.

Her orgasm imploded.

Unimaginable ecstasy erupted and blazed from her cunt to every nerve in her body. Rapture filled her with heat and light and savage pleasure. The bliss rolled over her again and again until she was breathless and spent.

The nymph fucking her lips stiffened. Mary clamped her lips on his thick member, licking and sucking the salty crown.

He exploded into her mouth.

His hot semen splashed down her throat and she sucked him all the way to the base. She slurped him clean, enjoyed the feel of his scaled skin against her tongue.

The nymph pumping into her pussy gurgled. His fingers clawed at her hips as his eyes rolled back into his head. As his cum filled her pussy, Tek thrust deeply into her ass and shouted, "Mary!"

Tek's come filled her ass and she clenched around his pulsing cock. The nymph occupying her mouth slipped out and backed away, watching their final act with avid eyes.

Slowly, the remaining two men released their hold on her. Her whole body felt shattered, but lord-a-mercy she felt utterly fantastic. Freed from the yummy cocks, Tek scooped her into his arms. The four of them rose to surface level and the air bubble popped. Water collapsed inward and refilled the tub.

"Thank you," she said to the nymphs. "That was...beyond words."

They both smiled then bowed to her then to their prince.

After they left, she snuggled in the strong arms of Tek. "Thank you," she murmured as she cupped his face and kissed him. "Thank you lots."

"You are most welcome." He returned her kiss. "You should know I have no intention of sharing you after we are wed."

"That's too bad," she replied.

He pinched her ass and she giggled. "Don't worry, darling. I have no intention of sharing you, either."

Tek rewarded her with another long, luscious kiss. But even as she melted into the arms of her lover and almost-husband, Mary thought about tomorrow. Would the people of Kratania accept her?

Or would someone challenge her for the heart of their king?

Chapter Three

෨

"I challenge Mary Jeanne Wolmack!" cried Rona. The sexy blonde rose from a front-row seat, dressed in a red gown designed to show off her big tits, and sauntered toward the dais.

Oh shit.

Mary, Tek and the Oracle stood on a large stage in the middle of a circular room that was half the size of a football field. In the middle of the dais were the thrones of the King and Queen, who looked like they could rule Kratania forever. They had been very nice to Mary, but she still felt intimidated by their beauty and power.

Determined now to meet her destiny head-on, Mary had gotten dressed in the royal blue robes and paraded herself on Tek's arm through the huge crowd. She'd listened to all the speeches and smiled until her lips ached. And finally, the announcement rang out in Tek's strong, deep voice, "The Chosen Crown Princess is Mary Jeanne Wolmack. She is my *harataya!*"

A loud cheer went up.

Then the Oracle—yeah, Miss-No-One-Challenges-My-Choice-For-Queen—pounded her staff onto the floor and announced, "All hail the *harataya* of Crown Prince Tek! Whosoever challenges his *harataya*, speak now or forever hold your peace!"

The Oracle hadn't expected anyone to challenge. The crowd hadn't expected it, either. Another cheer rose up along with thundering applause.

Then Rona's voice had boomed her challenge, silencing the joyful noise.

"Rona," said the King in a voice rife with censure. "You would dishonor your prince's choice as co-ruler?"

Rona bowed prettily, but her eyes flashed hatred at Mary. "She is not of our world, Your Highness. She knows nothing about our planet or our customs. It is my duty as a loyal citizen of Kratania to challenge the Earth woman."

"Loyal citizen?" snorted Mary. "You're loyal only to yourself. When's the last time you sent matra-patra tributes?"

Rona's lips tightened. "I have begged the forgiveness of my parents and made peace with them. If you knew anything about our culture, you would know that asking forgiveness negates the debt."

Mary rolled her eyes. Then she looked at the Oracle. "You said this was only a formality."

The Oracle shrugged. "I can't help the stupidity of this one." She sighed. "You must answer the challenge, Mary. Do you fight for your prince or do you relinquish your claim to Rona?"

Mary glared at Rona. "I fight for my prince."

* * * * *

"I'm going to lose," said Mary. She looked down at the tunic. It was sleeveless and very short. She wore a pair of panties that didn't even try to cover her ass. The garment offered freedom of movement and some coverage, so she wasn't going to complain about the getup.

She and Tek stood in a tent. Outside a warm breeze blew and tickled the cloth walls. In just a few moments, Mary would enter a roped-off circle and try to beat the tar out of Rona. The harem girl had fighting experience and she probably played dirty.

The only good thing about the battle was that it wasn't to the death. The first woman knocked down and pinned for ten seconds won the fight, the prince, and the right to rule Kratania.

"I want to win," she clarified, "but I've never fought anyone before."

"You will do well," assured Tek. He looked really worried.

"What if she wins?"

"I will give up my crown and move with you to Earth."

Shocked, Mary stared at him. "What about duty to your people? I know Rona's a bitch, but she's probably tolerable. You could live with her. You'll be a really good king, Tek."

"A good king needs a good queen." He hesitated. "I have realized something, Mary. I do not wish rule Kratania without you by my side. In fact, I do not wish to do anything without you."

Mary grinned, her heart alight with an emotion she dared not name. Aw, what the hell. She wrapped her arms about her prince and said, "You mean that you love me."

"Love." He nodded. "Yes, Mary. I love you."

"That's crazy," she said. "Nobody falls in love after two days and three-way sex."

He frowned. "It may not be so on Earth, but I know my own heart. I love you."

"So, if Rona wins…"

"I will win, either way," he said. "Because I will have you."

"And Kratania?"

"Sek will do right by my planet. In fact, all of my brothers are strong, valiant and noble. They are good leaders and good men."

Mary nodded, but she knew that Tek wanted to rule Kratania. He wanted to be king. Hell, he deserved to be king. And no matter what happened today, she would make sure that he stayed to rule.

* * * * *

The second time Rona pinned her, the Oracle counted to seven before Mary managed to kick the ferocious bitch off.

As she backed away from the grinning Rona, Mary spit out dirt and blood. The harem girl enjoyed hurting Mary. She'd punched and kicked and bitten and pulled hair, screaming like a banshee every time she smacked Mary around.

Mary had gotten a few good licks in, but she was seriously out of shape and fading fast. Rona, for all her girth, didn't look tired at all.

"What's the matter?" taunted Rona. "They don't teach Earth girls how to fight?"

Unless Mary included watching *Miss Congeniality* and the infamous SING scene, then no, Mary had never learned to fight.

Rona leapt forward, but Mary whirled out of the way. The woman switched directions, and screeching with victory, attempted to grab Mary by the shoulders.

Once again, Mary slipped out of the woman's grasp. She turned to run. Maybe if she kept Rona running and leaping and jumping, the hag would pass out from sheer exhaustion.

Instead, Rona caught Mary from behind, her arms clamping tightly around Mary's waist. Mary howled with anger and despair. She didn't want to lose, damn it. Rona squeezed harder and harder, probably trying to bruise ribs and puncture lungs. Gasping for breath, the face of Sandra Bullock floated through her blurry thoughts.

Wait a minute.

SING.

"Solar plexus," cried Mary, jabbing one elbow into the gut of Rona. "Instep!" She crushed Rona's bare foot under her heel and the woman wailed.

"Nose!" Mary bashed the back of her skull into Rona's face and heard a distinct crunch. "And groin!"

Her fist went back and up straight into Rona's vagina. The woman let go and staggered away. Mary turned around and let loose with a right hook that smashed into Rona's already battered nose.

Rona toppled face-first into the dirt. Mary sat on her and smiled gleefully as the Oracle counted to ten.

* * * * *

"By the power of the Great Geru," said the Oracle, "and the blessing of the King and Queen and people of Kratania, I pronounce you, Tek and Mary, forever bound."

Tek and Mary faced one another. Their jewels sparked, the blue lights meeting in the middle. She felt a jolt and full body tingle. Bound, heart, mind and soul. Yes, she had found her destiny. She was sure of that now. Tek was hers and together they would lead a full and happy life.

The filled-to-capacity ballroom erupted in cheers, laughs and claps. Tek cupped Mary's face and brushed his lips across hers. "I love you," he murmured.

"I love you too." Mary had never felt so happy. She kissed him again and grinned.

"It is time," said the Oracle. "Return to your chamber and enjoy this night."

"What about all these people?" asked Mary.

"Oh," said the Oracle, cackling, "we get to party until dawn. Free drinks and food courtesy of the King. Woo-hoo!"

Music blasted from the other end of the room and soon all the jostling bodies were singing and dancing. Tek led her from the dais and through the boisterous crowd. After many stops, congratulations, smooches and tributes, they finally made it into the hallway.

Tek held Mary's hand tightly as they hurried to their bedroom. Before the door closed behind them, Tek had unbuttoned the simple white wedding gown. The silky material pooled at her feet and left her quite naked. Mary was getting used to the idea of being nude all the time.

Mary fumbled with his tunic and he kicked off his boots and loose pants. Now Tek was gloriously naked. He was so yummy. *And he's all mine.*

"Crown Prince Tek," said a female voice. "We see you are ready to begin."

Mary whirled around and yelped. Three men and two women, all dressed in silver robes, stood in front of the huge bed. "What the holy hell!"

"The Guild," said Tek. "They must watch our first mating."

"Terrific." Feeling decidedly less enthusiastic, Mary marched over to the bed, dragging her beloved with her.

"Well," she said, "let's get this over with so they'll leave."

Tek laughed. "You are so romantic, my beautiful Mary."

She blushed, trying not to look at the five people watching them just a few feet away. This really sucked. She didn't want to have sex with her husband in front of those gawkers.

"I have never tried one of your chocolates," said Tek. "Perhaps your treats will make our first time as husband and wife more pleasurable."

"Everything's better with chocolate," agreed Mary.

She lay down on the bed and looked at Tek. She was not going to look at the Guild. He grabbed the box from the side table and placed it near her shoulder. He opened the box and chose one of the treats.

Tek scooted between her legs then he bent down to lick her pussy.

"Oh!" Mary closed her eyes and enjoyed the sensations of his flickering tongue. Her cunt welcomed every wet, hot stroke. Soon, she was squirming and wet.

Then she felt Tek tuck the chocolate into her pussy.

"Hey!" Her eyes popped open. "What are you doing?"

He grinned, squeezing the round sweet until it was crushed and melting in her crease. "Eating chocolate...and you."

She didn't protest again. He stretched out comfortably, as if he had all the time in the world and as if five people weren't watching them closely, and pushed apart her legs.

He parted her vulva to lick away the beads of her cream. He toyed with her clitoris too, and stroked her to her higher and higher pleasure.

Then...oh, then...he delved into her chocolate-covered opening.

He sucked and nibbled and licked. And when he had driven her mad with his lips and his tongue and wicked fingers, he crawled over her and slid his big cock inside her.

He didn't move, the rat. No, he decided to suckle her nipples, tormenting them until they ached.

Mary's hands were restless, touching every bit of his skin she could reach. And when she couldn't take any more of his lazy lovemaking, she smacked his ass.

"Fuck me," she demanded.

He kissed her, tasting of her essence and caramel-chocolate. She wrapped her legs around his waist and he thrust into her.

She met his every stroke, arching and rubbing as his cock pumped into her faster and harder. All she felt, all she knew was Tek. Sweat rolled of their bodies as they strained toward mutual peaks.

He plowed into her over and over and she felt the spark of her orgasm.

"Oh Mary," he cried, "I'm going to come!"

His declaration drove her over the edge. Together, they reached for rapture and fell into the sparkling heat of completion.

"It is done," said the same woman, speaking for the Guild.

Mary groaned and slapped a hand over her eyes. "Great," she said. "Now go the hell away."

"They're already gone," said Tek. He looked ravenous, as if he were a starving man presented with a buffet. He rolled off Mary then tucked her onto her side so that his chest pressed against her back. He fitted his half-hard cock against her swollen cunt and filled his hands with her breasts, tweaking her nipples. She moaned and wiggled against him.

"My seed is planted," he said, abandoning her breasts to stroke her stomach. "Soon, our child will grow within you."

As scary as it sounded to be a mother, Mary had to admit she loved the idea of carrying and bearing her husband's child. Maybe that's what love did you—made you all mooshy and weird and happy. And love made you reach a little higher and work a little harder.

In no time, Tek had another hard-on. She lifted her leg and guided his cock into her slick entrance. Once again, he cupped her breasts, twisting the peaks as he slid his cock in and out of her weeping pussy.

Mary panted and strained, enjoying every sensual movement. He kissed her neck, whispering sweet nothings, and she smiled.

Slowly, he pushed her onto her front, his cock still embedded. He fucked her like that—his dick squeezed between her thighs, his body pressed against hers. Mary's nipples scraped against the coverlet, her cheek pressed against the edge of a pillow. The pleasure was intense.

Yet again, her husband changed positions.

Bracing on either side of her, he lifted up. Holding onto her hips, he kept his cock buried in her pussy as he brought her up and back.

Before she knew it, she was sitting on his lap. He was kneeling and her legs butterflied on either side of his. He bucked upward, thrusting his cock so deep, she swore his crown brushed the entrance to her womb.

She moaned, holding onto his thighs as his cock plunged into her.

"Mary," he murmured. "Sweet, beautiful Mary."

Mary slid her hand down to her crotch and placed it so she could feel Tek's manhood pierce her cunt. She rubbed her clit, panting as she met Tek's every solid thrust. The orgasm welled and she increased the friction.

"Oh, Tek," she gasped. "I'm going to come on your cock, baby. Oh! Ooooh!"

The pleasure burst into a thousand hot fragments and as her pussy milked his cock, Tek cried out. He came hard, his breath harsh and his body stiffening as his cum shot hot and deep inside her.

"Well," she said trying to catch her breath, "if I wasn't pregnant before, I sure am now."

Tek laughed as he helped off Mary his lap. Together they lay on the bed and looked at each other. "You are very beautiful."

"So you've said." Mary smiled as she traced the skin around Tek's blue stone. "You're not so bad yourself."

He gathered her into his arms and held her tightly. Mary held him right back. Damn she was glad Tek had shoved her through that portal. They had both fought for the right to be together. And they had won. She snuggled deeper into his embrace, drowsy and jubilant.

Yeah, love definitely made you mooshy and weird and happy.

The End

WRONG GROOM

Kit Tunstall

ഌ

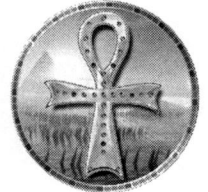

Trademarks Acknowledgement

The author acknowledges the trademarked status and trademark owners of the following wordmarks mentioned in this work of fiction:

Ben & Jerry's: Ben & Jerry's Homemade Holdings, Inc.

Jenny Craig: Jenny Craig, Inc.

Longhi Ballroom: Venetian Casino Resort, LLC Corporation

Rolex: Rolex Watch U.S.A., Inc.

Tao Nightclub: Venetian Casino Resort, LLC Corporation

The Venetian Hotel: Venetian Casino Resort, LLC Corporation

V Bar: Venetian Casino Resort, LLC Corporation

Venetian Wedding Chapel: Venetian Casino Resort, LLC Corporation

Chapter One

ဢ

Jayne Daux led her inebriated friend back to the hotel room Emmy had reserved at the Venetian on the Strip. It was quite a feat to get her to the eighth floor room because both women had imbibed more than a few appletinis at Emmy's bridal shower held in the V Bar downstairs.

"I love you Jayne," said Emmy, giving her an exuberant hug that nearly knocked them both off balance. The petite bride-to-be tottered in her four-inch heels but steadied herself against Jayne.

"I love you too." She was slightly more sober than her friend and managed to steer them to the right room. After all, it was her duty as maid of honor to make sure her friend survived until the wedding. That prevented her from drinking as freely.

"I love Rich so much." Emmy threw her arms wide, nearly taking a dive in the process. "I just love the whole world."

Jayne managed to catch her, supporting her tiny friend with her bigger frame. Next to Emmy, most women seemed large but she seemed huge in comparison. Most days, she tried not to draw comparisons between them but tonight, vulnerable from the alcohol and her own envy of Emmy's happiness, it was impossible to not come up wanting. A size two versus a size eighteen? Of course, she would feel inadequate.

She pushed Emmy gently against the wall so she could search for the keycards to their rooms in the impractical black bag she carried. It matched the plunging, sequined dress perfectly but had just enough space for a credit card, her ID, two keycards and a lipstick.

"You deserve to be as happy as I am." Emmy rubbed her face against the wall as if snuggling the elegantly striped gold and taupe wallpaper.

"I agree."

"Someday you'll meet the right man. He won't care about anything but who you are."

Emmy's comment sobered her up slightly. Jayne retrieved her friend's keycard and slid it through the reader on the first try. She put an arm around Emmy's waist to guide her into the luxurious room and dumped her a little less than gently onto the bed. Normally, her friend wouldn't have broached the topic of her weight and Jayne would never bring it up on her own. "I'm going to my room now. Call me if you need anything."

Without bothering to strip out of the slinky black and silver skirt or red velvet tank top, she kicked off her heels, curled up with the pillow and asked, "Whoever decided I couldn't see Rich before the wedding? It's a stupid tradition."

"It's not just the tradition, remember? His flight didn't arrive from the UK until this afternoon." Her fiancé had spent the last six months working in England, learning the banking industry. He had another six months of his assignment ahead of him but the two lovers decided they couldn't wait any longer to get married and had thrown together the upcoming ceremony in two weeks. "By the time he made it to his bachelor party, he wouldn't have had time to come see you tonight." She pushed the hair off Emmy's face. "You'll see him tomorrow afternoon in the chapel."

"'Going to the chapel...'" Emmy mumbled the rest of the lyrics into her pillow. That was one area where Jayne had no reason to envy her friend. She sounded like someone torturing a bullfrog whenever she burst into song.

"Good night, Emmy."

"'Night, Jayne." Almost immediately, her loud snores filled the room.

Jayne left her friend after covering her with a blanket. As she walked out of the suite and headed to her own room, she decided she wasn't yet ready to retire. It was almost three a.m. but the pleasant buzz she'd been riding the past few hours had mostly dissipated and she wanted it back. After all, she was young, single and in Sin City. It would be criminal not to take advantage of all the delights Vegas had to offer. Secretly, she hoped to finally have the chance to live out her wildest fantasy—a passionate, no-strings night with a handsome stranger.

Besides, it had been way too long since she'd gotten laid. She might not find a partner but she could at least test the waters.

* * * * *

Jayne walked into the Tao Nightclub a few minutes later. The last thing she wanted to do was put a damper on the men's fun. She scanned the room as quickly as she could, looking for remnants of Rich's bachelor party. Though she had never met the groom, she knew several of the men who would have attended, including Emmy's two brothers and cousins. No one looked familiar so she slipped into a free seat on one of the upholstered benches. Two men were a couple of cushions away. She considered making eye contact and trying to strike up a conversation. Her pussy quivered when she imagined what it would be like to have two lovers at one time.

The passionate kiss the men leaned forward to exchange soon broke up that fantasy. With a sigh, Jayne forced herself to look away from the strangely arousing display, not wanting to be a peeping Tom.

As she glanced across the room, her gaze collided with a set of piercing green eyes. They seemed to hold her spellbound and she couldn't break free from his stare. As the man the eyes belonged to raised his glass to her, she smiled a bit uncertainly in return. Even seated, he looked tall, with wavy brown hair, a nice tan and smooth, handsome features. His body looked lean and honed under the dark suit. That man could have his pick of any woman in the place—and there were several hotties still partying—so it seemed unbelievable that he could really be flirting with her.

She tried to dismiss the moment and let her gaze slide away. What she had deemed flirting might not be anything more than drunken friendliness on his part. It was just one of the many frustrating things about men. Jayne had no idea how to properly read their signals.

A server approached and she ordered a Cosmo from the tall, skinny woman. After she left, Jayne continued to look around the room, suddenly feeling out of place. The largest woman might have been a size six. The go-go dancers were probably in the negative sizes. It wasn't a place for a woman who preferred Ben & Jerry's to Jenny Craig.

Jayne attempted to shake herself out of her funk in the few minutes it took for her waitress to return with the drink. She knew she was being too hard on herself. Size eighteen wasn't that large. Most "normal" women wore a size twelve. She knew all the statistics but spouting them didn't do much for her.

"Don't be such an idiot," she said aloud but softly. "I am a beautiful and special woman." The litany felt ridiculous on her tongue and had never worked. It had originated with the fifth counselor her stepmother had taken her to as a teen in order to help her find the emotional roots of her excess weight. Jayne could say it all she wanted but believing it was another story.

Casually, she completed a circuit of the room, slowly letting her gaze return to the spot where she had exchanged glances with that hot man. Her tummy dipped with disappointment when she saw he had gone. So much for that imagined interplay.

"Is this seat taken?"

With a blink, Jayne jerked her gaze upward. It took every ounce of control not to let her mouth gape open when she saw the man from across the room now standing in front of her. He was taller than she had guessed but just as athletic and sexy up close. Reflexively, she looked to her left and right to make sure he wasn't talking to someone else standing behind her. Slowly, she nodded.

"It is?" He frowned, looking genuinely disappointed. "My apologies."

As he started to walk away, Jayne found her voice. "Um, wait...the seat is free."

He turned around and took the spot beside her as though none of the awkwardness had occurred. When he held out his hand, the flash of gold drew her eyes to the Rolex just peeking out from the cuff of his white shirt. She took the hand automatically, nearly jumping out of her seat at the sparks that arced between them when his palm touched hers.

"I am Patrick."

"Jayne Daux." She still couldn't quite believe he was sitting there, conjured as if by magic and it took her a moment to remember to let go of his hand. Sternly, she tried to compose herself and stop acting like an awestruck teenage girl.

Patrick laughed. "Jane Doe, huh? I see you want anonymity."

She shrugged, not bothering to explain it was her real name. Her mother and father had thought it clever to pair Jayne with their last name, hence she was forever cursed to be "Jane Doe" because of it.

"What brings you to Vegas?"

"A wedding," she said.

"Yours?" he asked with an arched brow before sipping the amber liquid from his crystal glass.

"Hardly." She nearly died when an unladylike snort escaped her.

"I would guess you don't hold much esteem for the institution?"

"It's fine for some, I guess." Jayne ruthlessly squashed the little-girl voice in her head that tried to remind her of all the years she'd spent planning a fantasy wedding that seemed unlikely to take place. Far better to be pragmatic about not getting married and embrace it. After all, with sixty percent of marriages ending in divorce, what was the point?

"Neither do I. Having experienced it once was enough for me."

She nodded. "Why are you here?"

Patrick's luscious-looking lips bowed into a rueful smile. "For a wedding—not my own," he added with a sparkle in his eye.

Jayne glanced at his left hand, finding it bare of a ring. "Divorced?"

"Yes." Patrick seemed to lean in closer than necessary when he put his empty glass on the long table in front of the bench. "You?" His breath washed across her cheek and he made no effort to move back.

"Not even close."

"Smart woman."

The conversation stuttered for a moment and Jayne cast about for something witty to say. Her brain seemed to be made of slush and she cursed the number of drinks she'd had. If ever there was a time to be clearheaded, it was now. "Would you like to dance?" Her eyes widened when she issued the invitation. What the hell was she thinking? Though she could dance passably, the last thing she wanted to do was press her body against his and so vividly reinforce how big she was.

"Yes." He took her hand, not giving her a chance to retract the invitation. Jayne tried to convince herself all would be well. Patrick already knew she was bigger than the stick women in the club. He'd have to be blind not to notice the discrepancy. The fact that he'd approached her had to mean something. Pressing her body against his probably wouldn't send him running away.

To her surprise, he bypassed the dance floor and led her up the staircase. As they neared the open door of the balcony, the cool desert wind beckoned, blowing against her flushed face in a welcoming caress. She followed him outside, averting her eyes politely from the couples in various clenches congregated around the balcony. Few eyes focused on the gorgeous view of Vegas.

The music was still audible but muted, allowing for conversation. Patrick didn't seem to want to talk as he took her into his arms. Jayne held herself stiffly, trying to keep her large breasts and her stomach from resting against his frame. When he started massaging the small of her back, she found it impossible to maintain her stiffness. With a small whimper of defeat, she melted against him.

"That's much better," he said through the thick fall of hair covering her ear.

"It's a lovely night." The inane observation was silly, especially considering her view was basically the cut of his dark suit. At five-nine, she was tall but he made her feel almost petite.

"Much lovelier now." The hand he'd had on her lower back inched downward. He paused at the curve of her hip, as if waiting to see if she would stop him.

Jayne held her breath, indecision making the choice for her. When she didn't speak up or step away, Patrick rested his hand on her buttocks, squeezing lightly. She shivered at the contact.

"Cold?" The huskiness in his tone revealed his own excitement.

"Hot," she said brazenly.

Patrick pulled her closer, moving both hands to massage her ass. "I couldn't agree more."

Jayne swore she had to be dreaming as Patrick eased her against the wall, somewhat in shadows. He kept a hand possessively on her right butt cheek but brought the other one around to rest just under her breast. She tipped back her head as he lowered his, parting her lips in invitation. His mouth was firm and sure against hers, his lips forming to hers as though they had been molded to fit together. She sighed into his mouth, overwhelmed by how perfect the kiss was.

Patrick slipped his tongue inside, stroking hers in a languorous fashion. Jayne darted her tongue around his, parrying and thrusting with lustful intensity. When he lifted his head, she whimpered at the lost contact.

He cupped her breast, his thumb stroking a circle just outside the boundary of her nipple. "I'd like to say something but I don't know whether to be blunt, or if I should tiptoe around it for a bit first."

Instinctively, Jayne tensed, preparing herself for a commentary on her body. It wouldn't be the first time a man had said something cruel in the heat of the moment, perhaps thinking he was doing her a favor by pointing out her flaws— as though she remained unaware of them. "I prefer honesty," she said coolly, already mentally disengaging from the handsome stranger who still held her so intimately.

"I want to have sex with you."

Chapter Two

ဆၵ

Her eyes widened and she blinked. "What?" It wasn't outside the realm of possibility, especially considering the proof of arousal pressed against her stomach but when she had been preparing herself for rejection, she couldn't quite wrap her mind around what he was saying so candidly. "I think I misheard."

A slow, sexy grin curved his lips upward. "No, you didn't. I want to take you up to your room—or mine—and strip off that dress. When I see what's underneath, I want to take that off too." He dipped his head to bring his mouth closer to her ear as a couple wandered by them. "My hands are aching to hold your luscious breasts and my cock is twitching just thinking about how it will feel to be inside your hot, wet heat."

Jayne's mouth was dry as the desert surrounding the oasis that was Las Vegas. She longed for something to drink. More than that, she longed to make his words a reality. "All right."

He brushed his lips against her cheek. "I didn't frighten you away with my frankness?"

She tipped her head back to meet his gaze. "Not at all. It's refreshing."

As Patrick curved his arm around her waist, Jayne fell into step with him, moving in harmonious rhythm as they reentered the club and walked through it, dodging people at every turn. "I think it's either all the whiskey I drank at the bachelor party, or maybe it's just this place. Whatever the reason, I'm not usually so brash back home in Boston."

"That's a pity." Jayne didn't admit she wasn't either. Never in thirty-four years had she indulged in a one-night stand. It was about time she did and what better place than here, with the perfect partner? "It might work every time."

They stopped to wait for the elevator, sharing the space with a couple embracing passionately. "I'm just happy it worked tonight."

"So am I." As they stepped onto the elevator, she fished inside her dinky purse for the keycard to her room. "I'm on eight."

"Ten." He shrugged. "You're closer."

By mutual agreement, they reached for the eight button at the same time. Jayne's body hummed with anticipation as the lift whisked them higher. Patrick maintained a slight distance between them until the fourth floor, where they lost their riding companions. As soon as the doors closed behind them, he pressed his body against hers, his cock pushing insistently into her lower back. With one big hand, he cupped her breast, squeezing the soft globe gently. "I can't wait to get you out of these clothes."

"I'm looking forward to it." She was excited about the coming encounter but nausea churned in her stomach. It would be a new experience to bare her body to a man she didn't know. The handful of lovers she'd had previously had all been friends first and their relationships had been well established before getting physical. Jayne had always given the men in her life ample opportunity to be on familiar terms with her first, so that if they found the outside disappointing, at least they would know the person she was. It had been her way of compensating. With Patrick, he would be accepting or rejecting her strictly on the basis of her physical form. The prospect was daunting.

At her room, she slid in the keycard and preceded him inside. Jayne tossed her purse on the ornate table by the door and turned on the light for the entryway. The sleeping area remained shrouded in shadows.

She turned to him, cocking her head. "Since we're being blunt, do you have protection?"

Patrick patted his pocket. "Sure do."

Relaxing marginally, she kicked off the stunning black heels that had been killing her feet half the night. Suddenly nervous, she walked to the phone. "Shall I call for something? Champagne?"

He shook his head, following her. Jayne tried to hide her anxiety behind boldness. With sure hands, she stripped away his suit jacket as soon as he came into range. Simultaneously, she stretched upward to capture his lips for a deep kiss. Now three inches shorter without the heels, he really did tower over her.

With expertise she didn't know she had, Jayne licked and teased his mouth and lips, alternately sucking on his tongue before nipping him. She kept her hands moving ceaselessly, first working at the knot precariously holding his crooked tie and then assigning her fingers the task of unbuttoning his shirt.

His cufflinks proved a challenge, forcing Jayne to break the kiss. She lowered her mouth to his chest, running her tongue across his skin in random patterns. Without looking down, she managed to undo each cufflink and button. Feeling an unreasoning sense of accomplishment, she dropped the shirt onto the floor and stretched to place the cufflinks on the dresser.

"You move fast, Jayne."

She smiled, looking up at him coyly through the fall of her lashes. "Sometimes...when I know what I want."

Patrick chuckled, though he sounded strained. A flush to his cheeks betrayed the state she had worked him into and she knew her face must reflect the same level of arousal. Unable to stop herself, she took a step closer, grasping the hair on his chest with her hands. Lightly, she scratched her manicured nails over one of his nipples, smiling with satisfaction at his harsh inhalation.

Jayne dipped her head to soothe the raw flesh with her tongue. Patrick tangled his hands into her elaborate coif, discarding pins with haste. She nipped his nipple in retaliation when he tugged her hair too hard.

"God, baby, do that again."

She arched a brow, amused that he found the act arousing. Gently, she bit him again and then gasped when he tangled his hand in her loose hair, pushing her face tighter against his chest.

"Harder."

Jayne sucked the nipple and surrounding flesh into her mouth, biting down on the bud with as much force as she dared. Patrick groaned but she didn't stop. There had been only a tiny measure of pain in the sound but far more enjoyment. She stopped biting for a moment to tease the nipple, stroking gently with her tongue. As she nurtured that one, she raked her nails across his neglected nipple, enjoying the way his body trembled. When she bit him again, Patrick said her name in what sounded more like a hoarse grunt than a word.

Bolstered by his response, she moved her hands to his waistband, undoing the leather belt quickly. Her fingers were nimble over the zipper and button of his trousers and she stripped them to his feet in seconds. Before continuing, Jayne took a step back. It seemed like her fingers stumbled over the simple process of undoing the button on her dress but the zipper slid down easily. She stepped out of it, feeling self-conscious of her voluptuousness. Patrick drew in a deep breath but she didn't wait to find out if it was one of appreciation or disappointment.

Dropping to her knees, she brought a hand up to his black briefs. His cock pulsed visibly through the fabric and she couldn't resist stroking the length of him. "I can't wait to taste you." She looked up at him from her subservient position, licking her lips. Patrick had tossed back his head and seemed on the verge of losing control. Jayne squeezed his cock head, grazing the tip with her nails. "You're so big. I bet your cock is going to fill me to the limit." The seductive way she purred the words hid the fact that she wasn't accustomed to such forthright carnal talk, in or out of the bedroom. Something about the man standing in front of her liberated her.

"Let's find out." The chords in his throat distended when he spoke, as though it was difficult to force out the words.

With a tsk of her tongue, she shook her head. "Not just yet. I'm going to suck you first."

"Jayne...let me..." He broke off as she lowered his briefs to meet his pants. "Seriously, I want to give you some attention."

"You'll have your opportunity." Not giving him a chance to lodge any more protests, Jayne put her mouth around his cock. The thick shaft pulsed in her mouth, and she swirled her tongue around the mushroomlike head. In the brief glimpse she'd had before taking him into her mouth, she had noticed his cock sprang from the thick growth of pubic hair shielding his testicles, straight and true, like an oak thrusting upward from the ground. Knowing that glorious member was in her mouth, at her mercy, sent a shiver of delight up her spine.

She inhaled deeply, suctioning air around the head. He jerked in response and she repeated the action. Patrick was stiff with tension and arousal, his entire body emitting waves of anticipation. Jayne swirled her tongue around the corona, warming him up.

Patrick put his hand against the back of her head, grasping a handful of her hair. "You're killing me."

"Just a little death." She breathed against his cock with each word, enjoying the way his body twitched. Jayne slid her mouth down the shaft, relaxing her throat as his cock head reached the back of her mouth. With one hand, she cupped his balls, rolling them in her hand with gentle pressure. She used the other hand to brace herself, cupping his ass. He groaned when she held all of him in her mouth and she let the moment lengthen until she could practically feel his body vibrating.

Jayne began sucking his cock, alternating the force of her suction as she worked the length of him, moving her head forward and back. Patrick arched against her face as she sucked. She scraped her teeth ever-so gently along the sides of his shaft, making him moan. His tight grip on her hair almost made her eyes water but she pushed past the discomfort to focus on her self-appointed task.

Working his balls, she thrust her mouth against him, taking in all of his cock and then withdrawing until she held just the bulbous head between her lips. Jayne flicked her tongue against the bundle of nerves at the head, making Patrick groan with pleasure. Once again, she took his full length, swallowing as much as she could greedily. His pre-ejaculate streamed into her mouth and she savored the salty tang.

"I'm about to come."

In response, she increased suction, crying out with surprise when Patrick jerked away from her. Jayne sat back on her heels, staring up at him with confusion and a touch of hurt. He twisted partially from her with his shoulders slumped. His ragged inhalations filled the room and it took him several moments before he turned back to her.

Jayne almost recoiled when he brushed his hand against her cheek.

"I'm sorry. I just didn't want it to be that way. I want to be inside you." The red stain on his cheeks seemed to come from embarrassment rather than exertion. "You make me feel like a horny teenager all over again. Only problem is, I'm afraid my hair trigger won't reset as fast as it did back then and you deserve better than that."

Charmed by the admission, Jayne smiled. She rubbed her cheek against his hand and then rose to her feet. "How do you want it to be?"

"Me inside you." He reached for her, putting his arms around her. Without a trace of hesitation, Patrick captured her mouth for a kiss, plunging his tongue inside her moist depths. Jayne returned it enthusiastically. Her pussy ached with the need for release and she shifted impatiently.

Apparently, Patrick wouldn't be rushed. He released her mouth and paused to take off his shoes, socks and pants. Then he stared at her corset with a look of deep concentration. "How do you get this thing off?"

"There's a button under here." Jayne showed him by folding down the edge of the corset. When she started to undo the cleverly hidden closure that kept the strip of satin around her torso, he pushed away her hand.

"My turn to do the undressing," he said for an explanation. His hands, seemingly more suited to a task like building a house, had no trouble with the delicate button. Once he had dispensed with that, Patrick found the zipper at the side and divested her of the garment.

She shivered, stomach clenched with dread, as she stood before him in the plunging velvet bra, matching lace and velvet panties and black pantyhose. Jayne hated to reveal herself so vividly. When he walked over to turn on the lamp by the bedside, the light made her vulnerability all the worse. She followed quickly, reaching to turn off the light he'd just turned on. Patrick intercepted her hand with a frown of confusion. "I like it dim. It's...cozier." It sounded lame even to her ears and she could tell he didn't believe her.

Patrick pulled her away from the lamp, leaving it on. "I want to see you. Every last inch."

It should have been sexy but the words just increased her anxiety. She always made love with the lights out. Until Patrick, no man had ever countered her unspoken edict.

Torn between fear and excitement, Jayne tried to remain relaxed as Patrick undid the clasp of her bra. The velvet underwire style opened, spilling forth her large breasts. With more haste than finesse, he tossed the undergarment aside and reached forward like a little boy eager to get his hands on sweets. She gasped when he took her breasts in his hands, pushing them together as he massaged the tender tissue.

"They're perfect, Jayne. Big, glorious and tipped with the most perfect pink buds." Patrick dipped his head to flick his tongue across one. "I could spend hours just feasting on your breasts."

A film of perspiration broke out on her body as he guided her back to the bed. Jayne sprawled across it, pushing aside worries of her appearance as he positioned his body above hers, his mouth at her breast. While he sucked one nipple, he paid equal attention to her other breast. His fingers worked magic on her skin, stroking, tugging and coaxing the bud to a hardened state she had never attained.

It was amazing to lose herself in his touch. At some point, Jayne realized she hadn't worried about whether her body secretly repulsed him for several minutes. It was a personal best for her and she strove to stay lost in sensation.

Eventually, Patrick seemed to get enough of her breasts, at least temporarily. He withdrew from her and Jayne turned to lie on her side so she could see what he was doing. She watched him walk to his clothes and search in his pants. When he walked back to her with a small strip of condoms, her thighs quivered with anticipation. Her pussy grew slicker yet with a new wave of arousal and she shifted impatiently. She patted the bed when he stood above her without moving.

"You are really incredible, Jayne." He tossed the condoms on the soft coverlet before bending over her. She caught her breath when he pulled down her pantyhose, lifting each leg to help him remove the thin silk. She couldn't help arching her hips upward as he stroked the sides of her pussy through the crotch. Patrick seemed to delight in his unhurried tactile exploration of the lace pattern, spending an inordinate amount of time running his thumb along the seam where lace met the velvet panel above her mound. She cried out when he pressed his thumb into the center of her slit, unerringly finding her clit. "So incredible."

Jayne writhed impatiently. "Please, Patrick."

With a chuckle, he stripped her of the panties. Jayne held her breath when he caressed the outside of her pussy with two fingers. She arched her hips to take the digits inside when he neared her opening. He evaded the maneuver by sliding his fingers north, once again seeking out her clit. She gasped when he circled the aching bud with his forefinger and then gasped again when he abruptly dipped his thumb inside her pussy. She watched through heavy eyes as he brought it to his mouth to lick off her essence.

"Mmm." He closed his eyes for a moment, as if savoring the taste. When the lids fluttered open, his eyes seemed like smoldering emeralds. "You're wet and ready, aren't you, baby?"

"I've been ready since our eyes met."

Patrick laughed but it was a strained sound that betrayed how much his apparent control was costing him. "If I'd had my way, I would have walked over to you, pinned you to that bench and fucked you senseless in front of everyone."

An intense jolt of pleasure shot through her as her mind supplied a visual to accompany his words. She giggled, imagining the shocked onlookers. If the bookmakers took the bet, she'd lay odds that not one of them would have looked away from such a startling sight as two people fucking in the middle of a trendy club.

In seconds, Patrick had torn open the condom and slid it on his cock. Jayne parted her thighs as he knelt between them. A last-minute dart of doubt tried to pierce the euphoric haze surrounding her but she successfully quashed it. Maybe all the years she'd spent working on her self-image were finally paying off.

Or maybe Patrick had made her so hot she couldn't think straight. It was a heady feeling.

Not as heady as having him surge inside her. Jayne's pussy stretched to accommodate his cock and aside from a twinge of discomfort, her body gave little indication that it had been more than two years since she'd had sex with a man. Her body fell into the age-old rhythm, following the pace he set. Patrick seemed to know instinctively when to vary his speed, or rotate his hips slightly to give her more stimulation. As she neared climax, he pushed her over the edge by bringing a hand between their bodies to squeeze her clit. With a shout of satisfaction, she convulsed around him. Her orgasm must have triggered his, because his cock twitched inside her several times, at first frenetically and then gradually slowing. The warmth of his ejaculate through the condom soothed her and she squeezed her muscles to milk every drop.

When it was over, they lay together, their harsh breathing slowing to normal. Jayne put her arms around Patrick, content in a way she had never been. She had no idea what time it was and didn't care. Even knowing he would probably leave sometime during the night and she would never see him again couldn't totally spoil the blissful aftermath. Sleep stole over her and she tried to fight it, not wanting to relinquish the night with Patrick just yet. Satisfaction and physical exhaustion, coupled with the unaccustomed amount of alcohol she had imbibed, combined to undo her resolve and her eyes closed. She was aware of slipping into slumber but powerless to fight it.

Chapter Three

ഇ

Patrick woke sometime later, still holding Jayne. She snored softly, oblivious to everything. Staring down at her beautiful face, his cock swelled with renewed arousal. A man driven by his senses, her perfection nearly overwhelmed him. Soft and smooth everywhere, with generous curves and a womanly frame, he could spend years getting acquainted with her body and never grow tired of it.

It killed him that she didn't see how beautiful she was. Jayne had made every effort to hide her self-consciousness but he'd seen through her façade. Everything she'd done, from turning the focus on him, to trying to put out the lights, had screamed that she wanted to hide from him. Patrick was thrilled she had wanted him enough to get past her issues but he yearned to show her just how sexy she was.

He stroked his fingers lightly across her stomach, smiling when she twitched in her sleep. He traced a circle around her bellybutton and she grunted. When Patrick moved his fingers up to her breast, lightly trailing his forefinger around her nipple, she made an indecipherable noise and turned over from her side to her stomach.

Undeterred by her remaining asleep, he shifted positions so he could lean over her. She jumped when he wafted a breath of hot air across her skin. Patrick blew again, concentrating on her lower back. Jayne tensed when he grazed her spine with his lips but didn't appear to wake. He ran his tongue across her lower back and down the cleft of her buttocks. Her harsh inhalation broke the silence, indicating he had succeeded in rousing her. One goal accomplished, he turned to the next, which was to arouse her.

She stiffened when he flicked his tongue across her anus. When her cheeks clenched around his tongue, he laughed. Determined to breach her defenses, he swirled his tongue around the puckered bud. She cried out with shock when he dipped his tongue inside, trying to rise to a sitting position. Patrick put a hand between her shoulder blades to discourage her from rising, while continuing to work at her back passage. He stroked the sides of her buttocks with his tongue, pleased when she gradually relaxed.

As her tension eased, he drew circles on her back, while moving his tongue lower. He chuckled again when she thrust her bottom into the air, giving him better access to her pussy. She was sweet, yet tangy, on his tongue and he lapped greedily. She squirmed, moaning each time he darted his tongue in and out of her opening. When he stretched his tongue higher, seeking out her clit, she thrust back to meet him. Patrick circled his tongue around the tight bud, enjoying her soft sighs. Unable to resist her heady flavor, he plunged his tongue into her again, thrusting in and out of her in mimicry of the way he wanted to drive his cock inside her.

She rolled onto her back and Patrick barely broke rhythm. Once she had settled, legs splayed, he grasped her soft thighs, kneading them as he sucked on her clit. Jayne arched off the bed, her hands balled around handfuls of the coverlet. Her obvious pleasure fed his own and he had to mentally count to ten to keep from blowing everything by driving his cock into her wet heat then and there.

Diligently, Patrick licked her pussy, sucking on her clit as he pushed two fingers into her snug sheath. She bucked her hips against his hand and face, guttural groans falling from her lips. He let out a groan of his own when she squeezed her thighs tightly around his head. Her pussy convulsed around his fingers and she whimpered, seemingly too out of breath to manage anything more taxing.

Patrick didn't give her a chance to compose herself or withdraw back into her shell. Tongue extended, he licked a trail from her neatly trimmed pussy to her left breast. He fastened his lips around the globe, sucking the nipple and part of the areola inside his mouth. While flicking his tongue across the hard bead, he thrust his fingers in and out of her pussy at a slow pace. His intent wasn't to make her come again—yet—but just to keep her stimulated.

"What are you doing to me, Patrick?" she asked hoarsely.

He lifted his mouth from her breast to look into her eyes. "I'm seducing you, baby."

Jayne blinked. "You've already had me."

"Not the right way." He lowered his head again, once more taking a generous mouthful of her breast, this time focusing his attention on the right one. Simultaneously, he wriggled his fingers inside her, probing as deeply as he could.

"What's that mean?" She let out a startled yelp, indicating he had found a particularly sensitive spot.

Ignoring her question, he raked his teeth across her nipple, pleased when she arched her back. Patrick swept his tongue around the hard pearl, finding her tastier than any ice cream. He had started out with the intent of seducing her senses but that didn't mean he couldn't enjoy his work. His cock ached, pulsing in time with the contractions of her pussy around his fingers as her body strove for orgasm.

When she buried her fingers in his hair, Patrick allowed her to pull his head up toward her mouth. He paused along the way to suck on her throat. She whimpered when he drew in a bit of flesh at the bend of her neck to nip it. Jayne's creamy skin had a faint taste of perspiration as he ran his tongue from her throat to her mouth, where he spent long minutes licking each plump contour. Finally, he responded to the invitation she issued with her open mouth and darted his tongue inside. Her unique taste got to him, making the blood rush through his head.

His thinking clouded by the intoxicating taste of her mouth, it took Patrick a moment to realize she had pushed away the hand he'd had in her slit, wrapped her thighs around his hips and was working on slipping a condom over his cock. Patrick tensed, trying to resist. "No."

She arched a brow and finished sheathing him in latex before asking, "Why not?"

Shaking his head, he pulled back from the wet heat trying to draw him in. "I want it to be special for you."

"It is, Patrick." She clutched his biceps and he couldn't keep resisting when she tightened her thighs to pull him closer. "This has been one of the best nights of my life. Please fuck me again."

The request melted his resolve. His cock swelled, the head nestling into her opening. Patrick sank inside her as she lifted her hips and he couldn't remember how to breathe for a second. It had been only a few hours but he had forgotten just how amazing she felt—hot, tight and so wet he could thrust into her for hours. Her soft body cushioned his and he experienced renewed appreciation for her beauty. His friends had sometimes mocked his taste in women but he pitied them for their ignorance. They would never know the delicious thrill of a voluptuous woman's embrace, of the softness of her skin and the erotic sensation of generous curves that welcomed him.

Their pace was slow, as if time had no meaning. Patrick lost himself in Jayne's wide blue eyes, enthralled by the depth of pleasure reflected through her veil of thick, black lashes. "You have the most beautiful eyes." He smiled when her cheeks flushed. "They remind me of the ocean in August, crashing against the sand at my parents' place in Nantucket."

She cleared her throat. "You don't have to work at seducing me anymore, hon."

He buried his face against the silkiness of her black hair, inhaling the fruity scent. Doing his best to memorize everything about the woman in his arms, he focused on all aspects of her. It was unlikely that he would ever see her again after tonight and he wanted to remember Jayne Daux. She was an unforgettable woman.

Her breathless cries and convulsing womb signaled her release, allowing Patrick to give in to the orgasm washing through him. His body shook under the onslaught and he nearly lost the ability to hold himself up on his arms for a moment. He couldn't help whispering her name repeatedly as he spilled his seed into the thin barrier of latex separating them. How he longed to feel her pussy clenching around his bare cock but it was too risky to do something like that with a one-night stand. If only he could see her again. But that was impossible. They were both in town for just a couple of days. He had no idea where she was from, or how far apart they lived. His own uncertainty kept him from suggesting any sort of serious relationship as they lay together in the sweet bliss of afterglow. Instead, he just held her, holding back the words his heart wanted him to utter.

Chapter Four

"Jayne!"

She jumped, focusing her eyes on Emmy, whose expression revealed she had been trying to get her attention for quite some time. Heat suffused her face when she realized she had been daydreaming about last night. Even worse, she'd been dwelling on the note she'd awakened to, where Patrick left his cell number and implied he wanted to see her again. She had been busy trying to work out the logistics of that. "Yes, what?"

"Do you know if the staff put out the right centerpieces? Yesterday, they had a hideous shade of orange mixed in with the white and coral flowers."

Jayne picked up the hairbrush on the vanity and began smoothing the long fall of Emmy's brown hair, which trailed down her back from the elegant knot atop her head. "They hadn't finished setting up everything but the centerpieces were out. They looked right when I checked out the ballroom before coming here to help you get ready."

"Thank goodness." Her shoulders, bared by the cut of the strapless princess dress, seemed to relax. "I tell you, I had no idea how stressful it would be to throw together a last-minute wedding like this. Maybe we should have waited until Rich finishes his internship and had the wedding in Boston like his mother wanted."

She shrugged, not looking up from smoothing the wrinkles from the back of Emmy's dress. "It might have been practical but you didn't want to wait for him, did you?"

"No." She let out a sigh that could have rivaled any schoolgirl, thinking of her crush. "He's so wonderful. I can't wait for you to meet him."

"I'd like that. All you've done is talk about him ever since you came back." Emmy had met Rich while she was visiting her father, an expatriate living in London. Theirs had evidently been a whirlwind romance and he had proposed before she flew back two weeks ago. Jayne emitted her own envious sigh, wishing something equally romantic could happen to her. For a moment, her mind conjured images of Patrick but she tried to ignore the thoughts. Last night had been wonderful and if she were lucky, they might have another night or two together in Vegas but she should resign herself to knowing that was all they could have.

"Did I tell you Rich's family flew in for the wedding? I thought his mother wouldn't come, because she was so angry that we were getting married like this, after only having known each other six weeks."

Jayne patted Emmy's shoulder, knowing how anxious she had been. "What changed her mind?"

She shrugged. "I guess Rich convinced her how in love we are." Emmy turned her head away from the mirror to look up at Jayne from her perch on the padded stool. "His parents are even letting us use their Nantucket cottage for our honeymoon."

She froze, trying to sound casual, though alarm bells rang in her mind. "Where is Rich from again?"

Emmy shook her head. "Honestly, you're not here today, are you? I must have said Boston a hundred times in the last few days. You should remember that I'm going back to London with Rich but after his internship, we're settling in Boston."

On autopilot, she dropped the section of lace she'd been fluffing. "Excuse me. I have to check something."

"What?" Emmy's mouth moved like a fish's out of water as Jayne rushed past her. "Jayne, what's wrong?" she called.

Jayne kept going, heading straight for the ballroom reserved for the post-ceremony reception. They had still been setting up everything for the wedding when she had been in the Longhi room earlier to check the centerpieces. One of Emmy's decorations included snapshots of her and Rich blown up to poster-size and mounted on the walls, to give their friends and family a sense of their courtship.

As she had expected, the staff, under the direction of the private coordinator Emmy had hired, were in the process of mounting the last few pictures. Multiple images of the happy couple already adorned the walls and Jayne's stomach churned with nausea when she saw the smiling face of the future groom. He looked different with the petite Emmy, against a European backdrop, than he had last night in her hotel room as he made love to her until she was limp but she couldn't deny Rich was Patrick.

She rushed from the ballroom, unable to stand the sight of Emmy and Patrick together. Anger and disgust thrummed through her. She had slept with her best friend's fiancé. God, how could Emmy ever forgive her? It crossed her mind not to confess to her friend. If she could just keep it all to herself, Emmy would never know.

The thought of keeping such an enormous secret had Jayne falling against a wall, doubling over from pain in her chest. She couldn't do it. She couldn't let Emmy blindly marry a man who would cheat on her the night before the wedding.

Blood pounded in her head and she was enraged with Patrick, or Rich...or whatever he went by. Why hadn't she realized he was a sleaze? Emmy had always been slightly naïve about people but Jayne seemed to have been born with natural cynicism. She always expected the worst to happen, so why had Patrick blindsided her?

Still feeling sick, Jayne stood up. She walked back toward the rooms set aside for the wedding party to use before the ceremony, scheduled to start in less than an hour at the Venetian Wedding Chapel. All too soon, she reached the brides' room and entered. To her relief, Emmy was still alone and was absorbed in fiddling with her hair.

She looked up with a puzzled expression at her return. "Where did you rush off to, Jayne?"

Jayne walked over to her and knelt beside the stool, barely noticing the way the fabric of her dress tightened uncomfortably around her hips. "I had to check on something."

"Well, what?" asked her friend, exasperation evident.

"Your pictures in the ballroom."

Emmy's eyes widened. "Oh no. The studio screwed them up, didn't they? I knew better than to do it all online. I should have gone in person—"

She cut into Emmy's panicked outburst. "They're fine." Jayne bent her head. "God, I don't know how to tell you this." She felt even worse when Emmy leaned forward to hug her.

"Whatever it is, I'm here for you. Just tell me."

Tears stung her eyes and her voice was a rough croak when she blurted out, "I slept with a man I didn't know last night."

Emmy blinked. "You?" She blinked again, sitting back. "Wow. That's not like you."

"I know."

She patted Jayne's shoulder. "It will be all right. We all do stupid things, you know? I ended up in bed with Rich on our first date. I couldn't believe it was happening at the time but I couldn't help myself."

So, the jerk always moved quickly. Anger reinforced her resolve and she looked into Emmy's eyes during her confession. "It was Rich. I didn't know it then but I slept with your fiancé."

Her pale face drained of all color and Emmy seemed to wilt. She bent over the vanity table. "What?" she asked in a whisper.

"I'm sorry." The tears broke past the dam that had held them in check, coursing down Jayne's face. "I really didn't know. I never—"

Emmy gained her feet abruptly, tossing her hairbrush at the mirror. The tinkle of glass was nothing compared to the loud shout her diminutive friend achieved. "How could you do that to me, Jayne? How could you two go behind my back? You're my best friend." She scooped up a bottle of moisturizer from the assortment of cosmetics spread on the table, pitching it against the wall.

Jayne cringed from Emmy. Her anger was frightening, especially since Emmy was usually collected and calm when faced with anything upsetting. She had never been one to throw things and scream. If not for the tears ruining her bridal makeup, she would have appeared just enraged. Jayne knew her well enough to know Emmy was only finding a physical outlet for her pain, because it was too great to hold inside.

She maintained her silence as Emmy ranted, just standing back from the chaos. It wasn't until the door slammed against the wall and the groom came rushing through that she took her gaze from her friend. "You," she snarled as soon as she saw Rich rushing toward Emmy.

"Emmy, what's going on in here?" Rich reached his bride, pulling a compact from her hand. "What's wrong?"

Jayne winced when Emmy slapped Rich hard enough to have the sound reverberate throughout the room.

"You lying, cheating bastard."

Rich frowned. "What? Are you crazy, Emmy?"

Emmy jerked away from him. "How dare you sleep with my friend the night before our wedding?"

Reeling backward, Rich's eyes settled on Jayne and he seemed confused. "What...her?"

"Yes, her." Emmy stamped her foot. "Why the pretense of wanting to settle down and raise a family if you were just going to sleep around?"

He shook his head. "Honey, I've never seen this woman before in my life and I haven't been with any woman since I met you. And it was a long damn time before you that I last had a lover." Rich glared at Jayne. "I don't know what your friend is trying to pull but I never touched her."

"You liar." It was all Jayne could do not to slap him herself. In the cold light of day, Patrick was completely different. His face even looked harder and his eyes, though green, weren't vibrant as they had been last night. How could she have found him so attractive before, when he left her cold now? It must be the harsh light of truth illuminating her thought processes.

Emmy seemed torn. "Jayne wouldn't lie."

"Neither would I," he said quietly, with so much sincerity that Jayne almost believed him. He looked back at her again, still befuddled. "No offense, lady but you aren't the type of girl I go for. You're more my..." He trailed off, a smile slowly forming on his face. "Wait right here."

"Where are you going?" Emmy reached out to try to stop him from leaving and Jayne shook her head in amazement at his departure. Did he really think he could just walk out on the situation and leave it all for her and Emmy to clean up?

Emmy looked at Jayne, her gaze searching. "You are telling me the truth, aren't you?"

Jayne nodded, wishing she had been lying when she saw the agony in her friend's eyes.

The return of Rich interrupted their exchange and he seemed excited. "I know what happened."

"So do I," said Jayne. She wouldn't waver. It might be easier to pretend it had never happened but Emmy deserved a faithful husband.

As another man entered the room, Rich put an arm around his shoulders and dragged him forward. "Is this the guy you were with last night?"

Jayne's mouth dropped open and it took her a moment to comprehend that her vision wasn't blurred. Twins! Dear God, they were nearly identical. In appearance, they were clones, though Patrick's eyes were warmer and his face more filled out. "Patrick?"

"Jayne?" He seemed confused. "What's going on? One minute, I'm squeezing into that darn tux and the next, Rich's telling me to get my butt into the brides' room."

Emmy gasped and it was a happy sound. She threw herself against Rich. "Oh, thank goodness."

Jayne looked down, embarrassed and uncertain how to proceed. "I am so sorry, Emmy...Rich. I had no idea you had a brother. A twin brother." To her relief, Emmy let go of Rich to come over for a hug.

"It's okay. I should have mentioned Rich has a twin but it just didn't occur to me. I guess it's 'cause I was so busy with the wedding, and I'd never met Patrick until this morning..." She withdrew, turning back to the two men. "You two clear out now and leave us to finish getting ready. And if you see the missing bridesmaids, send them in."

Rich was drawing his brother toward the door but Patrick's gaze hadn't left Jayne's. "Seriously, what is going on?"

"Come on, bro, I'll tell you while we get dressed."

The celebrant nodded to the bride and groom, who turned to face those assembled for the ceremony. "I present to you Richard and Emmy Maynard."

Jayne wasn't sure if she or Patrick clapped louder. Fortunately, he seemed to have taken the incident in stride and had even teased her about not being able to tell him apart from another man when they had reunited at the ceremony. She traded a glance with him from her side of the aisle, where she stood off to Emmy's side. Her body hummed with anticipation while she waited for him to take her arm and lead her from the chapel as they followed the bride and groom.

They walked to the Longhi room together, arm in arm. Her bliss from the previous night had returned, lending everything a rosy air. She remained bubbly with optimism as they entered the room. Even when the throng of people separated them, she was bolstered each time she met Patrick's gaze across the crowded room.

The first pinprick in her bubble of happiness appeared in the form of her stepmother. Jayne's stomach churned with nausea when she almost walked right into the smaller woman. Stella took an exaggerated step back. "I know you're not very graceful but please watch your step, dear."

That same tinkling laugh that always followed her digs grated on Jayne's nerves. She wanted to reply in a blithe manner, or even to just walk away from the woman who had made her teen years hell, but she couldn't seem to move her feet. Why did Stella always reduce her to this state?

What remained of her buoyant mood fled when the two stepsisters appeared on either side of Stella, completing the Trio of Evil, as she had dubbed them within days of meeting them. Stacia and Daisy were beautiful young women with willowy frames and shiny blonde hair—everything Jayne wasn't.

She attempted to be polite, greeting the women. "What are you doing here?" she asked after the requisite exchange of pleasantries.

"I couldn't miss dear little Emmy's wedding," said Stella. "She was over so often before you two left for college that I feel like she was one of my daughters."

Jayne took a sip of champagne to hide her grimace. She knew Emmy wouldn't have invited Stella or the stepsisters, so how had the other women found out? "How did you hear of it?"

"Emmy's mother. I ran into her at the spa. She invited me straightaway, as soon as she heard my invitation must have gotten lost." The flash in Stella's eyes indicated she knew she had been shunned. Maybe that's why she had flown from Beverly Hills to Vegas. Her own perversity had driven her to the act.

"It's lovely to see you." Somehow, Jayne managed to keep her tone civil. It was the same cool, distant voice she always used with Stella. They had never gotten along but all pretense of a warm relationship had lapsed the day her father died. Even at his funeral, they had been cold with each other. Jayne had only seen her stepmother a few times in the intervening years and each occasion was an ordeal.

"Speaking of weddings, did you get the card I sent to your little apartment in the Bronx?"

Jayne nodded, ignoring the insult directed toward her apartment. It was actually a roomy two-bedroom but Stella didn't believe any address outside of Manhattan could be anything but a hovel. "Congratulations are in order for you, Daisy?"

Daisy smiled and somehow it had the effect of making her seem even colder. "The wedding is late this year. I do hope you'll send a gift."

"Of course." She hid a dart of pain behind the fluted glass as she drained the last of the champagne. Why did these three still have the power to hurt her?

"I know you'll be much too busy to come."

"Yes. My job keeps me hopping."

"You're a secretary, aren't you?" asked Stacia with false sweetness.

"Assistant Director of IT for a major hospital, actually, but it's almost like being a secretary," she said with only a hint of mocking.

Stella looked her up and down. "I imagine it doesn't give you much time to get to the gym."

She looked away from Stella, in Daisy's direction. "Is your fiancé here?"

"No, he had to attend a business meeting in Prague."

Jayne nodded. "I'm sorry to hear that. It would have been nice to meet him." She began to look around the room, hoping to make eye contact with anyone in order to have an excuse to move on.

"My boyfriend is in the Bahamas, doing a photo shoot. He's representing one of the hottest designers of the year," said Stacia, her mouth curled into an unattractive sneer.

Jayne was certain she disappointed her stepsister by not asking the name of the designer. "Well, if you'll excuse me, I should see if Emmy needs anything." As she brushed past Stella, her stepmother caught her arm in a tight grip. She braced herself for whatever they wanted to say, praying they would get it over with quickly.

"Where is your date, dear Jayne?" Stella smirked and Daisy actually giggled, as if the idea was laughable.

"Are you still with Penrod, that scientist you were dating for so long?" asked Stacia.

"Perry," she corrected with quiet dignity. "No, we haven't been together for some time." It had been three years since they'd split, so it must have been longer than that since she'd seen the Trio of Evil.

Stella clicked her tongue. "Let me offer you advice, Jayne. You have to lose some weight. I know a good plastic surgeon who can do a tummy tuck, breast reduction and rhinoplasty. Within a year, if you work at it, you could be passably pretty. Maybe it will be your wedding someday." She tilted her head. "If you keep up your unhealthy lifestyle, you'll never find a man."

Jayne pursed her lips. She knew better than to argue, that the tirade would end faster if she maintained silence but she couldn't resist the compulsion to speak. "Why do you care, Stella? We never see each other. I'm no longer around you to embarrass you with my appearance, so why are you still doing this?"

Stella blinked. "I promised your father I'd watch out for you."

She snorted. "Yeah, thanks." Jayne started to walk past the three of them but froze when her stepsisters giggled.

"I told you she wouldn't have a date," said Daisy.

Stacia frowned. "Of course she doesn't, so don't make it sound like I was suggesting she would."

With a shake of her head, Jayne took a couple of steps, moving from the Trio of Evil straight into Patrick's arms. She looked up at him with a smile, feeling most of the sting of hurt dissipating under the calming light of his eyes. "I missed you," she whispered.

Stella managed to snatch her tentative happiness once more. Her trilling laugh caused Jayne to stiffen her spine when her stepmother approached.

"My goodness, Jayne, aren't you clumsy today?" She laughed again. "I did warn her to watch her step but she has no grace. Mr...?"

Patrick ignored the hand Stella extended in favor of shifting Jayne to one arm. "Patrick Maynard."

"The groom's brother?" Stacia fluttered her eyelashes at him.

He nodded and Jayne held her breath, waiting to see if he would find Stacia and Daisy as irresistible as every other man seemed to.

"Well, thank you for carrying familial duty above and beyond." Stella smiled in Jayne's direction but her glinting eyes held no warmth. "I'm so glad Jayne has had someone to keep her company today."

"Oh, it was no problem." Patrick put his hand on Jayne's buttocks. "Being with Jayne is a pleasure."

Daisy arched a brow. "Really? I grew up with her and I just can't imagine that."

Patrick smiled as he squeezed her bottom tenderly. "Perhaps that's because you're a shallow bitch who wouldn't know a genuine person if they fell on you." He inclined his head to Stella. "It was enlightening meeting you, ma'am, but we must go. There are still pictures to take and Emmy has to throw the bouquet before I can steal Jayne away and spend the night making love to her."

Jayne's eyes widened, though not as much as The Trio of Evil's. She couldn't contain a startled laugh at their identical gasps of shock and it turned to a giggle as Patrick drew her away.

"Jayne, you know those women aren't worth anything, don't you? Their opinion doesn't mean a damn thing," he said as he led her from the ballroom to a private alcove set up for pictures.

She nodded. "My head knows it but they still get to me."

He stopped in the hallway, turning her to face him. "You are beautiful, inside and out. They're just jealous."

Jayne shook her head, unable to hide her disbelief. "Why would any of them be jealous of me?"

Patrick bent his head to kiss her before answering. "Because you are a wonderful person and they aren't. They don't know how to be real like you, so they try to bring you down to their level. When you fail to respond to their taunts in a satisfying manner, they just get worse."

Impressed, she nodded. "It's like you lived with them yourself."

Patrick shook his head. "Fortunately, I've never endured it firsthand but I've seen several patients at my counseling practice who lived through similar experiences. The important thing is that you don't let them change you, or make you unhappy."

She hugged him. "At this moment, I don't think I could be unhappy if I tried, Patrick."

With impatience, they made it through the photo session and then it was finally time for Emmy to toss the bouquet before the newlyweds left for Nantucket. By mutual agreement, she and Patrick had set that as the point where they could officially retire to one of their rooms and spend the night in carnal bliss.

With some prodding from Emmy and Patrick, Jayne joined the gaggle of single women waiting to catch the bouquet. Stacia was nearby but she ignored her. She was annoyed to see Daisy in the crowd but her stepsister was an idiot. It wouldn't occur to her to sit out the bouquet toss since she was engaged.

Emmy climbed onto a chair with Rich's assistance, her back to the women. "Ready, girls?"

Jayne joined in with the rest to reply with an enthusiastic, "Yes."

"Here it comes." Emmy dramatically covered her eyes with her free hand before tossing the bouquet. It sailed through the crowd, over the heads of the grasping girls, including Stacia and Daisy. To Jayne's surprise, the bouquet seemed to fall into her hands as if propelled by magic.

She looked up, finding Patrick unerringly through the girls surrounding her with congratulations and hugs. There were a lot of details to work out yet, such as how they would build a relationship when he lived in Boston and she lived in New York but her heart had her convinced they would figure it out.

Staring into Patrick's eyes, the bride's words seemed prophetic to Jayne when Emmy shouted, "Jayne's going to be the next one married."

CLAIMING KATE

Zannie Adams

৯৩

Chapter One

ℬ

In just over a week, Kate Appleton would marry Mason Cooper.

They'd been engaged for almost a year, living together for six months. Because the construction on their new house had been delayed, they'd moved into the guesthouse on his parents' estate.

For months now, Kate had been planning the wedding, spending more time on that than on her job as a legal assistant. She'd wanted to get married since she was five years old and, because of the Cooper family connections, her wedding was going to be an elaborate, fairytale affair.

Everything was primed for this to be the happiest time of her life.

It wasn't.

Lately, she'd been spending more time with—and getting more attention from—her fiancé's cousin than from Mason himself.

At the moment, Bryce Cooper had her backed up against a wall in the guesthouse. One of his hands was planted next to her shoulder.

He was a handsome man—dark hair, high cheekbones, full lips. He looked like a model on a romance novel cover, larger than life and almost unnatural.

Kate wasn't really attracted to Bryce. His looks were too overblown for her taste. But she wasn't pushing him away at the moment—even though her fiancé could walk in at any moment.

Maybe she was letting Bryce get so close *because* Mason might walk in.

It had been a long time since any man had acted like he couldn't keep his hands off Kate. She missed the feeling. At one point, she'd believed Mason found her irresistibly sexy but she wasn't so sure anymore.

She wasn't actually going to *do* anything with Bryce—in fact, the idea of having sex with him made her giggle—but she wasn't pushing him away.

"Your hair is gorgeous," he murmured, stroking her honey-brown hair and then caressing downward until he was stroking something other than hair.

Kate wasn't remotely affected by the feel of his hand grazing her chest. But she had to restrain a snicker at such a brazen move. Adjusting to protect her breasts with one arm, she raised an eyebrow. "Uh, thank you. You realize Mason will be back any time now?"

"All the more reason to take advantage of his absence." Bryce's dark eyelashes seemed to thicken as he narrowed his eyes—in what she supposed was his sensual expression. "You have the most beautiful skin I've ever seen."

"It's one of my only good features."

It was certainly her *best* feature. Her skin—all over her body—was a nearly perfect ivory and she'd always been rather proud of it, since she wasn't beautiful or unusual in any other way.

He leaned closer, so close she could feel his breath against her cheek. "I beg to differ." His eyes focused on her breasts— on the outline of her nipples visible through her white tank top.

"Are those the best lines you have?" She was starting to get a nervous feeling in the pit of her stomach. It wasn't from lust or excitement. Rather, it was a jittery sensation caused by expecting Mason's appearance. "Do they work on the impressionable females you usually hit on?"

Bryce looked momentarily nonplused at her blunt question. But then he smirked. "I've never had any complaints before."

"I bet you haven't." Although she hadn't done anything wrong, she was starting to feel a little guilty. Just because she wanted to be this close to Mason—and hadn't been for a while—didn't mean she should amuse herself with Bryce's ineffective attempts at flirtation. "But would you mind backing up a little? I'd rather—"

Bryce didn't back up. "You'd rather what?"

"*I'd* rather you leave, as a matter of fact," came a familiar male voice from behind them. "We only have enough dinner for two."

Kate jumped at the sound of Mason's voice, even though she'd known to expect him. She tried to push Bryce away from her and he finally consented to step back, although he didn't withdraw as much as he should have after being caught leaning into his cousin's fiancée.

Kate peered over his shoulder at Mason Cooper, the man she was going to marry a week from today. He was as tall as Bryce but not so beefy. His muscle tone, like his personality, was smoothly efficient and competent. At the moment, he looked tired. He was dressed in his usual after-work clothes— slightly wrinkled khakis and a worn t-shirt. His thick brown hair was rumpled and he was carrying a bag of the Italian takeout he'd gone to get them for dinner.

He was staring at Kate and Bryce with slightly lifted eyebrows.

For just a moment, Kate thought he was going to get angry. The set of his broad shoulders looked tense and his steel-gray eyes looked hard.

The jittery tension in Kate's gut intensified and she held her breath. She hadn't deliberately set this scene up but now that Mason had caught them, she was hoping he would react.

She *wanted* him to get angry. To get jealous. To act possessive, defensive, even petty.

She wanted his control to snap.

She needed to know Mason still wanted her that much.

But he didn't break into an angry outburst. His eyes just flickered over Kate questioningly, from her long hair to her bare feet. Then he looked back at Bryce—who was doing his best to appear nonchalant, although Kate knew he'd always been intimidated by his older and far more accomplished cousin.

"I'm serious," Mason continued, "I'm hungry and there's not enough food. You aren't planning to stick around, are you?"

"I'll go. I can take a hint." Bryce gave Kate a smoldering look. "I'll see you tomorrow."

"We're trying to work out the landscaping on the house," Kate explained, seeing Mason's inquiring look. Bryce owned a landscaping company and Kate and Mason had hired him to do the work on their new house. "That's why he came over."

Mason nodded absentmindedly and set the bags on the table. "By the way," he mentioned, just as Bryce was about to walk out, "I moved your car. It's back by the garage. You'd left your keys in the ignition."

Bryce scowled. "Why did you move it? Now I have to walk a mile to get to it."

The Cooper estate was huge and sprawling and most of the parking was in front of the main house.

"You were parked in Kate's spot and I needed to park her car there."

Kate started to question this statement but Bryce beat her to it. His interest, however, was on a different part of Mason's comment. "The spot beneath the maple tree was empty. Why didn't you park her car there?"

144

"I parked there last night and this morning my car was covered with bird crap. I wasn't going to leave Kate's car there to be crapped on tonight."

Finally Kate couldn't hold back anymore. "Why did you take my car in the first place?"

"One of your tires looked low." Mason was already pulling containers of food out of the bag. "So I took it by the station, since I was going out anyway."

Kate hadn't noticed her tire being low and her shoulders stiffened in resentment. "You could have asked me before you made off with my car. What if I needed it?"

Bryce was looking on with interest and he likely would have stayed to witness the impending argument, but Mason had been serious about not wanting company. Without a word, he shouldered his cousin out the front door and locked the door behind him.

"I knew you weren't going anywhere," Mason said, moving back to the table and continuing the conversation, as if he hadn't just thrown his cousin out of the house. "You're already in your pajamas."

Kate glanced down at herself. She was wearing pink flannel pants, a tank and a hoodie sweatshirt. For no logical reason, she felt insulted. "I was tired. I had a long day. I worked on the damned wedding with your mother for hours. And, anyway, that's no reason to take my car without asking. I could have gone out like this."

Mason just rolled his eyes and bit into a breadstick. "You're not even wearing a bra. Some women might be able to get away with the braless look. Not you."

Kate sucked in an outraged breath. "What is that supposed to mean? Are you saying my boobs are saggy?"

This was the way it had been between them for weeks. Snipping and quibbling and getting defensive over the silliest things. They were both stressed—Kate from wedding plans and Mason from department politics at the university. They hadn't gone out on a date for a couple of months and they hadn't had sex since they'd moved into the guesthouse three weeks ago.

Kate was starting to wonder why they were even getting married.

Mason certainly wasn't acting like he wanted to.

He gave her an exasperated look and went over to stare into the refrigerator. "Don't be absurd. You know you have great boobs."

Kate put her hands on her hips and glared at his back. "Then what was that crack about a bra supposed to mean?"

"It didn't have an underlying meaning. Just that you wouldn't go out in public without a bra. At least, you never have before." He muttered something else but it was under his breath and she couldn't make out the words.

It sounded snide though. "What?" she snapped.

"Nothing."

"*What?*"

He let out an sigh she could hear from the other side of the room. "It was nothing."

"Would you shut the damned refrigerator!"

Mason finally grabbed a half-empty bottle of red wine and swung the refrigerator door closed. After pouring out two glasses, he returned to his breadstick. "What are we arguing about anyway?"

Kate had to think back but she soon remembered the source of her irritation. "You took my car without asking."

"Sorry about that." He carried his linguini into the living room and sank down onto the floor, leaning back against the sofa. "I'll make sure to ask you next time. I didn't think you'd mind."

His apology sounded sincere and he said no more as he started to eat.

Kate stood simmering for a few more seconds but then she relaxed too. It was ridiculous to have these arguments about nothing. They were both stressed but they could do better than this.

She could do better than this.

She picked up the glass of wine Mason had poured for her and the baked ziti he'd gone out to get her — even though he was just as tired as she was. Then she joined him on the floor.

Instead of leaning against the big chair, as she normally did, she sat next to Mason. She leaned against him, draping an arm across his belly. "Sorry I was snippy," she murmured, kissing the side of his jaw and then nuzzling his ear. He smelled warm and masculine — very Mason-like. "I guess I've been prickly lately."

Mason relaxed beside her and pulled her against him more snugly. He needed a haircut and his brown hair was falling over his forehead in the adorable way it had done for as long as she'd known him.

She'd known him for twenty of the thirty years she'd been alive.

They'd sat next to each other all through fourth grade and they'd been best friends ever since.

"Me too," he admitted, although Kate figured he was just being generous. He hadn't been particularly prickly lately. Distant and absentminded but not prickly.

She kissed him just beside his ear, tasting the salty bite of his skin. "Thank you for going to get dinner. And thank you for checking on my tire."

"You're welcome." He smiled at her and a familiar warmth filled Kate's belly — an absolute trust and security she only felt around Mason.

They ate in pleasant silence, broken only when Mason dropped a mushroom on his t-shirt. Kate giggled and dabbed at the spot with her napkin.

Then she giggled even more when Mason frowned at her for mocking him.

As Mason finished off his wine, he glanced over at her. "You mentioned problems with the wedding plans today?"

Kate thought back to what she'd said earlier. "Not problems. It's just getting to be a lot of work and your mom obsesses about such nitpicky details."

"Is she becoming a problem?" he asked slowly, carefully.

Kate swallowed hard. She was heartily sick of Mason's mother. She was a nice woman and meant well. But living with her—even in the relative privacy of the guesthouse—was not ideal. Mrs. Cooper had gotten far too involved in planning what was supposed to be Kate's wedding.

But Kate wasn't going to add another source of tension between them. "She's fine. I'm just getting tired of talking about flowers, menus, seating charts and music. It's all blown up out of control."

"We could have just eloped."

He spoke the words so casually, so offhandedly, that Kate experienced a surge of resentment. "I always wanted a simple wedding. It was your family who wanted the big one."

More specifically, it was his mother.

Something odd flickered in Mason's gray eyes but it disappeared so quickly she couldn't identify it. He just shrugged. "It will be over in a week. Let me know if you need me to talk to my mother."

And that was it. He'd dealt with the issue—the subject that had been making Kate crazy for the last few months—in a couple of seconds.

For the zillionth time, Kate wished Mason weren't so matter-of-fact and controlled about everything. She wanted to see him get mad or throw a fit. Wanted to know he was as human as she was.

She wanted to see him let go.

There didn't appear to be much chance of it happening at the moment. When she finished eating, Kate got up to go to the bathroom. She stared in the mirror for a moment, considering whether she should try to put on something sexier.

She wanted to have sex tonight but she didn't want to throw herself at Mason if he wasn't in the mood. She *really* didn't want a pity fuck.

She thought she looked cute enough. Her figure had always been good—curvier than fashion dictated but men had never complained. And her hair hung down in a sleek straight fall to the middle of her back, the honey color matching her eyes.

The flannel pants weren't her sexiest wardrobe choice but they were comfortable and the tank top revealed the lines of her breasts. So instead of changing clothes, she just took off the sweatshirt, baring a clear expanse of skin along her arms, neck and shoulders.

Deciding this would have to do to seduce her fiancé, she returned to the living room. Mason had shown her more attention this evening than he had lately so maybe he was starting to get horny too.

She hoped so. Three weeks was a really long time.

Mason was sitting in the same position she'd left him in, legs bent up, hair over his forehead, a spot of sauce on his shirt.

But now he'd put his glasses on and had a notebook in his lap.

He was evidently planning to work this evening.

Again.

With a pang of disappointment, Kate went to get the bestseller she'd been reading for the last few days. She'd been reading a lot lately, since there wasn't anything else to do in the evenings.

She wondered if other engaged couples were like this. All she and Mason did was argue and sit around. Surely it wasn't normal.

Maybe it was a sign they shouldn't get married.

Kate still wanted to marry Mason. More than anything.

But she wanted to marry a man who wanted her, who needed her, who felt passionately about her.

They'd been friends most of their lives. But maybe they'd been wrong to take it even further.

Sixteen months ago they'd been watching TV when Mason had kissed her out of the blue. They'd kept kissing—carried away by a wave of desire and intimacy that had swallowed them without warning.

They'd made love for the first time that night. And the following morning, instead of the awkward tension she would have expected after having sex with her best friend, they'd both been filled with a giddy excitement and the certainty that this was where their friendship had always been headed.

They'd had sex again that morning. And then again in the evening. And then the next evening. And the next. Until they were living together. Engaged.

Soon to be married.

But maybe the lust had been temporary—at least on Mason's part. Maybe he felt about her now as the friend he'd always been.

Maybe everyone was right when they'd warned her that falling in love with a friend was never a good idea.

Kate still loved him. Still lusted after him.

But a slow dread had been building up—in her chest, in her gut—telling her they were acting more like friends than like lovers.

Should she marry Mason, even if he wasn't crazy about her? If he didn't look at her and want to rip her clothes off? If he didn't even care that he'd just caught his cousin groping her?

He glanced up when she curled in the big chair with her book. She saw him note the absence of her hoodie, his gray eyes scanning over her bare skin and the heavy swell of her breasts through the thin top.

But then his focus returned to the notebook on his lap.

"What are you doing?" she asked, feeling the need to draw his attention again.

"Work."

She frowned, immediately prickly again. "What work?"

"Research," he explained, his gaze meeting hers matter-of-factly. "Do you want me to explain it?"

It was a serious question, although it might have sounded rude to someone else. Mason was a mathematics professor at the prestigious state university and most of his research was far beyond Kate's feeble math skills.

Mason had always been smart. Really smart. In high school, he'd been a little on the nerdy side. He hadn't been a cluelessly embarrassing geek but he'd never been one of the popular guys—football or soccer players—whom Kate had always dated. For years, she'd never dreamed he could be a romantic possibility.

But Mason was now confident, sexy and successful and most of those other guys weren't.

When they'd gone to their ten-year high school reunion a couple years ago, Kate had been so proud of him. They hadn't even been dating then but Kate had attached herself possessively to his arm, glaring at any woman who dared to approach.

A lot of women had tried to approach him.

Another man would have gloated to all of his former classmates who had looked down on him in high school. Not

Mason. He wasn't a saint. It just never occurred to him that he was now so much better than everyone else.

Kate shook her head, her thoughts returning to their conversation. "No. It's not worth the trouble."

Mason nodded agreeably and went back to his pencil and notebook.

Kate pretended to read and fiddled with the button on her flannel pants.

Evidently, equations and abstract mathematics were more compelling companions than she was.

Maybe he was regretting the turn in their relationship.

Maybe he secretly wanted his freedom back. She knew he could have any woman he wanted. Before they'd gotten together, the single women in town—from ages eighteen to forty—had been throwing themselves at him.

Maybe Kate should have realized all along how lucky she was to have him. Maybe she should have worked harder to be sexy and alluring.

Maybe he was hoping she would dump him so he wouldn't have to hurt her.

Maybe they should have left well enough alone. If they'd never become a couple, she wouldn't be paralyzed by these insecurities.

And she wouldn't be at risk of having her heart broken.

Why didn't Mason want to have sex with her? He hadn't made a move on her for weeks.

As she brooded endlessly, her tension grew so high she accidentally snapped the button off her pants.

It flew out of her hand and onto the hardwood floor, rolling halfway across the room and then under a bookcase.

Mason put down his notebook, automatically ready to retrieve it for her.

"I'll get it," she told him. She knelt on the floor in front of the bookcase and reached into the inch of space between the bottom shelf and the floor.

When she didn't feel the button, she lowered her head and shoulders to the floor to peer into the dark space.

The button, of course, had rolled all the way against the wall.

Her fingers could slide under the shelf but the heel of her hand didn't comfortably fit into the small space. She groaned and tried to force her hand in, adjusting her shoulders so she could see and reach at the same time.

When she finally felt the button with the tip of her longest finger, she was hit with the awareness of how she must look.

She was on her knees, her head to the floor, her ass in the air — the most ungainly, unattractive position imaginable.

So much for looking sexy this evening.

Maybe Mason was working and hadn't noticed her.

But when she drew the button out of its hiding place and straightened up, she saw that Mason was watching her.

"Find it?" His voice was kind of thick and she could see a muscle twitching in his cheek.

He must be laughing at her, trying to repress his hilarity out of pure decency.

"Yes." She sprawled out in a heap on the floor in front of bookcase, absently rubbing the back of her hand, which had scraped against the bottom of the bookcase.

As she did so, the button dropped out of her hand again, rolling its way toward Mason now.

"Fuck!" Her cheeks burned in embarrassment and exasperation. Why couldn't she be one of those graceful, enticing women who never made such fools of themselves?

Giving up any pretense of dignity, she scuttled after the button before it rolled under something else.

She caught it a few feet from Mason, slamming her hand down to trap it with a silly expression of victory. "Gotcha!"

Now she was on her hands and knees but at least this time she was facing Mason. The straps of her tank top had fallen over her shoulders and her hair fell over her face.

When she lifted her eyes, she saw Mason was biting his lower lip.

Evidently his hilarity now knew no bounds.

Deciding it was silly to take this absurdity too seriously, Kate chuckled. "Damned button. Thought it could make an escape."

"Indeed." His voice was still thick and his face more flushed than usual. From suppressed amusement, she assumed. He arched an eyebrow at her. "It was intent on making a getaway. But who am I to complain, having been treated to such a show?"

Kate *knew* he'd been laughing at her.

She gave him a good-natured scowl. "I thought you were working."

He cleared his throat and managed to tear his eyes away from where they'd been lingering on the ungainly sprawl of her body. "Right."

She hauled herself up and sat back down on the big chair. She peered suspiciously at Mason and decided, from the remaining tension in his shoulders, that he was still doing his best not to laugh.

She supposed it showed the kindness at the core of his nature that he was trying not to howl his head off at her clumsy display.

Although she would have preferred him to have been overwhelmed with desire, sweep her off her feet and carry her to bed to make passionate love to her, his reaction to this whole incident was very Mason-like.

He was very Mason-like. Especially in his glasses. He never wore them when he was trying to be sexy but Kate secretly found him irresistible in them.

A wave of tenderness washed over her as she watched him. She loved him. She wanted him so much. She couldn't give him up.

She just wished their relationship hadn't fallen back into this casual dynamic.

More than once, she'd considered just telling him, letting him know her concerns. But then, being Mason, he would go way out of his way to make her feel loved and cherished—if only out of pity.

And she would never be sure he even meant it.

After almost an hour, she put down her book. "I guess I'll go to bed." She paused before completing the thought, hoping he'd take the hesitance as a hint.

Surely he would want to have sex with her tonight.

He glanced up from his work. "All right."

He watched her, just as she was watching him. But she couldn't see anything like heat or interest in his gaze.

He was calm and matter-of-fact. Like he always was.

After a long moment, she let out the breath she'd been holding, feeling a crushing wave of disappointment. "I'll be in my room."

There were two bedrooms in the guesthouse and they were staying in different rooms. Mason's mother was old-fashioned. Although she must know they'd been having sex for months—they'd been sharing an apartment, after all—she preferred not to see any concrete proof of carnal relations between unmarried persons.

So they'd respected her preferences and kept separate rooms. They could, of course, sleep together whenever they wanted without Mason's mother being the wiser. And they often had, even in the last three weeks.

They just hadn't had sex.

And apparently they weren't having sex tonight either.

* * * * *

Kate brushed her teeth, washed her face and got into bed to wait. Maybe Mason would join her in bed eventually.

If he just made the smallest of moves, showed the slightest bit of interest, she would fill in the gaps and make the rest of the advances.

But if he didn't even act like he wanted her, she wasn't confident enough to jump him.

No matter how much she wanted to.

At about eleven-thirty, she heard him moving in the main room—putting dishes in the sink, checking to see if the doors were locked and then pausing, it seemed, in the hallway outside her room.

She held her breath, tensing up under the covers.

Then drooped again as she heard him moving to his room and closing the door quietly behind him.

She lay in bed in the dark and thought about Mason. Imagined his coming into her room, hauling her up into a kiss and then fucking the daylights out of her.

She imagined it so vividly that soon she was aroused and even more frustrated.

This was ridiculous. They were about to get married. Why the hell shouldn't she have sex with him?

So, before she could talk herself out of it, she got up and padded barefoot out of her room. Maybe she would just crawl into bed with him. If he didn't make a move, she could just sleep with him. That way, if he wasn't interested, she wouldn't have the humiliation of being rejected by her future husband.

She opened the door to his room without knocking, in case he was asleep.

He probably was. He usually went straight to sleep, while it always took her much longer.

It was so dark in the room after the dim light of the hall that she couldn't see her hand in front of her face. She scuffled blindly toward the bed, holding her hands out in front of her in an instinctive attempt to feel her way forward.

Her eyes adjusted slowly and could eventually make out the dark mass of the bed and even the outline of Mason's body.

She took one step too many, however and knocked her shin against the bed frame.

"Shit," she hissed, bringing up her right leg as the shock of pain hit her brain.

Mason rolled over. She couldn't make out his face but she tried to imagine what he must be thinking—his fiancée sneaking up on him in the dark like this.

She was still balanced on one leg when Mason made a wordless, guttural sound.

Then, before she knew what was happening, he had reached out and pulled her into bed with him.

She didn't resist. Couldn't have resisted, even if she'd wanted to. She was off balance from standing on one leg.

Feeling a swell of relief at his welcome, Kate opened her mouth to explain her presence.

But before she could get any words out Mason had rolled them both over so she was lying on her back. His weight on top of her was solid, warm and heavy and his face was so close she could feel his breath.

He gazed at her with silent intensity, something so hot and needy in his expression she could sense it in the dark.

Then he tangled his fingers in her hair, lifting her head up as he lowered his mouth into an urgent kiss.

Kate's arms wound around him, squeezing him in an embrace of matching intensity. She opened her lips beneath the invasion of his tongue, moaning deep in her throat as she squirmed to generate friction between their bodies wherever she could.

She was flushed all over and breathing quickly through her nose when he finally tore his mouth away. But her gasp of relief transformed into a gasp of surprised pleasure as his mouth descended to her neck, his lips sucking hard against her fluttering pulse.

Her hands grasped greedily at his bare back but she tried to soften her touch into a caress. She stroked the lean muscles and smooth planes of his shoulders and back, loving how strong and hot and solid he felt beneath her fingers.

Her hands slipped lower, to the waistband of his boxers. She edged her fingers under the fabric, pushing them down as she tried to reach the tight muscles of his ass.

But Mason moved lower on her body before she could reach, his mouth closing around one of her breasts. He sucked on one nipple, teasing it with his tongue through the thin cotton of her top.

Kate gasped again as she felt the corresponding tug between her legs. Her arousal was aching now — so strong it actually hurt.

She raised her hands until she was pulling on his shoulders, trying to bring him higher into a better position to ease the ache at her center.

He resisted, suckling and breathing loudly around her breast. Every flick of his tongue sent new sensations shooting down to her arousal and she writhed and arched up as her hands flew above her head to clutch the headboard.

He hummed against the damp cotton between his mouth and her flesh, one of his hands sliding down the side of her body until he was cupping her bottom. He used his grip and the weight of his body to hold her still as she wriggled frantically.

"Ah!" she gasped, wondering if she was going to come just from his mouthing her breast. She was afraid if she let go of the headboard, she might shatter completely.

He hummed again, the vibrations causing her to arch up and hook her legs around his thighs.

Then she felt his hand slip from her bottom to the space between her thighs. He palmed her groin and he must have felt how hot she was, even through the flannel of her pajamas.

She ground herself against his hand, exhaling in shaky relief as the pressure eased a little of her need.

Then his hand was gone. She mewed in disappointment and frustration, trying to pull him up higher over her body again.

This time, he moved at her urging, propping himself above her and then bending his elbows to kiss her again.

She clung to him, wanting him so much it felt like she could swallow him whole. He smelled like Mason, the warm, male scent heightened by the heat of his body and his urgency. The weight of his body on hers was a burden she never wanted to lose.

As they kissed he started to pull down her flannel pants and panties. She tried to help him by bending her legs and trying to kick them off. When one of her legs got tangled in the folds of fabric, she huffed in exasperation and reached down to yank them off her foot by force.

In the meantime Mason rid himself of his boxers and she spread her legs for him, pulling him into position between them.

He wasted time by slipping his hand down to finger her, checking to see if she was ready.

Her spine arched in pleasure when he stroked open her intimate folds, sliding his fingertips along the hot swollen flesh before sinking two fingers into her wet, pliant channel.

He grunted as he pumped his fingers, an oddly primitive sound that shot right to her pussy.

Her thighs tightened around him instinctively as she whimpered, her hips bucking up in response to his caress.

He didn't remove his hand as quickly as she'd expected. He kept up the intimate massage, causing her to whimper and buck up even more.

Soon her whimpers transformed to wordless pleas as the pleasure threatened to drive her crazy.

She let go of the headboard, which she'd been clinging to again, and reached to grab him low on the back.

She clawed at his ass and was rewarded when he pulled back his hand and braced himself on one elbow above her.

Reaching to the front of his body, she found his cock and something unclenched in her chest as she felt how hard and hot it was. He did want her after all. At least, one part of his body did. She stroked him, thrilling when he sucked in a quick breath in response.

She didn't have the time or leisure to fondle and tease him as much as she'd like. Instead, she tried to guide him into position. He reached down with his free hand to help her, lining up the tip of his cock at her entrance as she spread her thighs farther apart.

She cried out softly as he pitched his hips forward, pushing the hard length of his erection into her. Her wet passage yielded easily to the penetration.

Kate bent up her knees, drawing him in even deeper and she heard him grunt again. He was breathing heavily above her — the texture of his urgent panting matching her own.

Then he adjusted until his forearms were folded beneath her shoulders, holding her in a kind of embrace. She wrapped her arms around him and squirmed, the tight pressure of his cock inside her only fueling her desperate need.

He began to thrust then, responding to the demands of her bucking hips. He started slowly and evenly, his cock sliding slickly in her wet channel with sounds of wet suction. But his steady rhythm didn't last.

160

Kate squeezed him with her arms, her thighs and her inner muscles, huffing out eager sounds of pleasure and frustration. Mason's face tightened with effort and he jerked his head to the side instead of devouring her with his gaze, as he'd been doing before.

He was mid-stroke when Kate's frantically needy hands lowered again to his ass, her fingernails digging into the firm flesh there. He grunted and fell out of rhythm, driving into her in a short sequence of fast, clumsy thrusts.

The unexpected friction felt so good that Kate choked out, "Ah, ah, ah!" Her head tossed against the pillow and her eyes closed.

Then Mason jerked to a sudden halt, his cock still buried inside her. He breathed in ragged gasps through his nose and his body was so hot it burned her wherever they touched.

They were touching everywhere.

Kate understood he was having trouble keeping control—probably from going without sex for so long. But she was quickly approaching climax and she couldn't be patient.

She wanted to come. Wanted to make love to him. Wanted to see him lose control.

Wanted to know he really needed her. In every way.

She pumped her pelvis, causing lush friction as his cock moved inside her from the jerking of her body. She squeezed as hard as she could around the tight penetration, trying to silently urge him to move.

He rasped out an inarticulate noise—so desperate and primal she thought she might come just from the sound of it. Then he started to thrust again, no longer steady and controlled. His thrusts were hard, fast and uneven and his face lowered to the crook of her neck until he was panting against her throat.

More of his weight was resting on her now and it felt so good she wanted to melt into a puddle beneath him. Her nipples were chafing against his chest and she could feel his hair against her chin, his knotted muscles beneath her hands, the hair on his thighs against the smooth skin on hers.

She rocked beneath him, trying to get friction for her clit from the base of his cock, his pubic bone, anything.

Despite his own urgency, Mason must have sensed her need. He angled his hips so she got some hard pressure on her throbbing clit.

She could feel him try to slow down, try to sustain his control. His whole body was so tight it was shaking and he was now sucking down large gulps of air. She could both hear and feel his panting against the pulse in her neck.

She didn't want him to control himself. She wanted him to let go.

She wanted him to *need* to let go.

The speed of her frantic undulation accelerated until she was sweating and her chest felt like it might explode. But she was rewarded when she heard him make a guttural sound of desperation and then release the control he'd been striving for.

He drove into her fast and hard. She could feel his ass rise and fall in quick succession beneath her hands. He was huffing now in time with his rhythm and she knew it wouldn't be long before he came.

With that knowledge, her orgasm came hard and unexpectedly.

One minute she was rocking, pumping, trying to match his motion.

And the next minute she was slammed with waves of intense pleasure, the spiraling sensations starting at her center and pulsing out to overwhelm her whole body.

She bit her lip hard to keep from screaming in shocked pleasure but the involuntary sounds came out anyway, in rasps, mews and whimpers through her nose, as she shook through the duration of her climax. Her body convulsed beneath Mason's weight, her channel clamping down on his cock, pulling him into climax himself.

He made one more rasping sound — one that sounded like he was baring his teeth against her neck. Then he froze, his body tightened like a coil.

His release was hard and visceral. He reared up on straightened arms, his pelvis jerking clumsily against hers.

Her eyes were adjusted to the dark enough now that she saw his face change as she came, the tension transforming into a wash of pleasure and relief.

Her thighs were tight around him as she felt him come inside her. She loved the feel of it with a possessive neediness. Loved the kind of intimacy it implied.

And she loved how he collapsed over her afterwards, all of his weight suddenly pushing her into the mattress.

She clung to him as tightly as he was clinging to her. His body was still scorching but it was relaxed now, the hard, lean lines softening the way they only did after sex.

She loved him so much. And maybe this was all they'd needed to remind them both of why they were together.

Maybe he wasn't getting tired of her after all. Maybe he wasn't as matter-of-fact and cool about her as he usually acted.

She was just starting to get uncomfortable under his hot, sweaty heaviness when he raised his head from her neck. Her skin was wet from the moisture of his mouth.

He looked down on her and she was sure he was about to tell her he loved her.

That was all she needed to hear. It was all she needed for her silly insecurities to fade away completely.

She waited for it, her heart as full as it had ever been.

Instead of speaking, he kissed her. The kiss was as soft as his cock, still sheathed inside her, was becoming.

He pulled his face away from hers. "Thank you."

Kate blinked at him.

Had he just said "thank you"? *Thank you?*

After they'd had what she'd thought was loving, urgent, needy sex?

He'd *thanked* her — as if she'd just done him a favor?

"You're welcome," she managed to force out, since that was the only way she knew to respond to a "thank you".

But the pressure of dread that had been lurking in her belly and chest for the last few weeks rose with a surge into her throat. Tightened into unreleased sobs.

Starting to panic and not wanting him to see — since obviously this hadn't meant what she'd thought it meant — Kate squirmed beneath him, this time her movements obviously a request for release.

Mason didn't resist. He rolled off her, his cock easily sliding out of her slippery channel.

Kate rolled over onto her side, facing away from Mason.

What the hell was happening here? They were supposed to be as close, as happy, as romantic as two people could be. They were getting married in a week.

And instead everything was falling apart.

Was Mason even in love with her anymore?

She swallowed over the insistent sobs and hugged her arms to her chest. Then she felt Mason roll over until he was spooning her from behind.

He pushed her hair aside and kissed the back of her neck, draping his arm around her middle. His body was relaxed behind her. And his breathing had become slow and heavy.

He was already almost asleep.

While Kate had to struggle not to cry.

She lasted a minute, breathing with forced slowness and keeping her eyes wide open.

But finally her emotions caught up to her resolve and tears burned in her eyes.

She crawled out from under his arm and then out of bed.

Mason made a sleepy, questioning grunt.

"I'm hot. I'm going to sleep in my bedroom," she muttered, not bothering to offer a better explanation.

At this point, she didn't care what Mason thought. She just needed to get out.

She made it to her room before the silent sobs ripped from her throat.

She wasn't surprised when Mason didn't follow and didn't ask if anything was wrong.

Chapter Two

℀

Kate slept in late the following morning and Mason was gone when she got up. He'd left her a note, explaining he'd gone into his office at the university.

Since he worked in academia, he didn't always keep normal hours. His schedule was more flexible than it would have been in a business setting but there was always something he could be working on—even during semester breaks.

Kate stared at the scrawled note on the table for a long time, her throat aching with emotion. It was no big deal. He always worked some on the weekends.

But today the note stood out to her as a sign, a symbol of all her panicked insecurities about the wedding and their relationship.

She ate breakfast and took a shower, determined to be a mature adult and not break down and cry her eyes out because Mason had decided to go into work this morning.

Then she went into town to check on her wedding dress. After the most recent alterations, it fit perfectly so she took it home with her.

When she pulled up in front of the guesthouse, she saw Bryce's truck in her parking space again. She rolled her eyes and parked under the maple tree, hoping her car wouldn't get crapped on before she could reclaim her parking space from Bryce.

Mason still wasn't home when she returned. And Bryce was nowhere to be found. Feeling heavy and glum, she took her dress into her bedroom. Then decided to try it on again.

It was a beautiful dress. Not ornate or ostentatious but almost stark in its simplicity. It was sleeveless with thick straps and a deep square neckline. The fitted bodice shaped her figure perfectly and the full skirt fell to the floor in a smooth fall of heavy satin. There was no train and the only decorative elements were the intricate embroidery on the hem and the delicate pearl beading on the bodice.

She stared at herself in the full-length mirror. Her hair was going to be up on her wedding day, not falling over her shoulders the way it was now, but she still looked really good.

She wondered what Mason would say when he saw her in this dress. Would he be awed? Overwhelmed with love and desire? Feel like his dreams were coming true?

Would he even care?

With an ache in her throat, she figured he'd probably be as matter-of-fact about her wedding dress as he was about everything else. Maybe make a dry comment on how much more practically she could have spent so much money.

She sniffed, smoothing down her skirt and swinging her hips to make the fabric swirl around her bare feet.

When she heard someone at the door, she squealed—thinking Mason would catch her in her dress. But she heard a different male voice call from outside, "Kate! Are you there? Open up—I'm about to drop this!"

Bryce. He sounded annoyed so she hurried to open the front door.

He was carrying a huge potted plant. Some kind of ficus tree.

"What is that?" she asked, standing to the side to let him in.

He set down the tree with a melodramatic groan. "Wedding gift from Bill and Linda. Damn thing weighs a ton."

Kate stared at the ficus. "Oh. Thanks for bringing it by."

"You weren't here earlier so I went to say hello to Aunt Dora. I parked in your space so I wouldn't have to walk a mile carrying the damn heavy tree."

"Okay." With a shrug, she moved into the kitchen to get a drink.

"You look gorgeous," Bryce remarked, his voice growing husky and low. "Good enough to eat."

The double entendre was intentional and obvious—reinforced by the hot look in his eyes as they crawled over her body.

Kate leaned against the kitchen counter, feeling naked even though she was fully clothed.

She hadn't wanted Bryce to see her in her wedding dress. Not before Mason did.

Bryce came over, standing so close she was trapped between his body and the counter. "Are you sure you want to be wearing it for *him*? I'm not sure he can appreciate someone as sexy as you."

Kate had been worried herself about whether Mason still appreciated her sexually. But she certainly wasn't going to let Bryce speak that way about her fiancé.

About *Mason*—who was Bryce's superior in every way that mattered.

Mason, who was brilliant, with a dry humor and quick wit. Whose good looks were subtle and sophisticated, rather than crudely overblown. Who was eminently competent and coolly efficient. Who always thought about her before he thought about himself.

Mason, who would have parked under the tree himself so her car wouldn't be crapped on.

Bryce enjoyed flirting with her, and trying to seduce her was a challenge to him. But Mason really loved her.

He loved her. As much as she loved him.

"Bryce, don't," Kate said, her voice colder than usual. She put a hand on his chest to push him away, getting tired of this little game. "Mason is going to be back—"

"*Mason is already back.*"

The words were hard, cutting, snapped out like the slash of a blade. They'd come from the front door. From Mason.

Kate jumped with surprise and an odd sense of relief. But before she could react any further, Mason launched into action.

His expression stone cold and his jaw tightly clenched, he strode across the room into the adjoining kitchen. He moved purposefully and discreetly, like an animal stalking its prey.

Without a word, Mason grabbed the back of Bryce's t-shirt and hauled him away from Kate. Bryce stumbled back a few steps, clearly taken by surprise.

Kate was surprised too. Shocked, in fact. She gaped at Mason, a coil of excitement tightening in her belly.

Mason didn't look cool or matter-of-fact anymore. He was shaking with a frigid rage.

He pinned Bryce with hard gray eyes. "Kate is mine. You don't get to flirt with her. You don't get to hit on her. You don't get to touch her—*ever.*"

Bryce's mouth dropped open. "Look, man, you misunderstood—"

"I didn't misunderstand anything. I know exactly what has been happening." Mason hadn't even looked at Kate. "It stops now. Get out."

Bryce stood frozen, his eyes darting from Kate's breathless surprise to Mason's predatory face.

"*Now.*" Mason didn't even raise his voice but the one word was more powerful than a blow.

Bryce got out. Fast.

Kate barely registered his retreat. She was hypnotized by Mason's angry intensity, never having seen it before. Not in twenty years.

She'd wanted him to snap. But now that it had happened, she was a little nervous.

She breathed quickly, her heart racing and anxiety coiling in her belly. "Mason," she gasped, wanting to make sure he didn't think she had cheated on him. "It's not what you think. He's just been—"

Mason cut off her words. "Do you want to call things off between us?"

Kate's hand flew up to her mouth, her heart plummeting at the implication. "No! Mason, nothing happened! You can't think—"

"Fine," Mason interrupted again, taking two long strides toward her and backing her against the counter as Bryce had. Except he was nothing like Bryce. "If you don't want to call off the wedding, then you'll explain to me why I keep finding you rubbing up against my cousin."

Kate's nerves were still buzzing but something else was now growing inside her. Something passionately alive and resentful at the same time. "Let's get one thing straight. I was not rubbing up against him. *He* was rubbing up against me. And the asshole is *your* cousin."

Mason's voice grew silky and dangerous. "So you're telling me you've been suffering through his advances out of generosity toward *me*?"

"No," Kate replied, raising her voice in her exasperation. Mason's body seemed stronger and more substantial than Bryce's. And it was right there in front of her—its virile presence almost intimidating. "But he's been coming on to me. I certainly haven't encouraged it. And you haven't seemed to mind before now." The last comment slipped out, her tone involuntarily bitter.

"You haven't told him to stop." His sharp, controlled drawl shifted into gravelly rage again. "I'm tired of walking into my own home and finding my fiancée in the arms of another man." Before Kate could counter the outrageousness of his remark, Mason continued, planting both hands on the counter, trapping her. "I'm telling you right now—I'm not putting up with it anymore."

For some reason she couldn't process, Kate was a little turned on. She was annoyed and nervous and excited and disoriented and shocked by what was happening. But somewhere in the turmoil of all her emotions, an inexplicable arousal was starting to build.

Then she remembered she was wearing her wedding dress.

"Hey! Close your eyes. You're not supposed to see me in this!"

Mason narrowed his eyes, disregarding her words. "I'm still waiting for an explanation."

Kate felt dizzy and she hardly recognized her Mason in the angry, primal stranger in front of her. So she pushed him away and ducked under one of his arms. "Well, you can keep waiting," she snapped, starting toward her bedroom. "I'm going to change clothes. And I'm not going to talk to you when you're acting like a silly, jealous child."

She chose the words intentionally and figured they'd put Mason on hold until she pulled herself together some. The strategy had always worked before.

But she hadn't counted on this new side of Mason. He followed her. Instead of arguing, he unceremoniously scooped her up and hoisted her over his shoulder like a sack of grain.

She squealed and kicked out her legs, instinctively resisting his hold.

Securing his arms around her flailing legs, he said, "We *are* going to talk about this. Right now. I'm not going to let you keep running away from us." He strode through the hallway toward his bedroom.

Kate let out an exclamation of outrage, more from the injustice of this remark—after he'd spent the last few weeks running away from her—than from the indignity of her position. "Put me down, you disgusting Neanderthal. I'm not your possession. You can't just haul me around."

She squirmed as much as she could—wondering if something was wrong with her when she got even more turned on. His arms were like steel on her legs and his body beneath hers was hot and tense. Her helplessness and confusion only fueled her excitement. And she couldn't help responding to the intense passion radiating from him.

Her body didn't seem to understand the passion as anger, not lust.

When his arms tightened even more, hefting her back into place, Kate gasped, "My dress! If you ruin my dress with your caveman tactics, I swear I'll strangle you!"

Now in the bedroom, he set her on her feet in front of him.

Kate's knees buckled and she had to catch herself on the dresser behind her. Her first concern was for her dress, however, so she peered down, assessing the state of her precious dress.

"Your dress is fine." Mason's eyes were crawling over her body but she couldn't tell what he thought about her dress or how she looked in it.

"It's all wrinkled," she sniffed, her cheeks flaming and her fingers trembling. She brushed off the skirt and examined the beading to make sure it wasn't damaged. "And you're not supposed to see me in it until Saturday."

"My concern is hardly seeing you prematurely in your wedding dress." Mason stepped forward, standing very close but not actually touching her. "I've been holding back for weeks now but there's only so much a man can take. I figured you were having last-minute jitters about all the changes in your life. I was willing to be patient for as long as I could. But I'm not going to let you play me for a fool."

Kate gasped, reaching behind her to grip the edge of the dresser. "What? I've never played you for a fool."

"What do you call it then? When a man's fiancée ignores him but lets herself get groped by his oaf of a cousin?"

Choking on her outrage, Kate scowled into Mason's handsome, furious face. "Don't you dare blame this mess on me! You're the one who's been rethinking things. You're the one who's been ignoring me!"

"That is manifestly absurd. And a clear distortion of the facts." Mason's hands closed hard around her hips, pulling her pelvis against his. "Especially coming from the woman I just caught in a clinch with my cousin."

"We were not in a clinch!" Her words were rather strangled and not as strong as she'd intended. But she was brutally distracted by the feel of Mason's groin against her middle.

Evidently, their argument had aroused him as much as it had her.

Mason hadn't acknowledged his physical condition. His fingers tightened on the flesh of her ass through the expensive satin of her dress. "You seem to forget that I saw you together. Twice." There was a muscle twitching in his temple and a sheen of sweat on his face. "Tell me where he touched you."

Kate was so turned on now she was panting, her arousal pulsing almost painfully. This was what she'd wanted for weeks. What she'd needed. Evidence that Mason wanted her— so much he'd shed his civilized demeanor and claim her with instinctive possession.

She wanted—needed—to see this through, to let him claim her this way.

But she couldn't get past one major distraction. "Mason," she whimpered, praying she wasn't going to break his momentum with her plea, "My dress."

Something like understanding flickered across Mason's features but it was only there for a moment.

Then, "Take it off."

The brief command was as hard and textured as gravel.

Kate gulped. "What?"

"Take off the dress." The authority in his voice was as erotic as the feel of his hard body. "If you don't want it damaged, take it off." When she just gaped at him, he continued, pressing the bulge of his arousal insistently against her lower belly. "You can feel what kind of mood I'm in. I'm not going to be gentle. If that's not what you want, you can leave now. If you stay, take off your dress."

The sound of his thick voice and everything his words implied sent a pulse of hot desire to her pussy.

But there was no way she was gong to let him rip off her wedding dress.

"I'll take it off," she whispered.

Mason took a step back, freeing her from the dresser. Without a word, he waited, his eyes raking over her body with demanding possessiveness.

Kate's hands were still shaking as she reached behind her to unfasten the dress. The pearl buttons down the line of the back were purely decorative but she couldn't seem to unhook the hook-and-eye closure at the top. She worked on it with trembling fingers for almost a minute before she asked, "Can you help me?"

"Turn around."

She'd never been the submissive type but for some reason his blunt directives were as sexy as anything she'd ever heard. She was so aroused now she had trouble not squirming as she let Mason unhook the closure and then unfasten the rest of the dress.

He left it hanging open in the back. When she turned around again, he was standing in his former position. "Take it off."

Kate slipped the thick straps off her shoulders and let the dress slide down her body. After stepping out of it, she bent over to pick it up and carefully hung it up.

She was naked except for pink lace panties when she returned to stand in front of Mason. His eyes were sweeping over her, lingering on her smooth legs, swaying breasts and the juncture where her legs met her pelvis.

The juncture where her panties were damp.

"Now," he gritted out, pushing her against the dresser again. The edge poked her hard on the back of her thighs. "Tell me where he touched you."

"He didn't touch me," she insisted, feeling strangely naughty to be naked in the middle of the day when Mason was fully clothed in khakis and dress shirt. "Not *that* way."

"Don't assume you know what I'm talking about." He pushed into her. The bulge at the front of his pants felt even harder and tighter. "Tell me where he touched you."

"He touched my hair. He said it was gorgeous."

She added the last comment as an intentional goad, wanting to test Mason's reaction.

He made a low sound in his throat, almost like a growl. "It is gorgeous." He reached behind her for a handful of her hair, letting the shiny strands slip through his fingers. "But he doesn't get to touch it." He lifted it again as he leaned over, burying his face briefly in the soft hair. "It's mine."

"Uh," Kate objected — more on principle than any sincere feeling. Something small and wounded in her heart was knitting itself together at having Mason claim her this way. "Don't get carried away. The hair is mine."

He snarled and repeated, "Mine. Where else did he touch you?"

Kate took the demand seriously and tried to think back. "Nowhere. Wait, my arm, I guess." She paused, waiting to see what Mason would do.

She wasn't disappointed. He traced a line of kisses down the length of her right arm, murmuring rough, primitive endearments against her skin.

Kate was even more breathless when he finally reached her shoulder and her head lolled back in a ridiculous way. Limp with desire, she had to lean against the dresser for support.

"Oh," she choked, clinging to the back of Mason's neck. "He touched me here." She hesitated before her last word and then brought a hand to her left breast, which Bryce had brushed against the day before. "But it might have been an accident."

Mason bristled when he saw where she was pointing. "He *what*? You let him?"

"I didn't let him. I didn't expect it." Then her attempt at explanation broke off in a helpless whimper as Mason's head lowered to her breast. He took the bare flesh in his mouth, sucking softly and teasing the nipple with his tongue.

With his hand, he fondled her right breast at the same time until Kate shuddered and moaned in frustrated pleasure.

He was murmuring something against her skin. It sounded like a rough repetition of "mine".

Kate's back was arched so dramatically now she could barely stay on her feet. Her moans turned to whimpers and then to desperate sounds very close to sobs. She was so wet it felt like her pussy was dripping and she inhaled gulps of the hot, masculine scent of Mason.

She'd been gasping, "Oh God, oh God, oh God!" as Mason teased and sensually tortured her breasts. But finally she pleaded, "Mason, please! I never touched him. I never wanted him to touch me. You're the only man I want to touch me. Please! I'm dying here. Would you please fuck me now?" Then, hearing how pitiful she sounded, she couldn't help but add, "Domineering bastard."

It wasn't quite under her breath.

Mason obviously heard. His lips twitched and his eyes flared briefly with dry amusement but he recovered quickly. "I thought you wanted me to fuck you."

Kate's humor faded into panicked, lustful desperation when Mason took a step away from her. "I do! I'll be good. I promise."

This was apparently the right answer because he stepped forward, grabbing her by the hips and heaving her up until she was perched on the edge of the dresser. His hands moved possessively over her shoulders, her arms, her breasts, until one of them edged into the space between her thighs.

He fingered her through the thin lace of her panties, lingering on the place that was most wet and hot. "Did he ever touch you here?" His voice was no more than a hoarse whisper and his eyes were focused on his fingers, pushing against her swollen, intimate flesh through her panties.

Kate had released a mew of pleasure at his touch, so close to where she needed it. But at his question she sucked in her breath with a hiss. "No. Of course not. You didn't really think I would, did you? I was never even tempted by Bryce's dubious charms."

"I didn't think you would be," he admitted, his expression growing strangely still. "I always trusted you and never thought you would. But a couple of times, I—" He cut off whatever he'd intended to say and jerked his head to the side.

But Kate had seen that flicker of expression. Recognized it as insecurity.

Realized—for the first time—that Mason must have been suffering from the same kind of insecurities she had.

The final knot of uncertainty loosened in her chest.

"He's a selfish boy," she said quietly. "Why would I even consider him when I have a man like you?"

He met her eyes for a long moment and she saw his expression relax. Then soften into something fond and warm.

But she barely had time to register the swell of love that washed over her because Mason's expression transformed back into that hot, feral dominance.

Both of his hands started to move over the panties and she realized he must be searching for seams.

She knew she was right when Mason grabbed the fabric with both hands and pulled hard.

Kate cried out in response to the violent gesture, her arousal shooting back up to urgency. When he tore the second seam and dropped the remnants of fabric on the floor, Kate tried to wind her legs around Mason's thighs in an attempt to rub her clit against him.

He kissed her—long, hard and hungry—and when he finally tore his mouth away Kate's lips felt swollen and sore.

"Tell me what you want," Mason demanded, hooking one hand under her thigh to keep her from rubbing up against him.

Groaning in frustration and doing her best to hump his hip, Kate said, "Damn it, Mason, you know what I want."

"Tell me."

"I want you to fuck me."

"How?"

"Hard," she rasped, tangling her fingers in his thick hair and pulling on it in her urgency. "Hard and fast. Oh, God, Mason, I want to come." Her urgent wriggling had succeeded in finding the bulge of his arousal. She rocked against it as much as she could in her helpless position, feeling a thrill of victory when Mason closed his eyes and let out a low groan.

Before she could follow through, he had backed up slightly, grabbing her thighs and holding them apart. The move left her intimately exposed to his demanding gaze. He stared down at her pussy, his nostrils flaring with his heavy breathing.

Kate whimpered, bracing herself with her hands behind her on the dresser.

"You're wet," Mason said, his eyes never leaving the space between her legs.

Kate actually blushed. "Yes," she whispered, doing her best not to squirm. Then, her natural rebellion rising up, she added, "There's a shocker."

His lips quirked momentarily but he didn't break the mood. "How wet?"

Enjoying this far too much to not play along, Kate admitted, "Really, really wet."

"Let me see you touch yourself."

Giving a shaky moan of relief and heightened desire, Kate held herself balanced on one hand and moved the other down the line of her inner thigh. Mason was still gripping her legs, pulling them apart so she was splayed widely to his view.

Too eager to try to be sexy, Kate dipped one finger into her wet heat, drawing out more of the moisture collected there. Then she slid her slick finger up to her clit, letting out husky sigh of pleasure as she started to rub it hard.

"Not like that."

Kate gave a little sob but she responded to the rough authority in his voice. She moved her hand, leaving her clit aching even more.

"Fuck yourself with your finger."

She obeyed, sliding her finger back into her channel. She pumped it in and out, starting to pant as she picked up the rhythm.

"Two fingers." He was watching her hotly, his eyes never leaving her pussy as she joined the first finger with a second. The two fingers penetrated her entrance and slid in and out, glistening with her juices.

The sensations were building more slowly than if she'd been allowed to stimulate her clit, but Kate could feel an orgasm growing deep at her center as she masturbated for Mason's pleasure. Her cheeks were scorching and she was starting to sweat. But she couldn't remember ever feeling so hot, naughty and excited — all at once — in her life.

She was huffing out in intensifying pleasure when Mason moved his hand from her right thigh and closed his fingers around her wrist. "That's enough."

She almost cried in disappointment and frustration. She'd just been getting close to the orgasm she so desperately needed. Her body shook but she managed not to fight Mason's grip on her hand.

"Tell me what you want." He looked almost as hot and shaky as she felt.

"I want to come." She wanted so much to wiggle her fingers, which were still buried inside her, that tears were burning in her eyes. "Please, Mason, make me come."

"I will." He was about to say something else but Kate suddenly lost her balance, supported now in her precarious position by just one of her hands and one of Mason's. She almost toppled over. In catching her, Mason pulled the thigh he gripped a little too far from the other.

Her muscles protested the sudden pull of force and she cried out in unexpected pain.

Mason released her thigh and wrist immediately, wrapping his arms around her in automatic protection to keep her from falling.

Kate was disoriented and she buried her face in Mason's shirt and fisted her fingers in the fabric.

"Are you all right, baby?"

Despite her arousal, Kate couldn't help but snicker in fond tenderness. Mason was so instinctively considerate and protective—such a gentleman—that he couldn't force back that side of his nature, even when he was supposed to be dominant.

"I will be if you ever decide to fuck me," she complained, suppressing her reaction so she wouldn't break his mood.

She knew he needed this. And she needed it too.

He narrowed his eyes—suspiciously at first, as if he suspected she might have been laughing at him. Then the fire ignited once more and he released her, letting her slide to her feet off the dresser.

"Maybe we should move this to the bed," he suggested. "So I don't have to worry about your toppling over."

"Good plan."

He nodded to the bed. "Go on."

She walked slowly toward the double bed, feeling exposed and achingly aroused and still shaky on the feet.

When she sat on the side of the bed and looked expectantly at Mason, he shook his head. "Not like that. Get on your hands and knees at the foot of the bed."

Under normal circumstances, Kate never would have taken orders without question. It wasn't really her nature—in bed or any other aspect of life. But this afternoon every command he gave her made her even hotter—hotter than she'd ever felt in her life.

She crawled up on the bed and arranged herself on her hands and knees at the foot of the bed as he'd directed.

Now she was even more exposed. The position spread her open and the cool air against her hot flesh made her want to moan.

Her hair was falling over her shoulders and it kept sticking to her damp, heated face. She looked over her shoulder at Mason.

He was standing next to the foot of the bed, still dressed in his shirt and trousers. He looked as hot as she was—the edge of his hair was damp from sweat as were a couple of spots on his shirt.

"Mason, please."

"Bend your arms," he instructed, starting to unfasten his pants.

Kate bent her arms, lowering her shoulders and head, leaving her bottom in the air. It was as undignified a position as she could imagine, but she felt sexy and wild and naughty.

When Mason had rid himself of his pants, he got onto the bed behind her. He stroked the soft flesh of her ass, squeezing it. "Good girl. Now turn your head and look."

Her cheek was pressed against the mattress as she watched Mason with hungry urgency, but at his gesture she tilted her head away from him and looked toward the wall.

They were aligned perfectly with the large mirror and she could now see her naked body, folded and waiting for Mason to fuck her.

Her face was red and eager, something almost desperate in her eyes. Her hair was spilling around her shoulders and her bottom looked round and full, the flesh jiggling slightly beneath Mason's fingers.

A jolt of desire shot to her center at such a carnal display of her body.

"Watch," Mason rasped. "Keep watching yourself as I fuck you."

She groaned, clenching her inner muscles as if she could somehow pull him inside her. Licking her lips—watching as her tongue traced the swollen red line of her mouth—she wondered if it was possible for her to get any wetter. "Mason."

"Keep watching."

She did as he said. Didn't look away from her debauched reflection in the mirror, even as Mason moved closer behind her on his knees and stroked along the crease in her ass until he found her entrance.

"You're so wet," he murmured, slipping in a finger to check her readiness.

Kate was about to whine in impatience but she wisely bit her lip. Complaining might delay this even more and she wasn't sure she could handle waiting anymore.

She couldn't see Mason clearly in the mirror—he was mostly out of her line of sight—but from the rustling of fabric she heard behind her she assumed he was taking off his shirt.

He would be naked then. As naked as she was. She wanted to turn back to look at him but she didn't look away from the mirror.

Mason squeezed her bottom again, pulling the cheeks apart. Then she finally felt him lining up his cock at her entrance.

Felt the tight pressure of the penetration as he pushed his erection into her clinging channel.

"Ah, ah, ah," she gasped, as the pressure eased some of her empty ache. The throbbing of her arousal compelled her to jerk her hips in a shameless attempt to get more friction.

Mason's fingers dug into her bottom. "No," he gritted out. "Hold still."

Kate was almost sobbing as she tried to obey him. "Fuck, Mason. I don't think I can."

"Yes, you can, baby. Hold still this once. Let me fuck you."

She bit down on her lip so hard it was painful and her hands clawed at the bedding beneath her. But she managed to hold her pelvis still as Mason buried his cock in her body.

When he was in as far as he could go, he slid his hands from her ass down her back. "Good girl," he said again, leaning over so that she could see him in the mirror, draped over her body. "How's that?"

"Good," she choked, the inability to move almost torture. "So good." She could feel Mason's balls against her flesh and she could hear him panting next to her ear. "But I need more. Mason, please. Fuck me."

He eased back and then slid into her again, his thrust slow and luscious.

"Again," she begged. "Please, again."

He started up a rhythm—controlled, steady and pleasing. On each stroke, he hit her G-spot and spirals of pleasure would shoot out from the contact. Kate couldn't stop moaning, couldn't stop gasping, couldn't stop babbling out broken pleas for more.

She clenched around him as much as she could but all of her concentration was focused on not shaking her bottom or pumping her hips to match his rhythm. Her clit was aching with need and all her instincts screamed at her to bounce and jiggle as much as she could to generate friction.

She didn't though. She let Mason fuck her as he wanted and the orgasm that began to grow at her center was slow and powerful and torturous.

His grip on her ass was bruising and painful but the feel of his hands only increased her excitement. Mason's motion was shaking the bed, shaking her whole body and her breasts and thighs were jiggling from the momentum.

"Tell me how you want it," Mason rasped.

"Harder. Faster." Saliva was pooling in her mouth and hair was in her eyes and mouth. "Harder. Faster. Please."

With a groan, Mason accelerated his rhythm, pounding into her with more force and speed. The additional stimulation was exactly what Kate needed and she sobbed with pleasure as her developing orgasm surged forward.

Mason finally seemed to be losing control. He started to make animalistic grunts, timed to the rhythm of his thrusting. Occasionally he'd fall out of rhythm, bumping with erratic jerks against her bottom—usually when her sobs were particularly helpless.

"Are you coming?" He adjusted his knees for better leverage.

"Yeah, yeah, yeah," she huffed, staring in a wild stupor at the shameless reflection of her shaking body. "Gonna come. Gonna come hard."

He swallowed back another groan and leaned farther forward, bracing his weight with his hands on the bed. In this position, he couldn't make very long thrusts, but his hips pistoned into her from behind in short, fast jerks. His cock felt huge and tight in her overly sensitized channel and he kept slamming against her G-spot.

"Fuck," he muttered, his voice strangled. "Oh, fuck, baby. Come now."

She came — her climax spiraling out with the sound of his voice. She cried out in broken exclamations, her body convulsing and her inner walls clamping down around his cock.

He kept thrusting into her clenching muscles, extending her pleasure. And then, just as she was coming down from one of the hardest orgasms of her life, he wrapped one of his arms around her middle and pulled her upper body up toward his chest.

Completely off-balance, she reached up to cling to his neck, digging her fingernails into his skin.

Panting, sweating and even drooling a little, she babbled through the lingering pleasure.

Then his other hand moved down between her legs, stroking open her intimate folds and finding her still-throbbing clit.

She screamed as he pressed into it, another climax surging up on the heels of the first. His cock was still buried inside her, now at a different angle and he was jerking into her clumsily as he panted and grunted wetly against her ear.

As her second orgasm ripped through her, Kate clawed at the back of Mason's neck. The pain must have been what finally pushed him over the edge.

He roared out a rough, wordless exclamation and froze inside her for a moment. Then she felt him twitching and shuddering behind her as he came, felt his cock pulsing inside her, heard him muttering, "I love you. I love you. I love you."

She might have come again at the words.

They remained entwined for another minute, writhing and clinging to each other. Then Kate toppled forward onto her hands and Mason fell with her, his cock slipping out of her and his weight falling heavily onto her back.

Her eyes were burning with tears and her nose was running a little. Her pussy was raw and her lungs ached with her attempts to take a full breath. But she was flooded with visceral satisfaction. And with something deeper than that.

With absolute love and security.

Mason had adjusted their bodies so that he was spooning her from behind, their damp skin sticking wherever they connected. Occasionally, he would breathe a kiss into her hair, making Kate melt a little more.

"I love you," he said one more time, nuzzling the side of her head.

Kate grabbed one of his hands and hugged it to her chest. "I love you too."

She'd loved him for most of her life. Planned to love him for the rest of it.

"At least this time you didn't say thank you," Kate murmured wryly, after another minute of silence. Her ironic nature always presented itself whenever she threatened to lapse into pure sentiment.

"What?" Mason propped himself up on his elbow and turned her over so she was looking up at him. "What do you mean?"

"Last time. Last night. We made love and all you said was thank you. It made me feel… I thought… Why did you thank me like that?"

His brow was furrowed. "Why shouldn't I thank you? I thought you'd known how turned on I was by your chase after the button and had decided to help me out with it, even though you weren't in the mood for sex. Saying thank you was only polite."

Gasping in outrage, she said, "What? I wasn't doing it for you! You hadn't made a move on me in weeks. I was horny and needy and I wanted to make love to you. It was hard enough to make all the moves myself when I thought you weren't interested. But then I thought you needed it too. But then you said thank you and I got all confused again."

As explanations went, hers wasn't very coherent. But Mason seemed to follow what she meant. He cringed slightly. "I guess I read it wrong. Why didn't you tell me you were feeling insecure or that you wanted sex?"

Kate huffed at him. "Right. That's just what I wanted. A pity fuck." She paused. Then, "Is that what you thought I was giving you?"

Mason nodded reluctantly. "I've been dying to fuck you for weeks. But you were acting so prickly and all the hints I made fell flat."

"What hints? I never heard any hints!"

"What did you think it meant when I was appreciating the sexy show you gave me on the floor with that damned button?"

"You never said it was sexy! I thought you were laughing at me!"

Mason chuckled and stroked the hair back from her face. "Try to pay more attention next time. I was suffering from a painful hard-on. But then you told me to get back to work and you went to bed alone. What was I supposed to think?"

Kate considered this and decided she could understand where he'd gotten such a wrong impression. She *had* been awfully sensitive and cranky lately. "Well, you pay more attention next time too. I've been horny as hell and starting to think... I thought you wanted to go back to just being friends, that you didn't want to get married."

"Not want to get married! Are you insane? I was just trying to be patient and sensitive—letting you work through your jitters." He glanced away, as if he were struggling to say what came next. "And I guess I was afraid to push you too hard, for fear you'd decide you'd made a mistake. I didn't want to blow it now that my dreams were coming true, after being in love with you for twenty years."

Kate's heart thudded in her chest. She sat up straight on the bed and grabbed Mason by the shoulders. "What? What did you say? You weren't in love with me all that time."

"Of course I was. I've loved you all my life."

"No. No! We were friends. That's all."

"That's all *you* felt for me. But I always felt more. Don't you ever worry about us going back to just being friends. I've never thought about you as just a friend."

It was almost more than Kate could process. Mason was looking very Mason-like again, with rumpled hair, intelligent eyes and a dry smile. The dominant, primitive man he'd shown her before had retreated behind the surface but she could sense it still there. Always there. Ready to claim her whenever his possession of her was threatened.

He'd loved her the whole time. Through high school, college and the years that followed. And she'd never realized it. She'd always thought about him as just Mason.

He'd been waiting for her all along. And now that he had her, he wasn't going to let her go.

Kate had never felt so safe, so loved, so happy in all her life.

She wasn't sure if she wanted to cry or giggle hysterically. So she settled for a compromise.

She snorted. "Yeah, well, don't expect me to let you go all caveman on me very often. I don't respond well to taking orders."

Mason chuckled and pulled her into a hug. "I've noticed that. But don't expect me to ever let my wife entertain the attentions of another man."

He'd never called her his wife before. And right now Kate wanted nothing more than to be that. But all she said was, "Bryce's attentions were rather entertaining. You should have seen him give me a sultry look."

Mason growled, the noise vibrating in his chest.

"It was the funniest thing ever," Kate continued, patting him on the chest. "Not nearly as effective as yours. Plus, he's annoying and selfish. I hope his truck gets crapped on."

"It will." When Kate looked at Mason questioningly, he explained, "I switched the cars before I came in. His is now parked under the tree."

* * * * *

"Did I tell you how irresistible you look in that dress?"

Kate was wearing her wedding dress—this time on her wedding day. She couldn't believe the wedding was almost over. The ceremony had gone smoothly, only marred when Bryce had broken into a coughing fit as they'd been exchanging vows.

The reception took place in an old plantation house and gardens. The food was set up inside but most of the guests were mingling outside.

Kate pressed up shamelessly against her new husband. They were dancing on the parquet floor that had been set up beneath the tent in the middle of the formal gardens. They'd gone through all the traditional first dances and had made the rounds, greeting everyone. Now they were just enjoying themselves, since the reception was drawing to a close.

Kate was feeling rather giddy—an effect of her joyful excitement, the culmination of months of work and anxiety about the wedding and too much champagne. And Mason was looking as adorably sexy as he'd ever looked. He'd tried to tame his hair into order but by now it was hopelessly rumpled again, falling over his forehead. And his tux was a sleekly sophisticated contrast to his wry expression and lean, virile strength.

"No," she drawled, rubbing against him more provocatively than she should be doing in such a crowd. "You failed to mention it."

"I figured my speechless awe as you walked down the aisle should have covered it."

Despite misreading Mason in the past, Kate had recognized the look on his face in that moment as awe.

She'd felt rather awed herself. That he would feel that way about her. That he'd felt that way about her for so long.

She wound her arms around his neck and pressed a kiss on his throat. "It wouldn't hurt you to tell me occasionally instead of expecting me to read your expressions." She paused a beat. Then, "You didn't mention my dress the first time you saw it either."

Mason chuckled, his hands on her back tender and possessive. "I certainly noticed it. But I had other things to discuss at the time."

Kate couldn't resist pressing against his groin and was thrilled when she realized he'd grown slightly hard. "You certainly did." She blew into his ear, dug her fingernails into his neck and pushed her pelvis harder into his.

Flushed in delight when she felt him harden even more.

"I can't believe my husband has an erection at his own wedding," she teased him in a husky murmur. People were looking at the happy couple fondly, evidently unaware of the physical condition of one of them.

Both of them, actually—if Kate was honest with herself. She was getting a little turned on herself, no matter how inappropriate it might be.

"I can't believe my wife is such a tease," Mason replied, in a growl that both excited and amused her. "Someone needs to put you in your place."

"What place is that?" There was an obvious bulge at the front of his pants now and Kate rubbed against it relentlessly. "And who do you suppose is man enough to put me there?"

Mason's gray eyes flared deliciously. "Just wait until I get you alone."

Her intimate muscles tightened. But she taunted, "Empty words. That's hours from now. In the meantime, what will you do with that hard-on?"

"Don't push me, woman."

Kate snickered. "What exactly are you going to do in the midst of our gathered guests?"

She'd truly believed there was nothing he could do. But she'd once again underestimated her husband.

With a guttural sound, he released her. Then he hoisted her up—in her wedding dress, with everyone looking on—over his shoulder in the caveman carry he'd used on her before.

She squealed. In surprise. And embarrassment. And delight.

The wedding guests burst into laughter and applause, calling out teasing encouragement for what they saw as lighthearted fun.

Kate might have been the only one who realized her husband was carrying her off somewhere to fuck her.

She flailed her legs and pounded on his back with her fists, putting up an appropriate show of resistance to his presumptuous, primitive behavior.

She made sure he knew she wasn't truly resisting.

When they were alone and he put her down, she told him exactly what she thought about him.

Mason told her he loved her too.

SEDUCING A GOD

Taige Crenshaw

ຽວ

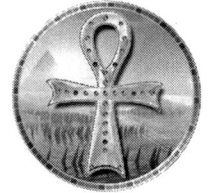

Dedication

შ

To my mother who has always been my number one fan. Although you are no longer with me I know you are smiling down at me every time I get published.

To Marilyn, my sister and second mother, who has always believed I would be a success.

To my lunch buddies, who listen to me ramble on about my writing ideas.

To the real Paula, who lent me her name. This one is for you.

How to Seduce

შ

Scope out the target you want to seduce.

Entice your target with your boldness.

Do nothing. Wait for your target to come to you.

Use any opportunity that presents itself to drive your target wild.

Conquer and don't stop even when the target begs for mercy.

Embrace your victory then go for it.

Chapter One

Scope out the target you want to seduce.

ℬ

With a barely stifled moan Paula Stroker wondered how much trouble she would get into if she jumped across the aisle and beat the wedding planner with that damn stick she was waving around. Everyone else was hanging onto every word the snotty piece of shit was saying. She couldn't figure out how many times you had to practice to walk down the aisle. Sheesh, you walked every day for God's sake. Frowning, she resisted her impulse although she would have liked to shock everyone who saw her as the well-behaved one.

You're just bitter it isn't you that's getting married. She almost snorted in laughter at that whopper. Her inner voice had a warped sense of humor. So what if she was single at thirty-five and her mother had resorted to throwing men at her who needed a zookeeper. As if she had heard her thoughts, her mother, Adrianna Stroker, glanced back at her with pity in her eyes. It took all Paula's control not to scream she would rather have her eyeballs plucked out than get married, then bolt out the door. She tried a smile instead. Her mother nodded then went back to watching the wedding planner like the words coming out of her mouth were gold.

She knew exactly what her mother was thinking when she looked at her. "If Paris was ready to settle down why couldn't Paula?" Glancing at Paris Stroker, her sister and the bride-to-be, Paula saw Paris roll her eyes. Stifling a laugh, Paula still couldn't believe it. Paris was getting married. Paris who had always said, "You won't get me down the aisle unless I have lost my mind." Yet here she stood, the wild child ready to tie the knot. Put on the old ball and chain or any of those other silly sayings. Something had to be seriously wrong.

Looking over at Nathan Randall, Paris' fiancé, she still couldn't figure out how he had convinced her. Yes, he was handsome with his chiseled good looks, he was head-over-heels in love with Paris and he was smart. He was in charge of the marketing department of Tantalize Me, the company she co-owned with Paris. Three years ago Nathan and Paris had met at work and fallen in love. They had been living together ever since. She knew that Nathan had asked Paris to marry him many times but she had refused. At least until a month ago when suddenly they announced they were getting married in a month. Mom had a fit, thinking Paris was pregnant. Since they had already been living together she and Paris hadn't understood what the big deal was.

When their mother had explained that living together before marriage was fine but being pregnant before marriage was a huge deal they had just looked at her like she was missing a few bricks. Her mother had a slanted way of looking at things. They already knew her view on marriage. She had been living with Christopher for fifteen years and still refused to marry him. Her claim that she couldn't dream of marrying anyone after their dad died was a load of shit since she could live with Christopher.

After realizing that Paris was not pregnant but wanted to get married, Mom had wondered how she could plan a wedding in that time. They had known she was just being coy. She liked nothing more than having a party. From the announcement to now, one week before the wedding, it had been non-stop preparations, fittings and all the wedding hoopla. Paula was sick of it. She couldn't even try to escape as she had planned from this, the engagement party. Her mother, the wedding general from hell, and her little minion the wedding planner, the devil's helper, had dragged them all into a separate ballroom away from the party to practice the walk down the aisle for the gazillionth time.

The wedding planner went from person to person, arranging them and telling them how to stand. When her turn came Paula gave the planner a look and she backed up, smiling tightly. They had already had a run-in with what Paula would and would not put up with. The planner went to the next person. Bored. Paula glanced around, looking at the rest of the wedding party who all seemed excited. She didn't get what turned people into smiling idiots when in a wedding. Shaking her head, she continued to look around, checking out some of the other people who had wandered in to take a look at what was going on. Paula shifted. She hated being the center of attention. She'd rather be locked in her lab working. Most of their audience was watching the show with a smile on their face. Continuing her perusal, Paula turned to her left, then her eyes widened.

His back was to her as he walked away. From the back alone he looked like a walking wet dream. His tightly braided hair swung between his broad shoulders, curling on the end to rest about mid-back. Paula licked her lips as she let her eyes wander down, then across those broad shoulders. She was a sucker for shoulders. He reached up with a sun-kissed colored hand to smooth back his hair, causing the muscles in his shoulders to ripple under his pale green dress shirt. He was one tall piece of eye candy.

Paula didn't think it could get any more delectable than those shoulders. Dropping her gaze, she realized how wrong she was. His tight hunter green slacks hugged his rear, detailing every nook and cranny. Her mouth went dry.

Was it hot in here? She wondered as she continued to look at him. He continued moving past all the people heading for the back of the room. He moved with a sense of grace, self-confidence and arrogance. She wished he would turn around so she could get a look from the front. *Have mercy on me if he looks as good as he does from the back.*

Suddenly the man turned and leaned on the wall. Paula couldn't catch her breath. He wasn't handsome. He was gorgeous.

His gray gaze roamed the room. Even from where she stood she could see he had thick curly lashes that offset those piercing eyes. His features were craggy and all masculine—broad forehead, sharp cheeks, full nose and firm lips pulled into a grim line. His broad shoulders looked even better in the frontal view. His chest was so broad it would inspire a woman to lay her head down and stay awhile.

I wonder if it feels as good as it looks?

The rest of him looked just as decadent. He looked like he was sporting a six-pack under that shirt. Thankful for the unobstructed view, she glanced at his firm muscular thighs and her mouth ached to take a bite along his skin.

Who was he?

Intrigued, Paula watched as he shifted where he leaned against the wall.

The look on his craggy face was miserable. She wondered why. Usually at parties like this she would find a corner and wait until she could make a graceful escape but now after seeing him Paula was looking forward to circulating so she could meet this luscious man. Being aggressive wasn't her style but she was definitely going to get an introduction. Paula frowned as a breathtakingly beautiful woman walked up to join him. The man gave the woman a hug then they leaned next to each other against the wall.

"Now line up, everyone." The wedding planner's voice cut in, distracting her.

Glancing back at the wedding planner, Paula's mind was on who the man was and what the woman was to him.

No respect. He got no respect. Markus M'ar Riage watched as the wedding coordinator flitted around trying to get everything to run smoothly.

The planner didn't have a clue about what it took to make a marriage. It had nothing to do with any of these silly trappings. Slumping farther onto the wall, he wished he was anywhere but here. He was only present because of the groom, Nathan Randall. Shaking his head, he still hadn't found out how the heck Nathan had known about him. When Nathan had called him out of desperation his soft heart wouldn't let him refuse. Damn it. Even though he knew that this family was nothing but trouble.

They were his biggest headache and worst shame. Out of the corner of his eye he saw a woman try to slide closer to him. Glancing at her, he gave her his "leave me the hell alone" look. She glanced at him, a panicked look on her face, and took off in the other direction, knocking people out of her way. He saw people glancing after her then at him. He turned his face away, trying to act like nothing happened.

Shit, he hadn't meant to scare her off, just have her leave him alone. This whole wedding business had him feeling out of control. Scowling, Markus decided it was time to hang up his rings and retire. Let the young bucks do all the work for a change. He was tired of being the clean-up crew. Let them get a taste of what it was like without him around. He felt someone come and stand by him. He sighed. Not another one. He cursed his handsome face.

"Why the pout, sweetie? You would think you would be happy at an occasion like this," a smoky voice teased.

Glancing at her, Markus couldn't help the grin that twitched on his lips. "Please. Men don't pout."

She laughed, throwing her head back and making her mane of kinky curly hair swing.

"What are you doing here, Fallon?"

Fallon M'ar Riage looked at him from head to foot. "Looking snazzy."

He sighed again and waited for her to reply. She looked at him, her silver gray eyes amused. She had a face that looked like she could launch any man into orbit. He knew for a fact that she did. She shifted, causing her rust-colored fitted dress to swirl around her. Absently he glanced up and was not surprised to see that most of the men in the room were staring at her.

Fallon's next statement brought his attention back to her. "Come on, bro, you did it. She's getting married. You should be happy." She glanced back at the bride and groom standing across the room.

He snorted. "Until she walks down the aisle and says I do, she's still my charge. Shit, this family has given me so many headaches. After this I'm retiring."

Fallon laughed and swatted him on the arm. "Where would the world be without you?"

He glared at her. "You think you're funny. I'm sick to death of being the fix-it man for the rest of you. Especially Claude and Leonardo. You all need to finish your own damn jobs."

She waved her hand carelessly. "You're too old-fashioned, Markus. Not everyone wants to end up married."

Markus looked at her like she was crazy and his head started to throb. "God, I can't believe we have the same parents."

She glanced at him and raised one eyebrow. "Live with it."

"I have, for over a thousand years, and I still don't get you." Markus stared at his sister and wondered where their parents had gone wrong.

She smiled, a devilish look in her eye, then reached up and patted him on his cheek. "And you never will."

Turning, she looked back at the bride and groom. "They make a lovely couple. Her daughter will be a firecracker."

Entice your target with your boldness.

Markus literally felt his eyes bug out of his head. "Christ, she's pregnant. No wonder that damn louse ZJ worked so hard to convince me to help Nathan after he called me."

Narrowing his eyes, he glared at her.

She was unruffled by his look. "What? That's what you're there for. We each have a job and we do it."

"Your job is not to populate the planet, Fallon."

"Yes it is. That's what the Goddess of Fertility does."

"No it isn't. Christ. At the rate you all are going we're going to be in major shit."

Fallon looked at him. "Unlike you some of us need more time to learn the full extent of our duties. We all can't be an overachiever like you. You think it's easy being the Goddess of Fertility? You should try it on for a day."

Running his hand over his face in agitation, Markus growled. "Fuck it, I don't have it any easier. These days everyone just jumps into bed, lives together or has kids without the benefits of marriage. How does that make me look? I'm the God of Matrimony for god sakes."

"Oh boo hoo, the poor God of Matrimony is so misunderstood. You need to loosen up, Markus. Stop being so stiff. You need a bout of knock-your-eyes-back-in-your-head sex. Get laid and laid well. Why don't you go out with Claude, no, better yet Leonardo?"

"You must be out of your ever-loving mind if you think I'd go out with those two to get laid. Hell, all Claude tries to do is live up to his name and make everyone fall in love. He doesn't realize being the God of Love doesn't mean shit without the follow-through. Leonardo is even worse. Fucking every woman in his path. Just because you're the God of Lust doesn't mean you have to act like a tomcat in heat. Neither one realizes that the correct end to love or lust should be marriage. I'm damn tired of being the clean-up guy. Damn that ZJ. Wait until Zeus hears about this. "

"Didn't you learn your lesson from last time? Zeus, Aphrodite, Hades and all the rest of the parents have retired. We're in charge now."

Markus felt his headache worsen. "We should all be able to work together by now. It's been two hundred and seventy-three years already. How much retirement does a person need?"

Fallon rolled her eyes. "With you testosterone-laden idiots involved, it's a miracle anything gets done." She patted his cheek again. "Retirement is forever, buddy." She laughed at him.

Opening his mouth to answer, Markus felt a weird sensation. Glancing toward the bride and groom, his eyes clashed with liquid honey. Taking in the woman staring at him in one glance, he noted that she was lovely. Her honey-toned skin glowed with vibrancy while her hazel eyes shone through her wire-framed glasses, impaling him. A small smile curved a lush mouth begging to be eaten. She turned, causing the light to shine off her dark reddish brown hair pulled back in a tight bun. He could see the impatience on her face.

His gaze dropped lower, taking in her prim black suit. Her full breasts would fit into his hands perfectly. His mouth watered thinking of taking a suck. They looked soft and delicious. His cock hardened to painful attention. Markus willed himself to calm down but it was useless. She made him feel primal.

He took a step forward before he realized it. Stopping, he glanced away and shook his head to clear the buzzing in his ears. Head clear, he glanced back at the woman. She was still watching him, her gaze steady.

Who was she? She was obviously part of the wedding party but he hadn't met her before. He had thought Nathan had introduced him to everyone. She looked away.

"What's wrong with you?" Fallon demanded, looking around.

Taking her by the elbow, Markus replied, "Nothing. Let's go back to the party."

"Why?"

With one last glance at the woman who was turned away from him now, Markus looked away then down at Fallon. "We have to discuss why you sent Zeus Jr. to me instead of coming to talk with me yourself."

Leading Fallon from the room, he ignored her protests.

* * * * *

Rushing down the hallway, Paula cursed the wedding planner for keeping her so long. When she had finally made it back to the party, she mingled to see if she could find the man. She hadn't. He was gone and she hadn't even gotten to speak with him. Since she had already played nice she was leaving.

Quickly climbing the stairs that led to the second floor, Paula walked away from the sounds of the party. Reaching the top, she turned right then left on the way to her old childhood room. The silence was welcome after all the noise. Glancing at her watch, she noted the time and figured she could go into the office for a little bit. Her current invention was giving her trouble and she wanted it finished before Paris' wedding at the end of the week.

Picking up her pace, she turned the corner to her room and felt like a brick wall hit her. She heard a grunt and as she started to fall strong arms grabbed her, holding her upright. Startled, she looked up into the face of her savior. Seeing it was the man from downstairs, her heart started to pound. He looked at her and a look of recognition passed between them.

Slowly he released her and stepped back. "Excuse me. Sorry. I didn't hear you coming." His voice was a rich molasses.

Silently he watched her.

Say something, you idiot. Paula returned his look, unable to come up with a thing to say. He nodded, then stepped around her and started to walk away.

Turning quickly, Paula cursed herself. B*e bold, be daring. Don't be shy. Come on.* "Paula."

The man turned and looked at her in question.

Cursing her shy nature, Paula tried again. "My name is Paula."

His answer was gruff. "Markus."

He looked at her, waiting. She thought of what she should say.

"I saw you in the ballroom earlier. Why'd you look so miserable?"

He smiled slightly. "Weddings."

She laughed in understanding. "You hate weddings too. Thank God. I thought I was the only one." Leaning against the wall, she looked at him and grinned. "Can you believe all the hoopla? I don't get it. All they need to do is get in front of a minister and say yes and be done with it."

He looked amused, walked closer then leaned against the wall beside her. Paula felt deliciously crowded. She stilled a shudder before it could escape.

"Yes. People don't realize that all this is not necessary." He shook his head, causing the braid that rested on his shoulder to move.

Before she could think about it her hand reached out to touch his hair. His hand flashed out and caught hers before she could touch it. Embarrassed at her boldness, Paula dropped her eyes and tried to pull away. He held firm. Raising her gaze, she locked eyes with his. This close up she noticed his eyes weren't pale gray as she assumed but silver with green flecks. She had never seen eyes that color before. Everything about him was intriguing. Swallowing, she realized how out of character she was acting.

He leaned closer, almost touching her lips with his. "I'm the God of Matrimony." Watching him to see if he was kidding, she saw he was serious.

She didn't believe him. "Really. I make sex toys for a living."

He titled his head to the side and continued to watch her intently then he grinned, threw back his head and started to laugh. Paula didn't appreciate it at all. It wasn't a joke. She did make sex toys and was damn good at it. Tantalize Me, the business she and Paris had started as a whim, had taken off and they were good at what they did. Paris dealt with the day-to-day administration and she created. She had fun making the various sex gadgets.

Narrowing her eyes, Paula did something that she was sure he would not expect. Stepping forward, she tugged out of his loosened grip, reached up and grabbed him by the shirt, stood on her toes and kissed him.

Not used to being the aggressor, Paula went with her instinct and kissed him thoroughly. She licked the seam of his lips and when he opened she swept her tongue deep inside. She devoured his mouth in a heated kiss. Markus' heart beat rapidly. Murmuring, she went closer to him and his arms wrapped around her. He wasn't participating, just taking her sensual assault. This wasn't about anything more than unadulterated, unbridled lust.

Drawing back, Paula looked at him to see what he would do. He said nothing, just looked at her through heated eyes. Uneasy, Paula wondered if she had overstepped a mark.

Finally he broke the silence. "Brace yourself." His voice was a hoarse raw sound.

Markus pulled her deeper into his body and aligned her into him until every part of them touched, then he kissed her. Delved deep and swift with no pretense. He lapped at each crevice in her mouth, sucking strongly at her tongue. He murmured, deepening the kiss, stroking in and out slowly then harder. Her body stiffened in shock as her pussy started to vibrate in time with his kiss.

His murmur was all the warning she got before he let out a soft purr. Shards of pleasure racked her with each decisive stroke of his tongue. Shocked, she felt an orgasm start to build. Markus tightened his hold on her. Paula went under. She murmured too while he ate at her mouth, sucking in her taste, trying to consume her.

God. Her body gushed as pleasure unlike anything she could ever imagine bombarded her. Growling deep in his throat, Markus gentled his assault, changing the texture of his kiss.

The contrast from wild to soft rolled over her with the tenderness of a summer breeze and the power of a lightning storm. Paula was lost in the sensuality of his kiss. From the moment she had seen him across the room she wanted him. He growled again, making her pussy pulse.

As she sank her hands into his silken hair, it loosened from its binding, spreading out, tickling her hands. Holding on tightly, Paula gripped him close. He purred in her mouth again, sending off shock waves of pleasure to her pussy. His tongue stroked softly along the sides of her tongue then he nipped it, startling her. Pleasure crashed into her as her orgasms overtook her, driving her body insane. Gasping, Paula bowed at the force of it. She hung onto him as pleasure jerked her body. Paula's mind blanked under the force of her release.

Markus stiffened and mumbled, "Christ, sorry."

Gently he leaned her against the wall, stepped back and walked rapidly away around the corner.

Leaning against the wall, Paula tried to catch her breath as small explosions of pleasure continued to rack her. *With a kiss he made me come.*

Raising a shaky hand, she pushed back her hair from her face. She couldn't imagine what would happen if they actually did the deed. On rubbery legs Paula pushed away from the wall, turned and walked to the door of her childhood bedroom. Fine shivers filled her as she walked. Tiny orgasms continued to flood her, making her pussy cream. She had to change her panties. They were soaked.

Do nothing. Wait for your target to come to you.

Striding down the hall, down the stairs then out the front door, Markus was thankful he didn't run into anyone. His cock was hard as a rock and he had no patience for niceties. Stopping just outside the doorway, Markus could still taste her, feel her body against his and smell the sweet scent of her orgasm. Although he'd had many women this had never happened to him before.

The instantaneous combustion.

The loss of control.

Clenching his fist, Markus fought to not go back inside and finish what they'd started. Furious at himself for being sucked in, he swore viciously. While kissing her he realized who she was. Paris' younger sister, Paula Stroker. He had never seen her. She was always at work in the lab or away. He should know better and steer clear of Stroker's family. When all his attempts years earlier to get Adrianna Stroker married off after her husband died had been disastrous, he had vowed not to have anything to do with the family again. To this day he couldn't understand why a woman who was so obviously in love refused to get married. Adrianna had passed the same feelings onto her daughter Paris.

Until Nathan had summoned him. He was still trying to figure out how Nathan knew about him and how to summon him. Very few mortals knew or even believed in him enough to ask for his help. They put their hopes in Claude Valentine. Most mortals knew Claude as Cupid but if you wanted his help you didn't dare call him Cupid to his face. Nathan had asked Markus for help. But when Markus found out who the woman Nathan was trying to convince to marry him was, Markus had decided to stay out of it. The Strokers were a sore subject since they were his only failure. He would have stuck to his initial inclination except Zeus Jr. came to him, asking him to take on the case.

Stupidly he had let his heart rule his head and worked on it. The rules for his help were simple. He only interfered when necessary. Follow what he said. And only the person he was helping was to know who he actually was. It had taken him a little over two long painful years to get Paris to agree to marry Nathan. Until she walked down the aisle he was still working to get the job done.

Yet within hours of seeing Paula for the first time she made him break his own rule of being unknown. She made him burn with things that he shouldn't. He had no time for distractions, especially one that was from the Stroker family. No matter how delectable they were. Striding down the stairs onto the street, Markus took in the quiet night. He took a deep breath, trying to clear her scent from his nose. Harlem Street was deserted as he shimmered and disappeared.

* * * * *

Two days later, sitting in his throne room, Markus still hadn't cleared her scent from his senses. Leaning forward, he put his hand under his chin and stared out at the empty area. Usually there was someone bustling around but he had ordered them all to leave him alone. He was out of sorts and his people knew it. Many of them had offered to help. Since he couldn't say he wanted to fuck Paula Stroker so hard she wouldn't be able to ever want any other man but him, he had declined their offers.

Restless, he shifted and let his eyes roam the richly decorated room. Pale yellow walls offset the gleaming hunter green marble floors. The various paintings and decorations were a profusion of colors, making the room seem alive. The pale green glass cutouts at different intervals all around the room gave him a view of his people passing outside. Markus could see them looking at the closed door in confusion. The doors were rarely closed and he always had time for everyone. Swearing, Markus couldn't even explain how she had gotten under his skin so deeply from their one meeting. He hadn't even been back to the Earth realm to check and see what was going on with Nathan and Paris.

Since he hadn't received any summons he assumed everything was moving on as planned with the wedding. Slouching back, he closed his eyes. He really didn't want to go to this wedding and chance seeing her again. There was no way he could afford to get near her again. It was too dangerous for his control.

"Why is it every time I see you these days you're frowning?"

Not even opening his eyes, Markus replied, "Go away, Fallon."

"No." She sounded very cheerful.

Opening his eyes, he saw she was floating with legs crossed above the table next to his throne. She was in what she liked to call her fertility getup. Which meant lots of bare skin and body paint.

Shaking his head, he looked at her. "Who are you impregnating now?"

Fallon laughed. "No one now. It's already done. Why are you sitting here by yourself?"

"No reason."

She rolled her eyes. "Come on, something has to be up for you not to be glued to the happy couple. Especially since it is in *that* family. I would think you would be there to make sure everything goes off without a hitch."

Guilt swamped him. "Nathan can handle it."

She raised an eyebrow. "Really? Or you hope he can?"

Markus knew she was right but refused to let her know. "Yes, he can handle it."

She shrugged. "Okay. What's wrong with you?" She blinked out then blinked in, leaning on the armrest of his chair.

She watched him closely then a huge grin curled her lips. "*Ah hah*, so you took my suggestion and got a little something-something." She slapped his arm. "Markus, you old dog, how did you find the time?"

"Go away, Fallon."

She pouted. "Fine. Don't tell me." She straightened. "But you need to go and check on Nathan and Paris."

Before he could ask her anything she blinked out. Swearing, Markus shimmered. Coming solid again, Markus saw he was at a combined bachelor and bachelorette party that Nathan and Paris had decided to throw at Tantalize Me. Glancing around for Nathan and Paris, he absently noted that Paula wasn't there. Locating Nathan and Paris, he narrowed his eyes then swore viciously when he saw that Nathan's and Paris' auras had changed. Snapping his fingers, he raised his blowpipe, inserted the dart then in quick succession he blew a dart at Paris then Nathan.

It hit her in the back of her neck and him in his shoulder. Paris raised her hand to her neck, rubbing it, while Nathan looked around. Sending his pipe away quickly, Markus was pleased to see they were back in the marriage frame of mind. When Nathan saw him he waved. Nathan nodded then returned to his conversation. Markus turned away and made his way around the room to circulate.

* * * * *

Frowning, Paula took off her goggles and rested them on her worktable. Although she couldn't hear the party going on upstairs, she could imagine they were all having fun. Earlier when the party started she had let the others go before making her way upstairs to check out the festivities.

To look for him you mean. Irritated, she pushed back her chair and stood. After getting nowhere with Nathan for more information on Markus or where he could be found, she had looked for him at each wedding event. Tonight was the same as it had been for the past two days. He hadn't shown up.

You would think after blowing her mind he would at least have the decency to come back and do it again. Since he wasn't at the party she wasn't inclined to stay or take part, instead choosing to come back to her lab and lock the doors. Walking over to the other side of the room, Paula pushed him out of her mind and focused on the one thing that didn't disappoint her — work. Taking a look at the two items on a table, she evaluated them. *The Stroker* was Tantalize Me's bestseller. Taking it off the table, she fingered the nipple clamps. They were much softer than most on the market.

Since she had extremely sensitive nipples she had wanted to create a clamp that was pleasurable. In production she had decided to take it a step further. After much trial and error she had come up with *The Stroker*, which was nipple clamps with a chain attached to each that led to a special clamp that could attach to the clit. It was made of a unique material so it was pleasurable. That wasn't the most special feature of *The Stroker*. With each step the wearer got the sensation of being lightly petted. Stroked softly as if by a lover's hand. It was a highly erotic feeling. To increase the sensation all you had to do was tap one of the nipple clamps and the strokes increased.

The clamps were offered in various colors with a variety of chains — some in solid gold, white gold or silver. At very special requests they would customize it to include precious jewels. Putting it down, Paula glanced at her newest invention, *The Xena*. She hoped it would do even better than *The Stroker*. The Xena and The Stroker were similar in design however in The Xena its functions had been enhanced to increase the wearer's pleasure. Quickly she went to the door and double-checked to make sure it was locked. Glancing around, she debated if she should wait and test it at home as she usually did. Although they had a set of volunteers to test the products on, she believed in performing her own private tests. She couldn't sell a product without knowing how it worked herself. They were already behind schedule for their anticipated release date in three weeks. The prototypes had just gone out to the testers yesterday.

Deciding it was worth the risk, she went back to the table, picked up *The Xena* and continued across the room to the back where her office was. Going inside the spacious area, she closed the door, locked it and walked rapidly over to her desk. Stopping in front of it, she set *The Xena* down and stripped quickly. Taking the two chairs in front of her desk, she positioned them to rest her legs on. Picking up *The Xena,* she attached the clamps to her nipples, hissing slightly at the feel of them being attached.

Taking a deep breath, Paula smoothed out the chains then picked up the clit clamp and leaned back against the desk. She spread her legs and stroked lightly along her clit then attached the clit clamp. She moaned at the feel of it. Raising herself, she sat on the desk, moaning as the clit clamp started to stroke. Lifting her feet, she rested one on each chair, spreading her thighs wider. Closing her eyes at the sensation of being lightly stroked, Paula moaned loudly.

Swallowing hard, she fought off her orgasm. She ran her right thumb along the right nipple clamp. The delicious tightening on the clit clamp was all the warning she had before a firm stroke then a deep suction made her back bow. The clit clamp sucked then stroked firmly along her aching pussy. It was like going from a gentle breeze to a gale-force wind. Dropping her hand back on the desk, Paula arched her back, screaming loud and long in orgasm. Absently she thanked God her office was soundproof.

Blearily she remembered to touch the left nipple clamp then fell back against the desk as the stroking and suction started on her tender clit. Brutal sounds ripped from her lips as she felt another orgasm approaching. Gasping for breath,

Paula braced herself for it. Suddenly the sensation stopped and a finger replaced the clamp, impaling her, causing her eyes to fly open. She looked up and locked eyes with silver gray.

Chapter Two
Use any opportunity that presents itself to drive your target wild.

ဆာ

Paula's heart thumped as she watched Markus' hungry gaze. He licked his lips while his gaze dropped, taking in her widespread soaking cunt. His look was like a physical touch, making an involuntary moan escape from Paula. His gaze snapped up to her face. The look in his eyes made her pussy cream even more. With a firm stroke Markus pulled out then back into her soaked pussy. Scrambling for something to hold onto, Paula grabbed the edge of the desk.

Markus smiled, a fierce twist of his lips. Paula tried to think but couldn't as he sunk another finger into her. Going in and out in rapid, rough motions.

"Gg.... Fu..." Paula screamed.

Markus leaned forward over her and flicked the nipple clamp with his tongue. It started to suck and stroke. It sent her over the edge. An orgasm rolled over her. Arching hard, Paula pressed down on his hand, grinding against it. He chuckled as he enveloped the nipple clamp in his mouth, sucked it off, spat it off to one side then curled his tongue around her hard nipple before starting a strong suction. He continued to stroke his fingers in and out of her.

"Uuuhhh...." Paula felt every suck and lick of his hot mouth pulsate in her pussy. His fingers were never still, driving her orgasm on and on.

Paula head thrashed from side to side while her hands came up and gripped his head, pinning him to her. "Fuck yes."

His muscles rippled as he moved from breast to breast, working the swollen tips until they were sore. His fingers swept in and out of her, stroking her inner pussy walls with delicate precision. Paula gripped him as shivers tore through her. Markus continued his sensual assault, using exquisite pressure that drove her to heightened frenzy. His tongue grew more insistent on her nipple then he let out a purr. Paula dropped back and let out a silent scream as the pressure inside her burst into an even more explosive red-hot release. He pinned her, keeping her in place while her orgasm ripped through her, making her jerk against the desk.

Before she could form a thought he stood back and, in one smooth motion, grabbed her and flipped her over, bending her knees so she knelt on the desk. He pushed her head down and arched her ass, then shimmered his clothing off.

Markus impaled her in one hard thrust. Paula screamed at the force of his thrust. It felt like he was at the end of her then her feverish pussy gripped his hard cock and he slid deeper. Her pussy milked him with the aftershocks of her previous orgasm. He gripped her hips and pushed forward, sliding even deeper inside her.

Leaning next to her ear, Markus whispered in his sensual voice, "No one but me will ever touch you again, Paula."

He nuzzled behind her ear and with a wet flick of his tongue licked slowly until he met her lips. He kissed her, a carnal clash of their tongues. Her cunt continued to clench around his cock in reaction.

He continued in a voice soft with purpose. "What's my name?"

Unable to speak, Paula whimpered. He licked along the side of her face then nipped on the bottom of her jaw.

"My name." He bit gently on her ear.

Paula shuddered as fine goose bumps rose all over.

"Look at me." Weakened with unbridled lust, Paula glanced sideways at him. His face was etched in harsh lines of desire. He lowered his head until their lips were barely an inch apart. Her lips parted, taking in each word he spoke.

"Say my name, Paula." His tone was darkly sensual.

He moved, riding her in a hard rhythm.

"Markussssss." Finding her voice, Paula's hands scrabbled, gripping the edge of the desk as she felt his cock stretch her feverish cunt to overflowing. She didn't think she could take it yet her body demanded she did. Cream flowed from her as she pushed back against him as he came forward. Her eyes rolled back in her head while her hips rolled to match his hard driving pace. Each plunge of his cock wrenched a scream from her throat until she was hoarse. And still he continued to impale her, never slowing.

Her eyes fluttered at the sensations of being taken so forcefully. He rode her so hard the desk was moving forward across the room. Markus didn't break momentum, just continued with their feverish lovemaking. With a loud roar she felt his hot cum explode inside her. His cock pulsed, stroking against her inner pussy walls, sending her into another fiery orgasm. All Paula could do was whimper as streams of his hot seed filled her, with more dripping down her legs. His hands gripped her hips as he continued to come. He slowed and continued to stroke in and out. Her pussy was feeling raw and well used but it still gripped him, wanting more. Paula rolled her hips and to her surprise and pleasure he hardened and lengthened again. With a slow stroke in and out he started again. Moaning, Paula smiled and held on for the ride.

Gazing down at Paula bent over on top of the desk for his pleasure, Markus shuddered. Stilling himself, he gritted his teeth, striving for control from the pleasure of her contracting around him. Instinct had taken over when he saw her prone on the desk. He had taken her hard and knew he should give her a rest but he couldn't. He continued to move, slowly grinding against her.

Paula moaned and arched her back, taking him deeper into her wetness. She drove him crazy. An involuntary groan ripped from his throat as she rolled her hips again. Looking at her honey-skin move as she rippled her back while her beautiful breasts bobbed, Markus grunted. The hunger for her increased until his cock felt like it was on fire. Shaking his head, he fought it with an iron will. Leaning forward, he licked down her sweat-soaked back. The sweet taste of her skin made power ripple under his skin. Steadying her, he plunged into her. Her short scream then moan played in his ears.

Biting down gently between her shoulders, he heard her breath catch. Paula's womb contracted around his penis, milking him. Lightning fire licked through his veins, heating his body to an unbearable pitch. Leaning forward, he aligned his body with hers and tangled his fingers with hers on the edge of the desk. He slid deeper. Using his knees, he spread her legs wider, fitting himself deeper into her. He rubbed against her, feeling every wet inch of her open wide for him. Pulling her back firmly, he showed her the rhythm he wanted. Their movements became frenzied once again as they fought to attain release.

Her screams of his name echoed in Markus' ears. Turning his head, he inhaled at the side of her neck, licked along it then bit her. Her body stiffened as she screamed and came in a strong gush. Her orgasm triggered his own. Roaring, Markus felt the continuous pumping as his body released within her sweet cavern. Paula slumped against the desk. Nuzzling into her neck, he kissed along her neck to her mouth. She moaned but was still. Looking at her, he realized she was asleep. Not wanting to be separated from her, Markus held her tightly. Trying to catch his breath, Markus stared at her. This woman who had brought him to his knees as no other woman ever had.

He knew something wasn't right about this. Swearing softly so as not to awaken her, Markus withdrew from her, clenching his teeth as her body gripped him. He held her close and took her to the couch. Laying her down gently, Markus covered her then leaned down and kissed her. He thought of clothing and was dressed. He shimmered. He had a man to see.

* * * * *

An hour later Markus shimmered in, dragged him up and grabbed him by his throat. "What the hell have you done to me?"

Leonardo Slavich said in a mild voice, "Don't make me kill you." Then he opened his hands palm out and sent a blast of power.

Before he could shield himself Markus found himself flipping through the air and across the room. Landing on his feet, Markus went after him again.

Leonardo raised his hand. "Before I kill you at least tell me why."

He said it in such a matter-of-fact way Markus stopped and looked at him.

Narrowing his eyes, he said in an insulting tone, "Like you don't know. You're the only one who could drive anyone to a lust frenzy."

Leonardo looked at him in confusion then threw back his head and laughed. "Christ, you finally got yourself turned out." Uncaring, he turned his back and went and slouched back on his throne.

Markus started for him again. "Fuck you, Leo. What have you done?"

He waved his hand. "No need to get nasty. Even if I wanted to I couldn't."

Markus stopped and looked at him, waiting for an explanation.

Leonardo looked at him like he was nuts. "What the hell did she do to you? Heck, I don't want to know. Give me her name so I can go see for myself."

Markus fist's clenched. "Stay the fuck away from her."

"Oh my, we're possessive." He stood in a graceful, boneless movement and sauntered over to him. "Markus, old buddy. It's called good old-fashioned can't-think-without-wanting-to-fuck-you-blind lust." He waved his hand. "And I didn't have a thing to do with it. Christ. I may be the God of Lust but if you were thinking clearly you would know our powers don't work on each other."

Sheepishly Markus realized he was right. "Fuck."

Leonardo laughed. "It seems you have been doing a lot of that. Details."

Markus grinned. "A gentleman doesn't kiss and tell."

Leonardo sighed. "You're so old-fashioned, Markie. Come on, buddy. Let's get a drink." He slung his hand over his shoulder.

Shrugging his arm off, Markus glanced at his buddy the God of Lust and shook his head. "Oh no. The last time I had a drink with you I couldn't function for days."

Leonardo grinned, a devilish quirk of his lips. "So."

Markus laughed. "I have a wedding to get to."

Leonardo shuddered. "You poor thing."

Markus looked around at the strangely empty room. "Where's your harem?"

The richly furnished room in gold and burgundy was usually crawling with scantily clad women. Leonardo was silent. Looking back at him, Markus could swear the face that women went crazy over was blushing. Nah, it couldn't be.

"Nothing. I needed some time alone," Leonardo replied, strangely somber.

Glancing at him, Markus realized something was different about him. Leonardo shifted under his perusal.

Swearing, Markus smacked him upside the head.

"Ouch." Leonardo rubbed his head.

Markus ignored him. "Please tell me you're not going after E—"

"Don't say it," Leonardo warned, a dangerous edge to his voice.

Knowing him well, Markus said nothing else on the subject.

"I have time for one drink," Markus said.

Leonardo looked at him and grinned. "Come on."

Leonardo!

Hearing that voice, they looked at each other. Leonardo had a pleased grin on his face. Markus shook his head, preparing for the new arrival.

On a swift wind he came in a blur of motion. Leonardo went flying and the new arrival jumped across the room after him.

Getting to his feet, Leonardo taunted, "Don't fuck with me, Cupid."

Claude watched him. "Bring it."

They flew at each other, blows going everywhere. Swearing, Markus went over to Leonardo's throne, poured a drink from the bottle, sat and watched them fight. He had learned not to interfere right away. They had to duke it out. He relaxed back in the throne, knowing this could take a while.

A smile curved his lips as his thoughts turned to Paula. The gusto she showed enticed him. Her ability to let herself go made him realize what he had been missing. The innate sensuality she displayed without knowing it made him want to strip her bare and take her. Putting his hand below his chin, Markus faced what he had known from his first look at her. She was his and he would make sure to show her what he felt for her.

Absently he looked at Claude and Leonardo still duking it out. He shook his head, seeing they were still going strong. Turning around, he looked out the window. The sun was going down and he figured she would be at the rehearsal dinner. Standing abruptly, Markus strode across to the door. He glanced back and saw Claude and Leonardo watching him.

He waved at them then went out the door. He had a woman he needed to see.

* * * * *

He fucking did it again.

In a bad mood Paula watched the people sitting at the long table in Herra's. It was Paris and Nathan's rehearsal dinner. She should be happy all the wedding hoopla was almost finished but all she could think about was Markus. He had fucked her blind and then disappeared again.

Pounding the table, she ignored the looks she was getting. She was tired of his disappearing act. As soon as she saw him again she was going to tell him so then tie him to a bed and fuck him blind so he couldn't disappear.

Rubbing her hand over her eyes, she didn't know what was wrong with her. She had never acted this way over any man. Heck, she barely knew him. Yet she felt like they were in tune with each other.

Taking up her wine, she took a sip. She almost choked on her wine as the barest kiss brushed her neck.

Conquer and don't stop even when the target begs for mercy.

Hunching forward, Paula knew who it was before she even turned. Looking over her shoulder, she saw his hot silver gaze. Balancing on his knees, Markus had a soft smile on his lips. He leaned forward to kiss her. Turning her head away, she let him kiss her cheek.

He sighed then said, "Come with me."

Watching him, Paula saw he was waiting patiently to see what she would do. Standing, she pushed back the chair and ignored the looks they were getting. He tried to touch her waist. She shrugged him off. Passing her mother, she didn't

221

say a word in response to her look. They went outside and around the corner from view. Turning around, Paula jumped, not realizing he was so close. Before she could say a word he crowded her against the wall and kissed her. A weird feeling of displacement made her head swim then she felt better. Grabbing onto his head, she kissed him back, devouring him.

He groaned in her mouth. Realizing what she was doing, Paula pushed him away. In that instant she realized that she wasn't outside the restaurant. Glancing around, she took in the humongous bed, heavy masculine furniture and rich decorations. Glancing to her left, she looked out the balcony that was in the place of a wall. Beyond was rich vegetation she had never seen before. Paula heard a sound and her eyes widened as she took in the huge iridescent silver dragon flying beyond the balcony.

Turning back to Markus, she looked at him. "Either I'm still passed out from the sex we had or you're really a god." She felt sick. "I need to sit down." She yelped as a chair rose under her butt, giving her a seat.

Paula started to laugh. Strangely it all made sense. Just her bad luck to find a man who was a god. Even if she wanted more with him it was impossible.

"I am the God of Matrimony."

"Crap. I'm batting a thousand. No, not any old god. You have netted the God of Matrimony. It can't get any better than this." Paula shook her head.

Markus looked amused. "Yes, I know your family's aversion to marriage."

Paula felt the need to explain. "It's not really an aversion but a choice."

He laughed. "An aversion. That's why Nathan called me in to help him get Paris to marry him."

She narrowed her eyes. "That was you. I knew something was wrong. So you're like some big matchmaker."

His look was affronted. "There is more to it than that."

"Okay, okay, no need to get huffy. So you have power and such."

"Yes."

She leaned back. "Okay, come on and show me something."

He watched her then a wicked grin curled his lips. He wiggled a finger. Nothing happened.

"What?" Paula asked.

He said nothing, just motioned to her. Looking down, Paula took in the hunter green bustier and hot pants. Glancing back at him, she grinned, "Handy trick."

She got off the chair and started to saunter over to him.

"Uh-uh. We have to talk before any more of that." Markus stated firmly.

Paula watched him, sure he was kidding. "So why the hell did you bring me here?"

Markus looked at her steadily. "I love you, Paula."

The breath whooshed out of her then she shook her head. "You can't."

He looked at her then walked up to her and cupped her right cheek with his hand. "I do."

"You don't even know me."

He took his other hand and put it over her heart. "I know your soul, heart and body."

Looking into his eyes, Paula saw him answer all her doubts and insecurities. With a laugh she reached up behind his head, loosened his hair so it fell in waves around his face then kissed him. She felt her own hair loosen, tumbling down her back, and his hands sank into it. His tongue speared her. Hungry and ravenous. He pulled back.

"I want to marry you someday, Paula, and unless you agree to that let's stop right here." Markus' voice was husky.

He was asking for her trust and faith in them.

Gazing at his silver eyes, she made a decision. "I will be happy to marry you someday, Markus."

He smiled then touched each of her wrists. She felt them heat and glanced down to see a gold etched bracelet circling each with a silver-colored gem with a jade embedded in its center. She glanced back at him and saw he had an identical bracelet on his wrist.

Raising her hand, she asked, "Is this your version of an engagement ring?"

He laughed. "The simple answer is yes but it is much more."

She looked at it. "I like it."

Taking his hand, she pulled him toward the bed. He went willingly. He snapped his fingers and the sweet smell of flowers filled the air. Paula glanced around and saw the room was filled with various flora. Some she recognized and others she didn't. Looking back at him, she felt her bracelets heat then dozens of mini candles floated in mid-air around the room. The smell of vanilla permeated the air.

Reaching the bed, Paula pushed him gently onto it. He waved his hand and they were both naked. Smiling, Paula left him and walked to the head of the bed. He turned to watch her. Climbing on the bed, she kneeled on the silk sheets and spread her legs. Lying back, she watched as he breathed harshly. His gaze scorched her as she lay, offering him herself.

Paula whispered softly, "Markus, I want us to be together forever. Not just today but for the rest of our lives."

Shocked, he looked up at her. A wicked grin flashed across his face before his gaze dropped, looking at her. Paula took her finger and ran it down her stomach and trailed it lower until she touched her wet heat. Dipping her finger inside, she stroked herself deeply. A moan rippled from her throat. She put her finger into her mouth and sucked on it while watching as he followed her movement. He tracked her hands as she returned her finger to her cleft again. She paused and waited for him to look at her.

Huskily Paula said, "Come take a taste."

Markus chuckled and, kneeling on the bed, he crawled up to her and dipped his head and licked along her clean-shaven slit from top to bottom before dipping inside and swirling. His tongue went to work on her swollen clit. He held her in place for his taking. A cry ripped from her as his tongue swept into her pussy with a precise move. He pulled out, lapping at her flowing juices.

Markus came up her body and spread her wide then sank himself in her. She savored the feel of his hard cock filling her. She moaned loudly. He locked eyes with her as he rocked against her. Of their own volition her eyes fluttered closed. He stopped until she looked at him.

Pressing against her clitoris, he murmured, "Watch."

Glancing down, she watched as he took her strongly. His thrusts alternated between soft and hard. As she neared her release he stopped. In frustration she grabbed his hips and tried to grind against him. Effortlessly he held her, withdrawing completely. Then surging forward in a burst of force, he embedded himself in one stroke again as he said, "I love you, Paula."

Sinking her hands into his hair, which framed them both, she kissed him then screamed in pleasure as his thrusts increased. He filled her until she didn't know where he ended and she began. The hungry look in his eyes was tempered by his love. Paula drew in a shallow breath in awe of the love she saw in his gaze.

Laughing in joy, she drew him to her. He rolled his hips and her breath hitched. She met him stroke for stroke. Waves of decadent pleasure crashed over her as she peaked strongly with her release. Keeping them connected, Markus pulled her back with him as he sat back on his knees. He continued to stroke deeply while her body continued to orgasm. Trying to get closer to him, she ground down against him, tightening around him as he raced toward his own release. Markus groaned while she kissed him in ravenous hunger. She leaned back away, giving him more leverage to sink deeper into her hot core.

Unable even to scream, Paula embraced the heat that scorched them as their release pulsated through them, driving them on and on. Markus pumped fiercely while his hot seed filled her up.

Still embedded in her, Markus, with an agile move, lay back until his back rested on the bed. Lazily he stroked her back then gripped her hips, moving her up and down his shaft. Feeling him lengthen again, Paula raised herself until she straddled him. Leaning forward, Paula took his hands and raised them above his head. She imagined him in chains. Her bracelets heated and she felt the cool touch of metal against her fingertips. Sitting back, she gasped as he slid deeper. Looking down at him stretched with his hands chained to the bed. Paula saw a white light that formed a bracelet encircling each of his wrists. Attached to each was a length of gold chain.

"Take me," Markus whispered.

The dark invitation in his voice played along her skin. Rolling her hips, she gasped, breathless from how he looked and the sensation of him inside her. Markus arched his hips to meet her downward stroke. Putting her hand on his chest, Paula moved herself up and down his hard shaft. She hissed as each motion of his hot, hard shaft pierced her.

In a glance at his face she saw his eyes dilate and his face harden with stark need. He watched her out of semi-closed eyes. Paula felt power fill her as she realized she could do whatever she wanted to him and he would let her. Watching his reaction, she raised herself up almost off his cock then sank back down swiftly.

"*Yes.*" His neck bulged with the force of his scream.

Paula smiled, determined she would wear him out. His mouth curled in response, a challenge in her eyes.

At the look of intent on Paula's face, Markus knew he was in for a wild ride. Wanting it to last, he ground his teeth, fighting the pleasure of her contracting around him. Paula arched her back, curling back, sucking him deeper into her pussy. A groan ripped from his throat as she set a hard pace to ride him. Looking at her sweaty mocha-colored face, he marveled at his luck in finding this woman. She was all he could want. Her bountiful, beautiful breasts bobbed as she rode him.

His mouth ached to taste her. He went to sit up then realized he couldn't. Her binding kept him in place. He was at her mercy.

"Let me taste you," he demanded.

Paula watched him and leaned forward until her breast was in perfect alignment with his mouth. Markus caught her breast in his mouth, sucking strongly. She gushed as an orgasm ripped through her. He smiled. He had noticed how sensitive her breasts were. Murmuring, he let the sweet taste of her skin fill him. Kissing down from her nipple, he nuzzled the underside of her breast. He licked, tasting the salty sweet taste of her. Finding the spot he was looking for, he bit her. A long and loud scream sounded as she came in a blinding rush.

Rocking his hips, he sped up to match her bucking body. Paula's womb contracted on his penis. Using his knees, he spread her wider, undulating his hips. Throwing back his head, he bucked as her orgasm swept over him. Paula swiveled against him then leaned forward and grabbed his head, sinking her hands into his hair. Countering her movement, Markus felt her body ripple with her orgasm once again. Turning his head, he captured her lips with his, drinking in her cries. Her body continued to quake as her orgasm ripped through her. Paula collapsed against him, whimpering.

Breathing harshly, she said, "I love you, Markus." Looking into his eyes, Paula put her hand over his heart as she spoke. "You see the real me. It isn't about the sexual chemistry we have," she chuckled, "although that is a plus. It is about what I see in your eyes as you look at me. The unconditional love for all of me. You watch the geek with the same hunger and tenderness that you do the sensual side of me. Your care makes me feel like a queen. The time you took to show me how you feel shows me the kind of man you are."

Paula paused, glancing around the room at the flowers and her own contribution of the candles. She turned and looked back at him. "A man who knows how to treat a true woman. Markus, I know your heart, body and soul. I want you. Only you, Markus. I will treat you as my king. I want the whole world to know how much I love you." Raising her hand, she cupped his cheek. "Markus, I know that we are meant to be together. Not just today but for the rest of our lives."

As she looked at his face, the love she felt for him welled up to overflowing. "I know it'll take time for us to know each other. I will revel in all those little moments we will share. We will be lovers, friends and partners."

Running her hand down his face, she let him see all she was feeling. His eyes heated as he looked at her and laughed in joy. He kissed her and he lengthened inside her again. Moaning, she deepened the kiss.

Chapter Three
Embrace your victory then go for it.

&

Standing in the vestibule, Paula waited for her turn to go down the aisle.

"Paula, I can't find Paris." Her mother's frantic voice made her turn around.

"What? Where the hell is she?" Running down the hall, Paula went to the bride's room. It was empty. Frantic, she looked around. Heading into the bathroom, she saw the note taped to the mirror. It had only two words.

I can't.

Her heart clenched. Paris had run.

"She's gone," a gruff male voice said behind her.

Turning around, she looked up into Nathan's pain-filled eyes.

"Nathan, I'm s—"

"Fuck it. She's not doing this to me." Nathan stormed out.

Following, she saw him pass Markus and go out the door. Continuing after him, she stopped when Markus grabbed her.

"Let him go. They have to work it out," Markus said quietly.

She nodded and watched after Nathan, sorry about the way things had worked out.

Her mother came into the room. "Where is Paris? Where is Nathan going? What about the wedding?"

Looking at her, Paula grinned and turned to Markus. "You're going to make an honest woman out of me, Markus."

Understanding, he grinned and nodded.

Turning to her mother, Paula said, "I'm getting married, Mom."

He mother beamed and rushed across the room toward her. "That's wonderful, my baby."

Smiling, Paula continued, "And so are you. Today."

Her mother stopped, her eyes rolled back in her head and she collapsed.

Shaking her head, Paula looked at Markus. "This may take a while. Go tell the minister and Christopher."

He laughed and went out. Turning to face her mother, she pushed back her sleeves and kneeled beside her.

* * * * *

Three hours later Paula watched as her mother danced with her new husband. It had taken some doing but she had gotten her married. Gazing up at her own husband, Paula raised her face for his kiss. Turning back to the room, she swayed in time to the smooth jazz piping into the room from hidden speakers as the guests mingled, laughing.

Scrumptious foods topped long tables covered by white lace tablecloths while ice sculptures gleamed wetly in the middle of each table. Tuxedo-clad servers handed out champagne to guests.

Taking in the guests, Paula had to ask, "Who are the two men with the bruises glaring at each other?"

Markus looked to where she nodded then laughed. "Claude Valentine, the God of Love."

"*Cupid is at my wedding.*"

"Shh… don't call him that. He hates it," Markus warned.

Confused, she looked at him. "Why?"

He shook his head. "It's the whole cherub baby thing. I'll explain later." He patted her hand and motioned to the other man. "Leonardo Slavich, the God of Lust."

"Hmm. I see why," Paula murmured.

Markus growled. "What?" He picked her up.

"Put her down," a languid voice said.

Glancing behind him, Paula watched as the same beautiful woman she had first seen with him walked up.

He put her down and introduced her. "My sister Fallon, the Goddess of Fertility."

Fallon smiled and hugged her. "I always wanted a sister."

Markus sighed and replied, "You already have one."

"Humph. She doesn't count," Fallon snapped. Turning her back on Markus, she looked at her then took her hand. "Your daughter will be a firecracker."

"What?" Paula sputtered.

Markus groaned. "Why do you always have to impregnate everyone? First Paris and now —"

Fallon cut him off. "I never said Paris was pregnant."

He looked confused. "You did."

Fallon shook her head. "No. I said her daughter would be a firecracker. You assumed I meant Paris."

"There is no way you could have known that then."

Fallon reached over and tapped his cheek. "What is your other name?"

Interested in his answer, Paula waited for his reply. His grin was sheepish. "Lord of Fertility."

"Exactly, bro. You have some super chargers." Fallon turned to the room and said loudly, "See, I told you it would work. Our job here is done." She turned back to them.

Eyes narrowed, Markus looked at her. "You all planned this."

Fallon shrugged. "Those boneheads," she indicated Claude and Leonardo and the other gods around the room, "wanted to just get you laid to mellow you out. The women and I," she indicated the other goddesses, "knowing how old-fashioned you are, knew you needed a wife." Fallon turned to her and hugged her once again. "Thanks for making him happy."

Paula returned the hug and replied, "It's my pleasure."

Fallon laughed and disappeared back into the crowd. Markus shook his head and laughed then turned back to look at her.

"I love you, Goddess of Matrimony. You are my soul, my heart and all I ever want. For now and always. Paula, you filled an emptiness inside me that I did not know I had. Thank you, Paula, for giving yourself into my keeping."

Looking up into Markus' eyes, Paula replied, "I love you, my God of Matrimony. I will love you and care for you as you deserve. My life is intermingled with yours. My heart is filled with all of you. The soul I have is more enriched with our joining." She put her hand over his heart. "I love you, my husband."

A smile blossomed on Markus' face as he leaned in and kissed her.

WEDDING NIGHT SURPRISE

Alice Gaines

ജ

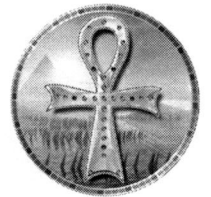

Chapter One

❧

Nothing like a good fucking to calm the wedding jitters.

Cass Gibson's fiancé did it like a pro, Steve's cock slid in and out of her wet pussy. She'd already come twice and he hadn't finished with her.

Slick with exertion, his body slid over hers while he thrust. "Damn, baby. I can't get enough of you."

"Come, lover. You know you want to."

"Not yet." He squeezed his eyes shut. Even in the dim light of the streetlight outside the bedroom, the concentration on his face showed plainly. He was near breaking point and fighting for control.

"One more for you," he said.

She clenched her pussy muscles, squeezing his cock. Hard and thick, it impaled her plunging deep. He'd fuck her like this all night if she asked. He'd screw her until she couldn't walk and then soothe her with kisses. He was the world's greatest lover and the best guy in the universe and in another week he'd be her husband.

She squeezed again, gripping every inch of him with her wet cunt.

"Shit," he groaned. "Don't do that or I'll lose it."

"Let it loose, Steve. I love you."

"Another way."

He pulled out of her and flopped onto his side next to her. Her pussy missed him immediately. Stretched to take his bulk, it felt empty now and ached to have him back inside. Cool air washed over her breasts and her nipples tingled — they'd grown tender from contact with his skin.

Before Cass could protest, Steve rolled her onto her side and pulled her rump against him. His hand snaked around her, his fingers finding the lips of her sex. When he parted them and found her clit, a shock of pleasure shot through her. Still sensitive after two orgasms she was primed and ready to come again. Unbelievable.

"Still want me to finish?" he murmured in her ear.

"Um…oh God…maybe not yet."

He rubbed harder and faster. Her pussy clenched tight, getting ready to explode again, while his fingers played over her clit. Now rubbing, now flicking. He even squeezed gently—just enough pressure to send it into overdrive.

"Still think you can't come again?" he asked.

"Don't stop. Please."

"Want me inside you when you come?"

"Jesus yes," she gasped.

"Want me fucking you?"

Damn what an image. Her cunt ached for him. Squeezing, empty, begging for his cock. His thick beautiful cock.

"Do you want me fucking you?" he repeated.

"God yes."

"Say it."

Shit, why did he have to torture her? She needed him pounding inside her. Now.

"Say it, baby," he groaned.

"Fuck me. Please fuck me."

He shifted his hips, bringing the head of his cock against her pussy. Still his fingers worked her clit. In a moment he'd push her over the edge and she needed all of him inside her.

"Fuck me, Steve," she cried. "Now please."

He growled and plunged into her. Deep. As far as he could go. Her whole body shuddered and threatened to come right then. Maybe if she could hold on—just for a bit—she could make it even better for both of them.

He moved like a maniac now, thrusting into her and sliding out only to pound back in. Hard as steel and smooth as velvet, his cock filled her. He seemed to grow even larger inside her. Hot and heavy. Ready to burst.

And oh his fingers. Plucking at her clit and teasing until every part of her burned. No resisting now. She was going to come.

The climax built, starting at her clit and coiling in her belly. Hot and liquid, it swelled. So intense she couldn't breathe. Gasping noises came out of her chest as she soared to completion. Finally her whole body came with a jolt. Her pussy erupted into spasms, gripping at the length of his cock. She came and came, gasping and crying.

Steve still pounded into her, faster and harder, drawing out her pleasure. Savage now, he stiffened and trembled. He came with a roar, thrusting wildly until he spilled hot come deep inside her. Finally he sagged, whimpering, as he held her hard against him.

Oh man. Ohmanohmanohman. Cass had to remind herself to breathe as she lay in the warmth of his arms. With what little strength she could muster, she turned over and buried her nose into his chest.

Steve sighed and rubbed her back. "And they say the sex gets even better once you're married."

"Impossible."

"Not only possible but inevitable," he said. "I'm going to make sure you're always satisfied."

She got a warm runny feeling inside. She'd loved this man since they were teenagers. Even separations for the college year hadn't driven them apart. In a week they'd be married, assuming she survived the wedding, and she'd be the luckiest woman alive.

"I'm going to make you happy, Cass," he whispered.

"You already do."

"No really." He yawned, the deep yawn of a satisfied man. "Really really happ…"

She looked up at his face. Asleep already. He smiled in his sleep, his lips curled and parted slightly. Oh hell, he'd worked so hard to give her incredible sex, could she blame him? Chuckling, Cass fished for the covers and pulled them up around their bodies. The perfect ending to a harried day of checking on flowers and caterers. Sighing herself, she closed her eyes.

Then a sound came to her. Footsteps below in the kitchen. The refrigerator opening, bottles clinking. Shit, Rafe. Why was he on the prowl?

She tossed aside the covers and sat up. Her robe lay beside the bed so Cass rose and slipped into it, the silk sliding over her skin. Without bothering with slippers, she padded out of the bedroom and closed the door behind her. On the landing the refrigerator light was visible. It went out again. The sounds of a drawer opening and utensils clattering around followed. Oh for crissake.

After descending the stairs, she walked to the kitchen and looked inside. Sure enough, Steve's best man stood with a bottle of beer in one hand and his other hand in the silverware drawer.

Wearing nothing but pajama bottoms, Rafe made quite a sight. Dark shaggy hair, broad shoulders and narrow hips— the perfect male specimen, if you liked the sort who wandered around nearly naked in someone else's kitchen. Somehow he managed to show off a tight ass under the baggy cotton. Even his bare feet were sexy. How did he manage that?

He stiffened and looked over his shoulder, spotting her.

"Can I help you with something?" she asked.

He turned and gave her a lazy smile. Insolent and knowing and way too intimate. The expression was rude and he'd been using it ever since he got off the plane and they'd met for the first time.

He held out the beer. "Doesn't Steve have any with twist off tops?"

"He...rather we do have a bottle opener." She pulled the magnetic opener from the refrigerator door and tossed it to him. He snatched it out of the air and opened the beer. After tossing the top and the opener into the sink he leaned back against the counter and took a long drink.

"I thought you were asleep," Cass said.

"The sounds of hot sex always wake me up."

Her face grew warm. In better light, he'd know she was blushing. Hell he probably guessed anyway. He was staring at her hard enough.

She pulled the belt of her robe tighter. "Your room isn't close to Ste...uh, ours."

"Yeah but you two made quite a bit of noise. Sounds like the boy scout is pretty good in the sack."

She didn't answer that. Wouldn't answer it. Their sex life wasn't any of his business.

"So how many times did you come?" he asked. "Could have been three but one was kind of soft so I couldn't tell for sure."

"Do you want Steve to hear us talking like this?"

Rafe shrugged. "If he's like most guys he's out like a light now. He came pretty hard himself."

"Enjoy your beer. I'm going back to bed."

She turned to go but his soft laughter stopped her.

"Do I scare you, little girl?" he asked.

She turned back and glared at him. "Of course not."

"Then why are you running away? Stay and have a drink with me."

"I don't drink beer."

"Brandy then." Without even looking away from her Rafe opened the cabinet where Steve kept a couple of bottles of liquor. It figured he would have found that already. "I dare you."

How ridiculous. How juvenile to dare her. She ought to ignore him and leave but if she did, would he continue to challenge her? Maybe she ought to accept his dare and show him he didn't frighten her. He didn't, did he?

Cass walked to the cupboard and brought down the brandy and a tumbler. He moved closer to her as she opened the bottle. The scent of him hit her—some kind of cologne or aftershave, a combination of leather and musk. Masculine. Something clenched in her gut and her hand trembled.

He might have laughed quietly or maybe he only sucked in a breath as his hand closed over hers. "Let me."

She pulled back. Hell, she took a step away from him and that scent. It had better be cologne. Heaven help all of womanhood if he smelled like that naturally.

Smiling, he poured some brandy into the glass—more than she would have served herself—and held it out to her. When Cass took it, Rafe picked up his beer again and lifted it in a toast. "To the happy bride and groom."

She took a sip of the brandy and looked back at him. "So how did you meet Steve?"

"We shared a dorm room freshman year. Later on we got an apartment together." He crossed his arms over his chest, and the beer almost grazed one of his pecs. "Didn't he tell you about me?"

He had. All about a hell raising girl-magnet. All night fuckfests in the bedroom down the hall. Steve had never minded. In fact he'd enjoyed telling the tales of Rafe's multiple conquests. He swore he'd never joined in and she trusted him. Still, she had the source right here in front of her. She might as well get corroboration.

"Steve calls you the stud," Cass said. "I never knew whether to believe the stories."

His eyebrow went up. "Stories?"

"The motorcycle, the parties, the women."

"I never drive my bike when I've been drinking."

She took a sip of her brandy. "What about the women?"

Rafe tipped his head back and laughed. "Intrigued?"

She shrugged but didn't answer.

"I do okay," he said. "I learned a few things over the years."

"Such as..."

"Always satisfy the woman." He smiled at her again. Maybe leer was a better word. "Takes some effort sometimes but it's always worth it."

The expression might be a leer, but it worked. Her heart did a little stutter-step in her chest but she looked back at him evenly. "Did you teach Steve how to do that?"

"Define 'teach'."

"You know." Shit, how was she going to put this? "Coach him."

"We talked about sex. I always had books around. I gave him some pointers."

"Talk and books only?"

He laughed. "You mean did he join in on the fun?"

"It's not too strange to ask."

Rafe swigged the rest of his beer and put the bottle on the counter. "I never saw him touch a woman."

She took a deep breath. She'd been true to him too although it had been hard as hell during long separations. Cass had gotten so horny sometimes she'd thought about other men. She'd had plenty of opportunity but when it came right down to it none of them appealed to her. She'd always hoped

Steve felt the same but he was a guy. She could have forgiven him if he'd strayed. Thank God she didn't have to.

"Steve read the books," he said. "I gave him some advice on how to make a woman come. He saved it all for you."

No wonder her man was so good in bed. He'd learned it all from a pro and each time he came home for the holidays or visited her at college he'd had a new idea. Some fresh technique or novel position. The sex got better and better. No wonder she hadn't wanted anyone else.

Rafe stared at her as if he could see through the silk of her robe. "I always wondered about that."

"About what?"

"What kind of woman could make a man want only her? My girlfriends had friends. Steve could have hooked up but he wasn't interested."

"He's a good man."

"The best, but there had to be more to it."

Cass clutched her drink and did her best not to tremble while Rafe continued undressing her with his gaze.

"You see, a guy that age is at his peak," he went on. "Saving it all up for holidays doesn't make any sense unless…"

"Unless what?"

"Unless he's taken a vow of chastity with a ball-busting bitch. Or she's so hot no one else is good enough."

She lifted her chin and glared at him. "I'm not a ball-buster."

"Yeah and you two haven't taken a vow of chastity either," he said. "I'm going to need earplugs."

"I'll get you some tomorrow."

"Thanks. And see if you can find me something to get you out of my fantasies."

She set her drink down on the counter with enough force to make the liquid slosh. "Don't do this."

"Do what?" Rafe leaned toward her. "Tell you that I get hard when you walk into a room."

"Steve might hear you."

"I have an erection right now. Want to see it?"

Cass deliberately kept her gaze on his face. She would not look at the front of his pajamas.

"You see, there's hot and there's hot," he said. "But what makes a horny guy refuse perfectly good sex?"

"Love maybe?"

He stared at her for another moment, looking as if he'd like to eat her. "Yeah that must be it."

He picked up her brandy and downed it in one swallow. "Maybe now that you two are done for the night I can get some sleep."

He turned and headed toward the guest bedroom in the back. Cass stood there for a while, waiting for some strength to come back into her knees.

* * * * *

Steve had to chuckle at the sight of his best man in a tux. He'd seen Rafe Walker in torn jeans, gym shorts and even in the buff. But a cummerbund and a shirt with studs?

Rafe turned, giving them a view of his back in the bank of mirrors. He looked at Steve and lifted his arms. "What?"

Steve let his laughter out. "That's so not you."

"You're kidding. I make this look good."

Sitting next to Steve in one of the chairs supplied by the formalwear store, his mother placed a hand on his arm. "Steven…"

"Yeah, Mom?"

She raised her hand to her mouth and leaned toward him to whisper in his ear. "Do you think you could get your friend to have his hair cut?"

Steve looked at Rafe. His hair was kind of shaggy and brushed the top of his shirt collar. It suited him. Still if he cut it, it would grow back.

"Hey, pal," he said. "You want to meet my hair stylist?"

"Come on, Steve. I already agreed to wear the monkey suit."

"I only get married once, Rafe."

Rafe looked over at Cass. "What does the bride think?"

Cass had been acting casual all day—as if none of this mattered to her—but her foot hadn't stopped wagging since she sat down. Something had gotten under her skin.

She looked at Rafe evenly but her foot didn't stop moving. "It's Rafe's hair."

"But Cassandra, dear," his mother said. "It's your wedding."

"Whatever Rafe wants to do is fine with me," Cass said.

Now that wasn't right. The love of his life had obsessed about this wedding for months. The last few weeks had been full of preparations and hot and heavy sex to blow off the tension. Things had taken a turn for the weird ever since they'd picked Rafe up at the airport, though. The two of them acted like oil and water—dancing around each other but never mixing. Could it be his two best friends didn't like each other? Or was something else entirely operating here?

Rafe stared at Cass and she stared right back. The air took on a charge. Even the little man with the measuring tape hanging around his neck seemed to notice.

"Would you prefer I show you another suit?" the man asked.

"The suit's fine," Steve answered. "Is there someplace I can talk to my fiancée in private?"

"Certainly, sir. This way please." He indicated a door toward the rear.

Steve rose and held out a hand to Cass. She hesitated before taking it and standing.

The door led to a storeroom with boxes and disassembled manikins standing around. The man left them alone and Steve pulled Cass into his arms. "Okay, what's up?"

She gave him a smile but it wasn't very convincing. "What makes you think something's wrong?"

"'I don't care about Rafe's hair'? What's up with that?"

"Well it is his hair."

"For months you've been agonizing about baby's breath versus Boston fern, pâté versus shrimp, and you're trying to tell me you don't care what the best man looks like?"

She hugged him, placing her cheek against his chest. "Maybe I finally chilled out."

He slipped a finger under her chin and lifted her face so that he could look into her eyes. "I've been in love with you since I was fourteen. You're not fooling me."

"You and your darned BS detector."

"So what's up?"

"Something about Rafe makes me uncomfortable."

"He makes all women uncomfortable. Care to be more specific?"

"I don't know." Case huffed. "He swaggers."

Steve chuckled. "He has a lot to swagger about."

"There's more." She wouldn't look him in the eye, either. "Does it seem to you that, maybe, Rafe looks at me funny?"

"Funny?"

"As if..." She gazed up at him. "Come on you're a guy. Do I have to explain?"

"Ah you mean The Look."

"You have a name for it?"

"Sure." Cass looked so confused at that, he had to laugh. "The Walker Patented Drop Dead with Lust Look. No female is immune to The Look."

"Oh brother."

"I watched him all through college. Co-eds, waitresses, even some professors. One look and they were in lust. I don't think he could turn it off if he tried."

"I'm your fiancée, Steve. I'm going to be your wife."

"And I trust you completely."

She sighed.

"Shouldn't I trust you?"

"Of course."

God how he loved this woman. She was getting massive doses of The Look and instead of giving in to it, she was confessing. He knew with everything inside him that she hadn't done anything wrong but she was worried about her thoughts. And she'd told him willingly. You couldn't have a better foundation than that.

"All the time we were in college you were true to me, right?" he said.

"I didn't want anyone but you."

"I didn't want anyone but you either." He kissed the tip of her nose. "We got through four years of off-and-on separation. I think we can survive The Look."

She took a deep breath and some of the tension went out of her shoulders. "You're right."

"I'll get Rafe to cut his hair."

"You don't have to. Really."

"I want to. Mom wants me to."

She smiled, really smiled this time. "Thanks."

"We'll have the best wedding the world has ever seen. Promise."

Her smile broadened. "I have the best groom. I know that."

"Want me to be the best right now?"

Her eyes got wide. "Huh?"

He put his hands on her buttocks and pulled her against him. "A little tension reduction might help you get through the rest of Rafe's fitting."

"Here?" She looked around the storeroom and then at the door. "Someone might come in."

"A quickie. You know it only takes me a minute to make you come."

She bit her lip for a second. "How?"

"Nothing fancy. My hand in your panties."

A slow smile spread over her face. "Good thing I wore slacks and not pantyhose."

"Put your arms around me. If anyone comes in they'll think we're kissing and go out again."

"You're evil." She lifted her arms and ran them around his neck. She also spread her legs so that he could unzip her slacks and slide his hand inside and under the silky fabric of her panties. When he found her clit she shivered and moaned.

"That's what you need, Cass."

She nodded and held on tight while he stroked her. Her sensitive nub hardened as he rubbed it and moisture pooled against his fingers. Tonight he'd do an even better job for her and draw out her pleasure for as long as she could stand it. Right now he only needed to take the edge off her nerves. Giving her the stroke she loved the most, he circled Cass' clit faster and harder until her moans turned to gasps. She was close.

"Now, baby?" he whispered.

"Uh-huh. Oh yeah. Do it, Steve."

"Here you go." Teasing, rubbing, circling, he pushed her until her breath came in gasps. She stiffened and did her best to swallow a cry as she climaxed, hanging onto his shoulders. Finally, she rested her head against his shoulder and sighed. He removed his hand from her panties and rezipped her fly.

"Rest a bit. Then we'll go back to the others," he said.

"What about you?"

"No time for me."

She put her hand against the front of his pants. "But you're hard."

"I'm always hard when I touch you."

"It's not fair that I get something and leave you unsatisfied."

That was his Cass. Always thinking of him, especially where sex was concerned. He kissed the tip of her nose. "You can take care of me tonight."

"Oops. I promised Sylvia I'd have a drink with her after work."

"After that then. I'll warm the bed for you."

She grinned at him. "You're on."

Chapter Two

ഇ

"Oh...my...gawd." Cass' maid of honor's jaw dropped as she looked over toward the entrance to the club.

Cass followed her friend's gaze and found Rafe standing there. Who else?

Sylvia's eyes widened as he approached the table. "Don't look now but Mr. Sex is headed this way."

Cass picked up her glass of wine and took a sip. He'd had his hair cut—or styled—but even shorter it looked sinful. The gentle waves wouldn't submit to scissors, it seemed. They fit with the faded jeans and denim jacket. The T-shirt underneath outlined every muscle of his chest—muscles she'd seen in the buff the night before.

Sylvia's smile grew downright eager as he approached. Another victim for The Look.

He stopped by the table and stared down at her. "You ready to go home?"

"I thought Steve was picking me up."

"He had to work late. He told me to borrow your car and pick you up."

A throat cleared. Sylvia.

"I'm sorry," Cass said. "Sylvia Thomas, this is Rafe Walker."

Sylvia held out her hand. "My pleasure."

Indeed she was almost purring.

Rafe shook hands. "Nice to meet you."

"Rafe is Steve's friend from college. He's going to serve as best man."

"Oh really." Sylvia's voice dropped an octave into lust territory. "We'll be spending time together. I'm Cass' maid of honor."

"Oh really," Rafe answered.

Oh gag.

"Pull up a chair, Rafe," Sylvia said. "Join us for a drink."

"I'll get it," he said. "What'll you have."

Sylvia held out her glass. "White wine."

Rafe looked at Cass. "You?"

"I'm fine."

He took Sylvia's glass and headed toward the bar.

Sylvia followed him with her eyes. "Why didn't you tell me about him?"

"I only met him yesterday."

"We've been here an hour. When were you going to talk?"

Good question. Sylvia was going to find out soon that her partner for the ceremony and reception was a guy who oozed sex. But how did you work that into a conversation? By the way, the best man is a major turn-on? Drool alert? What?

"Do you believe that ass?" Sylvia asked.

Cass checked it out. He was facing away at the bar and the jeans outlined his tight buttocks as if they'd been sprayed on. No healthy woman could look at that without her imagination going into hyperdrive about how it would move when he thrust into her.

"Well never mind," Sylvia said. "I know what he looks like now. Be sure to give Steve a big sloppy kiss for me."

Rafe turned back, a glass of wine in one hand and a bottle of beer sans glass in the other.

Sylvia covered her mouth with her hand and leaned toward Cass' ear. "Damn, look at the front of his pants."

Cass deliberately hadn't looked there but now she couldn't help herself. It was faded like the back but a line right up the center was even more faded. From the base of his torso almost up to his belt.

"Do you think?" Sylvia whispered. "Oh...my...gawd."

Shit. She needed this. Not. Maybe she could push Rafe and Sylvia together. Maybe they could work out their frustrations on each other and leave her the hell alone. Would that get her mind off the ridge over his fly? Or would it only cement the image in her brain?

Now at the table, Rafe set the wine in front of Sylvia and the beer at the empty seat next to her. He sat and gave Sylvia a bedroom smile. "So you're the maid of honor."

"Always a bridesmaid..." Sylvia said. Nice way to let Rafe know she was single.

"I'm new to this best man stuff so you can give me some pointers."

"Happy to," Sylvia said. "Do you dance?"

"Some." He lifted his beer and took a drink.

"We'll have to dance at the reception. Want to practice?"

It wasn't entirely clear from Sylvia's smile what dance she had in mind but if Rafe was going to give Sylvia The Look he'd have to take care of himself.

"No band," he said.

"There's a jukebox." Sylvia rose. "I'll put on a song."

She sauntered off swinging her hips in a seduction that wasn't the least bit subtle. Rafe watched her for a moment and then turned to Cass.

"You two good friends?" he asked.

"We've known each other since high school."

"She likes sex. You can always tell by the way a woman walks."

Cass almost choked on the wine she'd been sipping. "Is everything about sex with you?"

"She started this, not me."

"But you'll finish it, won't you?"

"You care?"

Damn it. If only she were a better liar she'd tell him no. He'd never believe her though and the denial would only make her look foolish. So she didn't say anything.

The music started up when Sylvia was only a few feet from the table. A sultry Latin sort of song. Too slow for a salsa dance, this one would require body contact.

Rafe stood, put his hand at the small of Sylvia's back and escorted her to the tiny dance floor. While Cass looked on he took Sylvia into his arms, curling their hands together over his chest.

What happened next might as well be a public fucking as the two of them rubbed chests and bellies and just about everything south from there. No one else in the bar seemed to notice but Cass couldn't have stopped looking to save her soul. Rafe slid his hands over Sylvia's ass and cupped her buttocks pulling her even harder against his pelvis. He had to be getting hard now—his cock swelling against the ridge of faded denim in his jeans. Sylvia wobbled a bit and rested the side of her face against his chest.

Cass looked away but that didn't help get the image of the two of them out of her mind. Her mind? Hell her pussy. She started throbbing as she imagined feeling his cock get thick and long against her hip then helping him guide it inside her. Rocking in time to the music as it drove them on. Her clit rubbing against the base of his hard-on while her breasts pushed against the muscles of his chest.

Heat spiraling inside her, she clutched at the stem of her wineglass and tried to breathe evenly. Damn this was torture. She had to get out of here. She could go to the ladies room and splash some water on her face. What was she thinking? That would ruin her makeup. She didn't want to leave anyway. Not really. As perverse as her fascination was, it held her in her seat watching her maid of honor rubbing her crotch against the cock that was haunting Cass' dreams.

The song ended finally. Sylvia and Rafe stopped moving but didn't step apart. After a moment Rafe moved Sylvia away from him as he stared into her face with a lazy smile that screamed lust. Sylvia opened her eyes and gazed back up. Her expression begged him to fuck her.

They turned and walked toward the table with Sylvia in front of Rafe, close enough to hide what had to be an obvious erection. Just as well. It wouldn't do Cass any good to look at the thing. She was wet enough already.

When they got to the table Sylvia picked up her purse. "Ready to go, Cass?"

"Ready." What the hell? Why not?

Sylvia smiled up at Rafe. "Can you give me lift home?"

"Your car's still at your office," Cass said.

"Battery's dead," Sylvia answered. That had to be a lie or she would have mentioned it before.

"I can pick it up tomorrow," Sylvia added.

Yeah and she and Rafe could give Sylvia a jump too but neither she nor Rafe seemed to have considered that.

"I'll drop Cass off and take you home," Rafe said.

What a knight in shining armor. What a load of crap.

* * * * *

Steve closed the door behind him and dropped his keys into the dish on the front hall table. "Cass?"

No one answered. Her car hadn't been in the driveway, and the house was dark and silent. Neither Cass nor Rafe appeared to be home. Could they still be out with Sylvia at this hour? Cass drank occasionally but she never stayed out long enough to get drunk.

Shoot. He'd been hot and hard all day thinking of finishing what he'd started in the storeroom at the formalwear shop. She'd been eager for a good fuck too. One way or another he would get laid tonight. First he had to find her.

Pulling his tie loose, he walked toward the back of the house. He'd call her cell phone and find out where she was. When he got to the kitchen and turned on the light he stopped in his tracks. The back door stood open. What the hell? Had someone broken in? Everything looked normal.

He stepped onto the deck and stopped dead again. This time he smiled. The whirlpool in the hot tub had the water churning and Cass sat in it giving him her best come-hither look.

She rested her elbows on the rim of the tub and pushed up to show her naked breasts slick with beads of water. "You're late."

"I didn't see your car outside."

"Rafe took Sylvia home." She brought her fingers to her nipples and toyed with them until they turned to stiff points. "That was over an hour ago."

"Rafe and Sylvia?" He chuckled. "Less than two days in town and already he's getting laid."

"The Look strikes again."

"If he's not back by morning I'll drive you to work."

"In the meantime there's something else you can do for me."

He started shucking out of his clothes. "I'll bet there is."

Cass lowered herself into the water and scooted to the near side of the tub finally resting her chin on the edge to watch him strip. She could always make him hot and hard with a look and the sin in her gaze went right to his cock. She had to have some kind of erection ray in her eyes because in no time at all he had a hard-on that pressed against the cotton of his briefs. She licked her lips. She knew damned well what that promise did to him too. Steve hadn't had another woman's mouth on his cock but if someone else was getting better head, heaven help the guy.

Finally naked, he walked to the hot tub and climbed in.

Before he could slide down into the water she slipped between his legs, grasped his cock and stroked it with strong fingers. "Thanks for bringing this home to me."

"My pleasure." He sat there watching her stroke his rod until it felt as if it would stretch out of its skin. "Oh hell yeah."

Her mouth opened and her tongue emerged. Slowly the tip approached the spot on his cock just under the head. After all their time together, she knew that place was the most sensitive on his whole body and she knew how to work it. Unable to breathe he waited for the feel of her tongue against it. He steeled himself to control his reaction but knew damned well he'd surrender the minute she licked him.

She flicked her tongue at exactly the right place and he almost came right out of his skin. Teasing him with the perfect pressure she licked at him. His balls tightened and his heart started thumping in his chest. He couldn't hold back a groan as she continued loving his cock. Hot and throbbing, his body started the climb to the inevitable.

She stopped that but kissed the head of his cock before laying it against her cheek. The flesh was a livid crimson, proof of how hot she'd made him so quickly and there was so much more still to enjoy.

"You're so beautiful," she said in a husky whisper. "So big and hard."

"You make me that way."

"You make me hot and wet."

"You're in steamy water."

"Nuh-huh." She bit her lip for a moment. "I was hot and wet before I got in here."

"I wasn't even home."

"I was thinking of you."

Hmmm. Thinking of him or thinking of Rafe fucking Sylvia? No woman was immune to Rafe's raw sexual power. Cass had always loved Steve completely. Nothing would change that. But she had the regular dose of female hormones and Rafe had slept under the same roof with her. They had some kind of chemistry that had upset her enough to act strange at the formalwear store. The stud had to have gotten to her at least a little. He'd just have to help her work out the kinks. Maybe things could get even more interesting.

Before Steve had a chance to follow that thought she opened her mouth and took his cock inside. Hot damn what a feeling. She slid her lips up and down his shaft swallowing as much of his cock as she could. As the pressure built inside him, he could hardly keep his eyes open. He managed to see through the haze of arousal well enough to watch her suck him, wetting his flesh and making it throb.

Holy shit. Every time was new with this woman. This time she rasped at his secret spot with her teeth. So gently he wouldn't even feel it on another part of his body. There it threatened to snap his control. And yet he couldn't make her stop. Not yet. Just a little bit more. He closed his eyes and gritted his teeth while she worked him. Hotter and higher the excitement spiraled upward from his balls and spread through the rest of him almost stopping his heart. He had to hold off. Had to find the strength to stop her before he creamed without satisfying her. He would stop her. Now. He would somehow. But damn.

Somewhere he found enough strength to take a breath and then another. "Stop, baby. You're going to make me come."

She didn't stop though. She kept right on sucking him deep into her mouth running her lips over him and teasing with her teeth.

He groaned and then growled. "Stop, Cass. I mean it."

She did finally and he pulled himself back from the brink taking her head between his hands and bending to press his forehead against hers. "Baby, you almost got my whole load down your throat."

She gave him a wicked smile. "Good huh?"

"I'll show you good."

He slid into the water and reached for her. She came to him immediately, her legs wrapping around him. He had to push her away a bit to make room for his hand between her thighs. As hot as she'd made him he wouldn't be able to control himself once he was inside her. He needed to make her ready first—massage her clit, stretch her pussy with his fingers. In the end he couldn't be gentle and she needed to want a rough fucking as much as he did.

When he parted the lips of her sex he found her clit already hard and distended. When he rubbed it Cass shuddered and almost lifted herself out of the water. He had to hold her close to keep up the pressure. She was aroused, near orgasm, even though he'd only just touched her.

"Something started your engine," Steve murmured, still toying with her clit in circular motions.

"Get inside me," she said. "Please."

"You tormented me. Now it's my turn."

"I'm going to come. I want to feel you filling me."

"You will."

"I want you now."

"Like this?" He slid two fingers into her and pumped. She was wet and hotter than the water around them. It wouldn't take much to make her snap but after years with Cass he knew how to draw her pleasure out until she begged for release. Slowly and with just enough pressure to make her crazy, he continued stroking her clit with his thumb while he moved his fingers in and out simulating what his cock would be doing in a moment.

"I need...oh God..." She whimpered and pressed her pelvis against his hand. More."

"More what?"

"Your cock. I can't stand this. Put it in me, please."

"My cock?" He kept on rubbing until she stiffened and her breath came in shallow gasps. She was close, hovering at the edge.

"Please," she whimpered. "Please."

He moved his hand and positioned her over him. With one slow and deliberate movement, he slid his cock into her an inch or two.

"Don't stop," she cried. "All of you."

Her muscles clenched around him as she tried to push herself down onto his shaft. Slick, hot, tight. He bit his lip and held onto his last shred of sanity while she pressed forward and down stretching to surround him with her heat.

Enough. No more waiting. He thrust inside her burying every inch of himself in her.

She shrieked with delight. "Yes yes. Fuck me."

There was no other word for it but fuck. She'd driven him too far and now he could only act like the beast she'd created. Over and over he plowed into her with enough force to send water splashing out of the tub. His cock was going to explode. Already the climax was building. He couldn't hold back, not even for her.

Eyes tightly closed, she leaned back and grabbed the edges of the tub for support while she moved in time with his thrusts.

Perfectly matched, he pounded into her while she slid along the length of his cock. Her pussy gripped him like a fist. Tight and hot. Irresistible.

The climax started in his balls. Too powerful to fight. He couldn't put it off any longer but gave in to the pressure.

Just as he thought he'd burst, she climaxed, screaming. Her pussy muscles clenched around him and then exploded into spasms.

Yes! He could come now. One more thrust and then another and another. All along the length of his cock until he shot lust out of the tip into her depths. It lasted forever as he gave and gave and she took it all. She milked him dry until they both went limp. Even then her sex continued fluttering around him in gentle aftershocks.

"Wow," he muttered finally.

She whimpered and ran her arms around his neck so that she floated in his arms.

"What got this started?" he asked.

"We are going to be newlyweds soon."

He nuzzled her ear. "That's all?"

"You always make me hot."

"Not like that."

"Come on, Steve. I love you."

"And I love you." But there was more to this than love. Much more. And that much more just might be named Rafe.

Chapter Three

ঙ

Cass sat at the head of the table observing the madness all around her. Some rehearsal dinner. With all the assembled Gibsons and Ballards it turned into more of a reception with people spread throughout the living room, dining room and family room. Even Dad's den held some of the diehard sports fans watching the baseball game. Mom shouldn't have gone to all that trouble but let Cass take the actual wedding party to a restaurant. She'd insisted though and now here they all were.

Cass reached over and squeezed Steve's hand before giving him a kiss on the cheek. Even when she did that she still caught a glimpse of Rafe and Sylvia at the other end of the table. He'd been sending her smoldering looks whenever he got the chance and he was still doing it in front of the others only more subtly. Bastard.

At least no one else seemed to notice. Oh hell. Maybe she was imagining the whole thing. She wasn't imagining how close he sat to Sylvia though nor the way her friend stared at him as if she'd like to have him for dessert. Both of them had a hand beneath the table. From the looks of things, they were touching under there and not each other's hands.

Steve rose and lifted his glass. "There'll be a lot of toasting after the wedding but there's one couple I don't want getting lost in the shuffle." He turned to her mom and dad. "Mr. And Mrs. Gibson. Fred and Camille. Thank you for welcoming me into your family."

With murmurs of agreement the crowd lifted their glasses. Even Rafe and Sylvia although they both kept one hand at doing whatever it was they were doing. Shit. Would she never get the image of that ridge of faded denim out of her mind?

"...another son."

Dad's voice. Cass snapped back to reality. Dad's smile was bright enough to fill the room and Mom was actually blushing. She'd have two sets of great parents now and the best husband in the world and all she could think of was Rafe sitting at the other end of the table getting an erection.

Damn it, she would *not* give in to him. She picked up her own glass and rose. "And to Mom and Pop Ballard the best in-laws a girl could hope for."

"Thank you, dear," Steve's mother answered. "Now make us a grandchild."

Laughter broke out at that. They already had five grandchildren by their other three children.

At the other end of the table, Sylvia whispered something in Rafe's ear and got up. "Excuse me a minute."

She left the room and Cass and Steve sat down. Finally Rafe's second hand emerged. His face wore the sleepy smile of a semi-aroused male with the scent of female in his nostrils. He always looked like that a bit, when you got right down to it. Part of *The Look*. This time was more obvious. They had been playing sex-right-out-in-public and now Sylvia had wandered off to... To what? Masturbate in the guest bathroom? Fuck.

"You okay, baby?" Steve whispered in her ear.

She took a sip of wine. Her mouth suddenly dry. "Fine."

"Soon all the pressure will be off."

"I know." What about the pressure in the pit of her stomach and below? Sitting here with Rafe staring at her with his heated gaze while her clit got overly sensitive in her panties.

She stood up a bit too fast almost tipping her plate over. "Let me help you get dessert, Mom."

"What?" Her mother's head snapped up. "Oh yes. That's a good idea."

Cass picked up her plate and headed toward the kitchen with her mother right behind her. Her sister Suzy showed up with more plates and she and Cass worked on stacking the dishes while Mom pulled the huge cake out of the fridge. From the corner of her eye—always the damned corner of her eye—she caught a movement in the back hallway. Rafe quietly let himself out the back door and closed it behind him. A crunch of gravel told her he'd headed down the path to the guest cottage. And Sylvia no doubt. She gripped the edge of the counter in her fists.

"Sis?" Suzy's hand stroked Cass' back. "What's up?"

"Nothing. Just nerves."

"Do you want me to get you an aspirin?" Mom asked.

Aspirin. Bathroom. Escape. "I'll do it. You get back to the guests."

"Are you sure, dear?"

"Sure. I'll be back in a minute." She nearly ran out of the kitchen and upstairs to her room. In her bathroom she opened the medicine cabinet and took out the bottle of pills. Who was she kidding? Over-the-counter medicine couldn't fix what was bothering her.

What the hell was she going to do? Here she was at her wedding rehearsal dinner and all she could think of was her husband's best man fucking her maid of honor. She ought to be happy for the two of them but all she wanted was some of what Sylvia was getting right now.

Maybe if she faced her jealousy head-on she could overcome it. Maybe she'd discover that Steve was better in bed than Rafe—better technique, more staying power, bigger cock. Maybe if she discovered the truth she could get the man out of her mind once and for all.

She put the aspirin bottle back into the cabinet and walked through her bedroom into the hall. The stairs and kitchen below sounded quiet. Mom and Suzy must have gone back into the dining room. With any luck she could get out the back door with no one seeing her.

She went quickly but quietly down the stairs and across the back hall. Once she got outside she pressed the door closed behind her and snuck down the gravel path to the guest cottage. The living room was dark so she let herself in and crept to the doorway of the bedroom. Rafe and Sylvia were in there all right and they were naked. Busy with each other, they wouldn't see her.

Rafe sat at the edge of the bed leaning back on his elbows while Sylvia knelt between his knees and sucked his cock into her mouth. The thing was every bit as big as she'd imagined. Thick and crimson with arousal it had a vein running along the underside. Sylvia could barely take a third of it into her mouth.

He reached a hand down and gathered Sylvia's hair away from her face. Now Cass could see her friend's cheeks working as she sucked him. She even got a clear view of the head of his cock when Sylvia flicked at it with her tongue before taking him into her mouth again.

Damn but she wanted him inside her—every inch of that hard flesh. Her clit ached and throbbed as she imagined her own mouth on his erection making him hot and hard. Making him swell even larger. She shouldn't have come out here but she sure as hell couldn't leave now.

He closed his eyes and tipped his head back, his face in a grimace of ecstasy. "Man you're good. Suck me, lady. Suck me."

Sylvia did, her hand working on the length of his shaft her mouth couldn't handle.

"Holy shit you're going to make me come," he said from between clenched teeth.

That didn't stop Sylvia. If anything she sucked harder and faster. Rafe's hips began to move, thrusting upward, plunging more of his cock into Sylvia's mouth.

"Fuck now. Oh yeah now!" he shouted.

Sylvia did take him out of her mouth then and kept working him with her fist. He arched upward—savage jerking motions—and roared as he shot semen into the air in spurts. It fell onto the carpet, onto the bedspread, onto Sylvia. She stroked him until he finished finally. Then, grinning, she rubbed his come into her breasts.

He fell back on the bed gasping. "Ah shit. Holy fucking shit."

Sylvia giggled. "Like it?"

"You took the top of my head off."

Well he might have been satisfied but the whole scene had driven Cass past lust to full-blown arousal. Her cunt ached and her clit had swollen. They'd better not be done now because she was in no state to just walk away.

Sure enough Sylvia climbed onto the bed next to Rafe. He flipped over, put his face between her legs and covered her pussy with his mouth.

All right this was bad. Very very bad. Cass had no choice but to slip her hand under her dress and into her panties. The material was soaking wet and her fingers easily found her throbbing clit. The shock of the contact nearly made her gasp but she managed to keep her breathing even as she stroked herself. She'd climax in a minute and then she could tiptoe out again and go back to the party.

Rafe must have been mighty good at giving head because after only a minute Sylvia was moaning with pleasure. Rafe slid his arms under Sylvia's hips and pulled her harder against his mouth.

"Oh God," Sylvia crooned. "Oh God."

Oh God was right. Cass' eyes half closed as a haze of lust settled around the edges of her vision. She slipped a finger inside her pussy plunging into the wet heat there and then used it on her clit. Faster and harder in rough circles. The way she liked it best. She had to finish herself before Rafe was done with Sylvia.

Suddenly a body bumped up against her back. What the...?

She looked over her shoulder to find Steve smiling down at her. He put a finger over his lips to command silence and looked over her head at Rafe licking Sylvia's pussy. He didn't seem angry. If anything he seemed to find the whole thing funny.

While Cass looked back at the couple on the bed Steve's arms went around her front and he slipped his hand into her panties. He took over for her, playing her clit like the master he was. Now she had only to concentrate on the scene before her and her own pleasure.

Just then Sylvia's moans turned to cries and her hips lifted off the bed. She screamed as her orgasm hit her and Rafe stayed with her licking until she fell back onto the bed.

Shit what now? They'd be done and they'd find her and Steve watching. Fuck. Fuck fuck fuck. She had to come now and get the hell out of here.

Rafe rose to his knees. Damned if he wasn't hard again. After only a few minutes he'd managed to get an erection as impressive as the first one. How was *that* possible? At least he wouldn't be going anyplace soon.

After a minute he leaned over Sylvia and kissed her. "You up for some doggy-style?"

Sylvia's face broke into a wicked grin. "Oh yeah."

He helped her to her knees, her legs spread, and positioned himself to enter her. Steve's hand left Cass' pussy and he bent behind her sliding her wet panties down her legs. After she stepped out of them he reached up to help her to a kneeling position. Genius. He'd enter her exactly the same way Rafe would enter Sylvia.

She waited, trembling, while he unzipped his pants and took out his cock. Just as Rafe sank into Sylvia, Steve pressed forward filling Cass.

Hot damn. Always well-endowed, Steve felt bigger than she could ever remember. So huge, so hard and yet she took every inch of him. She'd grown so wet he moved inside her easily making an unbelievable friction against the walls of her cunt. When he reached around her and stroked her clit again she almost screamed. The feeling was so powerful it melted her bones.

In the bedroom Rafe had set a slow rhythm. Clearly he was taking his time and she could watch his cock as Sylvia's juices moistened it. He slid himself all the way in her and nearly all the way out again. Every time he pulled away Sylvia whimpered until he surged forward again.

Behind Cass, Steve picked up the pace to fast powerful thrusts. His fingers continued to work her clit, now in circles as she'd done for herself. They'd finish first and escape. It wouldn't take long. She was almost there and he'd come right after her.

On the bed Rafe had closed his eyes again—the same look he'd worn when completely aroused by Sylvia's mouth. He moved faster and deeper. Sylvia gasped with each thrust wiggling her ass and pressing it against him. How utterly erotic to watch them near climax as she got ready to come. She knew Steve well enough to realize he'd reached the point where all he could do was fuck. But his fingers didn't stop, bless him. In another moment just another couple of seconds she'd come. A few more thrusts into her aching cunt a few more strokes of his fingers against her clit and she'd soar past the breaking point.

Now. Oh now! The climax took her with a fury that stole her breath. She shuddered as it started deep inside her and broke out into spasms all along her cunt. She gripped at the hard cock inside her and came, her wetness pouring over him.

Steve stiffened and thrust like mad until he came with her. Pulling her hips against him for maximum penetration, he spilled hot essence inside her.

He held her up while they recovered. Rafe had reached around Sylvia to toy with her clit as Steve had just done for her. From the looks on their faces and the force of their movements they wouldn't last too much longer. Steve quickly helped her to her feet and bent to grab her panties. As they crept out of the cottage the sound of Sylvia's screams came to them followed by Rafe's bellow of completion.

* * * * *

The sight of Cass' wedding gown on a hanger on the back of the door gave Steve a lump in his throat the size of Rhode Island. It got even bigger as he watched her at her dressing table. She was so damned beautiful and by the end of the day she'd be his wife.

His wife—he'd been saying it to himself all morning. She'd been his girlfriend since eighth grade, climbing trees together, watching scary movies, studying for tests. Now she'd be his wife and have his children. Life didn't get any better than that.

She caught his reflection in her makeup mirror and gasped. "You're not supposed to be here."

"I couldn't stay away."

She turned to face him. "It's bad luck."

"To see you in your gown. You're not in your gown." She wore a full-length slip of startling white. The fabric clung to her curves and emphasized the swell of her breasts. His cock hardened the way it always did when he looked at her but today he'd save his lust for their wedding night. After all the times they'd made love he had to make tonight extra special. Thanks to Rafe he had a good idea how. He only needed to test the waters with Cass a bit first to make sure the idea hadn't come from out of left field somewhere.

"You're not dressed yet," she said.

"No rush. It only takes a couple of minutes for a guy."

"It'll take me a lot longer than that. You'd better let me get to it."

"In a minute." He sat on the end of her bed and patted the space beside him. "We need to talk a little first."

She turned back to the mirror. "Really, Steve. I have a lot to do."

"We need to discuss what happened last night in your parents' guest house."

"We already did talk about it." She picked up a brush and feathered blusher over her cheeks. "It was fun. A little kinky. I don't think I want to do it every night."

"We talked about it. We didn't discuss it."

"Talking isn't discussing?" She rolled her eyes. "That's girl-speak, Steve."

"We talked about how hot the sex was. We talked about whether we want kink in our sex life. Kink isn't the issue. Rafe is."

She stared into the mirror. "Don't overestimate him. He might be a babe-magnet but he isn't an *issue*."

"Then why have you been avoiding talking about him?"

Still she didn't look at him. "I haven't."

"You're doing it right now." He patted the bed beside him again. "Come on, Cass."

She sighed and set down the brush. After turning to look into his face for a minute she got up and joined him on the bed. "Okay talk."

"I know you love me."

"When was that ever in doubt?"

"Doubt, never. But it might be a little niggling worry in here." He tapped the side of her head.

"Get real, Steve."

"You've responded to him. The guy puts out pheromones or something and you're not immune."

She made a little pfff of scorn. "Pheromones?"

"You've been as hot as a jalapeño since you laid eyes on him. Don't think I can't tell."

She wouldn't look at him. All along she hadn't faced what was going on in her own body. That dishonesty, not Rafe, was the real threat to their relationship. Their marriage would last for decades and she'd meet lots of attractive men. If she couldn't face her feelings straight on and share them with him they'd have secrets. They'd never had secrets from each other before and they weren't going to start now. In a way Rafe had done them both a favor by bringing this issue to the fore so they could work it out before they started their life as husband and wife.

"Rafe's a good-looking man," she said finally.

"You know lots of good-looking men. None of them turn you on."

"Rafe doesn't turn me on."

"The other night in the hot tub you were fully aroused before I even touched you."

She looked up at him. "I was fantasizing about you."

"Be honest, Cass. If you'd found anyone besides Rafe and Sylvia fucking in the guesthouse you would have crept out in embarrassment."

"Maybe. Maybe not."

"You want Rafe. Admit it."

"I've never wanted anyone but you." She said it too loudly, her expression full of bogus innocence. The more she protested the more she convinced him that this was indeed important.

"We love each other," he said. "Totally. That never changes."

She raised her hands in a futile gesture. "Then what is it you want from me?"

"Honesty."

She sighed again and her gaze traveled the room as if she might find answers in one of the corners. Finally she looked down at her hands. "All right. Maybe it's true. Just a little."

He lifted her chin so he could look into her eyes. "You wouldn't be a normal healthy woman if you didn't lust after Rafe."

"I said a little."

"And I said it's okay."

That seemed to confuse her as her eyebrows knitted together. "Okay?"

"Neither of us can help how we feel. What matters is what we do with those feelings."

"I wouldn't be unfaithful to you, Steve." She looked deep into his eyes. The way she always did when telling the truth about something important.

"I know that."

"Then what was the point of all this?"

"We needed to work through this. Get Rafe out of your system," he said.

"He's leaving after the ceremony. He'll take his pheromones with him."

She was right that Rafe would take his pheromones with him when he left but wrong about him leaving after the ceremony. At least he wouldn't leave right after. Rafe had one last wedding gift to give her. To give to both of them.

Chapter Four

‰

Cass sprayed cologne on the flesh above the neckline of her negligee, checked her reflection in the mirror one last time, and turned to join her new husband for their wedding night. After switching off the bathroom light she stepped into the hotel bedroom. Candlelight filled the room casting a warm glow on the dresser, the drapes and the naked man on the bed.

What the hell? Rafe? "What are you doing here?"

He gave her an evil grin. "I'm your wedding present."

Sure enough his erection sported a satin ribbon around the shaft. Tied into a bow with the ends hanging down over his balls. Another night he would have tempted her. This was her wedding night. Her fucking wedding night.

"Get out," she ordered.

"You want me, Cass." He grasped his cock near the base and stroked it. "You want this."

"I don't."

"Then why did you watch me with Sylvia?"

Shit he'd known she was there. She'd tried so hard not to make a sound. Had Sylvia known? Who the hell cared?

"If I hadn't heard you I would have known you were watching," he said. "I can feel it when you walk into a room."

"No this is wrong." It was. Horribly wrong. Not on her wedding night. And yet her feet wouldn't move and she couldn't look at anything else but his huge cock and his fingers sliding along its length. He had to leave. Now while she could still resist the temptation.

"I even held Sylvia's hair out of the way so you could see her sucking on me. Did it turn you on?"

271

It hadn't only turned her on then. It turned her on now. Damn but she'd like to take that ribbon off him and take his hardness into her mouth. She'd like to watch him come the way she had that night. This was her special night with Steve. Where in hell had he disappeared to?

"I'm married to your best friend," she said. "Doesn't that mean anything to you?"

"It means I'm jealous as all hell of the guy."

"Maybe you'd better get out of here before he comes back."

Too late. The lock on the exterior door clicked. She turned in time to see Steve enter the room, a bucket with a bottle of champagne in his hand. He took one look at the two of them and threw the privacy lock.

"I don't know how he got in here," she said. "I didn't let him in."

Steve walked to the dresser and set the bucket down. "I did."

Her jaw dropped. "You?"

"I knew you wanted Rafe. If you don't get him out of your system he's going to be a problem between us."

"So you were going to give me to him?" He couldn't mean for another man to have her on their wedding night. He couldn't. This was *their* night, not a night to spend with another man. "Damn it, Steve. You'd give me to another man tonight of all nights?"

"No, baby." He walked to her and took her into his arms. "I'm giving both of us to you."

"What?"

Smiling he stepped away, kicked out of his slippers and led his robe slide to the floor. When he got out of his pajamas he exposed an erection as impressive as Rafe's. A satin bow adorned it, the twin of Rafe's.

"Both of you?" she whispered. Stupid. What else could he mean? Her knees went weak as she looked at possibly the two most beautiful cocks in the world. She could have them both. No wonder her brain wouldn't work.

Steve pulled her against him and looked down into her face. "So you game?"

"You're really all right with this?"

"It was my idea."

'Wow."

He kissed her. He'd kissed her dozens of times since the minister had pronounced them man and wife. Innocent caresses until now. Innocence flew out the window now as he took her lips with his own. He pulled her hard against his pelvis pressing his erection into her belly. She melted inside. Heat pooled between her legs as she grew wet in anticipation. Her breasts pressed against his chest—a combination of smooth material and hard muscle teasing them to stiffness.

Steve eased a strap of her gown over her shoulder and down her arm then bent to take the nipple into his mouth. Sucking he urged a deeper response from the aching peak. She closed her eyes and tipped her head back scarcely able to breathe.

A throat cleared. Rafe. She'd almost forgotten about him.

"I think I can help," he said.

Steve straightened and chuckled. "That's the stud."

"Why don't you bring your wife over here and let me give her some head?"

"Sounds like a plan." Steve stripped her gown from her and scooped her up into his arms. In two strides he walked to the bed and lowered her onto it. When Steve sat beside her he filled most of the empty space. Surrounded by firm chests and erect cocks, testosterone and the scent of clean male, Cass took a moment to savor the ultimate—two sexy men devoted to her pleasure.

She propped herself up on one elbow. "When you guys lived together...did you...I mean the two of you?"

Rafe got her meaning first and tipped his head back and laughed. "Me and the boy scout here?"

Even in the dim light Steve blushed visibly. "You mean Rafe and me?"

She shrugged. "Stranger things have happened."

"What do you think, boy scout? Am I cute?"

Steve pulled a pillow from under the spread and threw it at Rafe.

"Because if you wanted to play a little I wouldn't mind watching," she said.

"I did wonder sometimes. You should have heard the noises coming out of his room," Steve said.

Rafe puckered his lips and made smooching sounds in Steve's direction.

"You were loud, asshole," Steve said. "Sometimes I had to jerk off to get to sleep."

Rafe reached over and untied the bow around Steve's cock. Steve looked uncertain but when Rafe's hand closed over his flesh and pumped he sucked in a harsh breath of pleasure.

Cass got out of the way so that Steve could stretch out beside Rafe. The second ribbon came off and Steve slid his fingers over Rafe's shaft, flicking his thumb on the head. They lay on their sides staring into each other's eyes as if in some kind of contest.

What a sight they made. Their cocks swelled even further as their fingers pumped — now faster now harder even twisting for more friction.

Nothing had ever looked so erotic. Two men, driving each other, neither giving up until the other begged for mercy.

Cass' clit throbbed watching them. She reached to her pussy and found she'd already grown wet. She'd have both of those cocks inside her soon but she couldn't wait for long. She palmed her sex, pressing and pushing her clit against the bone beneath. The room filled with harsh breathing as all three of them grew more and more excited.

Steve gritted his teeth and closed his eyes for a minute. Sensing victory. Rafe picked up the rhythm. Sweat broke out on his chest. "Give up?"

Steve opened his eyes again and smiled. With his free hand he cupped Rafe's balls, rolling them gently. "You give up."

"Fuck that," Rafe answered. They kept at it, hands sliding over cocks, chests working for air. Both men had obviously become highly aroused. She might have to stop them before they came but watching them excited her more and more.

Finally Rafe rolled onto his back in surrender. "You win. Shit you're good."

"I had more practice than you."

"I know one thing I've had more practice at," Rafe said. "Think Cass is ready?"

Steve looked at her face and then down at the hand still pressing against her cunt. "I think she is."

Rafe caught her feet and pulled her flat on her back in the middle of the bed. Moving upward, he guided himself between her legs and pushed her hand aside. "I'll take care of this."

Flicking at her with his fingers he parted the lips of her sex. She almost flew apart at his expert touch. Gentle yet effective. He teased her with just enough pressure to make her wild with needing more.

"Damn you smell good, lady." His voice sounded dark with lust. "Hot woman ready to come."

He licked her once. Just one stroke upward over her clit. So intense she gasped and her hips jerked.

"You need it, Cass, don't you?"

"Oh yes."

"You got it."

His mouth closed over her clit and she almost came. He sucked then used his tongue to send the pressure higher. He kept it up showing her no mercy while the heat coiled deep inside her. She ached and burned. Rafe knew how to work a clit.

With arousal clouding her mind she looked over at Steve. He watched her face, smiling at her. "Good, baby?"

Good? Heaven. She had to find a way to thank him. "Give me your cock."

Steve scooted toward her bringing his beautiful tool to her face. While Rafe continued caressing her clit with a touch that pushed her closer to the edge she took her husband's rock-hard cock into her hand and guided the head into her mouth. A tang of salt greeted her tongue. Pre-come. Rafe had aroused him to an explosive level just as he'd done with his mouth on her sex. She sucked gently—enough to take Steve to another level without making him come.

He moaned and pushed himself deeper into her mouth. "Shit you make me so *hot*."

She pumped him with her fist until he trembled and thrust harder.

"Stop, baby or I'll come," he gasped. "I can't...oh shit...stop."

She pulled his cock out of her mouth, still grasping it, while Rafe kept on teasing her clit. Sucking then licking then stopping when she got so close she could feel the climax building. Then he'd start all over again pushing her to a higher plateau. She hung there, a massive O only heartbeats away, but he wouldn't send her there.

She couldn't go any higher. Couldn't get any hotter. She needed to come but he wouldn't let her. Still clutching Steve's cock she lifted her hips to press her aching pussy against Rafe's face but he only stopped again.

"Don't...oh God," she begged. "Don't stop."

Instead of using his mouth he slid a finger deep inside her and pumped. She was wet, so wet. Throbbing, burning. Craving release. Cass fought for breath and moved her hips again as he plunged his finger in and out.

Then his mouth closed over her again and his tongue lapped at her clit. Finally he'd give her what she needed. She could only lie there as it built, crested, and washed over her in waves.

She screamed as the full force hit her. Huge convulsions in her pussy coursing along the length of his finger. She sobbed and wailed again as it went on forever. When it ended she lay limp against the bed whimpering.

Rafe moved up beside her and put his arms around her fitting her body to his. Steve snuggled at her back and threw a leg over both of them. She lay there enveloped in male warmth and floated in the afterglow of an orgasm that had sapped her strength. One erect cock pressed against her belly and another against her butt. They hadn't finished yet.

After a few minutes her brain cleared and strength returned. Both men held her as she returned to reality. A reality that promised even more delights. She'd never imagined her wedding night would turn out like this but man oh man she'd take advantage of everything they offered.

Steve's hand started wandering—cupping her breast and then traveling over her ribs to her belly and below. Her clit was always extra sensitive after a climax and over the years he'd learned how to stimulate it lightly. He didn't touch it directly but rubbed her mound enough to awaken her lust again.

"What next, baby?" he whispered.

She reached behind her to stroke his cock. "I want this inside me while I suck on Rafe."

Rafe chuckled. "Shy little thing, isn't she?"

"You're my present and you'll do what I say. On your knees."

He obeyed and Cass rose to all fours. She'd dreamed of this ever since watching him with Sylvia — one cock inside her while she feasted on another. Both men had amazing equipment. Sleek thick shafts and huge heads.

The head of Rafe's cock faced her now, the ultimate temptation. She closed her mouth around it and sucked then flicked at the underside with her tongue. Served him right for the way he'd driven her past distraction. Behind her, Steve parted her legs and brought his own cock to the entrance of her pussy. Even as wet as she'd become, Cass had to stretch to accept his bulk. While she swallowed as much of Rafe as she could manage, Steve pushed into her one inch at a time.

"Shit this is good." Rafe pushed forward giving her more of his hardness. Grasping his cock she rubbed along his shaft.

His hips kept moving as he sucked in a loud breath. "I can see why you didn't want another woman, boy scout. I've never had head like this."

Steve thrust deeper now. Harder. "Wait until you feel her cunt squeezing you. Oh yeah, baby. Fuck me."

As she loved Rafe's cock with her mouth, her imagination filled with memories of how he'd looked gliding in and out of Sylvia. The grimace of pleasure on his face, his cock slick and swollen, crimson as he shot semen everywhere. Did he look like that now? Hot and ready to spew.

She briefly took her mouth off his hardness. It had turned a livid color signaling his complete arousal. Guiding it upward, she licked the underside all the way from his balls to the spot just behind the head.

He groaned and pulled away gripping the base in a stranglehold. He took several huge breaths. "Shit I almost lost it."

Behind her Steve kept pumping. "Can't take it, stud?"

"I can take it, boy scout."

"Not this." Steve pounded into her hard and fast. He could always make her climax by doing that. He only did it when they were about to come together. She had to hold off, had to make it last, when every nerve inside her built to orgasm again.

He kept pummeling her, his hips slapping against her ass. "You couldn't take this roommate."

"I can take it."

Steve pulled out and moved aside. Suddenly she was empty. She moaned in frustration. She needed a cock filling her, driving her.

Rafe obliged. In seconds he positioned himself behind her and thrust into her, penetrating deep inside her. She gasped in shock and pleasure. He filled her so completely, surging forward and then pulling out again. He set a wild pace, picking up where Steve left off. Cass bit her lip and fought back against the approaching orgasm. More of this—as much as she could manage—and then she'd come. It was too wonderful, too savage to let it end.

Steve lay on the bed stroking himself while he watched Rafe plunge into her over and over. "I can see why all those noises came out of your room, stud."

"Shit, boy scout. I'm gonna come. Too soon."

"Knock yourself out."

"Your...wedding...night." He stopped thrusting and remained buried deep inside her while his whole body shook. After one more thrust he pulled out. "Fuck! What we planned. Fast!"

"Come here, baby." Steve snaked an arm around Cass and pulled her back against him. After lifting her leg over his hip he shoved his cock inside her from behind and rocked forward and back.

In this position he went even deeper and harder than he had before. Helpless to fight any more she surrendered to the pressure building inside her cunt. Then when she couldn't take another moment, Rafe buried his face in her mound and found her clit with his tongue.

Damn. Oh damn. Too much. She'd never in her life felt anything like this. The pressure of Steve's cock filling her, the rasp of Rafe's tongue against her clit. She'd shatter. She'd die. She'd die if they stopped.

"Let it happen," Steve whispered. "I'm coming with you."

"Yes."

"Now, baby. Can't wait. Now."

"Yesssss!"

She stiffened as the orgasm hit. So hard she couldn't scream, couldn't breathe. It tore her in two—a throbbing cunt, a burning clit. Both men kept going as she soared to an impossible peak and hung there. Her pussy clutched at the hardness inside.

Steve's roar came from behind as he spilled his soul into her in hot waves. She managed to open her eyes in time to see Rafe pulling on his own cock. He went rigid, growling, as a stream of come shot out of him and sprayed onto her hip and the bed between them.

The three of them lay there spent, Steve still buried inside her while Rafe's breath heated her mound. Heaven. Pure heaven.

* * * * *

Steve loaded the luggage onto the scale at the ticket counter and turned to shake Rafe's hand. "Thanks for everything stud. I do mean everything.

"I'd stick around but I have my own flight to catch," Rafe answered.

Cass rested a hand on Rafe's cheek and turned her face up for a kiss. They did it innocently enough that no one at the counter could guess what had passed between the three of them the night before. Then blushing, she slipped her arms around Steve's ribs. How on earth she could blush after *that* wedding night was beyond him. She'd married him the day before and after the gift he'd given her she seemed even more dedicated to him and their marriage. Rafe had helped them get a good start.

"I wish you could stay in the house until we get back," Steve said.

"I have a job you know."

"Come back when you can," Cass said. She looked up to Steve for approval and he nodded.

"You guys come visit me too," Rafe said. "I'll show you a good time."

That he would. The three of them had forged a bond the night before. None of them wanted it to end. Ever. Right now Steve and Cass needed time by themselves but they'd always have room for Rafe in their lives. And in their bed.

"Bring a date next time," Steve said.

Rafe laughed. "Oh yeah. She'd have to be someone special."

Someone adventurous. If anyone could find such a woman, it'd be Rafe.

Rafe looked at his watch. "I'd better go."

"Have a good trip," Steve answered.

"Right." Rafe put a hand on Cass' shoulder. "You take care of her, boy scout or I'll be back to kick your butt."

"I will."

Rafe picked up his bag, turned, and strode off. Steve might have imagined it but Rafe seemed to swagger a bit more than usual. He had a lot to swagger about.

GROOM'S GIFT
Beth Kery

ဢ

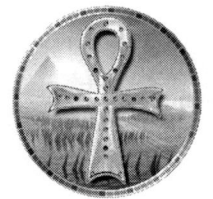

Dedication

ଐଠ

This is dedicated to my very dear friend D.J.C.

Trademarks Acknowledgement

ଐଠ

The author acknowledges the trademarked status and trademark owners of the following wordmarks mentioned in this work of fiction:

Newsweek: Newsweek, Inc.

Xtreme Sport: Honeywell International, Inc.

Chapter One

ဢ

"This is an inspiration. I'm going to use this in my summer line," Malcolm exclaimed as he walked around Libby and inspected her. "Talk about the gift of sex! If I were straight, I'd be on the floor in a sex-induced seizure right now. As it is, I'm considering proposing, Libby."

Libby blushed for the hundredth time that evening, causing her cheeks to turn the same shade as the cerise ribbon she wore — the cerise ribbon with not a stitch else. Unless one counted the black sheer thigh-highs and the stiletto heels...

"Ced will be thrilled to hear it, I'm sure."

"Not to mention my mother," Malcolm said.

"Quit joking around, Malcolm!" Libby squawked, scandalized that he had the audacity to tease her at *this*, of all moments. "I'm about to *do* this! Talk me out of it before I make the biggest mistake of my life."

"The groom is the one who is about to make the biggest mistake of his life by marrying Estelle. You're the best thing that could happen to him," Malcolm said calmly as he fluffed the confection of a bow that he'd created around her breasts.

"Thanks, Malcolm," Libby murmured with shaky gratitude.

"Think nothing of it."

"Malcolm!" Libby squealed in protest a second later. She slapped her friend's hand away from where he'd been tweaking one of her nipples which peeked out coyly between the cleverly arranged ribbons.

"Sorry," Malcolm said cheekily. "I had a little pot of nipple cream that I was ready to use on you, but you don't need it, Libby. Rosy as the ribbon, aren't you? And talk about responsive! John isn't going to know what hit him."

"I've lost my mind," Libby grated out.

"For seducing the man you love—even though you technically don't know him—before he throws away his life by marrying a silicone robot?"

"No, I'm *obviously* as sane as the church lady for that. I'm nuts for stripping down naked in front of you and letting you pinch and poke at me like I'm one of your mannequins And just for the record, I doubt Estelle's breasts are silicone. John's too much of a naturalist to go for that. They don't even use silicone anymore for fake boobs, do they?" Libby asked distractedly as she turned in the three-way mirror and inspected her ass. Malcolm had worked his magic there, as well. It must be magic, how else could he have managed to make her ass look like a firm, plump, gift-wrapped piece of sex-fruit?

"I wasn't talking about her boobs. I designed Estelle's wedding dress, so I would know. Those puppies are the real thing, all right. I meant that I think there's a computer chip behind Estelle's ginormous breasts instead of a beating heart. And crazy or not, Libby Taylor, you know you did the right thing in coming to me to prepare you for your little sex ambush of the gorgeous Johnny." Malcolm matter-of-factly rearranged the bow that topped her ass so that even more of her bare buttocks were exposed. He shook his head in wonderment.

"I'm a fucking *genius*."

Libby frowned into the mirror. She hated to stroke his already gargantuan ego, but Malcolm was right. As a clothing designer who had his own shop on Oak Street, an exclusive shopping area in the Gold Coast of Chicago, Malcolm had not only the talent but the materials necessary to pull off her little plot. He had been the perfect person to run to in her desperation…well, along with Nathan and Ced, that is. Or assist her in her madness…however you wanted to state it.

As the days that led up to John's wedding loomed closer, Libby increasingly felt like she was watching the train wreck that was her life from a distance, immobilized by horror. The fact that Ced—Malcolm's partner and her other dear friend—had been hired to cater John and Libby's wedding and that Malcolm had designed the bride's fabulous wedding dress made the nightmare all that much more close and real.

The funny thing about the whole situation was that it had been *her*—Libby—that was the spoke of the wheel bringing together Nathan—John's father—Malcolm, Ced, Estelle and John. She had no one but herself to blame for this ridiculous mess she found herself in. If it wasn't for *her*, Nathan would never have become friends with Malcolm and Ced. The three of them wouldn't have conspired to set up John and Libby, and Ced and Malcolm would had never hosted the party that was thrown with the sole purpose of introducing her to John, and, most of all, John would never have met that blonde bimbo that had proceeded to ruin Libby's life!

Of course, when John and Estelle became engaged, it had been Ced and Malcolm they'd hired as their wedding caterer and gown designer. They'd accepted, of course, because John had become a good friend. And since Libby lived down the hall from Ced and Malcolm, she had become the unwilling witness to all the intimate details of the marriage of the man she loved to another woman.

Talk about the definition of a nightmare.

And now, that awful wedding was only three days away!

She *couldn't* let John Waite get married to someone else—not without ever having at least kissed his lips once, smelled the scent on his neck, heard him say her name, seen the expression on his face when he came...

If she at least did that, she would have had her rare, special moment. She wouldn't die knowing she was the lamest, most gutless woman on the planet.

Oh God, she *was* out of her mind.

John Waite didn't know Libby Taylor. John Waite didn't care about Libby Taylor. What were the chances that Libby Taylor could talk John Waite into sleeping with her tonight when he was on the verge of marrying a drop-dead gorgeous heiress who was stacked like the wedding cake Ced had created?

Slim to none, no doubt.

Still…she had to try. Didn't she? He *was* the man of her dreams, after all.

The whole bizarre odyssey—the latest chapter of which involved down-to-earth, girl-next-door Libby standing stark naked—with the exception of a cerise ribbon—while her best friend poked at her nipples and ass—began a year and a half ago. That had been when Nathan Waite, John's father, had started treatment at the Low Vision Rehabilitation Center where Libby worked as an occupational therapist.

Nathan had quickly become one of her favorite, but most challenging patients. As a former partner in a law firm and active sportsman, his initial reaction to his functional blindness due to a stroke had been anger and depression. As an occupational therapist, it had been Libby's considerable challenge to help Nathan to accept the cards that had been dealt him so that he could move on to functioning as independently as possible by adapting his environment and habits to his new disability.

Nathan had spent his first two weeks of intensive daily therapy being as rude and uncooperative as possible toward Libby. But Libby hadn't wavered in her mission. She was used to dealing with all kinds of emotional reactions to newly acquired disabilities and figured it was actually best if people got it over with in their first couple weeks of rehabilitation so they could move on to the pertinent stuff in the last six weeks. She'd acquired thick skin over the years when it came to surliness.

Besides, she'd immediately liked the silver-haired, handsome man, despite his sour glares and vast stubbornness.

She'd finally gotten through to him one day when she'd set him up on a computer that magnified print and pictures so that Nathan could see them. He'd only scowled when she'd equipped him with a high-contrast watch, remote control and telephone, saying that he looked like an old coot using them out in public. But the computer...now that was something *of use*, according to workaholic Nathan Waite.

His mood had notably brightened the first time that he'd read out loud an article from *Newsweek* to her. He'd immediately asked if he could bring in some of his own items on disc for the next day. Libby had agreed, glad to see her patient showing some enthusiasm for once. Libby figured it was well worth it, even if she did have to listen to Nathan practice using the program by reading out loud boring legal briefs.

But what Nathan had brought with him the next day had rocked Libby's world. He hadn't only exposed Libby to legal documents on that day, he'd introduced her to the man who would become the love of Libby's life—Nathan's only son, John Waite. She'd learned about John in depth, not only through a loving father's eyes, but through photos, videos and, most crucially, John's own words.

Nathan had read to her every single thing that John had ever written as a reporter for *Xtreme Sport*, in addition to the more serious pieces he wrote as a freelance writer. As a gifted athlete, John not only *wrote* about exciting, death-defying sports such as skiing down vertical drops from mountains previously uncharted by man or kayaking Class VI whitewater rapids, John *participated* in them.

Libby knew she'd fallen hopelessly in love with him when she read his piece about becoming an accidental hero in the high, inaccessible mountain regions of Zarand in the Kerman province of Iran.

John had become an accomplished helicopter pilot during his stint with the Air Force in his early twenties. He had been doing a piece about skiing on some uncharted peaks on the

Turkish border when the lethal quake had occurred. John had immediately responded to the emergency when he heard of it, flying casualties with his helicopter in and out of the remote mountain villages and bringing in much-needed supplies and food.

Libby had realized early on that John was a gifted writer, but this particular piece — which had since gone on to win several journalistic awards — had emphasized not only his courage and humanity in the face of trauma and death, but his talent for conveying those same characteristics in the village people that he'd helped save, despite their vastly different cultures and way of life.

John Waite wasn't only a grade A hottie, he was a brave, compassionate, complex man and Estelle Gish didn't deserve to stand in his shadow.

Before she'd "met" John, via Nathan's computer, Libby would have scoffed at the idea of falling in love with someone solely through the means of technology. But it could happen. Oh yes, it could happen in spades.

Malcolm's voice brought her back to the present jarringly.

"When I left John's bachelor party at midnight, Ced and Nathan said that they were going to deliver John to his loft by two a.m."

"Oh my God, what time is it?"

"Calm down. It's only one-thirty. You'll have plenty of time to make it."

Malcolm shouted out in protest a moment later when Libby pulled on her coat.

"Watch what you're doing! You're squashing my creation!"

"Malcolm, I'm practically stark naked here! Surely you didn't expect me to walk out on Oak Street and catch a cab wearing nothing but a pink ribbon," Libby scolded.

"Sit on one hip," Malcolm ordered irritably a few minutes later as he held open the cab door for her.

Libby rolled her eyes but complied by tilting uncomfortably on her right side in order to protect the lush confection of a bow above her ass. She looked up at Malcolm desperately, realizing all too poignantly that the one chance was nearly upon her to touch John, to pleasure him, to love him as only she could before he became a married man.

She didn't allow herself to dream of the possibility of actually changing his mind about marrying Estelle. To succeed at that, she would have had to begun her mission at least a year ago. That had been when Nathan, Malcolm and Ced had plotted to introduce Libby and John at a party. Unfortunately, not only Libby's lack of nerve but Estelle Gish herself had backhanded Libby's dreams of a future with gorgeous John Waite.

Libby had stared on in rising horror from the distance as Estelle moved in like a lethal storm and proceeded to blind John with a flash of sex-lightning.

Damn Cedric straight to hell for becoming superficial friends with the socialite, even though Libby couldn't really blame him. Estelle Gish was a valuable contact for Ced to have for his catering business.

Despite Nathan's, Malcolm's and Ced's pleas, Libby had left the party that evening without saying so much as an *"it's such a pleasure to finally meet you"* to the man of her dreams.

Her chicken heart back then made her plans tonight all that much more desperate, lunatic and ludicrous.

"Wish me luck," she begged Malcolm wildly before he could shut the cab door.

"I wish you luck, phenomenal sex and everything else you deserve, Libby Taylor. Love you," Malcolm said as he gave her a quick kiss.

"And whatever else you do, don't you *dare* squash that bow until John has the chance to unwrap you!"

Chapter Two

ॐ

John Waite was just tipsy enough to have to set down on the floor the bag of sex toys and gag gifts he'd received from his bachelor party so that he could fully concentrate to get his key through the lock the first time around. It surprised him a little that the door to his loft swung inward after the first turn of his key. He usually double locked.

It wasn't too shocking he'd forgotten, though, as harried and flustered as he'd been when he'd left for the airport two days ago. He'd pretty much gotten into the rhythm of commuting back and forth between Chicago and the offices of *Xtreme Sport* in New York. That hadn't been what had made him so distracted as he left his loft earlier in the week for the airport. It had been the fact that Estelle had been furious with him for leaving Chicago the week before their wedding.

John had been relieved to be gone, though. Estelle's wedding plans were becoming so extravagant and bewildering to him that he felt as though he would be an outsider at his own marriage ceremony.

For the most part, John was glad he'd moved back to Chicago so he could be closer to his dad since his stroke. John was Nathan's only family now. His father and he had gone through some rough spots in their relationship when John was younger, but he figured they'd pretty much weathered the storms of his youth.

The problem was that both he and Nathan were fiercely independent men and their opinions clashed way too often. His father was always insufferably confident that he knew precisely what was best for John and John had spent way too much energy throughout his life trying to prove him wrong.

John hoped they were past that now, although there was the whole situation with Estelle. When Nathan had become functionally blind from his stroke, John had insisted that he move in with him when he relocated to Chicago. Nathan had refused and his protests had become even more forceful since John had proposed to Estelle.

John scowled at the thought as he flung his keys on the entry way table. His dad's staunch independence was only partially responsible for his refusal to move in with Estelle and him.

The fact of the matter was Nathan disliked Estelle with an almost alarming intensity, given the fact that she was going to be his daughter-in-law. And despite Estelle's bright smiles, John had occasionally seen the glitter of ice in her eyes when Nathan was in one of his irascible moods—which, when she was around, was pretty much all the time.

John closed his eyes briefly in mounting frustration before he determinedly headed back toward his bedroom. A hot shower would help him unwind. He'd been having far too many doubts and uncertainties about his marriage to Estelle over the past several months and the strained relationship between Nathan and her was only one ingredient in his boiling emotional brew.

But it was normal for a guy to have doubts before he took the final plunge into marriage, right?

So why did John get the feeling that his uncertainties weren't normal at all? Why did he feel like someone who was about to undertake an important, long journey only to get the nagging feeling that they'd forgotten something behind...or left something crucial unfinished?

The nipple clamps Ced had given him at his bachelor party fell out of the bag when John tossed it distractedly on the floor next to his bed. They weren't in a cardboard box like the other gifts but were, instead, encased in a luxurious velvet box like fine jewelry came in. John wondered why his friend had dropped so much cash on a sex toy.

Was it John's imagination, or had there been a curious *knowing* look on Ced's face when John opened the box earlier tonight and inspected the surprisingly delicate nipple clamps and silver bell attachments?

Of course, Ced and Malcolm made no secret of the fact that they enjoyed an adventurous sex life. Maybe Ced had noticed John's doubtful expression of longing and guessed the clamps would end up eventually with the rest of the sex toys he'd received tonight, gathering dust at the back of John's closet. John scowled as he whipped his shirt over his head.

Estelle may have breasts that, at first glance, seemed like prime male fantasy material, but John knew firsthand that her nipples weren't that sensitive.

Silly to use nipple clamps to increase the sensitivity of a part of her body when that particular portion of her wasn't that responsive to begin with.

Just like the rest of her.

John actually cursed out loud for allowing that ungenerous thought to pop into his mind.

He turned the water in the shower to extra hot in order to scald the thoughts from his brain. While he stood under the jets with his eyes closed, the nipple clamps inadvertently popped into his brain again. He pictured himself placing them on a pair of nipples that were already stiff and pointed just from the lightest brush of his fingertips. The clamps would make the peaks unbearably sensitive. John imagined the woman lying on his bed naked, her expression tight with arousal, her shining mahogany-colored hair spread upon his pillow.

He felt his cock stir. He unconsciously stroked himself. Why not? It was as good a way of any of getting his mind off his doubts about getting married.

About getting married to Estelle.

His erection became full and tight under the ministrations of his imagination and his hand, but the temperature in the shower became unbearably hot. He'd jerk off in the comforts of his own bed, he thought hazily as he exited the shower along with a cloud of steam. He toweled himself off, sprayed on deodorant in a perfunctory manner and padded into his bedroom nude.

And abruptly came face-to-face with the sexiest woman he'd ever seen, wearing nothing but a pink bow and a becoming blush that matched it to a T.

Chapter Three

ℬ

For a full ten seconds, they just stared at each other, both of them speechless.

"Hi," Libby eventually said throatily.

She mentally rolled her eyes, but quickly forgave herself for not giving a wittier greeting. Who could be glib standing in the face of all that glistening muscle and tumescent male flesh? She'd known John Waite would be a beautiful, sexy male animal, but this was...

She shook her head slightly to clear it as her gaze drifted from the golden skin covering a flat, ridged abdomen to his crotch. His cock looked full, aroused and unbelievably potent where it sprang from a thatch of light brown hair.

Her mouth went dry. Perhaps her body required every last bit of moisture from the periphery in order to adequately respond to the phenomenal surge of lust that flooded her sex.

That had been when she had croaked out her clever greeting.

She watched as his spiky, wet lashes narrowed over his green eyes, as though he was trying to bring a hallucination into clearer focus. To see those striking eyes up close in reality, instead of on a computer screen, felt surreal to Libby.

"Hi," he finally replied. "Who are you? And what are you doing in my loft?"

Libby cleared her throat, more affected by the sound of his deep, resonant voice than she'd prepared herself to be.

"I'm Olivia," she replied.

Nathan, Cedric, Malcolm and she had all agreed that John had heard the reference to "Libby" on too many occasions in the past, so she resorted to her given name. She bit at her lower lip nervously before she forced herself to plunge, once and for all, into the abyss.

"Cedric and Malcolm sent me as a gift."

She couldn't help but smile at the way his eyes popped when she spun around for him slowly, giving him the full benefit of Malcolm's genius.

"I'm yours for the night, John," she said when she finally faced him again.

John was still in the process of questioning his sanity and searching for something rational to say—difficult to do when his brain was inundated by animal lust when she smiled. His heart thudded madly in his chest. He'd already been far too affected by the sight of the lovely, luscious, near-naked auburn-haired woman that stood in his bedroom wearing nothing but a bow and stockings, but the sound of her low, husky voice and the sight of her full lips curving into a smile that was both shy and the essence of pure sex at once made some kind of powerful chemical reaction to cascade from his brain to his blood and straight to his crotch.

Against his will, his gaze dropped to where two of the prettiest, most pert nipples he'd ever seen in his life peeked out flirtatiously at him between the ribbons.

Until his dying day, he would swear that they were the precise nipples that he'd just been fantasizing about not two minutes ago in the shower. Well, not exactly the same. Olivia's nipples were even more perfect, because they pebbled and darkened in color from just from the stimulus of his gaze alone.

"That's a very...sweet gift on Malcolm and Ced's part," John muttered huskily, unable to remove his eyes from the delectable vision of the rosy crowns of her firm breasts, "but I'm afraid I'm going to have to refuse your offer, Olivia."

"I'm not a hooker, John," Libby said impulsively.

His eyes darted up to her face. Libby swallowed heavily at the impact of being the focus of his intelligent, penetrating gaze. She felt her knees weaken. God, was Estelle's last thought before falling asleep and her first upon awakening that she was the luckiest woman on the planet?

"If you're not a prostitute, why would you agree to come and have sex with me for one night only?" John challenged.

For a panicked second, she floundered.

"I saw you once in the distance at one of Ced's parties. I thought you were very sexy. When I heard Ced and Malcolm talking about sending you a prostitute on the night of your bachelor party, I volunteered to…pleasure you instead," Libby explained in a rush of partial honesty and complete embarrassment.

She wasn't in the habit of actually *saying* things like that, for God's sake!

Her eyes widened when John came closer to her. She swore she could feel the heat waving off his nude body. He stopped only a foot way. He studied her through narrowed eyelids. Even in her high heels, she had to crane her neck slightly to look up at him.

"You're that adventurous, Olivia? It's normal operating procedure for you to put on a getup like this," his eyes swept hotly down over her body, "and seduce a complete stranger into a single night of raw sex?"

"Oh, *yes*," Libby lied straight through her teeth. When she felt the heat begin to burn her cheeks, she boldly reached out and placed her hand on his chest, desperate to do something to distract him from noticing her embarrassment.

She felt a jolt of awareness shoot up through her arm.

He felt so hard. His skin was smooth and warm beneath the damp golden brown hairs on his chest. Instinctively, her sensitive fingertips sought out more of the exquisite sensation, rubbing against his skin in tight, small circles. She felt him inhale sharply. Her gaze shot up to meet his.

His green eyes glittered with simmering heat in a paradoxically rigid, cold face. She shivered in growing excitement when he raised his open hand and curved it around her neck.

"When?"

"When what?" Libby asked dazedly as she inhaled his scent. Her nostrils flared slightly, catching not only the obvious smell of the soap he'd used in the shower but the underlying, subtle scent that was John and John alone. Her pussy reacted by flooding with liquid heat. Much to her mortification, however, that wasn't her body's only reaction to the scent of John's body.

Tears also stung her eyes.

John's gaze sharpened. He tilted her jaw so that he could see her more clearly. Libby felt horribly exposed under his stare.

"When were we at the same party together at Ced's?" John asked starkly.

"Oh...it's hard to say exactly..." she stammered lamely.

His head lowered over her upturned lips.

"Make a guess then," he whispered harshly, his mouth just inches from hers.

Libby felt like she could barely inhale when she felt his breath, warm and fragrant, brush against her lips and nose.

"A year ago, maybe?" she squeaked out through a constricted throat. She watched him with huge eyes, her heart beating madly as he merely studied her features for several torturous seconds.

Finally, he sunk his fingers into the upswept hair at her nape.

"Okay," he murmured, "I'll be gracious and accept the gift wholeheartedly."

His mouth lowered to cover hers.

Libby felt as if every cell in her body vibrated with desire. How was it possible for a man to taste and feel so good? He shaped her lips with his own slowly at first, lazily, sipping at her, sandwiching her lips between his one at a time, plucking at them. He played with her until Libby lost patience and bit at his lower lip.

She moaned in triumph into his mouth a second later when he responded just as she'd hoped he would, practically falling on her mouth like it was a luscious piece of fruit and he was dying of thirst and hunger. It was as if a simultaneous sex-bomb exploded in both their bodies. His tongue probed between her lips and boldly explored her mouth. The fact that he groaned and pulled her against his nakedness when he fully registered her taste gave Libby hope that he liked her taste as much as she did his.

That and the fact that the column of his penis surged and stiffened next to her belly even beyond the already impressive erection that he'd been sporting since coming out of the bathroom.

Her hands rose to eagerly discover what she'd only dreamed about before. His lean, defined, hard muscles fascinated her exploring fingertips and palms. She traced his shoulders and gently dug her fingers between the muscle and the ridge of the flat bones at the back of them. He responded by palming a bare ass cheek and pushing their bodies almost roughly together, squashing Malcolm's bow above her breasts in the process—not that either of them noticed or cared. Libby scraped her fingernails down the long length of his spine and finished her arousing tour by squeezing both his taut, muscular ass cheeks just as lustily as he currently massaged one of hers.

John pressed his mouth to the fragrant skin at the side of her neck. The hand that wasn't happily squeezing her sweet, firm ass cheek swept along the side of her waist and ribs. He'd never experienced skin so silky and soft in his life.

"Olivia," he whispered heatedly as he moved his mouth to the back of her nape, capturing even more of her exquisite scent and taste at the same time that his palm curved around a bow-encased breast. She fit his hand perfectly, filling it with firm flesh. The erect, pointed nipple that pressed into the center of his palm scorched his consciousness.

He gritted his teeth to stifle a curse of protest when he felt her back out of his arms. He blinked once, fully taking in how lovely she looked with her cheeks glowing and her large liquid brown eyes gleaming with arousal. He saw her reach up to the ribbon, noticed the way her slender throat convulsed as she swallowed.

"You're supposed to pull here," she said simply.

John reluctantly released her peach of an ass cheek from his palm and grabbed the end of the ribbon. He pinned her with his stare.

"You'll give yourself to me for the whole night, Olivia?"

Libby nodded eagerly.

"And you'll do anything and everything that I desire?"

"Oh, yes," she promised.

He gave a small smile before he stepped back slightly and pulled on the ribbon, his eyes lowering in order to fully appreciate his gift as he unwrapped it.

Chapter Four

so

The bow melted away from her breasts first. John found himself staring at two high, pale breasts that thrust out proudly from the plane of her chest, capped by large, pink nipples. He experienced an almost feral lust at the sight. He perfectly envisioned himself licking and sucking on the pert beauties, knowing instinctively she would feed his hunger just as bountifully as she roused it.

He gathered more and more of the pink ribbon in his right hand as he pulled on it with his left. His eyes narrowed when he saw where the ribbon led next. It traveled between Olivia's ribs and smooth belly. At her crotch, the silk had been sewn to a patch of pink satin, a tiny tease of a piece of cloth that covered her pubic hair. Barely.

John's nostrils flared as he pulled up on the ribbon and she gasped. His eyes leapt to her face.

"Spread your legs," he ordered softly.

She spread her shapely thighs. He heard her stifled cry when he began to pull up with gentle pulsations on the ribbon, the action creating a firm pressure on her clit.

John watched her face as he stimulated her, fascinated by her expression of arousal.

"You have beautiful breasts. Touch yourself, Olivia," he rasped when she met his stare.

Libby responded just as much to the stark desire on his face as she did his verbal request. She cradled her breasts from below in an offering gesture, keeping her nipples exposed to his hot eyes as she kneaded her own flesh. The pace of his subtle tugging on the ribbon increased notably at her actions. She moaned. The pressure felt so good on her aching clit, but he was also stimulating all along her pussy, perineum and anus. She pinched her already erect nipples between her thumb and forefinger.

John jerked up energetically on the ribbon. She gasped in pleasure.

"Turn around," he grated.

He wasn't going to be able to take much more of this. His cock strained uncomfortably, stretching skin that had never been tested so sorely with this degree of desire. He made a muffled sound of arousal in his throat when Olivia turned, exposing her backside to him. The sweep of her naked back was elegant and sexy. His hands itched to run down the slope from her narrow waist to her hips. Her thighs were slender and lightly muscled and he couldn't wait to be buried between their silky softness.

And he forgave himself completely for his disloyalty to Estelle when he focused on Olivia's round, firm ass topped by the pink bow.

He came up behind her, the ribbon still in his hand.

Libby held her breath when she sensed John's body heat so close behind her. She glanced over her shoulder anxiously. He was staring down at her ass with a fixed, tense stare.

"John," she whispered helplessly when he spread his hands on the front of her thighs, caressing her lightly. The ribbon dropped to the floor while he stroked her for the next breathless seconds.

He then reached between her thighs from the back and recaptured the piece of pink silk. Libby leaned back into his solid chest, weak from desire. He pushed forward slightly on her hips so that he could continue with his mission, prying the piece of cloth from the folds of her damp sex and the crevice of her ass.

"You're soaking wet, Olivia."

Libby moaned as he ran his fingers over the ribbon where it had been buried in her sex. Somehow, the knowledge that he did so felt even more intimate at that moment than if he'd just plunged his fingers into her pussy.

He pulled on the ribbon once, then again more firmly and the bow above her ass collapsed. He made short work of the last, single strip that was affixed around her waist by ripping it savagely with both hands. Libby trembled when he pressed his hot, hard body tightly to her from behind. His hands ran avidly across her hips and belly while his mouth scorched the side of her neck.

"You're the *perfect* gift, Olivia," he praised between kisses.

"I'm so glad you're pleased," she whispered over her shoulder as she craned up for him.

They crashed together in a ravaging kiss.

John groaned gutturally as he flexed his hips and ass, pressing his balls into the plump cheeks of her ass. His cock throbbed between the upper swells of her buttocks and along the silky skin of her back.

He broke their kiss, gritting his teeth at the effort of restraining himself from bending her over then and now and impaling her soft body with his cock.

Libby cried out in surprise when he turned her to face him abruptly and lifted her in his arms. Her shock was relatively short-lived, however, as her legs naturally found a home encircling his hips and John's mouth was back on hers, making her forget everything but him and her sharp desire.

Their kiss was so wild and intense that Libby barely noticed that he'd moved to the bed. He sat down on the edge, her knees bent at his side as she straddled him. John fumbled in the nightstand for a condom. He moved so quickly that before she could catch her breath he encircled her waist and arrowed his cock into her pussy.

"Ohhh, *God!*" Libby muttered. She was wet and very aroused, but John wasn't a small man. The fat head of his cock carved into her flesh, stretching her tissues, forcing her to accept his powerful presence.

John saw her look of surprise. "You're my gift to do with as I please...aren't you, Olivia?" he whispered tautly.

Libby felt her cheeks flush with heat as he watched her so steadily at the same time that he gripped her hips and moved her up on his cock, the thick, defined head creating a vacuum in her narrow, liquid channel. Libby trembled uncontrollably. He grunted his pleasure as he pushed her hips up and then back down on him until she sheathed the first half of his straining erection.

"Answer me," John demanded.

"Yes...*God, yes,*" Libby moaned as they began to stroke each other in unison, using the first half of his cock. It hurt a little, but the pleasure of taking John into her body was so immense that the pain merely acted as piquant spice to her desire. She cried out when he thrust his hips at the same time that he gripped her ass, holding her steady as he sliced deeper into her melting depths, not satisfied until his balls pressed tightly to her damp hilt.

A groan tore at his throat. His arm, thigh and ass muscles bunched tightly as he struggled to keep his control.

He was encased in a mercilessly tight, hot pussy. It felt like heaven.

It felt like...*he'd come home.*

His eyes flashed open when he heard Olivia's muffled cry. He merely said her name, that's all, before he leaned forward and slipped one of her nipples between his lips.

Libby stared down at him in wonderment. He drew on her nipple hungrily, but so sweetly, it was as if a magical cord thrummed to life between where his tongue lashed at her nipple and where his cock throbbed near her womb. She whimpered helplessly. Her eyelids clenched shut as she rocked him ever-so gently in her body, giving herself the pressure that she needed.

John felt her begin to quake in his arms, heard her cry out in release. Her pussy shimmered around him, resonating heat

305

into him, tractoring him impossibly deeper as she came...testing his control beyond his endurance.

He began to fuck her, loving the way her climax pulled and teased at his cock as he did so. He couldn't wait to sink back into her after each stroke.

Libby still convulsed under the power of the strongest climax she'd ever experienced. The fact that John began to fuck her in the midst of it only prolonged the indescribable sensation.

The realization that this was *John Waite* fucking her oozed into the modicum of consciousness that remained after her brain-frying orgasm.

"John," she muttered as she clutched at his head and then his shoulders and began to move over him, matching his demanding thrusts.

"That's right," he answered. "Give it to me. Fuck me, Olivia."

They mated with a wild, mutual abandon, their flesh pounding together in a forceful rhythm. Their cries and shouts and the protesting screech of the mattress springs became their background percussion.

Yet, throughout their stormy joining, Libby was aware of his glittering green gaze fixed on her. There were times when she had to shut her eyes in the face of the intense pleasure and the rapidly building pressure, but somehow she always sensed his stare on her...penetrating and hot.

The friction created by his pounding cock finally reached the point of eruption. She cried out when he held her down tightly in his lap. He encircled her hip with one hand and reached with his thumb, rubbing her clit.

She screamed when she came again, this orgasm even more profound than the former one because she felt John swell and spasm deep inside her as he found his release as well.

John clamped his eyes closed as he finally surrendered. He'd wanted to make it last, but she was too tight...too sweet.

He growled harshly as he came at her furthest reaches and pleasure racked his flesh in sharp, crashing waves.

For a minute or two, only the sounds of their ragged breathing pierced the silence. Libby opened her eyes dazedly. John's forehead pressed at the juncture between her neck and shoulder. His short, golden brown hair was still damp from his shower and spiked out in various directions.

She smiled to herself and instinctively raised her hand to smooth it.

"Is it sticking up?" he asked directly into her neck.

Libby laughed softly at his muffled question. She felt like she was the Queen of the Universe when he pressed his lips to her throat, as though he liked the vibration of her laughter.

"Yes. You look like you have horns."

He leaned back and regarded her with a heavy-lidded gaze. His eyes ran with lazy appreciation over her mussed mahogany hair and flushed breasts.

"You bring out the devil in me, Olivia."

Libby swallowed. Another valuable lesson learned about John Waite. Before he had climaxed, his eyes had been fierce flames. After the edge was taken off, they were even more lethal in their impact on her.

Bedroom eyes, that's what John had.

Instinctively, she tightened around his cock where it still harbored snugly in her body. He went completely still at her unintentional caress.

"You bring out the devil in me, too, I think," she whispered. Her eyes rounded when he smiled. Oh, *yes*. This crazy escapade had been *so* worth it.

"The temptress, more like," he replied in a gravelly voice that made her shiver.

Libby licked at her lower lip in a mixture of anxiety, excitement and anticipation. John's green eyes sparked with fire as he watched the quick movement of her tongue.

"Would you let me tempt you, then, John?" she asked in a voice that was unintentionally throaty and sultry. She felt his cock surge inside her and gently rocked against him. His arms encircled her waist as he hugged her upper body closer to his.

"Put myself at your mercy, you mean?" John asked.

Libby smiled broadly as he pretended to deliberate on his decision.

"I don't know. A man could get into trouble putting himself into the hands of redheaded adventuress who doesn't think twice about seducing strangers," he said soberly.

"But then again, a man could end up regretting it sorely that he hadn't done every last thing that the redheaded adventuress demanded of him," Libby replied as she innocently batted her eyes.

"Good point," John admitted with a slashing grin and lascivious rise of his sandy eyebrows that Libby found utterly adorable. Nevertheless, she firmly stopped him when he spread his hands along her back and waist and began to move her up and down again on his cock.

"Uh, uh!" she warned gently as she rose on her knees and his cock slowly receded from her body. His absence felt terrible and when she saw John's expression of outrage, she momentarily relented and planted him back firmly within her...where he belonged.

For tonight, anyway, she reminded herself when her heart lurched unhappily in her chest at the unwelcome thought.

No time for feeling sorry for herself now. *This* was her moment. This was Libby's time, every precious second of it. She wanted to cherish all of it. She wanted to cherish all of John.

Libby may not be perfect, but she had some morals that she didn't waver on. One of them was that she didn't sleep with married man.

This night with John would have to last her a lifetime. She was determined to make it count.

"Lay back, John," she instructed as she withdrew and stood next to the bed. He looked like he was on the verge of arguing but seemed to think better of it when his gaze fixed on her breasts. She laughed softly.

"What's so funny?" he asked.

"You. Hasn't anyone ever told you that you're pretty transparent?"

"Meaning what?"

Libby shook her head, grinning. Her shoulder-length hair loosened from the twist at the back of her head at the motion. She distractedly pulled at the loose pins and set them on the bedside table.

"You broadcast your thoughts loud and clear," she said as she searched her hair for remaining pins and studied him with a warm glint in her eyes.

"I'll have you know, Ms. Temptress, that I'm known far and wide for my completely indecipherable poker face," John said as he bent his arms and rested his head in his hands. He liked watching her take her hair down. He couldn't wait to get back to some hot, explosive sex, but her teasing smile and the expression in her big, brown eyes when she looked at him kept him satisfied for the time being.

His eyes lingered on the glory of her shiny, bouncing hair. It looked exactly like he'd imagined it would. Her hair reminded him of the rest of her, sexy, saucy…naturally, utterly beautiful.

Libby shot him a wry expression as she placed the final pin on the table. "You were just thinking that you'd put up with me having my way with you because then you'd get to return the favor and have me at your mercy in return."

Her soft laughter resumed when she saw his handsome face collapse slightly with disbelief that she'd read him perfectly.

"What's all this?" Libby asked.

John's tight abdomen muscles flexed slightly as he glanced down to where she indicated.

"Oh. The stuff I got at my bachelor party tonight."

Something in his tone made her glance up at him sharply.

"Sexy stuff?" she asked. Her pussy experienced another major meltdown when he treated her to that slow smile. Her eyes zoomed down over his considerable length as he stretched out on the bed. God, she was so going to enjoy exploring every inch of his beautiful, hard, golden body.

"Well, I guess it depends on what you think is sexy," John replied huskily.

You, any way I can get you, John Waite, Libby thought. Still, she arched her eyebrows at him coyly.

"I'm sure I could find something in here to pique my adventurous spirit," Libby said with affected casualness as she began to rifle through the bag. The first item she held up was a pair of handcuffs.

"Possibly," she said coolly as she tossed them on the bedside table.

"Definitely," she murmured as she placed a bottle of lubricant next to the handcuffs. She smiled sweetly at him when she noticed the hot gleam in his eyes.

"*Oooh*, forget it!" she exclaimed when she took out a box containing the *Fist of Power*. Her eyelids narrowed suspiciously as she studied the impossibly large rubber fist. "Did Malcolm give this to you?"

John had turned on his side as he watched her, thoroughly enjoying himself. He merely shrugged lazily in lieu of saying *of course*.

"Figures," she muttered with a scowl. "Hmmm...what's this?" she asked with interest as she opened the next box and spilled out the contents. She examined a smooth, hard rubber protrusion that was about four inches long and nearly an inch wide with two curved handles at the end. The small dildo curved in and out, creating subtle bead-like swells on the surface.

"It says it's a prostate stimulator," Libby read. She noticed John's doubtful expression and smiled widely as she set it on the table with the other toys. "Come on, John, where's *your* sense of adventure?"

"Am I supposed to believe that you have everyday familiarity with prostate stimulators, Olivia?" John asked dryly. His eyebrows went up when he saw the pink flush of her cheeks. His smile turned smug. And she had the nerve to accuse *him* of being transparent.

"I'm a medical professional," Libby said imperiously, turning away to hide her flash of embarrassment. Temptresses weren't supposed to blush. "You'll be in good hands."

"Undoubtedly," John murmured.

"What's this?" She bent and picked up the blue velvet box from the floor. She hesitated when she saw the pretty, delicate nipple clamps. They obviously were a personal, intimate gift. Her eyes flashed up guiltily to John when she sensed the almost imperceptible tension that entered his nude body.

His eyes were like burning embers.

"Put them on the table, Olivia," he said softly. "And come here."

Chapter Five

∞

"John, I'm supposed to be taking advantage of *you!*" Libby protested weakly in dazed lust against his lips a minute later.

She'd been in the process of exploring his neck and chest with her fingers and tongue. He was delicious. Libby wanted to live off a diet of John alone. Her latest discovery had been how responsive his small, copper-colored nipples were beneath her lips, tongue and sucking mouth. She'd been in the process of gently nibbling the yummy nubbin with her front teeth when he growled her name, grabbed her shoulders and pushed her down to him. He kissed her with so much hunger, Libby had almost forgotten her desire to eat up every inch of him.

Almost.

The handcuffs rattled when she picked them up off the bedside table. Her expression told him clearly that he had no one to blame but himself.

"I'm going to have to force you to behave since you can't seem to do it yourself," she told him with mock regret.

His nostrils flared slightly as he stared at the dangling handcuffs. For a second, Libby thought he was going to refuse. She intuitively knew that John would much prefer to be cuffing her instead. But Libby wouldn't be denied unrestricted access to her sex playground on her one night with John.

His green eyes flashed up to meet hers before he held out a wrist.

"Okay. But this isn't my thing, Olivia. Just remember payback is hell."

He watched as she fumbled clumsily with the handcuffs, only successfully getting him anchored to one of the wrought iron posts of his bed because he tersely instructed her.

"There!" she said cheerfully, obviously pleased as punch with her accomplishment.

God, she looked as bright and innocent as a spring day, John thought. She did, anyway, until one glanced down and saw her firm breasts and fat, rosy nipples, or her beguilingly curving, completely feminine hips, or her flushed, swollen labia that gleamed with her sex oils and peeked at him teasingly through her well-trimmed, auburn pubic hair.

His cock throbbed almost painfully.

He gasped in pleasure when she knelt over him, her fingertips detailing every one of his ribs while her lips and tongue discovered how exquisitely sensitive his skin was from a few inches below his armpit down to the side of his waist.

"You know I'm not that convinced that you're a seasoned libertine, Olivia," John taunted raggedly, trying to suppress his grunt of pleasure when she scraped her teeth along the side of his ribs, raising goose bumps on his skin. He was desperate to say anything—even the truth—in order to get her to touch his cock before he exploded merely from her tortuous torso kisses alone.

Her soft hair tickled his belly when she whipped up her head, making his muscles jump with excitement.

"Why would you say that?" she asked in a hurt voice.

John unconsciously pulled on the cuffs. He really wanted to hold her at that moment, dammit.

"Male intuition," he replied dryly instead. He watched in fascination as she straightened until she was looking down at him from a kneeling position. His eyes widened slightly when he saw the determined fury in her liquid brown eyes.

He realized the anger he'd ignited might have Amazon proportions. He blinked in surprise when she abruptly dove for the bedside table.

313

"Olivia...I just meant that...Olivia?" he asked in rising trepidation when he saw her retrieve the prostate stimulator along with the lubricant.

Libby didn't answer him as he continued to call her name. She briskly lubed up the rubber dildo, not making eye contact with him. How mortifying to know that he could tell by her lovemaking she wasn't anywhere near the femme fatale she was pretending to be!

John pulled on the handcuffs, this time with rising frustration.

"Olivia, take these things off."

"No," she said with unnatural calmness as she curled up next to him. She hoped John didn't notice the way her hand trembled when she reached out and wrapped her hand around the base of his penis.

Both of them went very still for a moment.

"Olivia..." John muttered hoarsely when she began to stroke him, slowly at first, but then with an increasing tempo and force. Her touch felt magical—sensitive and curious one second, hard and sure the next.

Libby didn't answer. She was too filled with wonder at the experience of finally touching John's cock. His skin was stretched tight over the iron desire beneath. Her breathing escalated to a pant as she petted and worshipped that long, golden spear. She was thoroughly entranced by the velvety smooth texture of the fleshy arrow-tip of the head.

She bent down to sample the fat crown of his penis with her mouth. It had given her so much pleasure before to have that defined knob pushing in and out of her body. She longed to return the pleasure.

She closed her eyes and rapturously bathed the head of his cock with her tongue, running it along the defined ridge below the head, beating it briskly against the sensitive slit, circling and teasing mercilessly. And when her arousal finally overcame her, she held him firmly at the base and pushed her lips down over him.

Libby sighed in sheer ecstasy. The sheer weight of his cock on her tongue was exquisite. Her lips moved over him hungrily. Her suction was steady and strong because she was ravenous. For him.

For John.

John gave up calling her name and just stared down at her, his face tight and glazed with perspiration. He groaned at the sight of her hollowed out cheeks as she applied an eye-crossing suction on his cock. Her dark eyelashes formed a spiky crescent on her cheek, making her look strangely calm and focused even as she increased her tempo. She gobbled him greedily, her head thrusting down over him as she crammed more of his stalk into her warm, sucking cavern. She briskly slapped the head and the sensitive sweet spot below it with the wet lash of her tongue on her upstroke. The fingers of the hand that held him at the root reached, cradling and caressing his balls almost lovingly.

Watching her created a strange feeling in him that only magnified his tremendous arousal. He forced himself to look away. He stared up at the ceiling, panting and sweating as she flayed him alive with her tongue and mouth. He'd never experienced a woman pleasuring him with such an obvious hunger or such sharp, precise focus.

Libby's ecstatic trance broke slightly when she heard John curse under his breath. She glanced up at him while his cock still tickled her throat. She had determinedly kept him deep a moment ago, thwarting her body's natural urge to reject him. Her gag reflex had vibrated into him, and that had been the reason for his tense curse.

She slid her lips up to his rim and licked him avidly while she took a deep, much-needed inhalation.

She took advantage of the fact that he wasn't watching her. He jumped when she parted one tight ass cheek with her left hand and pressed the lubricated stimulator to his puckered asshole with the other.

"*Olivia*," John rasped, his head coming off the pillow.

His dense erection sprang against his belly when she released him from the ring of her tightly drawn lips.

"Shhh," she soothed softly.

The sound made a shiver of pure animal lust shimmer up John's spine. The cool lubricant and Olivia's sure touch felt unbearably exciting, but *dammit...*

"I was about to come," he protested as he watched her with fiery eyes.

"I know it," she replied huskily. "Let's see if we can't make it nicer for you."

He grunted when she pushed the first rubber swell into his ass. Libby watched his expression carefully as she continued to firmly feed the stimulator in until the front handle lodged against his perineum. She hazarded a guess from the sudden glazed, wild look that came into John's eyes that the pressure not only in his ass, but against the internal root of his cock was much appreciated.

Libby continued to watch him with wary fascination as she reached again for his cock with one hand. His eyes looked so fierce at that moment and his beautiful muscles were so tense and swollen with blood that Libby wondered with a thrill of fear and excitement if he was going to tear right through the bedpost to get at her.

"You're going to pay for this, Olivia," he hissed. He watched her with narrowed eyelids as she lowered her lips to his cock again.

Her only answer was an enigmatic smile before she took him again into her clinging heat. John closed his eyes and groaned gutturally as she sucked him deep and fast at the same time that she manipulated the handle of the rubber implement, stimulating his prostate from an interior and exterior angle.

"*God bless...it!*" he grated out in stark incredulity in the face of the exponentially amplified pressure.

He howled a few seconds later when the tight coils of his control powerfully sprang free.

He must have lost consciousness for a few seconds. When he came back to reality, he was still gloriously coming in Olivia's milking mouth. He abruptly choked on his pleasure when she yanked the first swell of the stimulator through the ring of his rectum and then pushed it in and out rapidly. Another shout of sheer ecstasy scored his throat as his orgasm shot up to its original, potent strength.

He blinked in disorientation a while later, blurrily taking in Olivia as she rose up over him. He noticed that she licked her lips in a satisfied manner as she placed the stimulator and lubricant on the bedside table.

The little minx.

"I think you liked that quite a bit, John," she said with a sunny smile as she knelt next to him. "It's a good thing I'm so innocent or you might have been downright overwhelmed."

John regarded her steadily as he willed his rapid heartbeat and panting breath to still.

"Time to unlock the handcuffs, Olivia," he finally murmured through rigid lips.

That increasingly familiar shiver ran through her at his tone and gleaming green eyes—the one that felt like some exciting combination of trepidation and anticipation. She bit her lip anxiously, but a deal was a deal, after all...

She reached for the little metal key on the table. Her heart beat pounded loudly in her ears.

He snatched the handcuffs from her fingers the second he was free. Her eyes rounded as he sat up abruptly.

"Are you going to handcuff me, too?" she asked shakily.

"No." He tossed the cuffs on the table carelessly. "I'm not going to need handcuffs to keep you under control, Olivia. Stand up next to the bed."

Chapter Six

ഇ

Libby swallowed convulsively. She wasn't sure exactly what he'd meant by his subtle threat, but despite her anxiety, she was all too willing to find out.

"Put your hands behind your head. Elbows out," he directed briskly as he came to the edge of the bed.

When Libby complied, he grabbed her hips and moved her between his long, spread thighs. She whimpered in arousal when he took both her breasts in his hands. He squeezed her gently, and then more tautly, popping her nipples between his curving thumb and forefinger. She groaned unevenly when he leaned forward and took her into his mouth.

He agitated one nipple with his rough, wet tongue and then sucked her with a steady pressure that varied in intensity. Just when it would become strong enough to verge on pain, he would soften and draw on her sweetly.

Libby groaned shakily as he continued to treat her nipple like a piece of rare sex candy. By the time the crown of her breast popped out of his mouth, it was stiff and red, the center tip more than twice its normal length.

"God, you're sweet," he mumbled before he turned hungrily to her other breast. By the time he was finished torturing and teasing her other nipple, Libby was sure she might explode if he just breathed on her clit. Her sex felt unbearably tight and achy.

"John," she whispered tensely when his head moved back from her distended, pointed peak.

"Hmmm?" he asked distractedly as he reached blindly for the bedside table. He fumbled around for a few seconds

319

because he couldn't seem to unglue his eyes from the sight of her breasts.

Libby's eyes widened when she realized he'd grabbed the velvet box. Oh, no. Not the nipple clamps. It was going to hurt!

John's eyes leapt up to her face when he heard her muffled sound of distress.

"There's a ring that adjusts the level of tightness, Olivia. I won't cause you any pain unless I think it will add to your pleasure. Do you trust me?" he asked her softly.

"Yes," she answered immediately.

He smiled as he drew out the silver clamps. The little bell on the end trilled sweetly as he adjusted the degree of pressure of the clamp on her nipple. It aroused him, that sound. It made him think of Olivia herself, so pure, delicate and sexy. Ced had known exactly what he was doing when he bought them. He'd had Olivia in mind and no one else, John realized as he slowly closed the rubber-coated tips on her rigid nipple.

Libby gasped. The sensation was much more subtle than she'd imagined, or at least it was on the adjustment setting that John had chosen. The clamp provided a steady, constant pressure to her sensitive nipple that was just below the threshold of pain.

It excited her greatly.

Besides, what sane woman wouldn't get excited at the hot look in John's eyes as he examined her once he'd affixed the clamp to her other nipple?

"*Oh!*" Libby cried out shakily when he abruptly reached up and jostled a bell. The weight of the swinging bell pulled on her nipple, creating a shiver of mixed pain and excitement to ripple through her. A sharp twinge of arousal bit at her clit.

John smiled at her responsiveness when he saw her instinctively clamp her thighs shut to alleviate the pressure at her sex.

"I told you payback was hell, Olivia," he murmured.

Libby merely moaned as lust stabbed through her.

"Back up, honey," John ordered.

Libby stepped back slowly, all too aware that any abrupt movement on her part would make the bells sway and pull on the clamps that tugged at her tender, sensitive flesh.

John stood up beside her.

"Bend over and put your hands on the bed."

He watched her with a tight focus as she slowly, carefully complied. No matter how hard she tried to keep the hanging bells still, however, they still tinkled sweetly.

"Is it too much?" he asked her quietly when he saw her tight expression.

"No...I can take it," Libby whispered.

As if to assure himself, he suddenly swept his fingers between her thighs.

Libby cried out in pleasure as he massaged her clit firmly before he plunged a finger into her pussy.

"You're so wet. *Olivia!*" he muttered the last in a voice thick with arousal as he felt the walls of her pussy start to convulse around him.

What an exquisite torture it was to come so thunderously with John's finger inside her while she tried to remain as still as possible. The bells shimmered in subtle sympathy with her body, nevertheless, trembling delicately, giving her ecstasy a song all its own. The pressure on her nipples added a sharp, forbidden edge to her climax.

"Okay?" John questioned a minute later when she'd finally caught her breath.

"Yes," she replied breathlessly, resisting the urge to nod her head.

"Good, because I'm going to have to punish you for cuffing me to the bed and teasing me like you did," he said gently.

Libby started at that. The bells rang and she grimaced at the taut pinch on her nipples. She forced herself to glance sideways using just her eyes.

"Hey!" she said in a miffed tone when she saw him draw something out of the bag that she hadn't noticed before...a round wooden paddle!

"I've wanted to paddle your ass from the moment I saw it topped with that pink bow. What an inspired gift," John said with a flashing grin. "Come on, Olivia. Where's your sense of adventure?" he teased. He reached out and smoothed his hand across a smooth ass cheek. His cock jutted forward in excitement. Oh yeah, Olivia's firm, round ass was made for a good spanking.

Air rushed from Libby's lungs in surprise when he abruptly smacked her in the middle of the ass. The bells tinkled merrily. She gasped in pain.

"You're going to have to keep yourself very, very still," John admonished.

"Thanks for the advice. I think I get the idea," Libby replied sourly. No wonder he'd told her he wouldn't have to tie her up to control her! The clamps on her nipples assured him that she'd keep perfectly motionless while she got her butt blistered, just like a...

"Good girl," John muttered through a slashing grin before he proceeded to paddle her repeatedly.

After a minute, Libby was panting like she'd just run a sprint. And it wasn't from discomfort, although her butt did burn with a slow, hot pain. No, she panted in pure lust. Because John didn't just punish her, he pleasured her in between the sharp smacks. He caressed and molded her burning buttocks in his palm, soothing her. After he'd subjected her ass to a particularly lusty round of spankings, he rubbed and stroked her very well-oiled clit until she begged him hoarsely for relief.

"Do you think you've had enough punishment, Olivia?" John asked eventually as he palmed and squeezed a bright pink butt cheek.

"Yes! *Fuck me*," she whispered raggedly. Every shred of her pride and self-consciousness had been burned to ashes by the inferno of her desire.

John went very still behind her. "Excuse me?"

"Fuck me! *Please*," she cried more loudly. She moaned when she felt his cock spring up and caress her tingling ass in response to her request. God, what it did to her to experience how much he wanted her.

"Okay," John said with forced calmness as he tossed the paddle on the bed. "But if I do, I'm going to fuck you hard, Libby," he said silkily as he moved behind her and grasped his cock. His erection throbbed in his hand.

He wouldn't last for long, that was for sure. Paddling and stroking her had pitched him once again into a gratifyingly sharp arousal. He pulled back a rosy, plump ass cheek and presented his cock to the narrow entrance of her juicy pussy. He grimaced at the erotic sensation.

"You're going to have to keep very, very still and be a — "

"*Good girl*, I know, I know!" Libby grated out through a frenzy of lust. "Just fuck me, dammit!"

"Well, since you asked so nicely…" he said grimly.

Libby's eyes clenched shut when he grabbed her hips and impaled himself into her, his pelvis smacking briskly into her ass. The bells rang briskly, but she didn't notice or care…because she was coming again.

His face was rigid with lust as he began crashing into her. He'd never felt anything so good…so sweet…so fucking *mandatory* to his existence as pounding his cock into this woman as she came around him at that moment.

Libby's mouth hung wide open as she stared blindly while John thoroughly possessed her. He hammered his cock into her so hard that she whimpered in helpless pleasure, submitting to the power of his desire, becoming transformed by it as she fully submitted to her own.

She let the bells ring freely as she joined him in their frenzied mating, holding back nothing of herself from her lover.

Her cry sounded incredulous when he reached around her and quickly removed one nipple clamp, and then the other. Pleasure and pain tore through her like lightning at the same moment that he drove his cock to the mouth of her womb.

"Come with me, Olivia," she heard him demand tautly.

He pinched at her clit rhythmically and she complied...all too gladly.

Chapter Seven

 හ

Libby struggled wildly for air, but she loved the sensation of John bending over her and wrapping her in his arms. His embrace felt so sweet…so secure.

By slow degrees, a foreign, powerful emotion began to swell in her chest. It slowly segued to a feeling of panic. She forced herself not to groan out loud.

God, she was such a fool! She'd given herself so completely, so fully to him. She would never, *ever* be free of John Waite now…

And his wedding to another woman was in two days.

"Let's lie down," she said shakily.

John's heavy eyelids sprang open at her tone.

"Are you okay?" he asked as he rose up off her and put his hands on her waist, encouraging her to stand and turn in his embrace. "I know I was a little rough with you, but I thought you were enjoying it—"

"Of course I *enjoyed* it, John," she said with a shrill laugh, cutting him off. When she noticed how his sweat-glistening, handsome face pulled tight with concern, she took a deep breath, willing herself into calm.

She had no one to blame but herself. She had no right to subject John to her misery.

"I think I'm just exhausted," she said with a small laugh.

John's heart went out to her when he saw the mute apology in her liquid eyes and the tremor in her full lower lip. He sank onto the bed without another word, bringing her with him.

"Of course you are," he murmured hoarsely when she'd settled in his arms, her head resting on his chest. "Go to sleep, Olivia."

Tears flooded her eyes when she felt his lips on her ear, his hand tenderly smoothing the hair at the back of her head.

Oh, God, it was heaven.

And it would be pure hell to walk away from him in a few hours.

* * * * *

Libby stirred in John's warm embrace when the gray dawn light shone through the blinds. They were both turned on their left sides, his big, warm body spooning hers, his arm around her waist. It felt so good, but she was going to have to leave him soon.

Her night with him was over.

Her face pinched in misery. *No, don't let it be over, not yet,* she thought desperately as she twisted around and ate up the dim, shadowed image of his face as he rested peacefully.

John groaned deep in his throat a moment later, going from sleep to intense arousal in a matter of seconds.

"Olivia," he mumbled groggily.

"Yes," she whispered softly. Her arm moved between their bodies as she stroked his cock into hardness. The abundant lubrication she'd poured in her palm assured him a firm but slippery glide through her tight fist.

"God, that feels good," he murmured thickly. His hand came up to palm her waist and slid down the curve of a smooth, naked hip. "You feel even better."

Libby smiled, despite the full, heavy feeling in her breast. They were still both lying on their left sides, only her arm reached back between their bodies to stroke him. She twisted her neck, searching him out in the dim light. He raised his head. Their mouths found each others and fused.

For Libby, it was the sweetest kiss of her life—extremely hot, but slow and unhurried and...soulful.

She broke it reluctantly a minute later. John froze when she resituated herself, pressing the thick head of his cock into the crevice of her ass. Her hand remained on the base of his cock, guiding him to where she'd never embraced a man before.

"Olivia, do you know what you're doing?" he hissed in disbelief and sharp lust when she pressed the tip of his cock to her tiny hole. Because of the abundant lubrication and her steady, firm pressure back on him, the first inch of the head penetrated the tight ring of her anus.

His body and consciousness sprung into full, total wakefulness.

"Are you sure?" he managed to get out in a strangled voice. The rim beneath the head of his cock slipped into her incredible heat.

"Yes," she whispered on an outward gasp.

Time seemed to stand still.

Together they worked his penis into her body, neither of them hurrying the process. Both of them seemed aware of a desire to make the experience last. They whispered to each other softly...intimately. He placed his hand on her jaw and turned her mouth to meet his again and again. His hand explored her body thoroughly, pleasuring her just as he found pleasure in the sensation of her curves and silky skin beneath his fingertips.

But they were only human. The pleasure eventually overtook them...overwhelmed them.

The same hand that had stroked her gently now held her hip steady as he pulsed and surged into her. Just when John knew he was going to have to submit to the tall wave of pleasure that was intent on crashing over him, he felt Olivia tighten around him, heard her sharp cries of release. He thrust into her one last time, holding her fast against his pelvis, his balls pressed tightly against the soft, firm flesh of her ass.

His shouts of disbelieving bliss mingled with hers.

Who *was* this phenomenal woman? John thought dazedly a while later as he drifted into a satiated stupor. He could tell that Olivia was already asleep by the soothing sound of her even breathing.

His unconscious mind was active and busy, because he answered his own question as he fell into a deep, satisfying sleep.

"*Libby*," he muttered.

Chapter Eight

ಸಿ

Libby was *furious* with Malcolm. She was never, *ever* going to speak to her best friend again, she promised herself.

"I'm never, *ever* going to speak to you again, Malcolm Dupres!" she hissed.

Of course, she only broke her original vow to ensure that the man who maneuvered his car through the crowded streets of downtown Chicago with such infuriating calmness and skill knew the consequences of his actions!

Malcolm merely wrinkled his nose and rolled down the window of his plush sedan.

"When is the last time you took a shower, young lady?"

Libby's jaw came unhinged. Of all the nerve! *He* was the one who had practically broke into her condominium that morning and then taunted and harried and forced her—yes, *forced* her—to leave with him.

"Malcolm, you know very well what I've been through for these past few days! You're the one who shoved me into the hallway and locked me out of my condo! How can you make fun of me for smelling bad, you jerk?" She surged against her seat belt wildly. "And I don't want to go anywhere, *you big shit*! Don't you know what today is?" she asked shrilly.

"Two days past the one where you should have taken a shower?"

"It's John and Estelle's wedding day, you fricking idiot!"

"I'm disappointed in you, Libby," he said firmly as he turned onto congested Michigan Avenue. "I never thought you were the type of woman to pull something like this. Don't you think you're being a bit dramatic, dear?"

Malcolm became unsettled by the ensuing silence. He thought he'd succeeded in bullying Libby out of the frightening zombie-like state that he'd found her in when she'd finally opened her condominium door to him less than an hour ago. She'd refused to answer his, Ced's or Nathan's phone calls.

He turned and looked at her distractedly.

His strong, stern façade melted like chocolate on the dashboard in August when he saw the expression of pain on her pretty face.

A second later it turned to stark terror.

"Malcolm!" Libby shrieked in panic when he nearly plowed into the bumper of a cab changing lanes.

"Oh God, Libby, I'm sorry!" Malcolm exclaimed.

Libby gave another muffled scream when he abruptly began to fumble in his pocket and the car swerved into the right lane. A bus sounded its horn furiously, but Malcolm seemed oblivious as he frantically combed her mussed hair.

"You really don't smell *that* bad, honey."

Malcolm gave her a twisted, eager grin that was supposed to be reassuring, Libby realized.

"Malcolm, what the hell is wrong with you? Keep your eyes on the road!" she screamed when he failed to notice that the light had turned red. He braked to a screeching halt, missing the car in front of him by a fraction of an inch.

Libby blinked in disorientation at something she saw across the street. Her inhalation scored her throat.

Not only were she and Malcolm at the corner of Michigan Avenue where the church was located where John was supposed to marry Estelle in twenty minutes, but Ced was at the curb waving madly at them.

And there was Nathan standing next to him, looking very distinguished in his father-of-the-groom tux, his white walking stick held tautly beneath his arm like a saber.

"Malcolm, how the hell could you have brought me to *John's wedding*?" she asked in shuddering, sheer disbelief.

"Everything is going to be just fine, Libby," Malcolm mumbled desperately. Libby hardly noticed that he'd unfastened the glove box until he abruptly reached up and sprayed her several times with his expensive men's cologne.

"Arghhh," she choked as she waved her hands in front of her wildly, her eyes instinctively clenching shut over the burning pain of the alcohol. "What are you doing, you fucking loon?"

She never received a reply because the door sprang open next to her and suddenly Ced was pulling her out into traffic.

Libby blinked in disorientation as Ced herded her along, blinded by Malcolm's strong cologne and the brightness of the sunny June day. She instinctively dug in her heels and tried to turn the other direction when they approached Nathan.

"*No!*" Libby hissed under her breath as Ced shoved her up on the curb.

"*Yes!*" Ced replied just as forcefully, unfazed by the furious glare she hurled at him through squinting eyes. Libby barely made out Ced's handsome face through her burning, blurry eyes when Nathan spoke next to her.

"Is Malcolm with you?" he asked her bluntly as he inhaled and grimaced at the odor that accompanied her.

"*No!*" Libby said again, this time more sourly. "What the hell do you three think you're doing dragging me to John's wedding? Have you lost your minds?"

Nathan just shook his handsome, gray head patiently and held out his arm for Libby to take. She gaped at him in disbelief through squinted eyes.

It was Ced's voice next to her that finally stilled her sense of disoriented panic.

"Everything is going to be okay, Libby. Just go with Nathan."

Libby stared back at Ced uncertainly as she took Nathan's arm.

"Ready, Libby?" Nathan asked with surprising gentleness.

Her heart quaked madly in her breast as she marched slowly down the pedestrian-crowded sidewalk with her handsome, distinguished escort.

Tears welled in her eyes that had nothing to do with Malcolm spraying her directly in the face with his cologne. The one of many of her emotions that surged uncontrollably was the fact that it had been Libby who had been the one who had first led Nathan when he was in rehabilitation after his stroke. She had guided him, at first with her touch and then with her voice, on countless occasions as they toured the neighborhood streets of the Low Vision Rehabilitation Center.

Nathan had become as dear to her as her own father was.

"Proud of me, aren't you, Libby?" Nathan asked gruffly as they progressed down Michigan Avenue, his tapping cane parting the crowd in front of him so efficiently that Libby never even considered caution as they moved along.

She swiped her cheek surreptitiously, even though she knew Nathan's vision was too poor to have actually seen the betraying tear. That was one of many characteristics that John had inherited from his father, she thought irritably. Both men were far too aware of emotions a woman tried to keep secret.

She looked up at the high-rises that towered over them blurrily, her lips frozen in a tense, insipid grin.

"Hmm? Proud? What'd make you say that?" she asked with in an unnaturally high voice.

"Ah, Libby," Nathan sighed sadly as he led her gently down a path to their right. He paused patiently when he felt her balk. She had just realized that he'd guided her onto the path of the lush, green, peaceful outdoor sanctuary of the church where John was to marry Estelle.

"Nathan!" Libby grated in protest.

But Nathan just pulled on her and continued on.

"You know there's only one thing I've regretted more than never telling you how much I appreciate what you did for me back when I was in rehab. Libby, I've always sorely regretted because of *both* of our stubborn natures that I've never had the official opportunity to introduce you to my son."

She gasped in surprise when Nathan suddenly shoved her in front of him.

"Olivia Grace Taylor, it is my great pleasure to *finally* present you to my son, John Maximillian Waite."

Chapter Nine

ဢ

Libby glanced up into a pair of stunned green eyes.

"*John*," she mumbled incoherently as she stumbled forward on the impetus of Nathan's firm push and her own disorientation.

"Dad, what the...*hey*...are you okay?" John asked anxiously when she fell into his chest with a thud.

Libby squinted up at him in rising horror. Her cheek pressed into a shirt that covered the hard chest that she recalled all too well from their night of raw, uninhibited, extremely intimate sex. His familiar clean, masculine scent pervaded her senses. Her lower lip trembled uncontrollably.

Oh, God, please let this not be happening, she prayed fervently.

She was wearing a soiled T-shirt and rumpled jeans. She'd showered briefly after she'd stumbled into her condominium early Thursday morning, numb with grief after leaving John's warm embrace as he slept peacefully. She hadn't done much else since then in the grooming department, however. She'd been too busy staring at television shows she didn't want to watch through a blurry window of tears.

Libby gave a small shriek and leapt away from John's warm body as though his flesh had burned her.

"Libby...Libby, calm down." John did his best to soothe the struggling, soft feminine form in his arms.

"Oh...*don't*, John!" Libby expelled miserably into his chest when he held her head firmly against him. "Malcolm said I *smelled!*"

"You do smell sort of...well...unusual," John admitted.

Her liquid brown eyes flashed up at him, meeting his gaze squarely for the first time. John took heart in the fact that they looked like they'd been injected with venom.

"Let go of me, John Waite!"

She pushed away from his embrace with the energy of a wild, trapped animal, but he held firm.

"Uh, uh, Libby. I want to talk to you."

She stilled in her frenetic struggle.

John watched as she looked up at him with one eye, the other occluded by a swatch of thick auburn hair.

"You know I'm called Libby?" she asked slowly.

He exhaled with barely restrained impatience and frustration. "Yeah. You might have heard me call you that the other morning if you hadn't left my bed like some kind of...sneaky thief."

Libby gasped in outrage. "*Sneaky thief?*" Tears spurted out of the bottom of her eyes onto her cheeks, but she didn't even notice she was so discombobulated. John Waite was the one who had stole her soul so coldheartedly.

"I'd like to know just what the hell you think I took from *you!*" she challenged hotly.

She wasn't prepared for his expression of concern and compassion to melt so quickly into an anger that easily matched her own. His green eyes scorched so hotly that she inadvertently flinched.

"What, Libby? You own the rights to heartbreak, is that it?" he demanded.

She averted her eyes in confusion, but his hand came up to the side of her neck, tilting her jaw up in a familiar gesture. Libby's teeth ground together in frustration when she realized she didn't have anything smart or profound to say in the face of his harsh question and lancing gaze. Her eyes lowered over his broad, T-shirt-covered shoulders.

The obvious was her inspiration.

"Why aren't you wearing your tux?" she asked shakily.

He might as well have backhanded her when he answered calmly.

"For the same reason you smell like a dirty sock that's been sprayed with men's cologne, I guess."

He waited until her big, brown eyes darted up to his in amazement.

"I'm not getting married today, Libby," he said gently.

"You're...not...getting...?"

He shook his head solemnly. "No. I called it off yesterday."

"Well...that's...that's just..."

John caught her when her knees gave out beneath her. The next thing she realized was that she was sitting on one of the stone steps in the verdant courtyard of the church while John's long fingers massaged the back of her neck.

"Libby...Libby?" He slapped her cheek gently. "Don't faint on me, okay?"

"Of course I won't!" she assured him with a mysterious upsurge of energy. "I'm not a weak-willed, idiotic...how come Nathan was wearing a tux if you aren't getting married today?" she asked abruptly.

John sighed with relief when he saw some color return to her cheeks. She'd been so pale.

"Dad can't resist a little drama to make a point," John replied wryly.

"What point?" Libby asked when he sat down next to her on the step. Her brain must have begun functioning again at the news that John—*her* John—wasn't planning on pledging himself for a lifetime to another woman because for the first time, she realized that he looked a little worse for wear himself.

"You probably know just as much as me that my dad—not to mention Ced and Malcolm—have been trying to set you and me up for well over a year now," John began dryly. He glanced over at her apologetically. "I'm not too fond of set-ups, Libby."

Libby pursed her lips as she studied him. "Your stubborn independence makes it that way," she sighed and glanced around the pretty courtyard, taking it in for the first time. "It's some kind of weird knee-jerk reaction. Must be a Waite gene. Every time I wanted to get your father to do something in rehab I had to tell him he couldn't."

"And he'd be biting at the bit to get at it, right?" John asked with a small smile. "Yeah, I guess you're right. Dad and I sort of have a long history of clashing opinions and refusing to budge an inch on them."

"And so when Nathan told you that he'd found the perfect li'l redheaded gal for you, and then Ced and Malcolm set up a party for an introduction, you..."

"Fell for the first blonde that came my way? It was a bit more complicated than that, but yeah, there's probably more truth in that than I care to admit."

She gave him a withering stare.

"You can't put all this on me, Libby," John said in a hard tone. "You ran out of that party without meeting me first. I saw you that night, you know...not all of you. I looked up and saw the back of your hair as you flew out the door. '*There goes the mysterious Libby*,' I remember thinking. I was already used to your elusiveness. My dad tried to introduce me to you three different times when I came to the Low Vision Center. I really wanted to thank the woman—I *still* want to thank the woman—who was responsible for giving me back my father, but you were always mysteriously absent. Once I waited for you for almost two hours."

It was Libby's turn to look apologetic. "I was...in the break room watching you. I thought you never were going to leave."

John laughed in disbelief. "Why in the heck would you do that?"

Her eyes ran over his face anxiously. "I...I was afraid you wouldn't like me."

He gave a final bark of harsh laughter and shook his head slowly. His hand came up to cradle her jaw. Libby went completely still as he leaned in closer.

"Newsflash, Libby. I like you."

She experienced the now-familiar meltdown between her thighs when John smiled slowly just before he placed a soft, lingering kiss on her mouth.

"So do you want go out on a date with me, or what?" John asked a moment later next to her lips.

"When?" Libby asked, wide-eyed.

John shrugged as he stood and pulled her up from the step. "Now. Let's go to lunch."

"I have to take a shower first," Libby said as she looked down at herself miserably.

"Good. I'll take one with you," he said with a flashing grin. He grabbed her hand and pulled her after him eagerly.

Ced murmured something to Nathan when he saw John and Libby approaching, hand in hand.

"Everything all right?" Nathan asked good-naturedly.

"Everything's great," John said briskly. He tugged on Libby's arm and started to walk past the two men. "Sorry to run, but I've got to help Libby take a shower. Emergency hygiene, you know."

"John!" Libby sputtered in surprise, but Nathan and Ced just laughed as he pulled her past them.

"Go on, Libby," Nathan called out, grinning madly. "I know my stubborn son. He just doesn't want to have to stand around long enough to hear me say '*I told you so*'."

Also by Desiree Holt

About the Author

ЄО

I always wonder what readers really want to know when I write one of these things. Getting to this point in my career has been an interesting journey. I've managed rock and roll bands and organized concerts. Been the only female on the sports staff of a university newspaper. Immersed myself in Nashville peddling a country singer. Lived in five different states. Married two very interesting but totally different men.

I think I must have lived in Texas in another life, because the minute I set foot on Texas soil I knew I was home. Living in Texas Hill Country gives me inspiration for more stories than I'll probably ever be able to tell, what with all the sexy cowboys who surround me and the gorgeous scenery that provides a great setting.

Each day is a new adventure for me, as my characters come to life on the pages of my current work in progress. I'm absolutely compulsive about it when I'm writing and thank all the gods and goddesses that I have such a terrific husband who encourages my writing and puts up with my obsession. As a multi-published author, I love to hear from my readers. Their input keeps my mind fresh and always hunting for new ideas.

Desiree welcomes comments from readers. You can find her website and email address on her author bio page at www.ellorascave.com.

Tell Us What You Think

We appreciate hearing reader opinions about our books. You can email us at Comments@EllorasCave.com.

About the Author

൭

Multi-published in several genres, award-winning author Michele Bardsley spends her days creating fictional worlds because, let's face it, reality sucks. A prime example is that no one has yet to figure out how to make calorie-free chocolate. What's up with THAT?

Michele lives in Oklahoma where she is held hostage by her two children, her husband, and three cats. Occasionally her family remembers to feed her, but mostly she's forced to nibble on copy paper while eking out her next story. The manacles make it difficult to type, but she manages.

Michele welcomes comments from readers. You can find her website and email address on her author bio page at www.ellorascave.com.

Tell Us What You Think

We appreciate hearing reader opinions about our books. You can email us at Comments@EllorasCave.com.

Also by Kit Tunstall

ɛɔ

A Christmas Phantasie

A Matter of Honor

Ablaze

Blood Lines 1: Blood Oath

Blood Lines 2: Blood Challenge

Blood Lines 3: Blood Bond

Blood Lines 4: Blood Price

Eye of Destiny

Heart of Midnight

Lions and Tigers and Bears *with Kate Steele & Jodi Lynn Copeland*

Pawn

Phantasie

Playing His Game

Sundown Pack 1: Only Love

Sundown Pack 2: Fortune's Fool

Sundown Pack 3: Asking For Trouble

Also see Kit's story at Cerridwen Press (www.cerridwenpress.com):

Beloved Forever

About the Author

ଛ

Kit Tunstall lives in Idaho with her husband, son and dog-children. She started reading at the age of three and hasn't stopped since. Love of the written word, and a smart marriage to a supportive man, led her to a full-time career in writing. Romances have always intrigued her, and erotic romance is a natural extension because it more completely explores the emotions between the hero and heroine. That, and it sure is fun to write.

Kit welcomes comments from readers. You can find her website and email address on her author bio page at www.ellorascave.com.

Tell Us What You Think

We appreciate hearing reader opinions about our books. You can email us at Comments@EllorasCave.com.

Also by Zannie Adams

৪০

Complicated
Hold
Inescapable
Renaissance

About the Author

ဿ

Zannie Adams writes, reads, and caters to her chocolate-brown cocker spaniel, and watches cooking shows on television. She has lived in eight different states, had far too much graduate-level education, and generally done her best not to settle down. She has been writing novels all her life, but only recently did she begin to write erotic romances--a genre that has allowed her to explore her love of both passion and commitment.

Zannie prefers to spend most of her time writing, but she has to stop occasionally to teach writing and literature at a liberal arts college and to walk her dog. She lives in the Midwest.

Zannie welcomes comments from readers. You can find her website and email address on her author bio page at www.ellorascave.com.

Tell Us What You Think
We appreciate hearing reader opinions about our books. You can email us at Comments@EllorasCave.com.

Also by Taige Crenshaw

ഉ

Carnal Awakening
God Style Temptation
Golden Seduction
Shadow Dance
Veils Rising

About the Author

෨

Taige Crenshaw has been enthralled with the written word from the time she picked up her first book. It wasn't long before she started to make up her own tales of romance.

Her novels are set in today between people who know what they want and how to get it. As well as in the future of vast universes between beautiful, strange and unique beings. There is lots of spice and sensuality added to her work.

Always hard at work creating new and exciting places, Taige can be found curled up with a hot novel with exciting characters when she is not creating her own. Join her in the fun, frolic, interesting people and far reaches of the world in her novels.

Taige welcomes comments from readers. You can find her website and email address on her author bio page at www.ellorascave.com.

Tell Us What You Think

We appreciate hearing reader opinions about our books. You can email us at Comments@EllorasCave.com.

Also by Alice Gaines

၈

Dr. Feelgood
Sans Regret

Also check out the author's book at Cerridwen Press
(www.cerridwenpress.com).

Child of Balance

About the Author

ജ

Award winning author, Alice Gaines has been published in other genres, including paranormal and historical romance. She's delighted to join Cerridwen/Ellora's Cave family with her fantasy work.

Alice loves stories that stretch the imagination, either through exotic or superhuman characters. She has a Ph.D. in psychology from U.C. Berkeley and lives in Oakland, California, with her collection of orchids and two pet corn snakes, Casper and Sheikh Yerbouti.

Alice welcomes comments from readers. You can find her website and email address on her author bio page at www.ellorascave.com.

Tell Us What You Think

We appreciate hearing reader opinions about our books. You can email us at Comments@EllorasCave.com.

About the Author

෨

Beth Kery grew up in a huge house built in the nineteenth century, where she cultivated her love of mystery and the paranormal. When she wasn't hunting for secret passageways and ghosts with her friends, she was gobbling up fantasy novels and any other books she could get her hands on. As an adult she learned about the vast mysteries of romance and sex and started to investigate that phenomenon thoroughly, as well. Her writing today reflects her passion for all of the above.

Beth welcomes comments from readers. You can find her website and email address on her author bio page at www.ellorascave.com.

Tell Us What You Think

We appreciate hearing reader opinions about our books. You can email us at Comments@EllorasCave.com.

Why an electronic book?

We live in the Information Age—an exciting time in the history of human civilization, in which technology rules supreme and continues to progress in leaps and bounds every minute of every day. For a multitude of reasons, more and more avid literary fans are opting to purchase e-books instead of paper books. The question from those not yet initiated into the world of electronic reading is simply: *Why?*

1. *Price.* An electronic title at Ellora's Cave Publishing and Cerridwen Press runs anywhere from 40% to 75% less than the cover price of the exact same title in paperback format. Why? Basic mathematics and cost. It is less expensive to publish an e-book (no paper and printing, no warehousing and shipping) than it is to publish a paperback, so the savings are passed along to the consumer.

2. *Space.* Running out of room in your house for your books? That is one worry you will never have with electronic books. For a low one-time cost, you can purchase a handheld device specifically designed for e-reading. Many e-readers have large, convenient screens for viewing. Better yet, hundreds of titles can be stored within your new library—on a single microchip. There are a variety of e-readers from different manufacturers. You can also read e-books on your PC or laptop computer. (Please note that Ellora's Cave does not endorse any specific brands. You can check our websites at www.ellorascave.com

or www.cerridwenpress.com for information we make available to new consumers.)

3. *Mobility.* Because your new e-library consists of only a microchip within a small, easily transportable e-reader, your entire cache of books can be taken with you wherever you go.

4. *Personal Viewing Preferences.* Are the words you are currently reading too small? Too large? Too… ANNOYING? Paperback books cannot be modified according to personal preferences, but e-books can.

5. *Instant Gratification.* Is it the middle of the night and all the bookstores near you are closed? Are you tired of waiting days, sometimes weeks, for bookstores to ship the novels you bought? Ellora's Cave Publishing sells instantaneous downloads twenty-four hours a day, seven days a week, every day of the year. Our webstore is never closed. Our e-book delivery system is 100% automated, meaning your order is filled as soon as you pay for it.

Those are a few of the top reasons why electronic books are replacing paperbacks for many avid readers.

As always, Ellora's Cave and Cerridwen Press welcome your questions and comments. We invite you to email us at Comments@ellorascave.com or write to us directly at Ellora's Cave Publishing Inc., 1056 Home Avenue, Akron, OH 44310-3502.

COMING TO A BOOKSTORE NEAR YOU!

ELLORA'S CAVE

Bestselling Authors Tour

Discover for yourself why readers can't get enough
of the multiple award-winning publisher

Ellora's Cave.

Whether you prefer e-books or paperbacks,

be sure to visit EC on the web at
www.ellorascave.com

for an erotic reading experience that will leave you
breathless.

LaVergne, TN USA
02 July 2010
188229LV00001B/152/P